BLUE THIEF

By S.E. McLean

Copyright

Published by Dome Tree Publishing

ISBN Paperback: 978-1-989447-03-1

ISBN Complete eBook: 978-1-989447-10-9

Freebie eBook (first episode of this book)

ISBN eBook Solitaire: 978-1-989447-04-8

The price of anything is the amount of life you exchange for it.

Henry David Thoreau.

American essayist, poet and philosopher

Some things,

the cost in human life is so dear

it makes them unthinkable.

Contents

EPISODE ONE — SOLITAIRE

There is no consuming fire like passion

No ravenous shark like hatred

No unrestrained torrent like greed

And no entangling snare like misconception.

Chapter 1 — The Impossible Blue

Lives would change forever over a primeval chunk of rock. As implausible as the Excalibur sword, this particular rock could thrust mere mortals to the stature of gods, or cast them down to the netherworld. And fate is mercurial in her choices.

Wednesday, March 4

In the middle of nowhere, baked by the equatorial sun and shrouded by acacia and sycamore trees a wretched sin played out. The only people aware were the desperate men, women and children risking their lives.

Mountains of red earth and dozens of narrow holes revealed the true nature of the crime. People trudged in daily with a pick, a frayed rope and hope. Longing to escape poverty, they dug like fevered meerkats, slipping down their narrow burrows for the tantalizing chance of fortune.

Elvis, a young man, arrived with the dawn to excavate his purchased artisanal mine. By noon the only thing he discovered was an unusual plum-sized stone. Turning it over several times he pondered if he should toss it and continued digging. He tucked it in the pocket of his ragged pants. Another swing of the pick. Another probing the clumps of earth. Another hour.

As the scorching heat of the sun faded behind the hazy horizon he headed out with only this single stone. He almost discarded it, but since he walked past the buyer anyway, he stopped in.

The man in the shack, Kareem Onai, looked at Elvis with eyes as dark as his heart. A survivor of Rwanda's civil war, he was tough and handled guns since he was eight. But there were a couple of things that uniquely qualified him as the stone buyer. He spent several years in Dubai, learning the gem trade and he proved himself an excellent appraiser of quality stones. More importantly, and for reasons Kareem never spoke about, he was fiercely loyal to his boss, known only as Jack. His loyalty ensured mountains of money filled Jack's bank account.

The moment he saw the raw stone his mouth went dry. It was an unbelievable find. The test results confirmed his instincts. A gem this size is extremely rare, but one of this pure clarity and stunning colour was unheard of. This single stone, still in its raw form, would command an unimaginable sum. Kareem did some quick calculations based on the recent sale of a smaller, less vivid gem and arrived at an estimated value of 120 million dollars on the legitimate market. His hands shook as he handled it.

Few people were aware of the stone's existence. Two, in fact. The young man who found it and Kareem – and he cleaned out his cash supply to pay the miner a bonus to not mention his find to anyone.

Normally, Kareem held all the stones in the safe until the weekly shipment, but this near-priceless treasure required careful handling. He chose to use his special safety deposit box instead.

Jack can afford to lose all that is in the safe. He wouldn't be happy, but he could afford it. He cannot afford to lose this stone. I cannot afford to lose this stone.

Instead, Kareem stashed the prize in a small box attached to the underside of the office latrine. Rarely had he need of his outhouse lock box, and he knew the sooner this find of a lifetime moved out of the camp the better.

With the gemstone as safe as it could be, Kareem called his boss. "We now own the Impossible Blue. It's huge – at least 150 or 160 carat beautiful vivid blue diamond. Hardly a flaw. Unbelievable size. Phenomenal clarity. There's not a word to describe it. No one has seen anything like this stone. We're talking over a hundred million dollars, just in its raw state. And the colour – incredible. The market will go crazy when they see this diamond." He slowed down to catch his breath. "Jack, You know I'm not a nervous man, but I don't want the responsibility of protecting this thing. You've got to get it out of here immediately."

Chapter 2 — On The Mountain

Hope cannot exist without fear, and fear without hope. This was as true in the hand-dug mines of Africa as it was on a West Virginia mountaintop half a world away.

Sunday, March 1

"Ten years ago you told me you met the perfect guy. For a decade I've determined to find his faults. All the time he works in Africa is the only one. And I'm not so sure that's such a bad thing." Libby carefully balanced her water bottle on the rough sandstone and let her eyes stretch across the gorge.

Libby and Dakota met each other during their first year of college. Their friendship celebrated dreams attained and mourned hopes lost. Libby, the more gregarious of the two dated a man pursuing a law degree. He came from a wealthy southern family of lawyers and judges. Despite the pull of his heart, he caved to family pressure and called off their wedding.

Dakota would say her friend never recovered from the pain and loss.

Libby blamed all men for the weakness of one.

Dakota smiled at her friend's assessment of Blake's virtues. The pungent smell of earthy woods warmed by the sun wafted up the cliff known as the Endless Wall. Dax lay back, resting her head on her backpack, closed her eyes and let the spring sun warm her face. "It's been tough with Blake away so much, but we're trying to get pregnant now. He says things will change soon and he'll be around more."

"And there goes his one imperfection." Libby stretched out, reaching down to her toes, keeping her muscles loose for the climb back down. "Pregnant you say? Dibs on being the godparent. The kid's bound to be an absolute angel who practically raises herself and becomes the doctor who finds the cure for cancer and splits half the money with her guardians."

"There's no guarantee I'll have a girl and she will be the saviour of the medical world. I'm not that lucky."

"Have you looked at your life lately?" Counting on her fingers she said, "Let's see now. Blake, an international financier. A house in D.C. Successful counselling practice. And did I mention, Blake? The perfect child is inevitable."

Dax grinned. "It sounds like you're a bigger fan than me. Should I be worried?"

She snorted. "You should know by now, I'm not marriage material. Until I met Blake I didn't believe in the existence of nice guys."

Feeling restless, Dax got up and stood inches from the cliff edge. "Lately, he's been – unsettled."

Libby scrutinized her friend, looking for clues to things not spoken. Finding the concealed story was her job and she was good at it. "Are you concerned?"

Dax hesitated. "No, it's probably work related. Providing financing to some of the struggling countries in central Africa has inherent stresses."

"Could he be feeling over his head? I would have thought that kind of job would require a background in economics or banking, not military."

"Apparently not. Uncle Logan assigned him the most difficult region when he started. I'm sure he wouldn't do so unless Blake could do the job."

She walked along the edge towards their climbing ropes. "For the past few weeks I've been feeling on the cusp of something significant. Something life-changing. I can't shake the feeling. It's almost overwhelming." She turned and faced her friend. "It's our tenth anniversary next weekend."

"Ten. That's a milestone. I think that's the tin or aluminum one, isn't it? Maybe he'll get you a roll of aluminum foil."

"Very funny. I'm thinking one of those big, beautiful African diamonds would be nice."

"Don't get your hopes up. You've got a long ways to go to reach the diamond anniversary. I think it's like 100 years of marriage."

Dax shielded her eyes from the sun and peered into the distant hazy line between sky and earth. "We need to plan that trip to Joshua Tree National Park soon, before I'm too pregnant to climb. Otherwise, it will be many years before I can go."

"Let me check my schedule when we get back. I think I have a bit of time in a few weeks." Libby stood up to scan the gorge, the bridge and the ancient tree-covered mountains beyond. She chose this rock-climbing route for the view. Her eyes settled on her friend. "You seem a little unsettled yourself. Distracted perhaps. Tell me more about this *on the edge of something significant* feeling."

Dax dropped her hand and looked down at her fingers. She always removed her wedding ring when climbing. The slight tan line from the missing ring caught her attention. "It's probably nothing more than my biological clock ticking." She stretched out her shoulders. "Ready to go?"

"Sure." Libby prepared the ropes.

Dax double-checked the setup. "All set. What do you want to climb next?"

An impish grin spread across Libby's face. "Cirque?" the site of nearly impossible climbs.

"Let's do it. We've got all afternoon."

She shook her head. "I'm joking. You are fearless. That's going to get you in trouble one day."

"Impossibly long reaches, hanging off big cliff roofs, heights, spiders, blood, clowns – no problem. What I fear is a snake in the toilet when I pee in the middle of the night. That, dark tight spaces and window perverts."

"Window perverts I get. And I remember the panic attack you had at camp the time you slept on top of the third bunk, just inches from the ceiling. But a snake in the toilet? Tell me, Dr. Dax, what outhouse incident from your past caused that fear?"

She laughed. "I'm many years short of being a doctor. Anyway, I stumbled upon a BBC article about an Australian woman who got bit by a carpet python when she sat on the toilet. Then there's the reptile expert who talked about a snake in the toilet of a 19th floor condo explaining that they are excellent swimmers, can hold their breath for a long time and can squeeze through tight spaces. Apparently they can slink through the pipes from the outside and end up in the toilet. The story kind of glommed on to my existent unease with snakes. And videos all over the Internet of snakes coming out of the toilet solidified the fear. Now, I imagine sitting down in the middle of the night, half asleep and hearing a slithering and slosh in the toilet bowl then as I leap to my feet, I discover a 20-foot python latched on to my butt. I spin to –"

"Stop right there. I don't need to hear this."

"– pull it off, but it won't let go. Then with my underwear down at my heels, the paramedics machete the coiling python at the neck, but its jaws are locked on and –"

"Alright, already. Too much information. I've already got enough visuals to haunt me at three in the morning. I probably have to turn the light on now. Let's move to a less traumatic topic."

"Okay. A new topic. What news story of deep political secrets are you investigating?"

"Ah, I'm chasing down a lead on a link between Bulgaria, Morocco and international aid tied to massive amounts of wealth pouring into Dubai. I'll be leaving for Europe in a couple of weeks to check out a few companies I think are fronts."

"I watched a show on Dubai. The super-wealthy are buying up property there."

"It's not about the wealthy living a decadent life in Dubai. No one cares. This foul smell comes from millions of Euro suddenly appearing in offshore bank accounts and the whispered associations to a handful of highly positioned politicians. It stinks of skimming and fraud."

"Be careful. People can be vicious when you go nosing into their money schemes."

"And unless someone shines a light on the villains of this world, avarice gives license to atrocity."

Chapter 3 — The Office

In the pursuit of happiness, avarice and ambition make the same mistake. Both soon forget about the light joy of happiness and instead pursue a dark, unquenchable lust for wealth and power as its own end.

Tuesday, March 3

Blake tapped the office door with his foot.

The two large Starbucks coffees caught Logan's eye. "Blake. You're a sight for these old eyes. Would that be a shot of espresso with my name on it?" Standing up from his desk he said, "It's good to have you home," and gestured toward the sitting area.

"You're finally acknowledging that you *are* the Old Man?"

"Old eyes, not an old man quite yet." Logan sat down in a club chair, set his papers on the end table and pulled the tab on the coffee lid. "All this desk time takes its toll. I envy you boys out there on the front lines of action."

Blake leaned back on the sofa, resting the ankle of his jeans across his knee. "You could spend some time with Wilberforce in Kyrgyzstan keeping an eye on the travelling nursery yurt."

Laughing, Logan said, "His name isn't Wilberforce."

"No? Gaylord then."

Still chuckling he said, "His name is Gale, and he's working with the president."

"Right, Gale – the guy that came to the office barbecue wearing a Squidward T-shirt. C'mon. You gotta see the joke."

"I don't know if you'll ever be ready for a management role."

"Not likely. I like my job in the field. I'd go squirrelly sitting behind a desk moving paper from one filing cabinet to another."

"Just think about it, please. I need someone here, someone of your calibre, with your skills."

"You ask me every time I come."

"I hope one of these times you'll agree." He looked at Blake over his reading glasses. "How's Dax? I haven't called her in a few weeks."

"She's good."

Logan pulled off his specs. "She mentioned you're hoping to start a family soon."

He grinned. "We're past the talking stage on that one. We're still negotiating on me spending more time at home. I promised her I would make an effort once we have kids."

"There's lots of work here that doesn't involve sitting behind a desk."

"I'll think about it."

"Ah, the standard answer." Sliding his glasses back on he said, "Now, tell me what's going on in Zimbula. How's my friend President Etienne Akleelu? The media paints a rough picture."

"It's Africa. You know how it is coming up to an election. Economic growth is non-existent. The unemployed rate is sky high. Poverty remains rampant and that, in itself, destabilizes. But it's not only the economic conditions. Things are heating up between the ethnic factions. And the go-to tactic is bombing. The airport has been a favourite target. It's barely operational, which is a concern for security. There are no commercial flights in or out. I still fly into Nairobi but now catch a flight to Kigoma in Tanzania then drive across the border to Mabezi."

Logan rubbed his chin. “Etienne continues to put in orders, but he complains he’s paying for air because they never arrive.”

“I’ve supervised the shipments and they are definitely in possession of everything they ordered.”

“What of this discrepancy? Is Etienne lying to me for some gain? Or has he lost control of his people?”

“It could be either. There is some talk that he has slipped over the edge. His opponent calls him President Akookoo.”

“What’s your assessment?”

He shrugged. “I don’t know. Maybe he’s developing dementia from some STD. He regularly entertains a parade of prostitutes. He’s not mentioned the missing shipments to me.”

“How’s your relationship with him?”

“Reasonably good. He still seeks advice. We talk every few days. And he leans on us heavily.”

“Is Ironwood on the ground?”

“No. Etienne would love for us to take a more active role, but I’ve kept to the mandate.”

“Good. Keep us in the background. Ensure nothing can stick if this goes south. What’s your sense of a military coup?”

“I’ll get in touch with Akleelu today. And as soon as I get back there, I’ll connect with the top boys. I’ve fostered solid connections with all of them. As to a coup, I know there’s talk. I think it’s just that – talk.”

“Good. Let me know if you want my involvement.”

“For sure. I know you had a strong relationship with him. So far, I’ve got his trust. I’m one on his speed dial. He calls for every random thing he wants.”

Logan laughed. “Years ago he called me in the middle of the night expecting me to bring him a Mickey Mouse hat. Maybe he’s had dementia for a long time.” He wrote a few notes. “Now, what’s Etienne’s issue with moving ahead on mining and exports. The potential of strong economic growth is enormous.”

"As well as expanding our contract. It's certainly a mineral rich country. Unfortunately, no mining company has been able to sign an agreeable contract with him. He insists on terms that are extremely unfavourable or unpalatable. I'm working on it and believe I'm making progress. But getting him to budge is like getting the Titanic to shift over a couple of feet."

"When do you go back?"

Blake grinned. "See? You need me there. My tickets are in about 10 days. I'd like to stay home longer, but I need to deal with a few things, and I'm still short a couple of men since the accident killed two men. Got any good new recruits ready to get out in the field?"

"I might. I hired a man last week. General Spicer highly recommended him. Turns out he's from your old special ops unit. The man became quite interested when he heard you work here. Asked a couple of times about you. Said he's really looking forward to connecting."

"My old unit?" Blake's hand tapped the back of the sofa. "What's his name?"

"Jamie Moore."

He leaned forward and rubbed his face. "Yeah, I vaguely remember someone by that name. If he's the guy I'm thinking of, he joined the unit shortly before I left. Might have done a mission or two with him."

"I'm thinking of deploying him in Zimbula, under you. He couldn't learn the ropes from anyone better."

Blake's face winced. "When would he be available?"

"He starts in a couple of weeks. With his background, maybe a week or two of orientation. So, three, maybe four weeks."

"That doesn't work for me. I need a couple of guys immediately. How about the young guys you mentioned about a month ago. Are they ready to go?"

"One is still available. I could give you him now and Jamie in a month."

Blake stood up and pitched his empty cup in the trash. "You're sure I can't have a couple of guys now?"

"Is there an issue with Jamie?"

Blake rubbed the back of his neck. "No. Nothing like that. I really need a couple of guys now." He pulled his wedding ring over the knuckle then shoved it back in place. "Yeah, sure. Give me the guy you got now. I'll get Justin to help cover in the interim."

"Tell Justin I'll throw in a bit extra this month for the added workload." As they walked to the door, Logan rested a fatherly hand on Blake's shoulder. "You and my favourite niece should come over one evening for dinner. Ask Dax to call and let me know what day works best for you two."

Blake nodded. "Sure. Is Trevor around? I need to follow up on a few things."

Logan nodded. "He's down in the warehouse."

"Thanks, Logan."

"Do you need some office space for the next couple of weeks?"

"Mostly I'll work from home. I have a meeting with procurement tomorrow about a couple of issues."

"Spoken like a manager."

As Blake left the office he said, "Flattery will get you nowhere."

Logan smiled as he turned back to his desk.

After chatting with Trevor, Blake headed for the parking lot. Once in his Ram pickup truck, he searched the Internet for James or Jamie Moore. He stared at the image of the man. "I remember you, you dirt bag." He threw his phone across the cab, slammed the truck into gear and squealed out of the parking lot.

Chapter 4 — The Note

Dakota and Blake lived in an upscale neighbourhood of Washington, D.C. with broad tree-lined streets and deep lawns where old money rubbed shoulders with Washington's brightest. They purchased their home seven years ago and were still considered the newcomers.

Setting their dirty dishes from dinner on the counter Dax said, "It's so good to have you home. I miss you, you know." She held Blake close, drinking in his face, his warmth, his presence.

Blake gave her a quick kiss. "I missed your cooking."

"You missed my cooking? After weeks away, that's all you got? Try again."

He looked in the air. "I missed your cold feet in bed?"

"Alright, socks and flannel pajamas tonight."

"Oh-oh. Not the ones with Tinker Bell. How about I miss your beautiful face and I dream about holding you close, reading poetry, sipping tea, eating cucumber sandwiches and whispering sweet nothings all evening long."

She smacked his butt. "Keep it up and I'll wear my new pink bunny rabbit onesie."

"Hmm. I deeply regret whatever I said. Please forgive me, oh queen of my heart."

"You're impossible. And I love you."

He held her tight. "Love you too, babe."

Dax melted into his long, pressing kiss. When he broke his hold, he winked. "Glass of wine?"

"That sounds good. There are a couple of bottles of white chilling in the fridge. How's Uncle Logan?"

"Good. He wants us to come over for dinner. We need to pick a date and you can let him know."

"Okay. I'll check my calendar and we can figure out what day works later. Did he say anything about decreasing your time overseas?" Dax began rinsing the dishes.

"We didn't get a chance to get into –" His phone buzzed with an incoming call. Glancing at the name he said, "It's Africa. I've got to take this. Hello."

He paced to the far end of the kitchen. "Yes. It's evening here and I'm now home with my family."

He watched Dax close up the dishwasher and wipe the counter. "This can't wait until I'm back?" He stepped into the front room.

"You did what?" He leaned on the window. His eyes followed a kid passing under the streetlight. "You used *my* name? What the –"

He listened. "Dammit – no, no, no. Bloody hell, Salama. Escalating him right now makes him unmanageable."

He rubbed his forehead. "Of course he did. You turned him into a freaked out monkey throwing his shit everywhere."

"Okay. How many? Three? Are you kidding? Three?" He pulled the phone away, muttering a string of obscenities. "Who?" Slowly, his head nodded with the enormity of the news. "I needed them. These guys were in my pocket. Do you have any idea what you've done?"

"No. I know you're trying to help. But you understand, this is a royal mess."

"No. Stop talking now. What I need is for you to shut up. Don't you try to fix it or you'll screw it beyond salvageable."

In a quieter voice he said, "No. I'll handle it. Listen, I need you to go over there and tell him you got it wrong. Give him a little sugar. Keep him quiet and distracted."

He glanced behind him to see if Dax was listening.

"I know it's hard, but I need you to do this. You'll take care of this for me, yeah?"

"See you soon."

Out of habit he started to pull the curtains closed then hesitated, listening to Dax settle in the family room. He searched the deepening shadows, remembering Dax's explanation of why the curtains need to close after sunset. *I'm not afraid of the dark, but of what lurks there.*

Wednesday, March 4

Blake stepped out of the shower. "How about Horatio?"

She pulled the toothbrush out of her mouth. "What? Like the English sailor guy? No."

"Dorcas?"

"Did you ever play in the school yard with other kids? You're such a dorkus."

"Fannie. Always thought that was a fabulous name."

She rinsed out her mouth. "No body parts."

"Moon Unit? Tank? Queen Precious Jewel Sunshine?" He pulled on a loose pair of track pants.

"Try to stick with ones that sound like a normal name." She headed to the kitchen with Blake close behind.

"Like Stiffany? Daisy Boo? Talula Does The Hula?"

"How long have you been thinking up these horrible names?"

"Huckleberry? Alfie? Egbert? Chester? Barney? Eanis?"

She poured two cups of coffee and popped down a couple of blueberry bagels. "Eanis? Think about what is going to be said on the playground with that name. No. Maybe you can do better with a little girl's name?"

"Griswalda? Bertha? Edith? Ethel? Birdie? Mabel?

"Mabel, the table? And Birdie? Really? That's almost as bad as Eanis. Clearly you get a limited vote on what we are going to call our baby." She leaned back on the counter, taking a sip of her coffee and watched Blake move about the kitchen.

He tapped the knife on the counter, waiting for the toaster.

She traced a red, half-moon scar on his left shoulder. "This is new."

He looked at the freshly healed wound and shrugged.

"International finance is surprisingly dangerous," she said.

"The hidden dangers of trading in money and shuffling paper. We financiers are under-appreciated."

She laughed. "All those paper cuts. Yes, the world has no idea what you have to deal with. Although, a moon-shaped paper cut on your shoulder is odd."

He didn't respond.

"When do you go back?"

He scratched his tousled hair. "I don't know. A week, maybe."

She wrapped her arms around his bare chest. "We'd better make the most of this week then."

The bagels popped up as he kissed the top of her head.

While he buttered she said, "Is it possible to come home for your birthday?"

"Mid April? No, not likely. I can probably be home to celebrate April 25."

"You'd rather celebrate your military discharge than your birthday?"

"You know I think of it as the first day of my life." Turning back to the bagels he muttered," Nothing worth remembering happened before that day."

He never spoke of his drug addict parents. There were painful things in his childhood with his aunt and uncle that he slammed the door shut on and refused to deal with. And Dax knew better than to poke that bear.

"Okay, plan on a party on April 25. Let me know who you'd like to invite. We can barbecue some steaks. Maybe we'll have some baby news to celebrate as well."

"Sure. Sounds great."

She glanced at the clock on the stove. "Oh look at the time. I've got to hop in the shower."

He flipped on the television, tuning to BBC. After the commercial, they recapped the breaking news that three top generals were killed in Zimbula, a central African country. The experts talked about the economic instability of the country and the long-term reign of the current president, Etienne Akleelu. The pundits engaged in an extended discussion on the possibility of a coup and the impact on surrounding countries.

One believed the middle ranks in the military slaughtered the three generals to clear the way to rise up against the president. Another suggested the generals were about to turn against the president, and Akleelu was responsible for their execution. A third man said there's the possibility that no coup was in the works. Coming up to the election the paranoid president lost it and killed his own.

Blake muted the television when Dax came in dressed for work.

She said, "I expect to be home around two. It's supposed to warm up to a beautiful afternoon. There's some beer in the fridge on the deck. Maybe we can kick back for awhile. I'm making a lasagne and salad for dinner. How does that sound?"

"Good, babe."

She kissed him goodbye and grabbed the keys for the BMW convertible.

She usually left earlier to avoid the heavy morning traffic on her drive to her Bethesda office. But when Blake was home she shifted to reduced hours. A bad accident brought traffic to a near standstill causing her to arrive just minutes before her first client. Her morning involved counselling a college woman with an eating disorder, a depressed housewife, and a teen with antisocial behaviour.

Between clients, she received a call. “Hello, Dakota Keyes speaking.”

A client suffering from schizophrenia whispered into the phone, “Snipers.”

“Tyrone?”

“I need your help. You need to tell them they have the wrong person.” She heard him yell, “I’m a veteran. You’ve got the wrong guy.”

“Who are you talking to?”

With his hand cupped over the mouthpiece he said, “The SWAT team. They’re in the yard. They’ve surrounded the house. Wait!”

“Tyrone?”

She heard him muttering.

“Tyrone, can you hear me?”

“They’re ordering me out of the house. Call them and tell them not to shoot me. They have snipers. Don’t shoot! It was just my flashlight.”

“Tyrone, do you remember how we talked about being mindful?”

“I’m coming out. Don’t shoot.”

She heard shuffling and grunting. “Tyrone, talk to me.”

“I’ve got to put you down now. They’ve ordered my hands behind my head.”

“Tyrone, I need you to pass a message to the SWAT leader. Can you do that for me?”

“The SWAT leader said, ‘That would be okay.’”

“Alright. I want you to tell him what you can smell. Do you smell grass?”

“No, I smell the garbage. Crap. Is it Thursday? I need to get it out front for pick up."

"Yes, it's Thursday. How about you take the garbage out front now?"

"I think that would make the snipers nervous."

"Focus for a moment. What do you hear? Can you hear any birds? You know how you love the tapping of the woodpecker? Can you hear one now?"

"Oh yes. He's busy in the trees. Yes. I can hear him."

"What else do you hear?"

"A big truck just passed by. And I can hear my neighbour cutting his grass."

"Good, Tyrone. Now talk to me about what you did this morning."

"I stayed in bed. I didn't sleep last night."

"Okay. Did you take your medication this morning?"

"No. I ran out a couple of days ago. I haven't picked up the new bottle yet."

"So without your medication, and without sleep –"

"I know what you're going to say. Maybe this isn't real?"

The phone dropped. She heard muffled sounds. "I'm back. It seems real."

"Yes. It seems very real. Do you think you can come in to see me right away? I'd like to talk with you."

"I'll ask if they'll let me go." She heard him talking. "Yes. Yes, I can go."

"Great. I'll see you soon. And Tyrone? Just ignore the voices."

"They seem so real." She heard him breathing.

"I know."

He broke down, quietly crying into the phone. "I'm trapped by these hallucinations. I want to find freedom from this nightmare. It feels like I'm looking for the escape door and I just can't find it. I'm pounding and pounding on the wall hoping it will suddenly change to a door. But it never does. It seemed better in Helmand. At least there I was fighting something real."

"I understand. Let's talk more about this when you come in."

Once off the phone with Tyrone, she called Blake.

"Hi Hon. What are you up to?"

Turning the television volume down Blake said, "I popped into the office this morning. Now I'm making some calls to clients and my team in Zimbula."

"Did I tell you today, I love having you home."

"I might have heard you mention something about that."

"Listen, I got a call from a client in crisis. I need to see him this afternoon. I'll be a little later getting home – maybe five or so. I'll start dinner when I get home."

"I thought you said you'd be home around two."

"That was the plan. Unfortunately I've got an emergency."

"I'm not home that much. It'd be nice if you could make an effort to be here."

"It's only another couple of hours. I'll pick up some steaks and a Greek salad. That won't take long to make."

"I come home and you're spending all your time at work. I've got plenty to do elsewhere too, but I'm making an effort to be here, to spend time with you. Isn't that what you want?"

"Yes, our time together is important to me. But ethically I can't put off a client in crisis. I won't be long."

"I'm disappointed that I'm the only one here making an effort. I'm trying Dax, but it feels like I'm the only one."

"You're not the only one. I've cleared all my afternoons for the week. The time is all yours."

"Until some old bat with dementia calls. It's not just today, Dax. It's the whole thing. There are days I want to buy a reindeer farm in Iceland and leave behind all this crap." Before she had a chance to respond he said, "I've got an important call from Africa coming in. I've got to go." He abruptly ended their call.

After checking Tyrone into the Bethesda hospital for overnight support, she stopped for a few groceries and was on her way home by 4:30. Waiting in a long line of traffic to make a left, she pondered the call with Blake. His comment about being the only one making an effort puzzled her. *Is he truly unhappy? Or is this stress talking?*

He believes he's the only one making an effort to spend time together. Could that be true, at least in part? While ethically required to deal with clients in crisis, I can see how it would feel like I'm putting my work ahead of our relationship. Maybe for a time, I need to reduce my caseload and handle only those clients less likely to have a crisis.

While stopped at a red light, something Tyrone said in the counselling session came to mind. *Death and darkness share one thing, our fear of the unknown. I imagine many in the military feel that way. Maybe Blake also fears the unknown and his frustration is simply a response to the changes associated with starting a family. I know he had a lousy childhood. Maybe that's unconsciously causing him to react.*

I've seen it many times where fear of the unknown spun a life out of control – whether it's a fear of death, darkness, entrapment in a delusional mind, a significant change to one's life – or a distressing call with a husband.

Okay. This is not going to spin me out of control. And I'll do all I can to reduce the tension for Blake. Once we have kids, I'd have to reduce my caseload anyway. I can certainly begin to make those changes now if that helps him.

She smiled as she thought about the promise of their evening ahead.

Having made a large detour around a car on fire, she arrived home around five thirty. As she removed her shoes she called out. "Hi honey, I'm home."

The house remained quiet.

In the kitchen, she flipped on the lights and laid out the dinner groceries on the counter. Thinking Blake might be napping, she called out again. Still no answer. Checking her phone for messages revealed nothing. She prepared the salad, seasoned the steak, and set the table. Excited to share her decision to further cut her caseload, her heart sang. With everything ready but the steaks, she phoned Blake. It went to voicemail. *Probably driving and can't answer.*

She looked over the food and the table, her hand tapping the counter. Glancing down at her pantsuit, she decided to change into her favourite little black dress. She touched up her makeup and looked at the effect in the mirror. *Earrings. That's what's missing.*

On the night table she noticed a folded note with her name on the front. With a sick feeling in the pit of her stomach, she picked it up. Blake's wedding ring fell out.

"If you're not going to make any effort to be here when I'm home, I'm done."

She fell to the bed. *I don't understand.* Reading the note a second and third time brought no clarity. *What does* I'm done *mean? Does it mean he can't deal with this tonight? Or this week?*

Her eyes settled on his ring. Her mind didn't want to embrace what its presence meant. The more she stared at it, the more it compelled her to think the unthinkable. She hurried to his closet. The suitcases were gone. Three shirts hung among dozens of jumbled empty hangers. The sock drawer – bare. Underwear – gone.

His footprint in the house had always been small. Now, nothing remained but three old plaid shirts.

It was one day short of ten years.

Chapter 5 — Missing

The ache reached deep, entwining itself not only around her heart, but her mind, firing off desperate reactionary thoughts. Like a building under demolition, Dax felt the first blow of the wrecking ball shattering the strong standing structure of her marriage. The entire building threatened to disintegrate.

She flinched at the forsaken sight of Blake's empty closet. Unable to look, her knees collapsed. Her face flushed and eyes blurred at the one thought screaming over and over in her head. "It's over."

She pulled one of the shirts off the hanger, buried her face in it, drawing in a deep breath. With a long exhale, she let her head fall back to the wall.

No, no, no. I just can't believe this is the end. I would have seen at least some signs of us falling apart before this.

Her breathing steadied as she combed through the past year in her mind for any indication that their marriage teetered on the precipice.

There's nothing. He's not spending any more time in Africa than he has in the last five years. No sign of emotional disengagement. Things are good in the bedroom. Money is not shifting out of the accounts. There just aren't any signs that he's been wanting out of the marriage.

She looked at the balled up shirt. "I don't get it." His note and disappearance didn't align to the ten years of their life together.

I guess this could be stress from work. Absently she touched her wedding ring, back on her finger after rock climbing. *Then again, I think things are about the same as always at work.*

I think.

Truth is, I don't actually know. He doesn't talk a lot about his work.

Actually, now that I think about it, he doesn't talk about work at all. I know very little about what he does and the challenges he faces. In my defense, it's not something he's ever volunteered. It's been that way for ten years. As far as that goes, there's no sign of a change.

This is actually rather troubling – I really don't know a lot about his work, the struggles or even the successes. How did I not notice? I guess because I never did know much about what he does. It's not a lack of interest, is it? If he wanted to talk about things, I would have happily discussed whatever he wanted to talk about. He just never talked – about anything. It's unknown to me, like his past.

I think because his work and challenges never came up in discussion I never thought about it. There's a simple fix for that. I could spend a month in Africa learning about what he does. Then we could go on that safari we talked about years ago.

She folded the crumpled shirt, stroking the worn cotton.

Ah, a trip to Africa – yeah, that is all grand and wonderful, but I honestly don't think his work is the issue.

She stretched out her legs and laid the folded shirt on her lap, adjusting the collar. "What's going on with you, Blake?"

I really don't think work is the issue. This whole thing could be a freak-out about starting a family. Yeah. That makes a whole lot more sense. He's always refused to talk about his childhood. I know there are horrible things in his past that he's not dealt with. Maybe he's afraid he'll revisit those horrors on his own kids.

We don't have to call it quits because of his past. We can put off having kids until we deal with whatever this is. We just need some time to talk things through. I could meet him in Paris. I'm sure he could take some time off work. We could kick about Europe for a month, resolve whatever the issues are and move ahead. Then we could do an African safari and I could join him in Zimbula for a couple of weeks.

She got up to look for her phone. She pulled up his number and drew in a deep breath. It rang four times and went to voice mail. "Hi hon. I got your note. I think we need to talk. Can you please call me? I love you."

On the Internet, she searched for flights and departure times to Nairobi. Figuring he left for the airport mid afternoon she thought, *He's probably in the air by now. Maybe six or seven hours to Paris or Frankfurt, and then a layover. I'll try calling around midnight and maybe catch him between flights.*

She changed out of her dress and into pajamas and made herself a tea. Thoughts, self-accusations, arguments and worry swirled through her mind like a funnel cloud, round and round, ruthlessly circling, threatening destruction, but never resolving anything.

Determined to not let her mind spiral out of control, she settled in to watch a top-rated five-season serial. While the opening credits rolled by she reminded herself, *we are going to be okay. I'll get a hold of Blake. We'll talk. We'll meet in Paris and work things out. And there's nothing more I can do until midnight.*

Trying to convince herself she repeated," Everything's going to be alright."

Five episodes later she tried calling again. Four rings and it went to voice mail. "Hi honey. I hoped to catch you between flights. Please call me when you get this message. It doesn't matter the time. I want to talk. Thanks, love."

Another no answer. He may not have his phone on.

She checked the front and back door locks then stood in their bedroom looking at the bed. Aching tendrils coiled tighter. Pushing down this overwhelming feeling she said to the empty air," This is not over. Everything's going to be alright." Returning to the family room with a pillow and blanket she watched three more episodes before falling asleep.

Thursday, March 5

An hour before her alarm, she awoke from a disturbing dream about being locked in an old abandoned house, searching for both Blake and a way out. An alarm kept ringing and although she searched every room, she was unable to find it and turn it off. She found Blake in the basement standing behind unlabeled boxes with his back to her. He wouldn't turn around and face her. Despite her calling and coaxing he refused to respond. She awoke still feeling confusion and hurt from the dream.

In the few moments it took for her mind to wake up, the heartache slammed her like a bulldozer in stealth mode.

Lying awake, the words *I'm done* steamrolled into her thoughts. She knew Blake was probably on his second leg of the trip, travelling from Europe to Africa. She'd have to wait until noon to catch him in Nairobi. She deliberately closed the door on the pain. Although it was still early, she headed into work to immerse herself in paperwork as a distraction until her first client.

Grateful for a break after three sessions, she went for a walk in a nearby park. Her favourite bench was perfectly positioned to watch the resident swans. The male swan pursued the female, copying her movements. They raised their bodies out of the water, facing each other, dancing an ancient ritual that bonded the two.

With images of the courtship dance imprinted on her mind, she tried calling again. "Hi love. I guess you're in Kenya by now. We do need to talk. Please call as soon as you can. Thanks. I love you."

A young mom and her daughter threw bread on the water, bringing the swans in close. She smiled at the toddler clapping.

She called Justin Forsythe, Blake's second in command in Zimbula. When his recorded message finished she said, "Hi Justin. It's Dakota Keyes. I've been trying to reach Blake, but he's travelling and I haven't connected yet. When you see him, could you ask him to call home. It's important. Thanks."

Since her afternoon schedule was clear, she stopped by a little specialist shop to pick out Blake's birthday present. Every year since they married, she bought him several investment bottles of whiskey, his favourite liquor. The collection, worth thousands of dollars, now topped 50 bottles. She spent an hour with the broker determining which collectibles she wished to purchase.

At home, she went for a long run and shower before dining on part of the uneaten meal from the night before. Rarely did she have trouble filling her time alone, but she now felt restless and disconnected. After rattling around the house, she settled in to watch more episodes of the serial.

Saturday, March 7

After leaving several messages with Blake and Justin on Friday, she couldn't settle her mind to sleep. From midnight on, she became increasingly distracted waiting for either Justin or Blake to phone. At two in the morning, she decided to call again, thinking they would be finished work and probably eating dinner. Neither answered.

Worry threatened to derail her. It took another two episodes to quieten her mind and fall asleep.

At seven in the morning she tried again. He didn't answer. *He's been there at least a day. Why doesn't he answer?*

She tried Justin. "Oh Justin, I'm so glad to get a hold of you. It's Dakota. I'm trying to get in touch with Blake, but haven't reached him. Could you let him know I really need to talk with him as soon as possible?"

"Yeah, I got your earlier messages. I'll certainly pass along your request when I see him."

"He hasn't been into the office? Is he at home?"

"No, he hasn't come to the office and hasn't checked in. To be really honest, I'm not sure where he is. I've called a couple of times, but he hasn't answered."

"You're saying he's missing?"

"Don't panic. I simply don't know where he is."

"That's the definition of missing."

"Well, yes. But when people think of a missing person, it implies something bad happened. I don't know that anything bad has happened, and I don't want you thinking so. There are a number of things that could prevent him from getting in touch. I tend to think it's something like a dead cell phone and jet lag induced sleep."

"Have you gone to his house to check?"

"I plan on stopping by after work. I don't think you have to worry. Africa is not like America where both travel and communication are easy. Often cell service is down here and the roads are rough. The vehicle may have broken down along the way. Or he could be at home in a deep sleep."

"Wasn't he flying directly to Mabezi?"

"No. Commercial flights no longer land in Mabezi. We now fly into Kigoma in Tanzania and drive a few hours across the border."

"Oh, I see. Will you call me after you check his house? Let me know either way? I know you think I shouldn't worry –"

"Um, sure. It'll be several hours before I leave the office."

"That's fine. Sooner, if you hear from him, okay?"

"Yes, ma'am."

"Thank you, Justin."

If his plane went down, there'd be news about it.

She checked the international news sites for any indication of a downed plane. Then she searched what to do if your loved one goes missing overseas. Once on the State Department website, she read all she could on Zimbula, Tanzania and Kenya. She knew certain countries in central Africa were undergoing economic and ethnic struggles, but she had not realized that Zimbula was considered one of the most dangerous because of crime, civil unrest, violence and kidnapping. Along with hotspots like Libya or Somalia, the State Department included Zimbula on its list of Do Not Travel countries.

Zimbula has a Do Not Travel advisory?

And has for years?

He's been working and living in a place that no one should be visiting?

I wonder if those advisories are like a weather warning – all hype and terrifying warnings for a storm that amounts to a few snowflakes. It can't be too bad if Blake has worked there for years with no problem.

Puzzled she thought, *what would a country in such civil unrest need with international financing directed at developing business and jobs? It doesn't make any sense. No, this hype is the U.S. government not wanting to be liable for anything that goes wrong overseas. They can always say, "We warned you."*

She looked up travel to Canada and Britain. For Canada, exercise normal precautions. For the United Kingdom, exercise increased caution due to terrorism.

Yeah, this is how they roll – overly precautious and guarded. And neither Blake nor uncle Logan ever spoke of Zimbula as an extremely dangerous area.

Yet I wonder – could something have gone horribly wrong? Am I going to be calling in Russell Crowe to negotiate a ransom with kidnappers? I can't even imagine negotiating for your husband's life.

Gotta stop this train of thought before it leaves the station.

She checked the Internet for news from Zimbula. She found many short articles about the murder of three generals, several editorials about the upcoming election, the civil unrest and the talk of a coup. And she found one article on a village in the northeast that was wiped out by floods and mudslides.

Chapter 6 — In Vino Veritas

Saturday, March 7 (morning)

Eager for the distraction of paperwork, she headed to her office. She spent more early morning hours surfing the Internet for an explanation for Blake's silence and little on sleep.

She expected to hear from Justin around noon. A couple of restless hours ticked by. She tried to call again. No answer.

The lack of communication and all the unknowns escalated her concern. She decided to try one more time then call the U.S. Embassies in Kenya, Tanzania and Zimbula and enlist their help in locating her husband.

A glance at her watch and quick calculation confirmed that it would be the end of the workday for Justin. She left another message asking that he call.

A couple of minutes later, her phone rang. She choked out an almost breathless," Hello?"

"Hi Dakota. This is Justin. Sorry I missed your call. I understand you're thinking of contacting the embassies here?"

"Unless you've located Blake, yes. I'd like their help. We don't know what's happened to him, or even if he's okay. He may be hurt or kidnapped. We need to get the experts involved."

"And you consider the staff at the embassies to be experts in field work? More than the staff of Ironwood?"

"I don't mean to insult anyone, but this is my husband's life on the line here. So yeah, I don't think a bunch of financiers are going to know diddly squat about finding a missing person and dealing with the criminal element if need be."

There was a long pause. "Uh-huh. Financiers. Right. Well – you certainly can call the embassies. It's been my experience they don't like to extend themselves far beyond the gates of the embassy. We are here on the ground and I assure you, we are your best bet for locating Blake. Give the team here another day to backtrack his travel plans. I'm sure we will find him with a dead cell phone and a broken down vehicle."

Something tugged at her pants-on-fire meter. Momentarily, she struggled to identify the cause. After some quick calculations she said, "My understanding of the typical travel itinerary is that Blake should have arrived in Mabezi well over 12 hours ago. Have you and the team done any of the backtracking, like you're suggesting?"

"Well, no. I assumed Blake was at home sleeping off the jet lag."

"But you'll go out now?"

"No, it's not really a good idea to do that kind of thing at night. I'll send some guys out at first light."

"By some guys you mean everyone, including you, right?"

"We can't –"

"Everyone including you, right Justin?"

He sighed. "Yes, ma'am."

As soon as she finished with Justin, she called Logan.

"Well, hello, darling. Have you and Blake decided on a day you want to come over for dinner?"

"What?" She shook her head. "No, Uncle Logan. I'm calling about Blake being missing."

"Maybe he's caught in traffic."

"He's not missing here. He's missing in Africa. He left Wednesday afternoon. I've tried calling him for two days now and he doesn't answer."

"He left for Africa? I didn't know. Let me try him. I'll call you right back." In a couple of minutes he said, "Listen, I'm coming over. I'll see you in 20 minutes."

Didn't Justin alert Uncle Logan? Wouldn't that be the logical thing to do when one of the employees goes missing in a foreign country? Either he's incompetent – or he doesn't want to find Blake. Oh my – maybe he's involved.

She paced the floor. Her mind raced, exploring tentacles of possibilities. Justin betrayed Blake. Justin is a criminal. Maybe he leads a roving band of murderous thugs.

Wow, that's going down a bad road. I cannot accept the logical conclusion of that rabbit trail. I'm shutting down this line of thinking right now.

Logan hugged her at the door. "You must be worried."

She nodded. "No one seems to know where he is."

He closed the door. "Yes, I spoke with Justin. He and the team will be working through the night to track him down. Don't worry, honey."

Funny how Justin kicks it into gear when Uncle Logan calls. "Thanks. I called him. He seemed a little reluctant."

Logan lifted his large foot. "You just need a big boot." He looked at the worried lines around her eyes. "We'll find him, Daxie. Don't worry."

They wandered into the kitchen. With her hands resting on the counter she said, "Can I get you anything? Coffee? Rye and Coke?"

He opened the fridge. "A beer will do. Thanks." Pitching the cap in the garbage he said, "Blake left Wednesday? I thought he was here for a couple of weeks. I wonder what happened that made him hurry back. I didn't hear of any emergency."

"I think it was me."

His brows knit together.

She headed for the front room. “He expected me home in the afternoon, but I had a client in crisis that delayed me. I called him. He seemed pretty upset. Another call came in for him, so we didn’t get much chance to talk. When I got home, he was gone. He left a note saying he’s done.”

“I wouldn’t get too upset about a note.”

She sat down. “He left his wedding ring. Cleaned out his closet.”

“I see.” He moved to sit beside her and pulled her close. “What’s going on with that boy? He’s too young for a midlife crisis.”

“I want to call the embassies in Kenya, Tanzania and Zimbula. Justin said they’re useless. What do you think?”

“Yes, we can call them. They may have quicker access to certain information. Do you have his flight numbers?”

“No. The only thing I know is approximately when he left home – some time Wednesday afternoon between 1:30 and 5 o’clock.”

Logan tapped and swiped his way to a list of flights leaving Dulles Friday afternoon or evening. “It’s one of three flights, one with United, one with British Airways and one with KLM.”

“He most often flies KLM or Lufthansa.”

“Okay.” He handed her the flight numbers for both airlines. “It’s likely one of those two. And I’d start with the embassy in Kenya.”

Relieved to have something to do she dialled the number and began pacing the floor. After explaining her situation, she was connected with Peter Wingham.

Peter listened closely to her story. “Who did you say he works for?”

“The Ironwood Group.”

“I gather they provide military support?”

“Military? No. They are an international financing company.”

Logan groaned and reached for the phone.

She said, “I’m going to let you speak with the owner of Ironwood, Logan Keyes."

Logan said, "Peter? Yes, I'm Logan Keyes." He noted Dax's crossed arms while he explained the nature of his company. "Yes, we provide military expertise and support."

Her frown deepened.

"No, Blake does not provide financing. His area is central and south Africa. Predominantly, he runs the team in Zimbula. We are heavily involved with strategy, tactics and training the military." He nodded. "Security, yes."

Dax rocked back on her feet.

"Yes, there is some instability at the top of the army." He watched Dax turn her back to him. "No, I don't believe the men are in a tenuous position."

Dax muttered something and stood in front of the window.

"No, there have been no threats. We have good working relations with the president, the military and the police." He listened for a moment. "Oh, about ten years now." Nodding, he said, "Of course." He handed the phone to Dax.

Peter said, "Okay, I understand your husband's role and, while Zimbula carries a do not travel advisory, your husband has been comfortably operating there for awhile. And it sounds like he can take care of himself. There is every possibility that he's broken down somewhere. It happens a lot in the less developed areas. I can check if there are any reports of a hospitalized or arrested U.S. citizen. I'll contact my counterpoints in both Tanzania and Zimbula, and they can check with the local authorities in their regions. They'll be more tuned in to things going on in their area – things that Blake may have got caught up in, like a flood wiping out a bridge or local gas shortages.

"Nairobi is one of the larger embassies in the region. I can be a point person here, if you like."

"Thank you. That would be great. I read that U.S. citizens are often the targets of kidnappers."

"Certainly there's the possibility that one of the groups involved in civil unrest kidnapped him for ransom. But let's check the basic things first. I've located a number of missing people over the last year, and none have been kidnapped. It's usually a simple explanation. I'm going to give you my direct number. Feel free to call anytime."

"Okay. Thank you, Peter."

She turned off her phone and stared out the window. "For my entire life you let me think you ran an international financing company. Why would you not tell me the truth? Why would Blake not be honest about what he does?" She turned around to face Logan. "What exactly does Blake do for you?"

Chapter 7 — Dead or Not Dead

Logan rubbed his face with his hand. "I'm sorry, Daxie. When you were young, your mom made me promise to keep that aspect of my work from you. After your father's death, she was concerned you would worry and have nightmares if you knew."

"I'm a long way from ten years old."

He studied his hands. "Yes. You are. I wanted to tell you the truth when you were 18, but that was the year your mom passed away. It was such a difficult year for you. I couldn't add to the load. Time passed and there seemed no right time to tell you. Then it became impossible to explain."

She tossed the phone on the sofa and headed for the kitchen.

Logan followed.

She opened the fridge. "I feel like a large glass of wine. Want one?"

"I still have some beer." He set the bottle on the counter and stuffed his hands into his pockets. "I'm sorry Dax. I never wanted to hurt you. I'm actually glad you know the truth."

She poured herself a full glass. "It explains why Blake never talked to me about his work."

"Can you forgive me?"

She shrugged. "You made a promise you had to honour. I get that." She stared unflinchingly at him then broke. "I love that you willingly bore the cost of that promise." She hugged him. "Of course

I forgive you. It's just a lot to get my head around."

She sipped her wine and considered all the people who work for Ironwood. There were very few women, and all the men were exceptionally buff. "I always thought of Ironwood as a male version of Hooters. For awhile I wondered if your hiring manager was gay. It sure explains a lot. Did you ask Blake to keep this from me?"

"Yes. I did." He cleared his throat.

"And he agreed?"

"Yes."

"He never said anything about needing to be honest in our marriage?"

"He understood the circumstances."

"It seems he found it easy to live a lie with me."

"Live a lie? No, Daxie."

"What would you call it when a husband's career is completely hidden from his wife?"

"In this instance, protection."

"Protecting everyone but his wife."

"Don't blame him. This was my promise and my doing."

"And here you are taking the blame for the lack of honesty in our marriage. That is not on you. He could have chosen to be truthful, valuing his and my relationship over some obsolete promise you made to protect a young child. But clearly he didn't value honesty, and he didn't want to talk about his work with me."

"No, it's not like that at all. I'm sure he wanted to protect you and all that you love, including your relationship with me. I see this as a sign of his deep care for you. Please don't take this out on him."

"Don't get me wrong. I still love him. I hope he and I can work things out – when we find him. I'm just disappointed that one lie from you and Mom twenty years ago could be a barrier to honesty between Blake and me."

"You're right – we will find him."

"Tell me one thing, and I need you to be completely honest."

"Anything."

"Are you two involved in anything illegal? Gun running? Drug smuggling? Anything criminal? Is there anything about his work that has put him in jeopardy? Is Zimbula dangerous?"

"No. I draw a hard line about what services we offer. We provide a lot of training, and security details – like protection for VIPs, and a few limited combat roles. We do acquire and sell weapons, but everything is completely above board.

"The truth is I've turned over the Central African operations to Blake. I get regular reports, but unless there's a problem I've left it all in his capable hands. Nevertheless, I'm not aware of anything that would put his life at risk. I worked there for over a decade and Blake's been there for almost as much time. I know what the State Department says about Zimbula, but Ironwood has worked there with no issue."

"Except the top generals have been shot and there's talk of a coup. Who do you work for there?"

"President Etienne Akleelu."

"If there is a coup then Ironwood people would be eliminated."

"A coup is always a possibility, but we would not be boots on ground if it looked like one was about to erupt. We're very connected to the players who could initiate a takeover. I spoke to Blake about the risks. His assessment is that this is nothing more than cage rattling coming up to the election."

"So you don't think the conditions in Zimbula have anything to do with Blake's disappearance."

"No, I don't."

"That's good, but he's still missing and we don't know why."

"We've got the embassies involved. And all my guys on the ground there are looking for him. We'll find him. It's going to be okay."

His phone rang. "Excuse me. I have to take this."

She poured herself another glass of wine.

"Hello. Hey Voodoo! How are you? Where are you these days?" He headed to the front room. "So, still grinding on the front lines and using that silver tongue to talk your way out of trouble? How long has it been?" Sitting with his legs stretched out, he rested his arm along the back of the sofa.

"Congo? No, we have no operations there."

Nodding he said, "Yes, Zimbula. Not me, but a man I have working for me."

His eyebrows shot up. "Whoa. Three hundred thousand refugees? I thought things were settling down."

"It seems it's in the DNA of the continent. What does this have to do with Ironwood?" He picked invisible lint from his jeans. "I see. Yes."

"Awamaki?" He stole a glance at Dax. "Not for many years. I – Oh, Awamaki Kubwa. No. I know nothing about this Kubwa. But I don't like anyone riding on the coattails."

"Uh-huh. Yep."

"No, but I will find out."

"Of course. There's a good chance I'll be in the area soon."

"No, Zimbula on other urgent business."

"I'll be in touch, for sure. I may need to tap into your information network."

"Thanks, Voodoo."

Sunday, March 8

Kareem stepped out of the ramshackle office. He signalled to a lithe fourteen-year-old girl, sending her through the warren of hand-dug shafts to the far end of the mine. She returned with the young man who found the Impossible Blue.

Kareem chucked her chin. "Come see me after dinner."

She stared at the ground.

He forced her to look at him. “I expect you after dinner.”

She gave him a slight nod of agreement.

He entered the shack with the young man. “Jack, this is Elvis, the man I told you about.”

Elvis wiped his hand on his pants and offered it with a beaming grin.

“Ah, the young man who found a rather large diamond.” Jack shook his hand.

“Yes sir, I am.”

“Have a seat.”

Elvis dusted off the back of his pants before sitting down on a wooden chair. He looked at Kareem then the boss.

Jack said, “I’d like to talk a bit about what this means to you.”

Elvis nodded and repeated to himself,” What this means, yes.”

“Do you have any family?”

Leaning forward in his chair, Elvis tried to find a comfortable place for his long arms. “Yes sir. I have a woman and two kids.”

“Call me Jack.” He scratched his chin. “Two kids. Where do they live?”

“Three hours from here.”

Jack nodded. “And you use what you earn from the mine to look after your family?”

“Yes sir – Jack.” He shifted in the seat, the chair creaked and wobbled.

“And you keep a little something for yourself. Maybe a lady or two on the side?”

Elvis shrugged. “Maybe one or two.”

Jack steepled his fingers in front of his lips. “How would you like to work for me as one of the drivers? It’s steady pay.”

Elvis scratched his sparse chin whiskers. He thought of the truck he saw arrive at the mine once or twice a week. “Just a couple of days a week? Could I still work my mine?”

“I can promise as a driver, you’ll earn five times the income you made last year. You'll drive for all of my mines here in Zimbula."

Elvis stood up and vigorously shook Jack's hand. "When do I start, boss?"

"How about today?"

"Yes, boss."

Kareem stepped forward. "There's one thing. As an employee, we don't talk to anyone about mine business. Do you understand?"

"Yes, keep my eyes on my own business, my ears closed and my mouth shut."

Kareem and Jack exchanged a look of satisfaction.

After making arrangements for other counsellors to carry her client load for a time, Dax called Peter in Nairobi. "I don't mean to be a bother, and I know we spoke yesterday, but I'm wondering if you have any news?"

"As matter of fact, I do. We've got some information from the airlines. A week ago Blake landed in Nairobi Saturday afternoon Eastern Africa time. He was booked on a flight to Kigoma that evening, but missed the flight. The police are processing the paperwork for permission to access the airport cameras. They're hoping that will give us a lead on what happened."

"So, he's in Kenya."

"Not necessarily. He may have caught a flight out on another day or caught a private commuter plane. We're still looking into those possibilities. We're also checking the hotels and hospitals here. I'm sorry I don't have more information, but it's a start."

"Thank you, Peter. It's more than I was able to find out. If you don't mind, I'd like to call tomorrow."

"Certainly. Like I said, call anytime."

Dax immediately called Logan to update him. "I want to go to Nairobi. Peter is making progress in tracking down what happened to Blake and I feel I need to be there."

Logan said, "What did he say?"

"That Blake arrived in Nairobi Thursday then missed his flight to Kigoma. They are still working on what happened after that."

"Going there alone – it's just not a good idea. There are areas of Kenya that have level 4 do not travel advisories, and level 3 areas of Nairobi that experience a lot of violent crime like armed carjacking, mugging, home invasions, and kidnapping. Street crime can happen anytime and anywhere. The local police are unable to respond. You would be a prime target and totally on your own. It's far too dangerous."

"You could come with me, or send a couple of the Ironwood guys."

"I need a few days to clear the decks here before I could go. And I don't have anyone available that has the experience needed to protect you in that environment. I'm sorry Dax. Maybe in a few days we can go."

Monday, March 9

A second update from Peter indicated that Blake took a private helicopter early Sunday morning from Nairobi, Kenya to the remote border of Tanzania, about 200 kilometres north east of Kigoma. The flight plan indicated the latitude and longitude of an uninhabited area west of a couple of massive game reserves.

Why would he travel to the remote hills of Tanzania?

She pulled out a map she bought years ago when they talked about going on a safari.

What would draw Blake to this isolated area? Checking Google Maps online for indication of habitation she thought, *there aren't even villages marked here.*

She called Logan. "Do you know anything about this area?"

"Not much." He pulled up a satellite image. "There's no development – no towns. And it's Tanzania, not Zimbula. We have no business going on in Tanzania right now. I can't imagine why he'd go there."

"Unless he's threatened, kidnapped, taken hostage, caught up in some ethnic squabble, or some other encounter gone wrong."

"Did Peter say anything about coercion?"

"No. But that doesn't mean maybe he stumbled on something he wasn't supposed to see or know and he was forced to go there instead of Kigoma."

"That just the stuff of movies. If you want to shut someone up, it takes three seconds and one bullet. There's no indication that he went unwillingly to this area."

"Maybe they're using him to get weapons."

Logan said nothing.

She said, "Okay. I don't know. Why do you think he went to Nowhere, Tanzania?"

"I have no idea. How about we wait until they track him down and we can ask him. I imagine that area of Tanzania has no cell phone service. And he probably doesn't take the satellite phone when he travels back and forth from the States. So he'd have no way to reach us, or us him."

She sighed, venting her frustration. "So we wait."

Tuesday, March 10

Peter called mid morning.

With a pounding heart, she answered. "You have news?"

"Yes. We confirmed Blake's passport information as a passenger on the helicopter flight to western Tanzania. We have CCTV footage of him boarding with three other passengers. As I mentioned yesterday, the flight plan indicates they were headed to the border hills of Tanzania and Zimbula." He cleared his throat. "I'm sorry to inform you they never arrived. The helicopter crashed about 70 km from their destination. The authorities in Tanzania have examined the crash site. No one survived."

She held onto the kitchen counter to stand. "They have his body? How did they identify him?" She thought of his wedding ring sitting on the dresser.

"They found Blake's passport in a lock box among the wreckage."

"Okay, but how does that prove he's one of the fatalities?"

"For private commercial flights, they collect the passports when passengers board, and return them when passengers disembark."

"I see."

"I'm so sorry, Ms. Keyes."

With a shaky voice she said, "Thank you. I appreciate your help."

"You're welcome. I wish I had better news. Do you have a pen? I'd like to give you the contact information of my counterpart in Tanzania. If you have any questions, you can contact her. She will be able to help you out with the logistics and paperwork to bring his body home, if that's what you wish to do."

She wrote down the name and number of Gladness Sibale and ended the call.

She sat stunned. No tears. Just stared out the window, very still and quiet, oblivious to the world.

An hour later, Logan came through the front door and called out. He found her in the front room.

"I phoned and you didn't answer. I became worried. Is everything okay?"

She slowly shook her head. "Peter called."

He sat beside her and took her hand.

In a quiet, steady voice she said, "They say he was aboard the helicopter. It crashed. There were no survivors." She turned and looked at him with a sharp thrust to her chin. "But how did they identify him? They are basing it on the presence of his passport in the lockbox. Maybe it wasn't him. Maybe he got off and forgot to get his passport. Maybe he's injured and lost in the jungle."

"Did you ask Peter how they identified him?"

"Everyone burned to death. Peter said because they have video of Blake boarding the chopper, and they did not make it to their first stop, and because Blake's passport was found in a lock box, they decided it must be him. I didn't ask for more details. He gave me the name of someone in U.S. embassy in Tanzania."

"I can call, if you want."

She handed him the paper. When finished the call he rubbed his forehead. "So, Gladness was quite helpful." He looked at the notes he made. "Nairobi has video of three passengers boarding the flight. She said although the bodies were severely burned, they found the bodies of the pilot and three passengers."

"But how do they know for sure Blake was one of them?"

"They know he boarded the helicopter, and it had not arrived at its first stop."

"But they don't *know* one of the bodies is Blake. Maybe it made an unscheduled stop. Maybe it's someone else. I want a DNA test. Does Tanzania do any forensic testing?"

"They are one of the strongest economies in Africa and quite advanced. I'm sure in Dar-es-Salaam they have forensic labs."

"Then I want testing done. I don't accept that he's dead."

Logan called Gladness to request a DNA test of the remains. Then he called Libby Kennedy.

When Libby arrived she noted the dark circles under Dax's eyes and the tension in her face. She hugged her exhausted chum. "Logan told me what's going on." She pushed back her friends hair. "I'm so sorry."

"There's nothing to be sorry for. Blake isn't dead."

Libby shot a look at Logan.

He said, "We've asked for a DNA test."

Libby nodded and turned back to Dax. "They have evidence he

got on the chopper?"

"Yes, but who knows what happened between boarding and when they crashed. Maybe he got off earlier. He could be injured and wandering lost in the jungle."

Libby looked at Logan for an explanation.

"Three passengers boarded. Four bodies were found at the crash – three passengers and one pilot."

Dax waved them off and headed to the bedroom. "But they don't know for sure." She closed the door behind her.

Logan poured himself and Libby a drink.

Libby said she was surprised he was back in Africa, considering this past weekend was their anniversary. Logan told her about the note, the wedding ring and how she's been trying to reach him for days.

"Oh, poor kid. He left a day before their tenth anniversary? And she's not talked to him? It must feel like he disappeared off the face of the earth and she doesn't know why." She poured a third glass of wine and headed down to the bedroom. "Can I come in?"

"Sure." Dax closed a drawer and opened another, searching through the contents.

"I brought you a glass of wine."

"Thanks." Another drawer opened.

She watched Dax finish with the dresser then move to the night table. "What are you looking for?"

"A money belt – you know, the kind you wear under your clothes."

Libby's eyebrows rose. "And why do you need that now?"

"I'm going to Africa." She momentarily stopped the search. "I don't believe Blake is dead, but if he is, I want to go and deal with his body and belongings at his house in Zimbula. And if he's not – and he's not – then there's a good chance he's hurt. At the very least I want to go talk with him face to face and work out whatever has him spooked about our marriage."

Libby took a big drink of her wine. She opened her mouth to say something then closed it again.

"Here it is." Dax set the money belt on the top of her dresser. Spotting Blake's wedding ring, she rummaged through her jewellery. "Oh, and I just found out that Ironwood provides military support services, not financial assistance."

Libby's brows furrowed. "What? So Blake's a mercenary?"

She shook her head. "That's an ugly word."

"It's what we call a professional soldier for hire."

"And it's what we call a person concerned with making money at the expense of ethics – and that doesn't fit."

"Hmm."

Dax turned back to the dresser and pulled out a silver necklace. Threading Blake's ring on, she read the inscription inside the ring, *For an eternity beyond forever* then clasped the chain around her neck.

Libby plumped up one of the pillows and got comfortable on the bed. "Tell me what's going on deep down inside."

Dax stopped, rested her hands on the dresser and looked down. "I haven't lost my grip on reality, if that's what you're wondering. I know it *looks* bad, but I'm not ready to throw it all away on circumstantial evidence." She turned to face her best friend. "No one knows *for sure* that one of those bodies is Blake. And until there's proof, I'm not willing to think the worst. I need to live with myself for another four or five decades. I want to rest easy knowing I pushed for facts, and feel confident that what I believe is the actual truth."

Libby nodded. "Yeah, I understand. I just wanted to know how you're really feeling. You know, about everything – his going back to Africa, the note and wedding ring. I know you're excited to start a family. And now, finding out the truth of his work. Those are really big issues. In light of all those stressors, it's a lot to deal with Blake missing and presumed dead."

Dax picked up her wine and sat on the bed beside Libby. "When you put it like that, it doesn't sound good. But I will continue to expect to find Blake alive and that we can work things out."

Libby clinked her glass with Dax. "To the eternal optimist who sees stars, particularly in the midst of a hurricane."

"Thank you, Lib. You're a good friend."

"I packed a bag to stay here with you for a few days if you can handle a bit of company. I'll be here if you want to talk and give you space when you need it. I can make my famous caramel double chocolate cheesecake. It's a perfect filler while waiting for news."

The tension in Dax's face eased. She leaned on her friend's shoulder. "You can have the room across the hall. And make it a big cheesecake. I'm going to need it."

Spotting the two emerge from the bedroom, Logan finished up a work phone call and joined them in the kitchen. Dax rinsed out her glass at the sink.

Logan silently inquired of Libby. She nodded and mouthed," It's okay."

He said, "I'm going to head back to work. You'll keep me posted?"

"Thanks, Uncle Logan." She glanced at Libby. "For everything, including calling Libby." She hugged him. "I promise I'll call as soon as I hear anything."

He kissed her cheek and waved goodbye on his way out.

She managed a bit of toast and tea for dinner. Libby lit the logs stacked in the fireplace and both curled up under blankets and filled their evening with movies.

Around midnight, they went to bed. Dax lay awake. Without the distraction of a movie, she tried to figure out all the possible scenarios that could explain how Blake could be alive.

Wednesday, March 11

In the morning, after a night filled with unresolved ruminations, she looked at herself in the mirror. Dark eyes, rimmed in red, looked back.

Gladness called to let her know that the lab agreed to run a DNA test on all three passengers, but due to the incinerated state of the bodies, the likelihood of recovering any DNA was extremely low. She asked if Dax would send a sample of Blake's DNA, his dental records and x-rays of any broken bones.

Now with something tangible to focus on, she spent the morning on the phone with a lawyer and the State Department getting legal permission to access Blake's medical and dental records. Then she spent the afternoon ensuring the DNA sample and various documents were forwarded to the forensic team in Tanzania.

Thursday Evening, March 12

A grey morning dawned, following a stormy night of brooding and stewing. The previous day's paper chase fuelled tumbling thoughts that kept pace with the rolling tempest outside.

After several nights without sleep, she looked burned out and felt drained. She tried napping in the afternoon, but sleep eluded her. Tylenol didn't touch the grinding headache. Her mind was scattered and unfocused. By dinner, Libby talked to her about taking sleeping pills for a few nights to get her back on track. Dax rarely took any medication. But when Libby said, "If they find Blake, you cannot be strung out on no sleep," she reconsidered.

Alone in her room that night, she dropped on the bed looking at the sleeping pill. At first she knew what she looked at, but fatigue beyond exhaustion drained away her thoughts. Unaware of how long she sat staring vacantly at the blue pill, reality broke through the numbness when Libby called out a "Goodnight." Before Dax could argue with herself, she took the pill.

In the darkness of a bedroom recently vacated by one, she lay on her back staring at the ceiling. Half an hour later, the swirl of the sleeping pill pulled her down into blessed oblivion.

At 3:37 am, her phone rang. The sound hauled her up from the whirling depths of sleep. Groggy, she looked at the number.

It's Blake!

She scrambled to pull herself loose of the covers and fumbled to answer the phone.

"Hello? Hello Blake? I'm so glad to hear from you. I was worried – I'm sorry, what?"

An accented voice said something muffled and distant. She heard Blake respond. "No, don't tell him where I am. I've tracked down a couple of connections that –" There were a few muffled words followed by," – the blue. It'll take several days to set up."

The phone beeped and the call failed.

EPISODE TWO — IMPOSSIBLE BLUE

Happiness is only found in today.

Yesterday's happiness is nostalgia,

Tomorrow's is but a glimmer of hope.

Chapter 1 — Jack Daniels

Friday, March 13 (early morning)

I heard Blake. He's alive.

Grasping at the tantalizing lifeline, Dax called back. While making the overseas connection her legs bounced in excitement. "C'mon, c'mon, c'mon." But the call repeatedly failed.

Now wide awake, she dialled every few minutes. When it finally connected, Blake didn't answer. It went to voice mail.

She cleared her throat. "Hi honey. I think you accidentally pocket called. It's such a relief to hear your voice. The Tanzanian authorities think you're dead. But I didn't believe it." She held her hand to her chest. "And now I know you're alive. Listen, I'm having trouble connecting. Could you please call as soon as possible? I really need to hear from you. I love you, Blake. We'll talk soon, okay? Bye."

She slid down under the covers and hugged his pillow. "He's alive. I knew it." With the phone beside her, she slipped into sleep with a smile on her face.

When Libby got up, she found Dax in the kitchen with coffee brewing and an omelette steaming on the cooktop. "Who are you, and what have you done with Dax?"

"You'll never guess what happened last night. Around 3:30 Blake called."

"What? Where is he? What happened? Is he okay?"

"I don't know. It was an accidental call. He didn't know he'd dialled. I heard him talking to someone then the call failed."

"So you didn't talk to him?"

"No, but I heard him. I know he's alive."

"Are you sure it wasn't a dream? Sleeping pills can play tricks on your mind."

She handed Libby her phone. "Look – a call from Blake at 3:37 last night. No, I didn't imagine it."

"I see you called back several times. You never talked to him?"

"No, the calls kept failing. Eventually one went through and I left a message."

Libby took a sip of her coffee. "Please don't be upset, but I have to ask. Are you sure it was Blake?" She held up her hand to stop any protest. "Hear me out. The evidence that Blake was onboard the helicopter when it crashed seems pretty solid, like he wouldn't get off without his passport. That there were no survivors also appears true. Maybe someone stole his phone, like in Europe, and that's why he didn't answer any of your calls. As to what you heard, you were in a pill-induced sleep and not operating on all cylinders. You saw Blake's number and expected to hear his voice, and that's what your medicated mind let you hear."

She vehemently shook her head. In a low, steady voice she said, "I know what I heard. It was Blake." She split the omelette in two and served it on two plates. Pouring two coffees she said, "I called the airlines and booked the flights to go to Zimbula. I need to be at the airport around noon." She looked at Libby, shoulders back and a glint in her eye. "I'll be in Zimbula Sunday morning their time."

In over twenty years of friendship, Libby had seen this kind of determination in Dax a handful of times. And she knew this was an unstoppable force. "Would you do me one favour?"

"You won't change my mind. I'm going."

"I know. Could you ask Logan to go with you?"

She smiled. "I already have. He's meeting me at the airport."

Libby hugged Dax. "It's good to see my old friend back. It's has been hard not knowing what happened to Blake, if anything. I'm glad you're going. You will find the truth. Just be careful, okay?"

"I will. I'll have Logan looking out for me."

Libby cocked her head. "I wonder. You know how you've been feeling on the cusp of something significant? Something life-changing? Maybe going to Africa is that thing."

Her eyebrows popped with surprise. "With all that's going on I'd forgotten about that. Yeah," she said nodding her head. "I think you're right. Proving Blake is alive and whether or not we go forward with our marriage. These are life-changing, significant things that will only be answered over there."

"Yes, Blake, your marriage and one more significant thing."

"What's that?"

"You're very likely to encounter a snake-infested toilet. And snakes are gargantuan there. I'd think confronting the reality of that nightmare is significant too."

"Yeah, thanks for reminding me. You're a great help."

"I'm always here for you." She gave her a bright, cheery smile. "When we're done breakfast, I'll help get you packed."

Dax gathered her clothes on the bed, including her little black dress and shoes. She smiled. *Perfect for celebrating our anniversary.*

While Libby packed, Dax collected all the documents she thought she might need – her passport and driver's license, vaccination certificates, their marriage certificate, photos of Blake, his will, and copies of his medical and dental records.

Libby drove her to the airport, helped her unload her luggage and hugged her goodbye. "You go kick butt in equatorial Africa."

"Thanks, Libby. I couldn't ask for a better best friend. Thank you for standing with me."

"Keep me posted on how things go."

Dax waved her phone. "As best as I can."

She checked in at the Lufthansa counter, dropped off her luggage, and picked up the boarding passes for her four flights. It would take 40 hours to get to Zimbula, and half of those hours would be in the air. She met Logan at the gate.

They flew to Frankfurt then Nairobi then a short flight to Dar-es-Salaam on the east coast of Tanzania and another across the country to Kigoma, Tanzania followed by a three hour drive north across the Zimbula border to Mabezi.

Friday, March 13

On a dark moonless evening, two men met in front of the Monk's Cellar, a downtown bar in Mabezi.

The younger man said, "You just get back in town?"

The other man nodded. "Yeah. Been up at the mines. How are things here in Mabezi?"

"President Akleelu wants to meet as soon as you can."

Checking his phone he said, "Okay. Anything else?"

"The helicopter from Nairobi crashed and no one aboard survived."

That caught the man's interest. He pocketed his phone. "I've heard. I think we will let Blake rest in peace in the hills of Tanzania. That simplifies things. Justin, I'm getting out. If you want, the operation is yours."

"You're getting out? Wow."

The man glanced around, assuring himself that no one on the street was listening. "Do you understand what I'm telling you?"

The men locked eyes for a moment. "Yes. Blake is now dead and you're pulling up your tent pegs and getting out of Africa."

The man nodded, satisfied his younger compatriot fully understood the unspoken ramifications.

"Jack, it's been a wild ride."

The man smiled. *Smart lad. He gets it.*

Justin offered his hand. "Thank you - for everything. What do I owe you for the operation?"

Jack rested his hand on Justin's shoulder, directing him into the bar. "Consider it a one time birthday gift. It's yours. It'll take a week or two to clean up a few loose ends then I disappear. Keep alert and let me know if anything surrounding Blake needs my attention. I hope to keep these couple of weeks quiet and uneventful."

"You'll have to keep Phil on a short leash. He's getting restless."

They sat in their usual spot, a dark corner with a view of the bar and all who enter. A beautiful waitress approached the table.

Jack smiled. "You're new."

"I started last week."

"Well hello beautiful. What's your name?"

Her eyes twinkled. "Brandy."

One eyebrow lifted. "Brandy, a spicy amber." He nodded. "Nice to meet you, Brandy."

She played with her pendant necklace, dropping it into a generous valley. "And you are?"

"Well, if you're Brandy, I guess I'm Jack Daniels."

"Mmm. A smoky smooth whiskey."

"Spicy and smoky. Sounds like a match made in heaven."

Resting a hand on her slim hip she said, "Well Jack, what can I get you?"

"I'll have a double Jack Daniels."

"A pair of Jacks for the captain."

"Gorgeous and quick wit. I think I'm in love."

She winked then turned to Justin.

"Ice Fox Vodka with a twist of lemon, thanks."

Jack watched her sashay to the bar then turned back to Justin. "Ice Fox. That's not a man's drink."

"Tell that to Putin."

"Putin drinks potato moonshine straight from the back alley still, not this girlie San Francisco diluted dishwater you drink."

"It's good to have you back. I missed the abuse."

"Abuse," he chuckled. "You're such a little girl. So what's the word on the street?"

"Aw, you know – talk about the possibility of a coup, a rigged election, lots of chatter about who killed the generals. And that resurrected the talk about all the people who have gone missing – like the Natural Resources Director."

He rubbed his face, looking at Justin. "If that idiot doesn't win the election, the easy money is over. Bad timing for all of this talk."

Justin shifted in his seat. "That's not everything."

Jack watched Brandy deliver food to a nearby table. "Uh-huh."

Justin's eyes narrowed. "Awamaki is back."

Jack leaned forward on the table. "Have you seen him?"

"Not yet."

"That will heat things up for everyone."

Brandy delivered their drinks. With a focused look she said, "Let me know if you want anything – anything at all."

Jack slowly ran his eyes over her body. "Thanks Brandy. I might just do that." After she left he said, "I'll talk to Akleelu. Get him repositioned to win this election and set things up for you."

"I'll monitor things from the office."

Jack clinked his glass with Justin's. "You're a good wing man."

Three rounds later Jack checked the time, stood up and threw several bills on the table. "I've got you covered."

"You staying at Salama's?"

"Unless a better offer comes along." He stole a look at Brandy behind the bar. "I need to settle Salama, clean up a mess and contain that idiot president. And there's a few things I need to deal with before I can get out." He tucked his wallet in his back pocket. "I'll do a shot of spicy amber another day."

Sunday, March 15

March ushered in the rainy season in central Africa. A heavy downpour hit many areas of Tanzania overnight, which caused widespread flooding. Their plane landed in Kigoma Sunday morning on the tail end of a deluge. Dax and Logan picked up their luggage from the cart on the tarmac then walked out to the taxi stand.

Even early in the day, the rising heat turned the dampness into banks of steam evaporating from the drenched earth. The thick air made it difficult to breathe.

After negotiating with one of the cabbies for a ride to the border, Logan climbed in the front of the SUV and Dax in the back. He shifted in his seat and watched the cabbie round the front of the vehicle. "For $20 these guys will drive you to hell and back." He glanced back at her. "How are you feeling? Tired?"

"I'm fine. It's good to be so close now. How long to get to Mabezi?"

"The border is about an hour and a half from here, depending on the condition of the road. With all the rain, there may be some damage that slows us down. It can take up to an hour at the border getting our visas. Then another hour to Mabezi. I think we'll go to the Ironwood warehouse first. We keep the spare vehicles there. So another three or four hours."

Once out of the city, the roads suffered from the deluge. Each dip held pools of water and red mud that slowed their progress.

An hour later they approached the bridge over the Kigoma River. The driver became excited, yelling something in his native language. He stopped about 50 feet from the tumultuous river's edge. The swirling tawny waters roared past, creating treacherous eddies and ever-changing mountainous spikes. A chair tumbled past in a matter of seconds. A tree slammed into the bridge supports, blocking the flow of water. Water piled up and washed over the bridge. Under enormous pressure, the tree snapped. It disappeared under the bridge abating the flood of water over the bridge.

The driver, while wildly gesturing, spoke to Logan. He peppered his words with frequent head shaking and much pointing. Logan offered him another $10 and the man quickly composed himself and put the truck into gear.

Dax thought, *seems the price to drive to hell has gone up.*

Once on the bridge, she could feel the power of the turbulent flow vibrating the structure and was relieved when they reached the other side.

The Tanzanian cabbie dropped them at the border. They carried their luggage to the guard station where they could purchase visitor visas. An older border guard called out," Stop right where your are, mzungu."

Dax moved close to Logan. "Is this going to be a problem?"

A burly uniformed man burst out of the guardhouse and, charging toward them like a Russian tank, he called his men to fall in behind him.

Logan peeled off his sunglasses.

Dax tried swallowing, but found her mouth instantly dry.

Chapter 2 — Welcome to Zimbula

The man stood in front of Logan, his men readied their weapons. "You old mongrel. What are you doing here?" He broke into a grin and clasped Logan in a bear hug. "Boys, meet my good friend Logan Keyes. I learned much under this man. Come, come inside." He gestured for the young men to carry their luggage into the office. He ordered one guy to arrange for a cab to come take them into Mabezi.

Logan said, "Jumai. Excuse me. Colonel Jumai."

"Yes, I'm in charge of Zimbuli security. Are you here on vacation with your beautiful young wife?"

"Not a vacation, I'm afraid. This is my niece, Dakota Keyes."

Jumai laughed. "Ah, your niece. I understand, my friend."

"You flatter me, but she really is my niece. We've come because her husband, one of my men, is missing and thought to be dead."

"And you're here to find him." He scratched his scruffy day's growth. "You will need a couple of visitor visas. How about a month?"

Logan nodded. "That should do. We can always extend it if we need to."

Jumai handed him a business card. "If you do, you call me and I will take care of everything."

Pocketing the card Logan said, "Thank you. How are your three boys? They must be young men by now."

"Following in their old man's footsteps."

The two men caught up on news of family and work while Dax filled in the three pages of forms. The man at the desk informed her that Zimbula had a few unique visa rules. Visitors were permitted to leave the country at anytime. But leaving before the end date on the visa cancelled the visa. To return legally, a person could not apply for a new visa until the cancelled visa reached its stated expiry date. A new visa could not be open in the same time frame as a cancelled one. It had something to do with limitations in their administrative processes. If caught in country without a valid visa, the offender would be sent directly to prison for two years. There would be no trial.

"So once we leave, that's it. We cannot come back into the country."

"That is correct. Not until you qualify to apply for another visa."

She signed to indicate her understanding and agreement.

The cab arrived and they completed the final leg of their journey to Mabezi, the largest city in Zimbula. Considering the economic conditions and the do not travel advisory, the modern brick and glass buildings in the core of downtown impressed. Minivans, Toyota pickups, motorcycles and bicycles hustled about the city. Cobble streets and plaster buildings with iron gates defined the wealthier neighbourhoods. Dirt roads cut through the slums overflowing with teetering assemblies of corrugated metal, plastic tarps, wood and sagging wet cardboard.

The taxi dropped them off at the Ironwood warehouse, a painted block structure. Using a passcode, they entered the large facility. Logan pocketed the keys for one of the SUVs and threw their luggage in the back. He helped himself to a couple of pistols, ammunition and knife, which he strapped to his ankle.

Noting the ease with which he became a warrior she said, "I've never seen this side of you before."

"I've never been with you in a situation where this was necessary." He opened the large bay door. "I've been thinking about how to track down Blake."

Dax heard the unsaid finish to his sentence, *if he is still alive.*

He pulled the vehicle out of the warehouse and locked it up behind him. "Something other than Ironwood business took him into the hills of Tanzania. We need to get familiar with his usual activities. That will open up leads, or at least possibilities of what happened to him and where he is."

"Would Justin know that information?"

"I think the best place to start is with the most reliable source of current information in the country."

He took her to an NGO director, Rosa Romano. At the front desk he asked for Rosa then wandered away to chat with some of the guys working in the yard.

An older Italian woman deeply tanned by years labouring under the hot African sun sized up Dax. "How can I help you?"

Dax showed Rosa a photo of Blake. She looked at it for a moment then said, "This man is your husband?"

"Yes. Do you know him? Have you seen him in the last few days?"

The corners of the woman's eyes squinted as she looked at Dax a long moment. "You know, in Zimbula, there's a saying. 'Only the dead have open mouths.'" She handed the photo back and said, "I cannot help you."

"Please. If you know anything, I beg of you. I won't tell anyone where I got the information."

"There's a boatload of reasons why this country is considered one of the most dangerous places to live. I do not need to add to my list of dangers by telling what I know about the activities or locations of people. Now if you have no actual business with this organization, I have work to do."

Dax grabbed her arm and held her back. "If your husband went missing, you'd do everything you could to find him."

"Everyone in Zimbula has missing loved ones. We know better than to ask questions. I'd advise you to do the same. Your American passport is no protection. In fact, your pretty white skin, blue eyes, and blond hair make you zuri kuku. I'd leave Zimbula before you can't." Her leathery, gnarled hands fingered a strand of her blond hair then walked away.

Calling after the woman Dax said, "Zuri kuku? What does that mean?"

But Rosa continued out of sight.

Dax looked at the photo of Blake for a moment then scanned the warehouse. She approached a local woman packing first aid supplies. "Do you speak English?"

The woman nodded.

"What does zuri kuku mean?"

"A pretty chicken. It's what the Inkurosha call the girls they sell for sex."

"Who are the Inkurosha?"

The woman's eyes grew large and darted about the room. In a loud voice she said, "The Honourable Wind of the Supreme," then grabbed the first aid kits and hurried away.

Dax watched her disappear behind pallets of rice then looked in the direction the leader fled. "Zero for two. Apparently not a country of talkers."

She found Logan leaning against an open bed truck speaking with a couple of men loading supplies. When he saw her approaching, he thanked the men for their time and walked her out to the street.

Dax said, "What is the Honourable Wind of the Supreme?"

"Ah, well – let's get something cool to drink and I will tell you." He turned the opposite direction from their vehicle. "The Inkurosha are something between police and royal guard. They do the president's bidding. They call themselves the Honourable Wind of the Supreme, referring to their undefined work for the president. Behind closed doors, some people replace the word wind with their word for passing gas. They used to be a stabilizing factor. That's changed in the last decade. Now the Inkurosha are not well-liked – actually, feared is probably more accurate."

The rough cobblestone road with deep gullies on either side stretched through commercial and residential neighbourhoods. In the distance, hazy hills crowned with a backdrop of clouds stood in stark contrast to the muddy city streets lined with rusted out vehicles, abandoned bicycle tires and strewn garbage. It was as though the promise of prosperity lay just beyond their reach.

They walked past a couple of properties lined with fences, even if only a collection of rickety sticks woven together. A narrow alley separated the barricaded properties from an old hotel. As they navigated past several street vendors in front, Dax noted distinctive gunshot pockmarks scattered across the stucco wall.

Logan steered her to an empty table in front of the grocery store ahead. After positioning the chairs to face the road, he held one for Dax. "I'll go get us a couple of sodas." A bell jingled as he entered the store.

Down the street, beyond the gates of the NGO, she watched a white flatbed truck slowly roll along the road toward the hotel and store. There were several men standing in the bed, each of them talking excitedly, one pointing, and one leaning around to talk to the driver.

From the other direction a couple approached her on foot. She turned from watching the truck when the young couple broke into laughter. Making eye contact, she smiled at the woman.

A loud explosion ripped through the air. Spinning around, she saw the gates of the aid complex catapulting across the street, followed by billowing smoke. Fence boards dropped out of the air like autumn leaves.

Dax scrambled to hide behind a boulevard tree. The truck continued toward the hotel, the men's enthusiasm now at a fever pitch. She kept her eye on the truck, occasionally glancing behind to check for Logan.

Several men readied to throw grenades into the hotel. One man pointed at the grocery store. Realizing the tree was inadequate protection should a grenade blow out the store, she ducked and ran along the narrow passage on the far side of the shop to the back alley. Once on the narrow lane, she was swept up in a mob of desperate people, storming past the back of the hotel and NGO, everyone trying to escape the rolling demolition.

She scanned the crowd for Logan, but the surge of people pushed her along.

When the pell-mell pace slowed, she walked backwards straining her neck to look. With senses on alert, she became aware of a beefy, bull-necked man moving along side her, his hair shaved short and a scruffy few day's growth of beard. She felt his cold blue eyes intently boring into her. Hoping an acknowledgment would satisfy him, she nodded and looked away. Still feeling his icy stare she glanced back.

"Hey sugar, buy you a drink?"

Her brow dropped at the proposition in bizarre circumstances. "Not interested." She eased her way through the crowd to put some distance between them. With the helter-skelter movement of people, she lost track of him. She spun around several times, scanning everyone, but couldn't spot him or Logan.

Beyond the NGO, the crowd slowed to a walk and began thinning out. A tall slim African man wearing a blue Miami shirt pressed a note into her hand and said "Blake," then gestured behind them and held up two fingers. She gasped at his mutilated hand – the missing ring and little fingers and the scarred skin that wrapped over the ragged amputation.

He glanced around. "Awamaki Kubwa." He signalled her to be quiet then disappeared.

Awamaki Kubwa. I must try to remember that.

Another grenade blast further down the street reignited terrified screams and a headlong retreat.

Chapter 3 – The Safe Cracker

Nearly alone on the red-mud side street, Dax realized she and Logan had not agreed to what they would do in the event they became separated. She wasn't even sure that Logan survived the blasts. Considering her options, she decided to wait at the SUV. Within minutes she saw Logan hurrying down the street.

He pulled her into his arms. "I am so glad to see you. Are you okay?"

"I'm pretty glad to see you too. Yes, I'm okay. You?"

"I'm a tough old dog. When I heard the blast in the hotel next door, I cleared everyone out of the store and into the back yard."

They climbed into the Ironwood vehicle. "There are elections in a few months and the people are deeply divided. Violence commonly ramps up as the day approaches. Drive-by bombings are standard practice. Each side is looking to intimidate the other. It's become much worse in the last decade."

Realizing his sunglasses were missing, he searched through the glove compartment. With borrowed glasses on, he shifted into gear. "This everyday violence is why I didn't think you coming here alone was a good idea."

She rested her arm on the open window, enjoying the breeze. "I'm grateful for your help, Uncle Logan. I wouldn't know where to start. I don't have your knowledge of the country nor your contacts. You're right, I don't know how to navigate these waters, but I know I had to come. I have to find Blake." She twirled his ring hanging from her necklace. *For an eternity beyond forever – I meant it ten years ago and still mean it today.*

"Did Rosa give you any meaningful information?"

"No. She told me to leave the country. Called me a pretty chicken."

His head spun to look at her then back at the road. After considering why Rosa would say such a thing he said, "There are men that make plenty of money from selling pretty girls. I'm sorry she couldn't help."

They drove in silence for a couple of minutes then Dax said, "Where are we going?"

"To the hotel. I thought you might be feeling a bit jet lagged."

"Could you take me to Blake's house?"

He checked his watch. "Sure. We might catch Nakato there. Years ago when I lived here I employed Nakato's twin sister as a maid and cook. Lesedi was killed by stray gunfire before I left and for a short time, Nakato worked for me. When Blake started, he hired her to look after his place."

Dax watched the passing houses, the children playing on the streets and people going about their business.

I knew Blake had a house here – he has to live somewhere. I get it. But I never thought about his life here beyond work – and as it turns out, I actually know nothing about his work, let alone his life here. I didn't know about the maid that looks after him and his house, a paid woman cooking for him, doing his laundry, making a home really. Most of his life is spent here – in a house I've never been in, enjoying meals shared with people I don't know, spending his evenings with friends I've never heard of. This is not a business trip. It's a full and rich life lived a world away from our scant few days together in Washington. I never looked beyond the days together in Washington. I know so little about the bulk of his life.

It's like I know nothing about him, and I have very little involvement in his life.

Logan pressed the buzzer on the gate. Dax held her breath hoping to hear Blake answer. A melodic voice said, "Bwakeye."

"Mwiriwe. Is this Nakato?"

"It is."

"Hi darlin'. It's Logan Keyes."

She squealed and moments later the gate swung open. A middle-aged woman ran out dancing and clapping her hands. "Mr. Logan. I cannot believe my eyes."

Logan bent to give her a noisy kiss on the cheek and a bear hug, lifting her feet off the ground. "How are you, beautiful?"

"My heart is singing." She tenderly touched the grey on his temples. "This is new."

He pressed his hand into her salt and pepper kinky hair. "So is yours." Her eyes twinkled.

Their friendly flirtation amused Dax. Their familiarity intrigued her.

Logan said, "Nakato, this is my niece, and Blake's wife, Dakota Keyes."

Nakato took Dax's hand in both of hers. "My, my, my. Blake's wife. Aren't you a pretty one." She looked at Logan. "Good looks sure runs in your family."

Logan grinned. "I've missed you, kasuku mdogo."

"Come in. Come in. Blake's not here. I haven't seen him for – oh a couple of weeks, I guess. Is he expecting you?"

Logan said, "I guess you haven't heard. There is some concern that Blake was onboard a helicopter that crashed in Tanzania. We've come to find out the truth."

"Tsk, tsk, tsk." She wrapped an arm around Dax. "Oh my darling, you must be so worried."

She nodded. "Would it be okay if I stayed here?"

"Yes, of course. This is your house." She rummaged through

a kitchen drawer and pulled out a spare set of keys. "Here you go. Take these. You can come and go as you please. This is for the front door, this one for the garage, one for the gate and this is the key for the truck. I can get in some food this afternoon and make dinner for you both."

Logan said, "Dax, I've booked us a couple of rooms at the hotel."

"Thanks. I think I'll pass. I want to be here when Blake shows up." She looked around the unfamiliar setting, the African textures and decor. "At least here I feel closer to him." *Actually I need to understand his life here. It's like those women who discover their husband has a second family. This is a whole separate life from the one we share. If we're going to hold our marriage together, I need to embrace this life. I need to be a part of this world.*

He said, "Are you going to be okay here on your own? Do you want me to stay here with you?"

"No, I think I need some time alone here."

Nakato said, "When Blake is home, I come in every day from nine to four. I keep the place, wash the laundry, do the shopping and get his meals ready. I'd like to take care of you while you're here, if you don't mind the intrusion."

"Thank you, Nakato. That would be wonderful."

She gave a firm nod. "Good, I'll be on my way now to get the shopping done. When I get back, I'll make dinner." She patted Dax's hand. "You have much on your mind right now. You don't need to be thinking about such day-to-day things as food or cleaning, Yes, it is good that I will take care of you."

Nakato left Logan and Dax to settle in the living room with their coffees while she ran her errands. Dax leaned her head back. "I think you're right. The jet lag is catching up with me."

"Why don't you go lie down. Nakato will be back in an hour or two."

"I think I will."

"I think I'll head back to the hotel and grab a couple of hours of sleep." He wrote on the back of one of his business cards. "Here. This is how to reach me at the hotel. Call if you need anything. We can get a good start in the morning. How about I come by around nine tomorrow morning?"

"Sounds good."

He kissed her head. "Sweet dreams."

"You too."

Within minutes she fell into a deep sleep. She awoke to sounds and smells of Nakato in the kitchen.

After dinner, she wandered through the house, looking at the vibrant paintings, many by the same artist. Like an outsider intruding into a stranger's private life, she drew in a deep breath and stepped into his office. "Blake, it's time to get familiar with your usual activities. Maybe I can find what took you to the hills of Tanzania."

She fingered through the papers on his desk then rummaged through the drawers. Finding nothing of particular interest, she sat back in his chair and looked around the room. The lifeless white walls and near-empty room left her with a cold, disconnected feeling.

Her eyes settled on a lone painting. She tilted her head. There was something about it that struck her odd.

I know. It's a painting of reindeer. Every other painting in the house is of Africa – like he slapped up whatever local art he could find. But this seems intentional. Like, where in the jungles of central Africa would one find a painting of reindeer?

She got up to take a closer look and noticed one side of the frame sat away from the wall. She pushed it back against the wall. It sprang out. Swinging on its hinges it exposed a wall safe. "Well now. What have we here?"

What would Blake use as a combination?

She tried her birthday first, then his. *What else?* She stood back, her hands on her hips. The painting slowly swung back against the wall. *Reindeer. That's just so bizarre. What is it Blake always says when he's frustrated with life? He's going to go buy a reindeer farm in Iceland – a new life. Oh, I know. April 25th – his military discharge date. First day of his life as he tells it.*

She punched in the day month year combination and the safe popped open. "Looks like I do know something about you after all."

She sat at the desk with the stack of papers from the safe.

On top of the pile lay a note in Blake's handwriting. It was two long strings of letters and numbers looking much like access to the WiFi. She checked the available networks and logged into the one listed on the paper. Satisfied that her phone had access to the Internet, she set aside the paper.

"Okay. Let's see what I can find out about your life here." The top folder contained statements from a Swiss bank. They showed monthly deposits of 25,000 U.S. dollars from Ironwood and withdrawals of $20,000, which matched up with the deposits into their joint account.

Okay, so he kept some money for himself. Probably uses it for travel and the cost of living here.

She set aside the folder and opened the next one. It held statements for a numbered account at the same Swiss bank. This one received monthly deposits of $200,000 to $300,000. Her eyes widened at the magnitude of the numbers. *That's about three million a year.*

The statements went back almost eight years. In the last year a couple of withdrawals totalled almost $20 million leaving a balance of a little under $5 million. She double-checked. It was in U.S. dollars.

Twenty million dollars.

Holy Hannah.

Where did all this money come from? Is this some secret Ironwood thing?

She checked the account holder list to see if Logan was involved. *Oh yeah, no name. It's a numbered account.* Then she checked the depositor identification – a numbered company.

Numbered account. Numbered depositor. I don't think this would have anything to do with Ironwood.

I don't understand. Every month he's receiving the equivalent of a year's pay. This is a boatload of money. She stared at the pile of papers. *And what did he do with nearly $20 million this past year? Is he investing in some business? Buying collectibles?*

She glanced at one of the local paintings in the hall.

They're good, but nowhere near 20 million dollars good.

She lifted the folder and saw yet another one filled with bank statements.

A third one?

It was another numbered account with the same bank. This account received over a million dollars every month and had a balance of more than a $100 million.

She sat back in the chair and stared at the balance, counting the zeros several times to be sure she got it right.

A hundred million! Oh Blake. What are you involved in? And is this all connected to why you're missing? Are you out there somewhere in trouble?

Almost afraid to dig further into the contents of the safe, she gave the stack a flip through. There were two accounting journals, a couple of envelopes, a few loose sheets of paper, and a cash box.

I came to find the truth. And there's more truth yet to discover.

The next item in the stack was a small brown banking envelope. She squeezed the folded edges to pop it open and dropped the contents on the desk. Out fell a key stamped with the number D735 and a folded receipt, which detailed the instructions for accessing a safety deposit box at the Swiss bank. *Probably another box of equally perplexing papers. I wonder what impossible truth those documents tell.*

She put the key and instructions back in the envelope and moved on to a second envelope. It was a couple of small photos of Blake.

The first of the journals, the red one, was divided into seven sections – Blue Moon, Tardis, Sonic, Dory, Pandora, Milky Way and Salt Shaker. The pages detailed transactions going back more than eight years for the first five sections. She took a look in the second blue journal. It had exactly the same categories.

Flipping to a random page in the blue journal, the final column for the month totalled $302,400. Turning to the same month in the red journal, the final column totalled $1,230,700.

On the remote chance the journals were linked to the numbered bank accounts, she pulled that month's bank statements.

Bingo. Exactly the same amounts.

Two journals. Two bank accounts.

Checking the blue journal, there were no expenses, only income. In the red journal, each month showed a number of expenses. She ran a finger down the column, looking for clues for the source of the money. The monthly debits repeated every month and were paid to cryptic entities only listed with three digit numbers.

That's not helpful.

So the money is coming from these seven sources – but sources of what? There's a ton of cash coming in and comparatively very little going out. What kind of business brings in millions and not much in the way of expenses? Something online? Is Blake some kind of YouTube phenomena? Did he write some best-selling app? Maybe seven apps?

She searched the Internet for each of the names in the journals and found a wide range of apps from streaming music to a child's game, even one that positioned a blue TARDIS phone box in your photos. Each sold under a different company name.

So, he's probably not an app developer.

She searched for a place called Pandora in Africa then in the world and found nothing.

Setting aside the journals and bank statements, she wondered what enigma awaited in the cash box. Inside she found a stack of Zimbula money.

She rocked back in the chair, rubbing her eyes.

What does all this mean? Oh Blake. Are you an honest man?

She leaned forward in the chair to look at the pile.

Who are you?

She fingered the journals.

Numbered bank accounts. Numbered depositors. Coded payables. No names. Maybe all this numbered company stuff isn't yours.

She paled at her next thought.

Maybe you discovered someone doing something illegal. And this is the evidence you plan to use to expose them. Someone like Justin.

Her eyes grew wide. Fingertips rested on her mouth as she contemplated the implications of Blake crossing a criminal.

That would explain why he's missing and Justin's done nothing to find him. That means he's in incredible danger, if he's still alive.

An uncontrolled shutter ran through her body.

Pushing the pile of folders and papers aside, she pulled his laptop open and tried various passwords until locked out. With little else to hold her focus, exhaustion caught up. She locked everything back in the safe then wandered out to the kitchen in search of a glass of wine. She found a couple of bottles of white from South Africa chilling in the fridge. "Bless you, Nakato."

Looking for a place to sit and think she drifted into the living room. Instinctively, she moved to close the curtains on the dark night, but stopped in the middle of the room, staring at the window.

No curtains?

Wow.

This is his *house. Not* ours.

She retreated to the bedroom. The presence of grey-striped drapes hanging in the bedroom brought relief. Pulling them closed, she got ready for bed. As she stepped out of her shorts a paper in her pocket rattled – *the paper from the Miami shirt man.*

With the distraction of the puzzling safe contents she'd forgotten about this strange encounter. She strained to remember what the man said, but it eluded her.

In a hasty scribble the note said, "Munyegera R2T14. I have the information you seek."

Chapter 4 – There's Something About Phil

Sunday, March 15

At a cafe in downtown Mabezi a well-dressed, East Indian business man in a white lightweight suit smoked a cigar in the rising heat of the very early morning. After carefully reading the details of a story, he closed the newspaper and leaned back, contemplating the world. He spoke with the waiter, inquiring of the man's family, when his phone rang. He looked at the name. "Awamaki, it's been a long time," he said, squinting as he blew wisps of smoke that hung in the humid air slowly curling before fading.

"It has, Ravi. Listen, I need some information. If you don't have the answers, I need to know who does."

"I'll do my best." He set the cigar on the ashtray.

"I've heard whispers of a man they call Awamaki Kubwa."

Ravi nodded at a person passing by. "The god's bigger dog, yes."

"Who is this runt?"

"I don't know who he is. He stays in the shadows. He's either American or European, but his operations are very shrouded. He's far more secretive than you. No one seems to know who he is, or is willing to say. Some say the president is his puppet."

"And what grisly deeds is this mongrel up to?"

Ravi finished his coffee. "Rumours suggest he's responsible for the slaughter of the generals. Singlehanded, he's turned the ethnic factions into a seething, boiling magma that's about to violently erupt. This country's ready to mushroom cloud. There'll be nothing left but dead bodies." He sighed. "We've missed you, Awamaki. I've missed you."

"Indeed. Sounds like it's time to pull the curtains back on this dark puppet master."

"It can't happen too soon. Only light can expose truth, and only in truth can we find forgiveness."

"Still the philosopher."

Ravi glanced at the article in the newspaper. "And you, the warrior."

"You used to tell me, 'Even the devil needs a friend.' I never knew which one of us was the devil and which one the friend."

Ravi picked up his cigar and rolled it free of ash. "Hmm. I live on the river. So I befriend the crocodile." He took a long draw, savouring the clear taste of a morning cigar.

"Birds raise their voice above the din not because they have the answers but because they have songs. You will not save the world with your noble words. The truth is that an ounce of action is worth far more than a pound of your fanciful words."

Ravi laughed. "Dear, dear confused man. You always got Gandhi's quote wrong. Here's the truth. When hatred is no longer inflamed and the wars recede into history, the butterfly will still be known for her beauty." He glanced at the headline of the paper. Leaning back, he sighed and blew out another long double stream of smoke from his nose. "Sadly, most of the butterflies of truth have long left this country. My eyes and ears expect utter devastation, but you're back and again my heart hopes for this country. It's good you're here, you old crocodile."

"Thank you, my friend."

In the morning, Dax tucked the Miami man's note in her pocket. On her phone she searched the Internet finding an unofficial refugee camp by the same name, a short distance inside the Tanzanian border. While waiting for Logan, she wandered into the living room and perused Blake's small collection of books on the coffee table. *He always has two or three books on the go, always the likes of Robert Ludlum and usually from a used bookstore.*

Picking up the well-worn one entitled *Bourne Identity*, she flipped the pages and noticed some writing on the first page.

"King of my life

"My heart beats with yours

"I discovered myself in your arms

"Eternal lovers

"Like the sun and moon

"Together forever

"Love Salama."

There's an intriguing story. I wonder what happened between the king of her life and Salama that this book ended up in a second hand shop.

Laughter announced the arrival of Nakato and Logan together. *Did they just run into each other now, or did they meet up last night. Maybe she's the reason Uncle Logan never married. Probably good I'm not staying at the hotel – leaves him free to do whatever.*

Over coffee he said, "I want to check the CCTV to see when the last time Blake was here, and who has come since then."

When Dax commented on how easily he logged into Blake's laptop he said, "All Ironwood laptops can be accessed with a master password. He wrote it out for her then scanned through the available video.

"Something shut the closed circuit system down three days ago. There's nothing since then. That wasn't much help." He stood up. "I thought we could stop by the office and talk with Justin, before we go to the American embassy and see if they have any new information."

When they walked through the Ironwood office door, a tall, broad-shouldered man in his late twenties came out from one of the offices.

"Sir! What are you doing here? I had no idea you were coming."

"Is there a problem?"

"No. No sir. No problem."

"Justin, this is Dakota Keyes, Blake's wife."

Logan noticed the forced smile on Justin's lips, a smile that didn't involve the rest of his face. Justin offered his hand. "Good to meet you," he said while shaking his head as though he didn't agree with his words.

Dax accepted his greeting. "Thank you. Have you any news on Blake?"

Justin's eyes darted to Logan. "I – thought he was killed in a helicopter crash in Tanzania." He turned back to an envelop on the front desk. "They sent these photos asking if I could identify anything of Blake's." He handed the photos to Dax.

She looked at a photo of a few surviving personal items arranged on the ground. The second image showed wreckage strewn in a 150 ft. swath. The rest were close ups of the incinerated bodies. She handed the photos to Logan. Seeing the ash piles that were once bodies, Logan slapped the photos on Justin's chest. "What are you thinking, giving these to Dax? Where did you leave your brains?"

She said, "It doesn't matter." She turned to Justin. "He's not dead. I heard him on the phone a couple of days ago."

"Um. Okay." Staring at the photos he said, "Well, he hasn't shown up here."

Logan said, "Did you and the boys go out and look for him?"

He nodded. "We did – until we heard he was killed in the crash."

"I see. I want you to get together a team and get yourselves to the crash site and actually do what I asked. Go look for him."

"Yes, sir." Justin nodded to Dax. "Ma'am." He excused himself and made a few calls.

With the phone to his ear, Jack sat on the balcony of a mansion overlooking Malawandi Lake waiting for an answer. He popped a white caviar laden cracker in his mouth, washing it down with straight whiskey.

A man finally answered. "Hello, Jack."

"Adrian. How's your bank account looking?"

He laughed. "Very good. All my kids are going to Stanford and Harvard."

"I'm about to bump it up enormously. I have something – let's call it the Impossible Blue – that I need to move."

"How impossible?"

"Kareem says it will sell raw for over $100 million."

A long pause made Jack say," Adrian? You still there?"

"I am. Are you serious?"

"Yeah. It's a 150 or 160 carat beautiful vivid blue diamond. It's size, clarity and colour are phenomenal."

"I don't know if I can help you. It's one thing to slide a stone with a handful of carats among the mine's output to legitimize it, but a blue that size is huge. Jack, I'd love a piece of it, but this is out of my range to slip into our product and get the money back to you."

"Any thoughts on where to sell it?"

"Yeah. You won't get the $100 million, but maybe half, maybe more on the black market. I'll get in touch with the top diamond dealer. If he's interested he'll call you. Can you send me a photo?"

Fifteen minutes later the dealer called. "You Jack?"

"Yes."

"I'm Xander. We have a shared acquaintance, I believe."

"Adrian, yes. I gather you've seen the photo? Are you interested?"

"Enough to take a look."

Jack smiled.

They made arrangements to meet in three days in Malawandi, the second largest city in Zimbula to assess the stone and negotiate a deal.

A few minutes after Logan and Dax left the Ironwood offices, an enormous African man sporting a gold front tooth and heavy gold jewellery entered the office and asked to speak with Blake.

Justin thought, *Looks like that huge black guy from the Green Mile movie.* "He's not here right now. Can I help you?"

He pulled out a handgun and held it inches from Justin's head. "You get him on the phone. I want to meet him."

This is so not my day today. He picked up the phone and dialled the number for Jack. "Umm. Hello, Blake. Someone here wants to meet with you." Keeping his eyes on the man, he shook his head. "No, I have no idea who he is, but I think it best you meet with him."

He hung up and said, "He'll meet you at the Monk's Cellar in two hours. He's coming from Malawandi."

The man holstered his gun. "You'd better pray he's there."

When the man left, Justin redialled. "Sorry about that call, Jack. This 10 ft. wall of solid black muscle held a gun to my head and asked to speak with Blake. I figured you'd want to deal with him."

"Good decision. I don't want him raising a stink."

Logan and Dax entered the two-storey embassy building and spoke with the uniformed man at the information desk. The lithe body seemed in conflict with the thick wired-framed glasses on the man moving with the grace of an athlete. He introduced himself as David Perry and led them to his second-floor office.

"Yes, I spoke with both Gladness Sibale and Peter Wingham about your husband, Blake Talbot. I understand the Tanzanian authorities believe Blake died in the crash, and you believe he's still alive."

She explained why she believed he didn't die in the crash and that they are searching for the truth.

"I see. Gladness said they will be running some tests, some comparisons with the medical information you sent as a courtesy to you, but they have issued the death certificate."

"How can they say he's dead when we don't know for sure it was Blake?"

He held a large brown envelope, arms resting on the desk. "Seems they are sure enough. They forwarded it to me this morning. Thought maybe I could get it to you while you're in country." He handed her the envelope. "There are several signed copies to help execute the will."

"But he's not dead. I heard him on the phone. I hoped all of you would make every effort to find him, not issue death certificates with little evidence."

"They are running the tests you requested."

"But after they issued a death certificate. What do you think they will find, when they've already declared him dead?"

"I understand your concern. I have always found Tanzania to be trustworthy." He set the envelope down in front of her.

She pushed it back. "I don't want this meaningless paper."

David looked at Logan.

"It's just a piece of paper, Daxie. He's neither dead nor alive because of what it says. I think you should take it. When you can prove he's alive then rip it up. Until then, it doesn't hurt to hang on to it. If you need it, you will have it."

She sighed. "Fine," and tucked it in her purse. "Let's assume for a moment that we know nothing of a helicopter crash. Where would you recommend we search for a missing person?"

"The non-governmental organizations. Here and in Tanzania, the NGO folks operate throughout the country and are pretty tapped in to what's happening on the ground."

"We visited one yesterday. No one was willing to talk."

He nodded. "I'm sure you're aware the State Department issued a do not travel advisory for Zimbula because of the pervasive violence. The constant stories of torture, mutilation and bloodshed cause a reluctance to talk." He pulled out a pad of paper. "There is an organization we've worked with on a number of occasions." He wrote out their address and a contact name for Help Me Find Them. "You may find they're more willing to talk."

David walked them to doors, stepping outside into the front courtyard. Logan thanked him for his help.

"For what little help I'm able to give, you're welcome." He extended his hand to Dax. "I am truly sorry that you're visiting under such trying circumstances. I hope you find Blake. I know this probably sounds hollow, but if I can be of any help here in Zimbula, please don't hesitate to ask."

"Thank you, David."

Beyond the iron fence of the embassy, a man built like a 220-lb. bulldog stared unblinking from icy blue eyes. A long scar divided his face in two. He stood motionless, except for his hand jingling something that sounded not quite metallic in his pocket. When he saw Dax leave the building he shook himself. "Time to work."

Absently his tongue repeatedly darted out between his lips like a lizard tasting the air. He took a number of pictures of Dax talking to David with a telephoto lens.

"The pretty chicken and the old dog meet the man from the embassy." He rubbed his temples. "Mata Hari with Ethan Hunt and the grand spymaster." Unaware, his face briefly grimaced. "I know who you are and why you're here, you honey bait spy."

A sudden coldness ran through his veins. He muttered," Obliteration – extermination – annihilation" He let out five quick bursts of air. "Identification, violation, complications, disorientation, revolution." Reaching into his pocket, he fondled the loose items and chose a longer one. "Forty seven of sixty four."

He released the item, dropping it in his pocket. "No tooth today. Just watch and report. Nothing more."

His fingers began twitching. It spread up his arms. "Ah, come, sweet mesmo." His back arched, his arms outstretched, his tongue rapidly flicked in and out of his mouth. A long low moan rose from his chest as he gave into the sensation. He began to sway when his phone rang. Scrambling he said, "No, no, no. No mesmo now."

"Yes?"

He watched Dax and Logan get into the SUV. "Monk's Cellar? On my way." He packed his camera.

As Logan and Dax drove past him he tapped his temple. "Everyone thinks you're Blake's wife. I'm going to prove you are a CIA agent planning a government takeover. I'll show everyone I'm not crazy. You don't fool me."

Chapter 5 – Evil Approaches

Jack entered the Monk's Cellar and nodded acknowledgment to the man with a long facial scar sitting in the corner.

In the shadows, Phil sat unmoving, his brows creased, his thin lips pressed into a hard line to keep his tongue constrained.

Brandy touched Jack on his back letting her hand drift down to his waist. "Good to see you again. Pair of Jacks?"

He turned. "Beautiful Brandy. You're looking particularly delicious. Double shot sounds good. Thank you."

He chose a table and seat that would position his appointment facing away from the dark corner and the man with the scar.

Jack smiled at the sight of the 6'5" African man as he walked in. *How did Justin describe him? A ten-ft. wall of solid black muscle.* Leaning back with a half-closed hand loosely resting on his lips, Jack studied the man as he approached.

"Blake?"

He nodded. "Can I order you something to drink, Mr. –"

A deep bass voice rumbling from the man's chest reminded Jack of the powerful roar of a lion. "You can call me Kalfou. A Johnny Walker will do."

"Kalfou – where good and evil intersect. Interesting name."

"Are you white voodoo?"

"No, I have friends who practice." He caught Brandy's attention and ordered the drink. "So Kalfou, what urgent thing did you want to talk to me about?"

The man sat rock still, staring at his quarry, his jaw clenching. Finally he pulled out his phone. He spit out," Big white man – big important white bwana. I know where you live."

Jack listened, a loose hand resting along the side of his face, his finger stretched up his cheek. He blinked slowly. "So?"

Kalfou handed over his phone with a movie cued up.

Jack pressed the play button and watched a video of Dax entering a house.

He handed the phone to Kalfou and sat back in his chair.

Kalfou said, "I want $25,000 American dollars."

"I imagine everyone in here would like 25 grand."

"I will snap your wife's pretty little neck if you do not pay me."

"That means nothing to me."

The man pushed his phone back in front of Jack. "Give me what I want, or I promise you there won't be much left of her."

"She is not my wife. Do what you wish. You'll not get anything from me."

The man raged, spittle foaming out of his mouth. "Her blood is on you. You just remember that. You had a chance to stop this and you didn't. It's all on you."

Jack watched the man leave then nodded at Phil who came to sit down across from his boss.

"Phil."

"Jack."

"How goes the surveillance?"

Phil thought about where he'd followed Dax and the unexpected evidence he gathered. "Good."

"No problems?"

"No. She's not that hard to tail."

Jack nodded. "I have another job for you – in addition to keeping track of Dakota."

Phil's tongue flicked.

"Yeah, Phil. It's a job you'll like. I need you to smoke the man that just left. Ensure he's never seen again. You understand?"

"Yes. Kalfou is dead and no one is to know."

"Now, as for Dakota, I want you to frighten her into going back to the States immediately."

A slow wicked smile crept across his face.

"Frighten her into leaving. Not frighten her to death. Am I clear?"

"Yes."

"Yes. Okay. Make her aware you are following her, hang outside the house, run into her when she's out, talk to her, let her know you're around."

"A stalker." Grinning like a boy with a mitt full of cookies," A peeping tom watching the government agent." His words tumbled out fast. "You're blind to the truth. You know she's a –"

"Don't drift into crazyville, Phil. Don't start your mesmerization thing."

"No mesmo." His finger and thumb rapidly tapped.

"This is a straight up job of scaring her – Phil look at me. Anything happens to her – you do anything that I have not ordered, I will ensure you will regret it. You don't want me to hurt you, do you?"

Phil shook his head.

"Now, what are you going to do?"

Phil fingered the knife on the table. "I'm going to kill the big man and scare the little woman."

Jack patted him on the shoulder. "Good man."

Shortly after Phil left Justin arrived. "I saw Phil tailing the big guy."

"Kalfou will not talk again."

Justin nodded. "Dakota and Logan will soon become a problem. They stopped by the office."

"I've asked Hannibal to scare Dakota off. I just need a few days. No Blake. And soon, no Jack. Nothing for them to discover. I want to get out clean. Do nothing that will draw attention if I can help it."

Logan and Dax stopped by the organization David Perry suggested, Help Me Find Them. A note on the door indicated it would be open the next day. They visited a number of NGOs throughout the city – CARE, Amnesty International, Community Health Watch, and the African Salvation Group. Most people either didn't recognize Blake or didn't want to talk.

At the Red Cross they spoke with one of the team leaders. Like others, he said he didn't know Blake. Dax asked if they could talk with the workers gathered around a table.

He waved toward the diners. "Help yourself."

Dax passed Blake's photo around the table. "This is my husband. He's missing and I'm trying to find out anything about the places he went and what he was doing. I want to know what happened to him. Have any of you seen him?"

Each looked at the image, said no and passed it on. A young woman looked and tapped the photo excitedly. "I've seen him." She showed the photo to another woman sitting across from her. "Remember? About two and half, no, three weeks ago."

Her friend looked and shook her head. "No, I've never seen that man."

"Yeah. You remember? When we delivered all those bags of beans."

A man at the end of the table cleared his throat. When the young woman looked, he gave her a brief shake of the head.

"Oh." She looked down at the photo, over at the man then handed the photo to Dax. "I – I must be mistaken. I don't think I've seen him before."

Dax said, "I promise to not say anything about where I got the information." She looked at the man at the end of the table. "Please. I don't even know if he's alive or dead." He took a sip of his coffee and said nothing.

Dax squatted beside the young woman. "Can you tell me where you dropped off the beans? Maybe you didn't see him at all, but at least tell me where you were and let me find out for myself if he was ever there."

The man said, "She's only been here a couple of months. She has no idea the names of the places we go. She cannot help you. None of us can give you the information you're looking for."

"But you know the places. Please. I'm just asking for –"

Logan pulled her toward the door. "Thank you for your time. We appreciate it."

Once outside Dax said, "She saw him. She knows where he was just before he came home. Why aren't you in there pressing for that information?"

"I know Africa. People are constantly threatened for talking. They are not going to tell you anything more. I've seen that I-know-nothing reaction many times. It stems from fear. Those who have been here for any length of time become afraid to talk. There's something going on that has folks scared."

"And you think Blake's a part of it?"

"Who knows? He's either involved directly or indirectly in something that's frightening people into silence, or he's very unlucky and at the wrong place and wrong time."

Something frightening – like gathering the evidence of corruption and criminal activity. And having an encrypted list of people involved. How powerful and widespread is this corruption that everyone is afraid? This is huge. "That woman knows something. Maybe we can wait for her to leave and talk to her alone."

"No. They'll make sure she understands the risks of talking. She will tell you nothing more."

At the last NGO, they spoke with one of the truck drivers. He looked at the photo.

"Yeah, I saw him about a year ago."

"You're sure? Where was he?"

"At Munyegera. It's a refugee camp about seven kilometres over the Tanzania border." He pulled off his baseball cap and wiped the sweat off his forehead with his elbow. "My sister was a relief worker at Munyegera. About eight months ago, she disappeared and no one knows what happened to her. I believe this man might be the last person to see her." He handed back the photo. "I tried to find her. Never did. I wish you luck. Most people never find their loved ones again. Zimbula is like the Bermuda triangle of central Africa. People disappear and are never heard of again."

On the way home Dax said, "Another day passes and we've learned so little. It's frustrating. Blake could be in trouble and needing help. We flash his photo all over town yet we are unable to get any relevant information from anyone. At this rate we'll need to extend our visas. One month isn't going to be enough."

"I know it's frustrating. Africa came to be known as the dark continent because of the enigma that swirls around just about every activity and the savagery that infects a man's heart."

"Beyond frustrating. Exasperating. Disheartening. How many people have lost loved ones and, like that man, never know what happened. The Zimbula triangle. I don't know if Blake's alive and suffering or dead and tossed out as an appetizer for the crocodiles. This is horrible."

Logan glanced at her.

"No. I'm not ready to go home."

He nodded.

"I think I need some chocolate though. Can we stop at a store? I'd like to get a few things."

As they walked into the biggest grocery store in the city, Logan's phone rang. He stepped outside to take the call. Dax signalled she'd only be a few minutes.

Wandering the aisles she got a couple of bags worth of snacks, granola bars, dried fruit, chocolate bars, baked goods, several South African wines and a bottle of rye for Logan. While she made her way up and down the aisles, stopping occasionally to read the labels that had English, Phil stalked her. His tongue darted in and out.

As she walked toward the exit after paying, he blocked her. "A pretty woman like you shouldn't have to carry those heavy groceries. Let me help you." Phil reached for the bags.

She stepped back. "No, thanks. I'm okay." She tried to move around him, but he held his ground. He eyed her like a lion on a gazelle.

Licking his lips added to the white crust piling in the corners of his mouth. "I've been waiting for – I think you need someone looking out for you. This is a dangerous place. You shouldn't be alone. What man left you unattended?"

"Get lost." She tried pushing past him, but he shifted in front of her.

"Ah, you wish to dance." He touched her hair. "I'm a very sexy dance partner."

"I'm not interested. I'm married."

"And yet you are alone here with me." His tongue flicked. "We could do some hugging, kissing and not hard squeezing."

"Let me past."

He reached for the bags again. "I will walk you to your car and get you safely home."

"Don't you have a job or somewhere you need to be?"

A slow grin snaked across his face. "I'm a taxidermist, but business is a little slow right now." He touched his neck.

Her eyes immediately settled on his unusual necklace. *Those white bones? What the – they're human teeth!* She looked out the door for Logan. *This is Jeffrey Dahmer's soul mate.*

His tongue slowly moistened his lips. "Dakota. That's your

name?"

Her mouth almost fell open. *You know my name?*

"I know why women like you come to Africa. Looking for a bull elephant." He wagged his eyebrows. "You can call me Jumbo."

"Alright Dumbo, get out of my way or you'll be singing soprano."

He smiled and stepped aside. As she passed he leaned toward her ear, clicked his teeth and whispered," Ah, you're into the rough stuff. Tasty."

She turned back, her knee making a sudden movement toward him. He quickly turned away.

"My knee connecting with the family jewels is the only rough stuff you'll get. Now stay away from me or you will deeply regret it."

Phil's tongue flicked excitedly.

She hopped in the vehicle beside Logan. "There are some truly sick people here."

"You okay?"

"Yeah. But I gather Zimbula has no mental health program. Just ran into a prime candidate for inmate of the year award."

When Logan left after dinner, Dax combed through Blake's computer looking for clues. She found a folder named utilities. Inside there were 14 sediment bed drill reports and two audio files. She pulled up a map on Google and marked the locations of the drilling based on their latitude and longitude. The points scattered along the northeast border of Zimbula. She scanned each report trying to decipher all the abbreviations and geological language, but drew no conclusions.

One of the audio files dated almost ten years ago. A man with an African accent spoke. "Blake, I need you to do something – something discreet. Understand?"

Blake said, "What do you want, Mr. President?"

The quality of the recording degraded with gaps of clicks, pops and buzzing. "I need — mining. Get everything you can out of the ground. Sell — the black market and — in my account. Keep — for yourself."

On the second file from eight years ago, the same man raged. "That land belongs to Zimbula, not Tanzania — the border means nothing — riches belong to Zimbula."

She sat back in the chair. *President? The president of Zimbula asked Blake to secretly mine the natural resources, making the president rich? Stealing from the people? Is that what this is all about?*

Blake isn't a criminal. So the president must have found someone else.

Nausea rolled her stomach.

Did the president try to kill Blake? It's coming up to the election. Maybe he's afraid he won't be re-elected and needs to cover his tracks. And Blake threatened to disclose the truth. These two files alone could end his political career and probably land him in jail.

She listened to the two recordings again.

Blake's been gathering evidence against a corrupt dictator who found someone to help him embezzle the natural wealth. Looks like Blake got his hands on the journals, and all those bank statements. But who did the president find to do his dirty work?

Slamming her hands on the desk she said, "The obvious person is Justin."

Yes! I'm sure that's why he doesn't want to find Blake, why he's so reluctant.

"We've got to find Blake – before the president or Justin does."

She randomly opened computer folders, looking for other information that may help her locate Blake. In a folder marked housing expenses she found 17 core sample reports on Tanzania locations in two clusters on the strip of land between Lake Victoria and Rwanda.

Core samples in Tanzania and sediment bed drill reports from

Zimbula. And the helicopter went down between the two locations. I wonder. Maybe Blake decided to go to the area and investigate. He's playing a very dangerous game in trying to expose the president and Justin.

Yawning, she stretched and checked the time on her watch. The next hour was spent on reading various articles about President Akleelu from BBC and other news outlets. After several assassinated Zimbula presidents, he won the election in the mid 1990s and held power since. Despite elections every six years, he has retained power by landslide votes. Many articles question the legitimacy of the elections and detail the extensive intimidation around the elections. One election, his only opponent stepped down then disappeared and was presumed dead.

And the next election is quickly coming. Nothing sticks to this guy. Oh Blake, what are you doing going after this lunatic on your own?

Several organizations concerned with human rights discussed the pervasive nature of the violations in Zimbula. One organization identified over 4,000 burial sites and an estimated 145,000 Zimbuli people slaughtered and disposed of in these locations. The violence didn't stop at slaughter. The articles discussed countless cases of torture and mutilation.

This truly is a country where there is no boundary on the dark depravity of power. No wonder there's guys like the human-tooth-necklace wearing creep running loose here. They have an open door to fully engage their darkest desires.

A few articles traced the president's drift into tyrannical and despotic behaviour, forcing hundreds of thousands of people to flee into Tanzania, Rwanda, even into the Democratic Republic of the Congo.

The buzz of someone at the gate interrupted her reading. She peeked out to see if it was Logan, but didn't recognize the African man.

Through the intercom she said, "Hello?"

"Hello. I'm looking for Blake. I have something for him."

"I'm sorry. He's not here right now."

He leaned into the speaker and whispered, "It's the information he wanted."

She released the gate.

The man looked up and down the street then met her at the door. He handed her a large brown envelope pulled out from under his dirty white T-shirt. "Tell him you got this from Jimmy James."

"Okay, Jimmy."

He wiped his hands down the sides of his shirt. Stilling his nervous arms and legs for a moment he gave her a deep nod. "Thank you, ma'am." He took a couple steps to the gate and turned back. "Yes. Thank you."

She opened the package and pulled out a number of shocking photos of President Akleelu. The series of ten images captured a minute of time – a line up of three decorated military men blind-folded and on their knees, a gang of ragtag men milling about with automatic weapons, President Akleelu arriving in a Jeep, shouting and waving at the men, pulling his handgun and executing the three men. The final images clearly showed three dead men.

This was on the news just days ago! Blake's gathering all the evidence he can. This is heavy-duty, witness-protection kind of stuff. They make movies of this kind of sting operation.

She stuffed the images back in the envelope and put them in the safe.

Sitting at Blake's desk, she stared at the locked safe. "That folder is like gasoline on a fire. This situation is set to blow. We've got to find Blake then get out before the blast."

Monday, March 16

The next morning she looked for her watch – an Omega from Blake – and couldn't find it on the night table where she always put it. She lifted everything on the table then checked the floor around the table. Getting on the floor, she looked under the bed, but couldn't find it. She finally gave up, thinking she must have put it down elsewhere.

Expecting Logan any moment for an early morning pick up, she looked out the front window and saw two shoeless legs sticking out from behind the gate. Up and down, the street remained quiet. She buzzed the gate open and headed out to see if the person needed help. On her way, she called to the man, but got no response. As she rounded the corner she gasped at the scene.

"Oh Jimmy. What happened?"

Logan pulled up and rushed out of the truck with gun drawn. "Are you okay?"

"Yes."

He scanned the surroundings then holstered his weapon and approached the dead man. "Did you see what happened?"

"No, I found him here. He dropped off something for Blake last night." She pointed to blood smudged writing in the dirt. "Awamaki Kubwa's dog Phi –" His finger lay on an unformed letter.

Logan's jaw clenched while he considered the message. *Awamaki Kubwa. The undercurrents are worse than I expected. And it's now at Blake's doorstep – our doorstep.* He glanced at Dax and decided to keep his concerns to himself.

"What's this?" She pointed to a long tooth beside the body.

Logan squatted beside the body. "Looks like a crocodile tooth. Some guys kill a croc and collect the teeth as a display of manhood." He patted the man down.

In the dead man's pocket Logan found a small raw diamond

and handed it to Dax. "Seems he came into some wealth. You say he dropped something off?"

"A bunch of photos of President Akleelu shooting and killing those three generals we heard about on the news just a week ago."

He shot her a look. "What?" He glanced around to ensure no one could overhear their conversation. He quickly steered her back to the house. "What did you do with the photos?"

"I put them in the safe."

He nodded. "Let me pull the truck into the driveway then I'd like to take a look at them."

After examining each image he told her to lock them up and not to speak of them to anyone. "These photos are like an alarm and flashing lights. No, it's more like a bright-as-day nuclear flash just over the horizon. It's a powerful warning sign. You and I don't want to get caught up in the impending thermal blast that instantly incinerates." He ran his fingers through his hair. "I wonder if we should get out now while we can."

"I can't leave without finding Blake. You can go, but I'm staying."

"Daxie, when you see a brilliant flash turning the night sky into day, you don't stand around waiting for the melt-like-wax heat and radiation to hit. The flash is your warning to take cover. Honey, I couldn't bear it if anything happened to you. This –" He tapped the photos in her hand. "– is the tip of the iceberg. The situation here is way more dangerous and complicated than you know." *And I don't want to scare you with my suspicions of what we're stumbling into.*

"I'm not leaving without Blake."

She grabbed her purse from the bedroom. *I know far more than Uncle Logan. But he's already nervous about my being here, so I can't tell him about any of what I found in the safe. Nothing about all the evidence Blake is gathering against the president. And that means I can't tell him about my suspicions of Justin. He would march us out of here in a heartbeat if he knew the danger Blake is in. And I can't tell him I think Blake was up in the remote Tanzanian hills gathering more evidence. For now, information will be on a need to know basis and Uncle Logan, you don't need to know just yet."*

When they left to visit the Help Me Find Them organization, Logan erased the words written in the dirt by the dead man. They stopped at a police station to report his death. He doubted they would do much to investigate, but at least they would remove the body.

At the non-profit's office, they saw a 20-ft. wall of images of missing people. Dax thought of the articles detailing the pits with thousands of people buried without record or marker.

While waiting to speak with the director, Dax chatted with one of the volunteers. The young woman got involved when one of the roving bands of armed men took her sister. Another volunteer told how her parents were killed and her two brothers taken. She found the younger one riddled with bullets on the side of the road. She never found the other one.

Dax spoke with another young man who provides information he learns during his travels as a cabbie. When he saw Blake's photo, he thought for a moment then said, "My sister is a teacher at the Munyegera refugee camp. I go see her a couple of times a month. I've seen this man there a few times."

"What's the name of the camp again?"

"Munyegera."

She pulled out the scribbled note from the Miami shirt man who said he had the information she needs. "Is this the place you're talking about? Is this where you saw Blake?" she said, pointing to the piece of paper.

"Yes. Munyegera."

Another point to this camp. We need to go there. "How far is it to this camp?"

"About three hours. It's a few kilometres into Tanzania. There are so many refugees flowing out of Zimbula that there's no room left in the official camp. So this one is where the rest of the refugees wait until they can get into the official camp where there is better food and accommodations."

She turned to Logan. "We've got to go there. That truck driver said he saw Blake there too. If Blake knows this camp, he may head there for help. Maybe someone there has seen him recently. Maybe he's unconscious in the hospital." She showed Logan the paper. "And a man handed me this note after we visited the first NGO. He said Blake's name. Look. He says he has information I'm looking for. That's three different people who have mentioned this place."

Logan said, "It's impossible. Once we leave Zimbula, we cannot return until early April."

She turned back to the cabbie. "You go across and come back without a problem?"

Logan said, "He's a citizen. We are on visitor visas. It's a mandatory two year sentence in jail if they catch us coming back in."

Ignoring Logan she said, "Is there anyone official guarding the border there?"

The cabbie shook his head.

She looked at Logan. "We've got to take the risk."

"No. This is not a good idea. You haven't seen their prisons."

When Logan stood up to stretch, she signalled and the man slipped his name and number to Dax. "You want to go, I will take you."

She pocketed the information. *I don't care about the risk. I must get to the refugee camp. I might find Blake there and won't need to come back.*

"Bring money. Information is never free."

EPISODE THREE – HARDNESS OF TRUTH

When fact conflicts with perception

and one does not embrace the truth,

they willingly vacate the realm of reality.

Chapter 1 — On Her Own

Monday, March 16 (continued)

Logan set up a late morning meeting with his old friend Etienne at his presidential palace in Malawandi. He dropped Dax at Blake's and made the two-hour trip to the capital city.

Within minutes of Logan's truck disappearing down the street Dax called the cabbie. She remembered what Logan said about the taxi drivers being willing to go anywhere for $20 US. He agreed to drive her to the border.

She left a note for Logan. "I'm sorry, but I must go to Munyegera. No lead left unturned. I know you want to protect me, so I'm officially letting you off the hook if anything goes wrong. I promise to get in touch as soon as I can. Love you, D."

Terrence, the taxi driver arrived in an old Toyota sedan. They chatted about his life in Zimbula and her life in the States.

As conversations do, it meandered to the pre-election strains in the country.

Terrence said, "The tensions between the Abeesa who used to be the rulers and the more populous Jika erupt regularly. A decades-long civil war involved the Jika rising up against the Abeesa who retained the power after independence. Much like nearby Rwanda, it became a bloodbath. In an attempt to equalize the relationship between the two ethnic groups, the Central Eastern Africa Coalition brokered a peace accord. But President Etienne Akleelu disregarded the accord, and has held the country with an iron grip. The Abeesa are now being slaughtered by the Jika. Even the words, Jika and Abeesa, enflame the long held hatred. Abeesa means above or higher and Jika means waters. The Jika say they are a roaring mighty sea. There is nothing above them, only the vultures that live off the dead. The Abeesa say they are the mighty winds that carry the eagles and Jika are mud dwellers – they have their feet in the sludge.

"I'm both and neither. I am lower than the mud dwellers and the vultures. People of mixed heritage are called maggots and the first to be slaughtered – everyone, that is, except President Akleelu. Although of mixed heritage, he decided he's Jika and uses his position to support the ongoing extermination of the Abeesa. There was one Abeesa man in the government, which allowed the president to claim an ethnically mixed government. Anyway, this man was in charge of developing our natural resources and we saw prosperity for the country on the horizon. But Akleelu removed him from office. Then the man disappeared. No one has seen him for nine years. Without anyone in that position, our country has remained economically poor, even though we are incredibly wealthy in mineral and mined resources."

The miles slowly ticked by, the road often cut through 8 ft. high grasses. Dax expected to see elephants wander across the road, but Terrence told her even the elephants have fled the violence of Zimbula.

They drove through several half vacant villages. As they approached one, Terrence slowed. "If you have any amount of cash on you, give it to me."

She hesitated.

"Even in a money belt, it won't be safe if they search you. They won't search me for money."

Several guys with assault rifles congregating on the road ahead convinced her. Terrence tucked the bills in his front pants pocket. "Stay cool and these boys will remain cool."

As they got closer, she could see most were in their mid to late teens. Their leader, a man in his twenties, wore dark sunglasses, a kofia head cap of colourful fabric and a loose fitting tribal shirt. He casually stood in the middle of the road with his gun hanging loosely at his side. He threw his cigarette on the ground, blew out a long stream of smoke and came to Terrence's window. She didn't understand any of what they said to each other.

The younger lads gathered on her side of the road. She smiled and nodded. One took a long swig of liquor, lurched forward and with bravado yelled something, the tendons in his neck straining. The others laughed, jostling each other, tripping over several empty bottles. One lad fired his weapon in the air and stumbled backwards laughing. His young compatriots joined in. Dax willed herself to hold steady and not react. The boys swayed, reeled and stumbled over each other.

Excellent. Fourteen year old drunk boys with assault weapons. About as smart as roller-skating on the edge of the Grand Canyon.

The youngest one accidentally fired several shots across the road within feet of the vehicle. No longer able to ignore the dangerous horseplay, the leader rounded the front of their car and yelled. He raised his weapon.

Dax gasped.

The man fired a spray of bullets at the kids' feet.

The boys backed up and lowered their weapons.

The leader ripped the gun from the offending boy. He smashed the lad's face with butt of his gun.

Terrence firmly grabbed Dax' hand. "Do not move. Say nothing."

She looked at the boy, now on the ground and bleeding from several deep wounds. His eyes filled with tears, but he determined to not give the leader any reason for further punishment.

The other boys sobered up and quietly gave the leader a wide berth.

The man returned to Terrence, grumbling loudly and occasionally shouting at the boys. Standing at the car window he continued shouting and gesturing at the boys. Finally, leaning in the window he said something to Terrence, pointing at the young lad on the ground. Terrence nodded in agreement.

They talked briefly then Terrence offered the leader his hand. They shook and the man waved them through.

Once out of sight of the village, Terrence returned her money.

"Thank you." She watched the passing rain-soaked vegetation. The stiff grasses rustled as they drove past. The smell of earth and reed gave the illusion of a peaceful summer day. "That boy –"

He looked at her and said, "A fly that dances carelessly in front of a spider's web risks the wrath of a spider's teeth."

"I knew of the violence here, but never expected to see the cruelty first hand. From what I've read, this was fairly light."

"Yes, considering the boy came close to shooting his leader."

"Who are they?"

"They are Abeesa defending their families' homes."

"Bit of a challenge with drunk 14 year olds."

"Other than old women and babies, these are the only people left to defend their homes. The men are gone."

"Gone where?"

"Dead mostly. Or in the refugee camps in hopes of avoiding an amputated arm or an acid burned face."

"Would you mind telling me about the wind of the supreme God? Who are they?"

"Now that's a question most people will not answer truthfully."

"Like many questions in Zimbula."

"Most will say they are the presidents royal guard."

"But they do more than guard the president, I gather."

"They don't actually guard the palace. In truth, they've become the unchained, often rabid dogs of the president."

"And the pretty chickens?"

"Ah, yes. Many young women have been taken and sold for cash."

"So neither gender and no age is safe."

"That is true, but the elections may bring change."

He turned off the main dirt road onto a two-track path over potholes, rocks and mud pits. At the end of this winding course he stopped at the edge of a river. "This is the border. Call me when you're ready to return and I'll be back to pick you up." He nodded across the roiling waters. "The camp is about a 7 km walk."

She stared at the turbulent river, remembering the thunderous power of the Kigoma pounding against the bridge just a few days ago. "How do I get across?"

He pointed up the river. "There's a path you follow. Around the bend there's a rope bridge. Then follow the trail through the jungle. You'll eventually come to the camp."

"Don't suppose you'd like to go with me and visit your sister?"

"I need to get back to Mabezi tonight." The concern on her face moved him. "Okay. C'mon."

"Thank you, Terrence. I will certainly recommend you as a first class cab driver."

When Terrence said rope bridge, Dax envisioned 2 ft. wide slats of wood to walk on and structured walls, all supported by thick strong ropes secured across the river. When they rounded the bend her heart fell.

"Are you sure this is safe? It looks like it's made of thread."

Three thin ropes acted as anchors, two to hang on to and one to walk on.

She wryly thought, *And now for a death-defying wire act by one of the Flying Wallendas.*

The ropes were homemade, with thick and disturbingly thin stretches. Dead leaves clung to the vines. Every so often there were bits of cord attaching the hand lines to the foot rope. While the safety of the ropes concerned her, the dip of the bridge into the river for about ten feet and the green algae greasing the rope made her uneasy.

Terrence grinned and hopped on, bouncing several times to demonstrate its strength.

She looked as far as she could upstream. *I don't want to be in the middle of this thing, knee deep in water, when a fallen tree comes hurtling down the river.*

He turned back to help her on.

"You go ahead first. I don't know that this thing is strong enough to hold both of us."

He lightly stepped across with the grace of a ballet dancer. As he neared the other side he turned to wave her across. She stepped onto the rope and steadied herself from the sway. She could feel the pounding of the water pulling at the centre section.

How did he manage to cross with no sway?

With her first step the base rope swung out from under her feet. She crashed onto the side rope. It rolled and grated its way into her armpit. Pushing herself back into an upright position, she pointed her toes outward, like a balance beam gymnast. Slowly she moved her first foot ahead. The rope wobbled, but at least it didn't swing out from underneath her. As she progressed, the rope soon became slick with green slime, causing her to slide forward. She caught herself and pulled back upright. Placing a bit more weight on the hand lines helped her navigate the slippery section, but required extra strength to hold the ropes close and not let them splay out.

At the centre point, with the water rushing around her legs, Terrence urged her to hurry. She glanced up river. A wide-eyed young zebra, thrashing in the fast current, swept toward the bridge.

"Hurry!"

A couple of rushed steps caused her foot to slip off the rope. She scrambled on hands and knees along the base rope. The zebra slammed into the bridge within inches of her. She gripped the wet vines, riding out the shudder of impact. The animal wildly thrashed trying to gain a footing. One hoof slammed into her thigh, leaving a gash. She tried to grab its mane and pull it toward the shore. In panic, it screamed. Its front hooves tangled in the ropes of the bridge. The current sucked it under water, rolling it on its back.

Tired and unable to fight, its head slipped under. Hoping to prevent drowning, she quickly untangled its hoof, letting the creature pass under the bridge. When it surfaced 30 feet down river, it bobbed lifelessly.

Shocked and disappointed, Dax stared for a moment. *Life is quickly expendable here. It's a hard country.*

She pressed on to the shore.

Stepping on firm ground, her knees gave out under her. The sharp hoof left a deep wound. Rivers of blood and water trailed down her leg.

Terrence wrapped his shirt snugly around her thigh to slow the bleeding. "Let's get you to the medical station at the camp." He helped her stand up. "It'll take about an hour to walk to the camp." He watched her try out her injured leg. "Maybe a bit longer with that leg. Do you think you can make it?"

"Yes. It hurts, but I think the bleeding is under control. Let's go."

A steady rain blanketed the tree canopy. Wisps of mist rose slowly from the jungle floor. About an hour closer to Munyegera they rounded a bend and found themselves surrounded by three armed men.

Dax thought, *they have men on patrol to help those fleeing.*

Terrence raised his arms.

Oh-oh. These men have no intention to help.

Terrence repeatedly gestured forward. The leader argued for a couple of minutes. One of the men moved in close to Dax and fondled her long hair, winding it around his finger. She turned her head away.

She could smell the pungent odour of days' old sweat. He said something that made the others laugh then snaked his arm around her waist, pulling her close to him.

She struggled.

He pulled her closer.

She kneed him hard, dropping the man to the ground.

The leader took a step toward her with his fist drawn.

Terrence pulled her behind him.

The leader hit Terrence with a blow to his jaw that sent him reeling backwards. Dax steadied him.

The leader followed with a direct kick to the knees and Terrence was down.

Stepping over Terrence, the man grinned at Dax. "Now you belong to me."

Terrence raised his hand to get Dax's attention. "Run."

"Shut up." The leader shot him in the head. A pool a blood formed then seeped into the moist earth.

Chapter 2 — Enigmatic Despot

Logan presented his identification at the gates of the president's palace. A guard escorted him through the extensive gardens and through the opulent mansion to a library with comfortable chairs. The expressionless guard stood at the door. Logan waited for half an hour before amusing himself by examining the titles of books in the collection. After the first shelf he concluded it was all for show. *Not likely Akleelu reads Nancy Drew in Spanish.*

The door burst open. "Ah, here you are, my friend."

"Etienne. Good to see you. This is quite a place you've built."

"Yes. You have not visited for many years. You like it?" He gestured with a gold handled flywhisk.

"It is beautiful."

"Come. Sit. Tell me what brings you to my country and to my home today."

"A couple of things. I wanted to find out how things are going and how you're feeling about the election."

"I will win, of course. Do you think otherwise?"

"The news of the three dead generals is concerning. Do you have a sense of whether this is connected to the election? I am thinking of your safety."

"Those three snakes? They are nothing. Loyalty. That is important don't you think? The three cobras were not loyal. What do you do with an ill-natured cobra about to strike? It does not matter that they are dead."

Logan nodded. *So he believes they no longer served in his best interest and killed them. This was not done in the heat of the moment.* "I imagine you've heard that Blake was aboard a helicopter coming in from Nairobi. It crashed in Tanzania. There were no survivors." Logan watched for a reaction.

Akleelu looked as though he heard his cousin twice removed had beans for dinner. "No, I had not heard this news. When did this happen?"

"Ten days ago." Logan watched for any indication of contact with Blake since then.

Akleelu nodded slowly. "I see. So you believe Blake is dead?"

"His wife thinks he is alive."

"Interesting." He sat back, tapping the flywhisk on the arm of the chair. "Yes, that is interesting. You are not here to see me. You are here to determine if Blake is dead or alive."

"My friend, we go back many, many years – over two decades. And I have been a faithful friend over those many years. And nothing has changed today. Do you fault me for visiting one of my oldest friends while in the area?"

"No, of course not. I would be disappointed if I heard you came to Zimbula and did not stop in to see me." He forced a smile. "Indeed, you are my dear faithful friend."

Logan had seen his crooked smile many times. It appeared when the man said something he himself didn't believe.

"Has Blake done a good job for you?"

"Ah, now the old dog is checking up on the young dog."

Interesting. Old dog and young dog.

Logan smiled. "The old dog must be sure the young pups are behaving themselves."

"Indeed. That is true." His eyes turned cold. "An old dog who keeps to the comfort of his bed is not the pack leader for long." He waved his hand. "It is good you are here to let them know you still have teeth." He drew a breath. "In answer to your question, Blake is a good man. We have had our differences over the years, but he has proven to be an asset. Look around. I am one of the wealthiest presidents in Africa." He cocked his head. "You have changed your staffing policy?"

"No. Is there someone you're concerned about?"

Akleelu looked out the window. "I fear nothing. I am not concerned for myself, you understand. Like a caring father, I have the care and responsibility for my people. I know Phil is a good informant and I presume he provides numerous dark services. I know Blake keeps him on a short leash, yet he's had a few run-ins with the police. Does he reflect a new standard in Ironwood?"

Phil who? I've not hired anyone by that name. "What makes you think Phil works for Ironwood?"

"So you know of Phil?"

This is becoming quite uncomfortable. What is going on here? "No one by the name of Phil works for Ironwood. Did he say he works for me?"

Akleelu crossed his leg. "No one by the name of Phil works for you. Hmm." Waving the flywhisk in the air, he said, "Tell me about this young pup, Justin. I assume he will fill Blake's shoes, being as he is dead?"

My clear lack of knowledge puts him at an advantage. I'm like a toy poodle jumping through his hoops. This is not good. I need to gain some control here. "As you know, he has been Blake's second in command for 4 years now. He's a good man. Intuitive. Smart. And of course, loyal. He's done well under Blake and holding his own in Blake's absence. Should Blake prove to be dead, we can talk about Justin."

Akleelu's foot tapped the air. "Yes, my dealings with him have been positive. But he is much younger, and I think not worth the same billing rate as Blake."

"True, he is younger than Blake, but he is about the same age as Blake when he took over. If you wish we can discuss the value of my people again."

"As I recall, you won that discussion and I paid full price." He shrugged. "It is not important. It is a matter of curiosity." He stood up. "So how long are you here for? You must stop by before you go back to America."

"I'm here until we get to the truth about Blake."

They walked to the door. "We?"

"Blake's wife, my niece, is here with me."

Akleelu passed through the door. "Ah, I see. Blake married the big dog's niece. He is a sly pup." He called over a stunning young woman waiting in the great room outside the library. "Logan, this is Salama, our most beautiful resource." He fondled her cheek. "She was Miss Africa four years ago and since then, a world-renowned supermodel. Salama, meet my dear friend Logan Keyes."

Logan noted the large diamond on her delicate hand.

In a silky voice she said, "Nafurahi kukuona. Nice to meet you."

Logan held her tapered fingers. "You too." He turned to Akleelu. "Thank you for your time, and I'll be sure to drop in before I leave and let you know what is happening with Ironwood leadership."

Logan left Salama draped on Akleelu's arm.

His life has definitely improved over the last ten years.

On his drive back he considered all that Akleelu said and the volumes left unsaid. *First, he killed the generals because he thought them disloyal, but he's not admitting to what he's done. Two, he seemed barely interested in the news that Blake may have died. Where most people would respond with concerned questions like, " Are you sure," he simply said, "So you believe he is dead." I think he knows Blake is alive and is intrigued that I do not.*

And who is Phil? It's as though Akleelu knew I wouldn't know about him and made sure I realized I don't know what is going on under my nose. So, Blake if I find you alive, you will have a lot of explaining to do. There's a swirl of dirty business – what did Akleelu call it? Dark Services.

So, if this Phil works for Blake, the stench of Dark Services is now attached to Ironwood. And you Blake will find yourself accountable for any tarnish of my company name.

What did he say? 'Blake is a proven asset. Just look around. I am one of the wealthiest presidents in Africa.' Now what did Blake do that produced that kind of wealth? It can't be legal.

Then there's Akleelu's forced smile that suggests he doesn't really think of me as a faithful friend. Has Blake turned Akleelu against me?

And his jab about keeping to the comfort of my bed – does he think I've lost control? Does he think of Blake as the big dog? Did he just drop a hint that Blake is Awamaki Kubwa, the god's bigger dog? An Ironwood man is the destructive Awamaki Kubwa?

Is it possible? The man whom I placed my trust for 10 years? Dirty deeds, hand in a big money pot, and it looks like you've taken advantage of my trust by hiring your own people. Yes, you could be the mongrel Awamaki Kubwa.

If that proves true, I personally will make you regret all that you've done to me, to Dax, and to Zimbula. I will bring you to your knees.

Logan expected Dax to answer the gate intercom and was surprised to hear Nakato greet him. She gave him the note Dax left. "At first a note left for you made me think Dax left for home, but her clothes and luggage are still here. I'm surprised she's not with you. Is she okay?"

"As far as I know." He ripped open and read the note. "Do you know when she left?"

She shrugged. "I was out all morning. She was gone when I arrived after lunch."

He checked his watch. “She’s probably to the border by now. I should never have left her alone.”

“Will she be home for dinner?”

“No, she’ll be gone for at least a day, maybe two. Maybe two years if she gets caught sneaking back into Zimbula. She’s gone to Tanzania.”

“Oh dear. I guess the apple doesn’t fall far from the tree. I remember you dancing near the edge many times.”

“True. But I’m better equipped to handle things if they become tense.”

“Ah, only men can handle themselves in difficult situations.”

“That’s not what I’m saying.”

With a hand on her hip and an elevated brow, she stared at him.

He raised his hands. “Okay. Let’s just hope you’re right and I’m reading too much into this.”

“You’re afraid to say that I am right and women can handle themselves in difficult situations.”

“I will be happy to say you’re right and I’m wrong when Dax is safely back here.”

“And I will be happy to listen.”

Chapter 3 — The Great Escape

Terrence's life quickly oozed into the damp earth.

Dax stood stunned.

The leader grabbed her arm and led her into the jungle. The second man helped his friend follow, injured from a knee to the groin.

Dax determined to track the general direction to the camp despite the twists and turns they took through the bush to a hidden camp.

At a small shack, they searched her and removed her purse and money belt. *Terrence was right. They found the money.*

The leader lifted a trap door and threw her into a 14-ft. deep pit. She bounced off the wall on the way down and landed on her hands and knees. She rolled onto her butt and leaned against the wall, trying to catch her breath. *Why did it have to be a confined space?* It took a couple of minutes to complete a progressive relaxation technique.

Her eyes slowly adjusted to the few slim shafts of dim light. The walls were rough cut exposing a couple of larger rocks and the occasional root.

What was it that Libby said? Fearless will get me in trouble one day. Looks like today's the day.

She stood up to study the walls for a couple of minutes. "I'll be outta here in a heartbeat." She grabbed a large root about halfway up the wall. Using the larger stones as footholds, she clambered to stand on the root. Shuffling up the root as high as she could, she stretched sideways to another root closer to the top. With a firm grip she explored the wall with her foot to find purchase on the lip of a stone.

She edged her weight over. A twig caught the T-shirt bandage on her leg and pulled the newly formed scab. She groaned. Pausing for a moment to let the pain pass, she drew in a long breath then pressed on.

With stable footing, she pushed up to the top. Listening for a moment, she pressed the trap door. Half expecting it to be locked in some manner, she smiled when it easily lifted. "Guess they don't expect pretty chickens to scale walls."

Seeing no indication of the men, she pushed the boards higher to get a good view. The shack was empty. She tried to swing the trap door fully open, but the weight caused it to pull out of her hands and crash to the floor.

She froze.

No one came to investigate. She scrambled out of the hole and closed it behind her. Relief shuddered down her back. She tightened the dirty bandage on her leg to staunch the fresh bleeding.

On a small table sat her cell phone and her purse emptied out, but no money belt. She returned everything to her purse and pocketed her phone. She creaked across the floor to crack the door open.

Only two men were visible. The leader sat in a truck smoking. The other man sat on the edge of the flatbed cleaning his gun.

I don't see the guy I kneed. He's probably not much of a threat. One gun is apart, so that eliminates that hazard. Probably dealing with one gun and two men.

She slowly moved along the walls of the shack peeking through the boards to find the nearest bush. With a plan in mind, she moved back to the door to watch for an opportunity when both men were distracted.

The leader's phone rang. He talked for a moment then slid out of the truck. While still talking he headed toward the shack.

She glanced around for something she could use as a weapon, but saw nothing. She considered hiding behind the door, but that would make it harder to slip outside. Instead, she flattened herself against the wall near the door and readied herself to dash out behind him.

Her heart pounded. She could hardly breathe.

When he opened the door, she crouched.

He paused.

The wound on her leg ached. The muscles quivered.

He turned and yelled at the other man.

He shrugged.

They exchanged a few words.

The other man hopped off the truck and went into a tent.

The leader waited then yelled. In exasperation, he turned back to the truck letting the shack door close.

She wiped the sweat off her brow.

He climbed into the truck and leaned to open the glove box.

It's now or never.

She carefully slipped out and circled behind the shack. With the building blocking their view, she ran for the cover of the jungle bush.

A few feet from the protection of the undergrowth, the leader spotted her. He barrelled toward her, calling the other man.

Twenty feet into the thick bush, she sharply turned to circle the clearing. She focused on finding a zigzag path that would not leave broken branches as a trail. Hiding behind a large trunk, she stopped to catch her breath and listen. She heard them heading away from her. Moving carefully, she put more distance between them.

Soon she could no longer hear them. As best as she could figure, she turned toward where she presumed the refugee camp to be, avoiding the main trail. She hoped to circle around the camp and approach from the far side. After walking twenty minutes, she turned. Expecting to find the refugee camp within 15 minutes she found herself still forging through thick jungle half an hour later. Apprehension crept in.

I think I'm lost. I may not be heading in the right direction. Maybe I'm walking deeper into the jungle.

She sat down to consider her next move and rest her leg. Blood soaked the T-shirt bandage. She closed her eyes and focused on listening. She hoped to hear noises from a large refugee camp, but heard nothing but creatures in the canopy.

Maybe if I could find a high point. She glanced around, but could only see a few dozen feet in any direction.

I think I need to keep moving in one direction until I come to the camp, or a trail, or the river – or the human traffickers.

She pushed her herself up and pressed on.

A wave of nausea hit. The little contents in her stomach churned. She stopped, leaning on a tree she emptied her stomach, spitting to clear the taste.

As she rested a distant sound of a low truck engine whispered through the trees. She turned to listen.

Yes, that is the sound of humans. If it's the refugee camp it's not where I thought it would be – or I'm not where I think I am. Let's hope that's not the kidnappers' truck.

She walked toward the noise. A glimpse of white caught her eye. As she neared, she saw an expanse of tents. She sighed in relief.

She froze at the snap of a twig immediately behind her.

Chapter 4 — The Good Doctor

"Ciao."

She whirled around. "Oh thank you, God."

A tall European man in his mid thirties stared at Dax, his hair still dripping from a swim in a nearby river.

She suddenly became aware of the dried mud on her clothes, the dried blood on her leg, and the stench of stress. "I – there's some men who kidnapped me. I guess I got lost running through the jungle. I'm looking for Munyegera."

One of the man's eyebrows lifted.

She drew a breath. "Do you speak English?"

"That is a quite a wound on your leg."

"Yes, a young zebra panicked on the rope bridge."

"A zebra was crossing the bridge?"

"No, not crossing the bridge." She laughed. "No, that would be silly. It floated down the river and went under the bridge."

"Ah. Yes. I see. You were swimming with the zebra."

"No. I was crossing the bridge and it was swimming. Well, not exactly swimming. More like drowning."

"Sì, sì. You were on the bridge and it was in the water."

"Have you seen the rope bridge from Zimbula?"

He nodded.

"Well, the zebra became tangled in the ropes."

"And you tried to help?"

"Yes! Well, actually it kicked me before it became tangled." She rubbed her leg. "Anyway, I am glad to run into you. Could you point me in the direction of the entrance?"

He moved in beside her and wrapped his arm around her waist. "Let me help you."

She rested her arm across his shoulders and fell into his strength. "Thank you."

"Looks like you have lost a bit of blood, no?"

"Some, yes."

"I will take you to the medical tent."

She pointed in the general direction of the river. The man that brought me here – they shot him. He's dead on the path to the bridge."

"I'll inform security."

He helped her check into the camp, registering her as his guest.

She looked at the rows upon rows of tarpaulin tents, some with a Red Cross logo, some with United Nations, and many makeshift, were organized in long rows. String lines swayed in the breeze with torn and stained clothes they called laundry. *Humanity on the edge of hopeless, and yet people press on with living.*

He left her waiting in the clinic for the doctor. The nurse called her into the examination room and introduced her to Dr. Ferrara. He offered her his hand.

The man who brought me here? "You didn't mention you're a doctor."

"My apologies. I was intrigued by the swimming zebra story."

"Drowning. The zebra was drowning."

He grinned. "Sì. And you tried to save it. Now –" He referred to her chart. "Dakota Keyes, how about I take a look at the damage?"

Libby won't believe I was in the middle of the African jungle with a devastatingly handsome Italian doctor treating my zebra wound.

He carefully cut and lifted the crusted T-shirt bandage. "Tell me, what do you do for a living when you are not mixing it up with zebras?"

"I'm a psychologist and have a counselling practice in Washington, D.C."

"A doctor of the mind." He carefully pressed the tissue around the wound. "I think you are lucky. Your zebra friend didn't hit the artery – no large pockets of internal bleeding. That is good. But the wound is quite dirty." He reached for a squirt bottle. "This will sting. Ready?"

She nodded.

Despite the biting sting of alcohol, she noted his gentle touch as he worked. "Now that it's clean, it does not look too bad. I'll freeze the area and give you a few stitches. When was your last tetanus shot?"

"I don't know. Probably the weekend when a picnic table buried a three inch sliver in my butt and jumping in the lake drove a nail through my foot."

He tapped and plunged the air out of the syringe. "Rough weekend. How old were you?"

"Oh let's see. That would be the year when the exploding kite gouged my wrist, so when I was 15."

He smiled. "You attract unusual karma." After checking her chart he said, "I'll give you a TDAP shot as well." He leaned into her direct line of vision. "It will cover you and your karma for another 10 years."

"Thanks."

When done, he helped her off the table. "Here is ten days of antibiotics." On their way out, he thanked the nurse.

Grinning she said, "Thank you, Dr. Ferrara, for seeing one of our patients," nodding at Dax.

Dax said, "Were you not on duty?"

"Oh I do not work here – just a visitor."

Dax stopped him. "They let just anyone treat patients?"

"No. Only doctors. They're particular about that. I am a doctor and a director with Doctors For Africa, the Italian organization that operates this camp. Every year I come to the Sub-Sahara to check in on all our operations. And what are you doing in Africa, Dakota?"

"Call me Dax. My husband works in Zimbula. He was aboard a helicopter flight from Nairobi that crashed northeast of here. The authorities say he's dead, but I heard him on a pocket call."

"And you are here looking for him. Do you believe he is at this refugee camp?"

"I've been in Zimbula for a few days. Several people mentioned he has been seen in Munyegera in the past. And I thought since the crash happened in Tanzania, maybe he found his way here. As well, there's a man located here who says he has information I'm looking for."

He steered them toward the workers' mess tent. "And you came on this search alone? Zimbula is a very dangerous place."

"My uncle came to Zimbula with me, but he wasn't in favour of crossing the border."

They got in the coffee line up. "Ah yes, the visitor visa restrictions. I gather because you crossed illegally on the refugee rope bridge that you plan on going back?"

"I need the truth. And yes, that will probably take me back to Zimbula."

"Before becoming a director I spent five years providing medical care in Zimbula. It is a dangerous country."

"A wise man once said, 'Death and darkness share one thing – a fear of the unknown.' Not knowing what happened to Blake, not knowing the truth is a darkness. I cannot face a lifetime of not knowing the truth. Going back is a risk I'm willing to take to get to the truth."

"Then I pray Zimbula is kind to you, and you will be okay. Your uncle let you come to the refugee camp on your own?" He handed her a paper cup.

"No. I paid a man to drive me to the border crossing. I left a note for my uncle."

Amedeo poured their drinks. "And this man who drove you, he is the dead one?"

"His name was Terrence. One of the kidnappers shot him in the head when he tried to help me. Poor Terrence." They stopped at the cream and sugar. "Terrence's sister works here. She should be informed."

He led her to a table with a couple of older women. "You are very brave, Bella."

"Determination more than bravery. The authorities are doing nothing to find Blake. And I have to know the truth."

He introduced her to Francesca, the head of administration. Dax gave her all the information she could about Terrence.

Amedeo introduced the other woman. "Emma has worked as a nurse at this camp since it opened." He gestured toward Dax's purse. "Do you have a photo of your husband?" He turned to Emma. "I thought you might be able to help Dakota. She's looking for her missing husband."

Emma wiped her hands on a napkin to look at the photo. Staring at the image she said, "Yes, I know this man." She hesitated, setting the photo down. "He is missing?"

"Yes. No one has seen him since a helicopter crash somewhere northeast of here. It happened over a week ago. But I heard him on a pocket dial."

When Emma looked puzzled Amedeo said, "Pocket dial – accidentalmente chiamato quando il suo telefono è in tasca."

"Ah." Emma nodded. "You would like to know if your husband is here. He is not."

"Do you remember when you saw him last? And do you know what he was doing here?"

Emma glanced at Amedeo. He gave her a brief wave of encouragement. Emma leaned forward, pushing her drink aside. "The last time I saw him was maybe four months ago. He came regularly to hire men."

Dax frowned. "Hire men to do what?"

"I keep my nose out of these dealings. If you want more information, you talk with one of the traders – Black Rat, I think."

"And you're positive my husband is not in the infirmary?"

"Yes. There are no white men in our care. If he's injured, he might be at the sanctioned camp. It's located further northeast from here."

Amedeo took her find Black Rat. As they moved through the camp Amedeo felt the presence of someone observing them, but never saw anyone tracking their movements.

A rotund hairy man sat outside Black Rat's tent.

Dax quietly said, "I can see why they call him Black Rat."

Amused at her comment, Amedeo controlled his smile. Directing his attention to the seated man he said, "We are looking for Black Rat."

The man called inside the tent then held the flap for them to enter. A near identical man sat inside at a makeshift desk. "I am Black Rat. How can I help you?"

Dax explained the purpose of their visit – that she was seeking any information he had on the man who regularly visited to hire men.

Black Rat sat back pondering her request.

Amedeo turned to Dax. "I think money will warm up his memory."

She searched her purse before realizing the kidnappers cleaned her out. Amedeo pulled out his wallet and handed over a couple of bills.

The man eased the money into his pocket in one fluid move.

"The white bwana. Yes, I know this man. He comes here to recruit young men."

Dax showed him the picture of Blake. "Is this the man?"

He looked at the photo. "Maybe. Maybe not."

"Which is it?"

He scratched under his chin. "I'm not recalling that information right now."

Amedeo threw down another bill. "Perhaps this will clear your memory."

He picked up the money. "Yes, yes it's coming to me now. As a matter of fact, that is the man, the white bwana."

"Where does he take these men?"

"Not my business. I never see them again. And many men come here and pay me for the opportunity to work for the bwana." Puffing on a large cigar he said, "The white bwana always pays well for what he wants…unlike some people." He tapped the table.

Amedeo threw more money on the table.

"He offers the opportunity of working in artisanal mines."

Dax said, "Do you know where the mines are?" *Let me guess, up by Lake Victoria and along the Zimbuli border.*

He ashed the cigar. "I have no idea and I have no interest in knowing. You can talk with Naga who sells maps. He may know."

"Does Pandora sound familiar? Or Tardis? Sonic? Blue Moon? Dory? Salt Shaker? Milky Way? Do you recognize any of these names?"

He ran his eyes up and down her, taking measure. He smiled a cold, lifeless grin. "Could be. I do not remember." He sat back and took a deep draw on the cigar.

He knows. But I don't think he's going to say anything more about the mines. Tapping the photograph she said, "When was the last time you saw him?"

"He does not come so often now, sends one of his mining managers instead."

"Where can we find this Naga?"

"He's in one of the *accommodations* in the sixth row – over that way."

Outside the tent and out of earshot of Black Rat's twin Dax said, "Thank you, Amedeo. Keep track of what I owe you. I can get you the money when I get back to Zimbula."

"Don't worry about it. I'm glad to help, Bella." His eyes cast over the tents looking for the source of his renewed sense of unease. *Is there someone following us? Or is this just an apprehension about a white bwana who hires desperate men to work mines – a man even the thieves claim little knowledge of.* "You know of these mines?"

"No. Not really. I read some paperwork Blake had in his safe. There were lots of geological reports, and evidence he gathered on the money the president of Zimbula is stealing from secret mining operations."

"He investigated President Akleelu?" *Investigated. I doubt it. That is not what he was doing here hiring men to work the mines.*

"I think so, but –" Her brows furrowed. "Why would he be hiring men if he was gathering evidence?"

Cannot see the ocean for all the water. The truth will shake her to the core.

They checked a number of tents, but couldn't find Naga. Someone pointed to the next row.

In the next line of tents a thin black man dressed only in a white loincloth blocked the road ahead. White paint covered his entire body except for unpainted eye sockets and a thin stripe extending from his lips to his ears.

Dax thought, *His weird face paint reminds me of something disturbing...I can't quite place it.*

His bizarre movement started slow. He shrank his shoulders together and curved his body first to one side then the other like a snake weaving before a charmer.

That's it. The long unpainted line makes his face look like a snake with dark lifeless eyes. Dax leaned in close to Amedeo. "They really need mental health practitioners here."

He put his hand on the small of her back. "Interested in the job? I know the director."

She grinned. "I'll think about it."

Amedeo said to the painted man," We're looking for Naga. Do know him or where we can find him?"

"Ssstep forward pleassse. The tent with the sssnake in front."

She grabbed Amedeo's arm. "I have a thing about snakes. A paranoia really – that they lurk in toilet bowls. You can imagine the resulting concerns. I won't do well with a snake on the loose."

Amedeo snickered. "Snake in the toilet. I have never had this thought." He looked at the coiled snake in front of the tent. "I think your back side is safe. It looks dead."

"You go first." They slipped past the painted man, Amedeo in the lead. He called into the tent. "Ciao? Hello?"

The painted man squeezed past them and entered the tent. "I am Naga, part human, part cobra. Yesss, pleassse sssit. What do you ssseek?"

Dax looked around at the snake-themed items. "The Black Rat suggested –" Her eyes fixated on an unusual chair. *No way I'm sitting on a bunch of hooded snake heads Too close to the terror of the toilet.* She forced her eyes back to Naga. "He suggested we see you. I understand you have maps to the mines of Blake Talbot."

Naga moved like a mesmerized cobra. "I have many mapsss. Tell me what you want and I will have it ready in 10 minutesss."

She said, "The location of the artisanal mines of Blake Talbot. You have maps showing how to get to them?"

"Which minesss do you wishhh?"

"Pan –"

Amedeo interrupted. "You tell us the names of the mines you know and we will tell you which maps we want. No money for fake maps."

He retracted his head into his shoulders and hissed. "Are you sssaying my mapsss are not real?"

"I have lots of money, but I only pay for the real thing. No fake maps. So, tell us the names of the mines or we leave."

With his hands moving wildly Naga made an attempt. "The pan–da mine." He watched them closely, shifting from side to side, like a mamba under threat.

Dax said, "There is no panda mine. The truth is you know nothing of the mines."

Amedeo took her arm. "We're done here. Thank you for your time, Naga. We will not be buying maps today."

They left with no further information than when they entered.

Dax glanced back at Naga's tent. "I've seen some strange behaviour, but he brings weird to an art form."

"Welcome to Africa. There is much need here and little help. Where to now, Bella?"

She pulled a crumpled piece of paper out of her pocket. "In Mabezi, a man handed me this note. He mentioned Blake's name and said I could get the information I'm looking for here."

He read the note. "R2T14 is the tent number – row 2, tent 14." He scanned the camp. "Over that way."

Even in the setting sun, they could see a limp hand poking out of number 14.

Amedeo hurried to the tent, pulling back the flaps to assess the man. He noted the two missing fingers when he checked for a pulse.

She peered in at the man wearing the familiar Miami shirt.

He shook his head. "He is dead."

"He was the man who handed me the note."

"I am sorry." He sat back on his heels and looked around the tent.

She bent to examine something on the ground beside the dead

man. When she realized what it was, she paled.

Chapter 5 — Truth and Daring

"Bella. Are you okay?"

She pointed to the object. "It's a warning to me."

Amedeo moved beside Dax, concerned she might faint.

"I'm okay."

He picked up a long tooth. "Do not worry, Bella. Some believe killing a crocodile and collecting all the teeth is a sign of manhood."

"That may be. But this is the second dead man I've found today and both had a crocodile tooth beside them. Last night, the other man dropped off some damning evidence. I found him this morning dead on the street in front of Blake's house with a crocodile tooth. And now this man wanted to get some information to me and again, dead with a crocodile tooth."

Amedeo rubbed his facial stubble. "So, this is not a coincidence." He stepped out of the tent and glanced over the camp. "I cannot escape the sense that someone follows us."

Despite the heat, a shudder rippled down her back.

He led her away. *Two dead men at her feet in one day? She's right. Warning bells are blaring. She's too innocent to know of the depth of evil she'll face when crossing swords with corruption here. This place deals in violence. Death lurks just a breath away.*

The image of her, covered in mud stumbling out of the jungle desperate for a safe place sprang to mind. *Like a small terrified rabbit, and now she's wandering into a pack of salivating hyenas.*

Dax watched the equatorial sun swiftly disappearing. *Two dead men. Two crocodile teeth. Secret mines. How do I wrap my head around Blake hiring men for some secret mining operation? But then, how can I believe everything that trader said. Who knows? Maybe nothing he said is true. Maybe he's part of the cover up. The answer is to go to the mines and see for myself whether Blake is a victim or a criminal.*

At the end of the row of tents Amedeo said, "Anyone else you want to see?"

"No." She gestured to the tents behind them. "He was my last lead. I may as well head back to Mabezi."

"It's too dark to travel the jungle. You can have my tent tonight."

"Thank you." Her eyebrows flashed up. "With the kidnapping and all, I hadn't considered how I'm going to get back. Even if I get through the jungle, I have no transport back to Mabezi. I'll have to call my uncle to pick me up tomorrow."

"Unless you have other plans, may I take you for dinner?"

She laughed. "Yes, thanks. Strangely enough, I have no plans and early breakfast was my last meal."

Amedeo stopped to inform the camp authorities of the dead man in his tent. On the way to the mess tent he cautioned her about mentioning who she's looking for. "I am concerned the death of these two men are directly connected with your search for Blake. The killer is probably still in camp."

Her eyes swept over the people heading to the mess tent. "A killer following me here is concerning. But I must know the truth, no matter how ugly that may be."

"Then keep conversation – " He waved his hand as though searching. "Easy, yes?"

"Casual conversation?"

"Sì. Casual conversation about where the young men here find work, and maybe the conditions of artisanal mining."

"I've certainly heard about artisanal mines in the Congo, so I can take that angle. Okay. I'll be careful."

They chatted with their table mates about the future of the young refugees, where young men find work. They carefully steered the conversation to the dangerous practice of hand-dug mines. They discreetly tried to find out if there were any local operations and where they are. One person spoke of a vague impression of a couple of diamond mines up near Lake Victoria, but she gained no new concrete information.

A young man who worked in the medical clinic sat behind Amedeo and Dakota and overheard their discussion. He followed them when they left the tent. "Excuse me. I heard you asking about mines in the area. I know about two here in Tanzania and several more in Zimbula. There's a bwana called Jack who comes here to hire men. I have a friend who went with him."

Amedeo led them to a quiet area out of the people traffic.

Dax thought, a *white man called Jack? Maybe Black Rat told us a couple of lies to gain more money. Doesn't sound like Blake is the man hiring. It's this guy named Jack.*

She showed him the photo of Blake. "Is this the man?"

He shrugged. "I never met him."

"Do you know the names of the mines?"

"One of my friends went to one called Milky Way. I've talked with other men who went to other mines. I don't remember all the names, but one man I know went to another one called Pandora. And one is called Blue Moon."

These are all the names from the journals. "Do you know where they are located?"

"Milky Way is northeast, here in Tanzania, somewhere up near the lake. I don't know exactly where. The other two are in Zimbula. Pandora is the only one I know how to get to. I went once to visit my friend."

"Could you show us where it is?"

"If you have a map, yes."

Amedeo said, "I've got one in my tent."

Inside his quarters, Amedeo flattened out his map on the table and brought a lamp in close. The young man bent over the map, studying the landmarks to orient himself. He traced along the Tanzania Zimbula border north. "The roads I used are not marked on this map. Here –" He pointed to a remote area. "There is a road here, just outside of this village."

Amedeo handed him a pen. He marked a road with several turns and an X where the Pandora mine was located.

Dax said, "Do you know what they are mining?"

"Copper and cobalt."

She shook the young man's hand. "Thank you. Thank you so much."

He ducked his head, smiling. "Yes, miss."

Amedeo handed him some money.

"Thank you, sir. Thank you, miss."

Amedeo folded the map and gave it to Dax. "This is dangerous. The people who operate illegal mines will not hesitate to kill unwelcome visitors."

"I'll ask my uncle to come. I'll be safe with him. He's operates a military consulting company. On a different topic, is there a shower I could use?"

Amedeo dropped her off at the women's showers with some borrowed clothes. While waiting on a bench outside he called his friend working in Zimbula.

"Greg. It's Amedeo."

"Hey, good to hear from you. Are you on your way here?"

He leaned forward, speaking quietly into the phone. "Not yet. I'm looking for some information."

"Sure."

"Do you know of any mining operations in Zimbula?"

"You probably remember this. About nine or ten years ago, Akleelu dismissed the Director of Natural Resources. The man disappeared in suspicious circumstances. Since then, no mines are registered with the government and there are no pending contracts, because there is no one in the government concerned with natural resource development.

"But there are several illegal artisanal mines in the remote areas of the northeast, somewhere along the Tanzanian border. Desperate men purchase the rights to dig in an assigned plot. The start up costs are pretty steep for the miners, so the men get a loan to cover the costs of digging rights and equipment. Then they pay processing and handling fees to sell the copper and cobalt they hand dig out of the ground. They earn so little and owe so much they never pay off their debt and become permanently indentured. I know of no one who has made enough money to get out."

Amedeo nodded at a passing person. "Do you know anything about the people running them?"

"It is rumoured they are operated by a man in partnership with President Akleelu. I've only heard his first name – Jack. These mines have made two very wealthy men – Jack and Akleelu. No money has come into the coffers of the country for things like health. Greed has blinded Akleelu to the desperate state of the people. He now lives in a gold gilded palace, while the country falls apart.

"Few men survive the work. And despite several organizations' complaints about lack of safety equipment and procedures, these mines operate with impunity. It's a dirty secret that isn't so secret."

Amedeo considered the implications of the information. "One other thing. Are you aware of a killer who leaves a crocodile tooth beside the victim?"

"Well now, that's an interesting question. A couple of months ago my friend, the chief of police, told me about a large number of murders with a crocodile tooth placed near the head of the victim. They can't say how many so far, since they didn't notice the teeth at first. But he said there have been more than three dozen murders, each one a little different, but always with a tooth. Questions about the mines and about a serial killer – what's up?"

With a crowd of people heading his way, he moved out of hearing range, but still kept a visual on the showers. "There is a woman here who is trying to find her husband. He is thought to have crashed in a helicopter accident, but she says she heard him on a pocket call."

"And she's searching the refugee camp?"

"Someone mentioned that people here would be able to provide information. She thought because he has been here before he might have made his way to the camp seeking medical help. A couple of informants confirmed he hired men to work some artisanal mines.

"Last night a man gave her what she calls incriminating evidence. This morning she found him dead at her door in Mabezi with a crocodile tooth calling card.

"A few days ago a man passed her a message that told her to come here because he had information she wanted. We found him dead in his tent with a crocodile tooth. So it seems the killer is tracking her.

"And he's close by at the camp."

He paced the drip line of the tree. "Yes. Now she plans on visiting one of the artisanal mines tomorrow to find out the truth about her husband – if he is involved in this illegal operation. Showing up at one of the mines is dangerous whether or not he is in charge, but she now has a serial killer on her tail."

"This woman is in deep waters. She should not go to any mine."

"I agree, but I doubt I can prevent her."

"You're going with her, aren't you. Like a moth to the light. You can't resist, can you."

"I can resist if I want. I haven't decided if I will go."

"If you go? I'm your oldest friend. You forget, I know you. You cannot refuse a woman in distress and the lure of adventure. I wondered how long it would take for a good mystery to pull you in. I'm surprised you lasted this long. What? Five years since Maria exited out of your life. She never understood you. You're a thrill junkie, my friend, and directing a non-profit offers very little excitement. Does this woman know of your background?"

"No, she doesn't." Ignoring the comments about his former girlfriend he said, "Thanks for the info, Greg."

"Stay safe and let me know how things work out."

Chapter 6 — Intentions

Monday, March 16

Over a bottle of wine, Amedeo spoke of his days in Zimbula. He told of a number of atrocities he witnessed and the many horribly injured patients he patched up.

Late in the evening he said, "Zimbula is worse now than when I was there. While you were in the shower I spoke with a colleague about the mines. They are illegal. A significant amount of money fills the president's bank account and he's not going to want anyone interfering. You cannot go up against that dictator. He has a long trail of dead and missing people."

"I have to find my husband. They say he's dead. I heard him. I know he's alive."

"What about the crocodile tooth killer who follows you? He's killed over 36 people in Zimbula. I don't want him to have the opportunity to put a tooth beside your head."

"I will be with my uncle."

"Will your uncle cross the border to meet you here?"

"No, I will have to meet him in Zimbula."

"And between here and Zimbula? What of the kidnappers you encountered in the jungle? And if the crocodile killer follows you?"

She considered how she would get from the camp to Zimbula

where she could meet Logan. “I could hire another driver.”

“This is a refugee camp. Vehicles here are rare.”

“I have to know the truth.” She spun Blake’s wedding ring on the chain around her neck. “I thought our marriage was solid. We were planning on starting a family. But on his last visit home, he left a note that said he’s done. He had a rough childhood and I wonder if he’s running from starting a family and not from the marriage.”

She looked at her glass of wine. “I don’t know why I’m telling you all this.” Another mouthful of wine slipped down her throat. “I want to talk with him. It’s impossible to go forward with my life without knowing the truth – is he alive, is he afraid of starting a family?” She hesitated. “Is he involved in something illegal here? Or is he collecting evidence to expose those who are?” She looked down at her drink and downed the last third. “The naked truth is better than any well-dressed lie that I could tell myself. I don’t know how, but I’m going to Pandora. You’ve stitched me up. I can quietly sneak through the jungle to the bridge.”

After a long silence he said, “Bella, you cannot go on your own. It’s too dangerous. I will go with you.”

“What about your work here?”

“The site visits can wait. I will drive you to Pandora.”

“Really? Thank you, but what about all the danger you just warned me about?”

“You stand a better chance with me than alone.” A grin pulled at the corners of his mouth. “Someone must protect you from drowning zebras and frisky elephants.”

“Ah, you can calm the heart of the wild beast?”

Nonchalantly he put a hand on his chest. “It is one of my many talents.”

She laughed. “Okay. Tomorrow we go to Pandora. By the way, where are we crossing? I need to get in without my passport and without them knowing I’ve violated the terms of the visitor visa.”

"With the river running high, even a SUV needs a bridge. That means we will be using a proper border crossing. There's one about 15 minutes from here."

"But I don't have any ID." She shook here head. "I'm not looking to do jail time here. Tell me you have a plan."

"I have a plan."

"Care to share some details?"

"It rather depends on what's going on when we arrive. I need to get a feel from the guards."

"So, you don't have a plan."

"Trust me. I have crossed in and out of Zimbula and many other African countries countless times without ID. No problem."

"No problem?"

"Sí, no problem." He split the last of the wine between them and held up his glass. "To the brave who live free."

"To us, the brave and free."

Wanting to make arrangements with Logan to meet them at Pandora she looked at her phone. "No service out here. Is there a phone in the office I could use?"

Amedeo ducked into his tent and brought out a satellite phone.

Logan answered after a couple of rings. "Hello?"

"Hi Uncle Logan."

"Daxie. It's good to hear your voice. Where are you?"

"I'm still at the refugee camp. Blake's not here, but I've learned that he's been here many times. One man says he came to recruit young men to work in illegal mines."

Logan thought, *that would explain the massive amount of money into Akleelu's bank account. It looks like Blake has his hands in an extremely lucrative money pot.*

She continued. "While that's a possibility, I don't agree. Another man said the white man who hires is named Jack, so I it's hard to determine what is true. Here's what I think. Blake has been gathering evidence against Justin and the Zimbuli president for making huge money from these illegal mines. Some of that evidence is in his safe."

"I see." *I doubt a young pup like Justin can operate illegal mines for the president under Blake's nose. Justin doesn't strike me as that intelligent or gutsy. But Blake certainly has the smarts and the balls. And Akleelu named Blake.*

"I've learned the location of one of the mines. Will you meet me there tomorrow?"

"Your driver will take you there?"

"No. He's dead. An Italian doctor here is going to take me."

"And you can trust this man to protect you?"

"Yes."

"Okay. Where is this mine?"

"Do you have a map?"

"Hang on a minute." Logan set the phone down and rummaged around for a map.

Amedeo said, "Your uncle has worked in Zimbula, yes?"

She nodded.

"I can talk to him if you wish."

Logan came back. "Okay. Go ahead."

She said, "I'm going to let you speak to Amedeo. He used to work in Zimbula and can better describe where the mine is."

Amedeo said, "Hello Logan. I understand you know Zimbula?"

"Hello, Amedeo is it?"

"Sí, Dr. Amedeo Ferrara."

"Yes Amedeo, it's been awhile since I worked here, but not a lot has changed."

He gave clear directions, using familiar landmarks. They settled on a meet up location a half a mile out from the mine.

Logan said, "Thank you for taking care of my niece. She managed to slip away before I could stop her. I'm grateful she ran into you before her determination bought her more trouble than she could handle."

"Prego." He thought of her run in with the zebra and the kidnappers, but said nothing. "We will see you tomorrow. Here's Dakota."

Logan waited for Dax. "Please take care crossing the border. Both of you could land in jail."

"We'll be careful. I promise. He says he's crossed borders without ID."

"He sounds like he can handle himself. Love you, Daxie. I hope I will see you tomorrow."

"Me too. Love you, Uncle Logan. Bye."

Under a dark tree on the edge of the camp, Phil settled in for the night. He watched Dax and an Italian man toast each other in the warm light spilling out of his tent. They talked into the wee hours of the morning. Finally she went inside and the Italian stretched out on an old lounge chair.

With nothing more to watch outside, Phil scrolled through his photos of the day. *The kidnappers confronting and shooting the cab driver, secret agent Dax and the visiting Italian man with a medical cover story. The two of them with the trader, and then the mapmaker. Photos of her at the dead man's tent.* His tongue flicked over his curling lips. "Ah, you like my handiwork." A few more images flashed by. "This is the one. The three of them, the CIA agent, the Italian agent and the mapmaker, all plotting over a map. This is the nail in your coffin, you female traitor."

He scrolled back to earlier images. Dax with the American at the U.S. embassy, *the CIA spy master*. Pictures of her and Logan. "Yes, I know who you are. I know who you all are.

He tapped the image of Logan. "You. I know you from before. You dismissed me like I was garbage. You never gave me a chance to prove to you my value. Well, I know more than you think. You old dog. The god's dog. A CIA plant, manipulating governments and dictators. You're back to take down the president. You and this pretty little honey trap agent you call your niece. I have the evidence right here of the three secret agents meeting and planning a coup.

"And now the sweet little CIA agent comes directly here and meets with a visiting Italian man. I know of the false documents you Italians sent to the U.S. to justify the invasion of Iraq. This stinks of an international dark operation, an armed insurrection in Zimbula.

"Well, I'm not young and stupid. I will have my revenge, Mr. I'm-So-Important. Logan, the old toothless dog. I will bring you down, you jack hole."

Over the next few hours a radical plan formed. Before dawn he crossed the rope bridge and returned to Mabezi to prepare for his big take down of the man he'd hated for more years than he could remember.

Logan checked the time. *Akleelu claims Blake helped him become rich. So it appears Blake is in bed with the president. And the two of them are stealing millions of dollars worth from covert mining operations.*

I wonder when Blake came up with his get rich scheme? Did he have a plan before he started with Ironwood? And Dax and I were simply pawns. Or did an opportunity arise that he couldn't resist?

Bottom line is he used both of us and spit us out.

He looked out the hotel window at Mabezi blanketed in night.

Through immoral and illegal means, he's become wealthy. And now he's decided to walk away from his marriage. He's not afraid of starting a family. Pure greed drives him, not fear. I wonder if he staged his death because he no longer needs Ironwood nor Dax.

He hit the table with his fist. *If I find out the only reason you married Dax was to get to me, you will pay.*

His eyes narrowed. *I will make you pay for any of these dark services done in my company name. I will bring you to your knees. You will never work in this field again. If I can, I will ensure you spend the next 20 years in a rotting jail and stripped of all the money.*

He stepped out on the balcony, leaning over to look at the empty pool below. *Focus on what I know and what is next. Daxie has evidence of these mining operations? Excellent. We will go investigate this Pandora mine tomorrow.*

Now if Blake is alive, where is he? At Pandora?

He paced across the balcony.

At one of the other mines? No. Rolling in millions, I doubt he spends much time in the jungle. And he's not at home. So where is he and how do I flush him out? If I'm going to bring him down, I need him out in the open, not hiding away somewhere.

Pulling him out of hiding simply requires putting his millions in jeopardy. Now, how do I put your money at risk?

A smile pulled at the corners of his mouth then spread across his face.

He called Justin and offered to meet him for drinks at the Monk's Cellar. After their drinks arrived Logan said, "What's the latest on your search for Blake?"

Justin studied his glass for a moment. "Not much to tell. None of the guys have seen him. It's looking like he may have died on that crash like they say."

"Have *you* heard from him?"

"No, sir. I would have told you if I had." He leaned back in his chair. "What's this about?"

"How do you find working with Akleelu?"

"Blake deals with him mostly. He's been relatively easy to work with. He's a bit scrambled and chaotic with the elections coming."

Logan took a sip of his drink. "Listen. I'm here because I have two main concerns. Naturally my company is important to me, but so are Dax and Blake."

"I am concerned as well."

Logan sighed deeply, hesitating to speak. He circled the rim of his glass with a finger. "Something has come up." Another long pause while he struggled to find the words. "I – " The muscles around his eyes pulled tight. He shook his head and blew out a long breath. "Have you heard or seen Blake at all."

"No, sir. Nothing."

Logan nodded. He bit his lower lip. "Listen. I've been contacted by the International Criminal Court in Hague."

For a brief second, Justin's eyebrows raised.

"Yeah. This is serious. They are investigating crimes against humanity and genocide here in Zimbula. The NGOs lodged complaints about the escalating slaughter of Abeesa – but also that Akleelu forces Abeesa to work in dangerous conditions hand digging for valuable minerals and gems. I need to know what Blake knows about this." He rubbed the back of his neck. "They are coming down hard." He looked at Justin, waiting for a reaction. When he failed to respond Logan said, "I need to speak with Blake. Are you sure you know nothing about where he is holed up?"

"Like I said, I've heard nothing from him to even suggest he is alive."

"Do you know where he would stay if in hiding?"

Justin shrugged. "No idea."

"Uh-huh." Logan studied the young man. *A small twitch in the corner of your eye. So you do have a tell.* Logan stroked a couple of day's growth. "To be honest, I'm not just looking for information from Blake. The Hague is directly investigating him for crimes. They suggest he is one of two people they will be charging. I'm concerned. So you can see, it's important I find Blake. I want to ensure he's not convicted. If you know anything –"

"Yes. I can see it is important, but as I've said, I know nothing about where he is, let alone if he's even alive. If he's alive and not at home, I know of no place he would be."

"I know Blake is alive. And Akleelu shared a number of things that suggest the light of the criminal court will not shine kindly on Blake."

Justin looked surprised. "You spoke with Akleelu?"

Logan nodded. "Yes. He was very confident the investigators will find him innocent of any charges. He said he knows nothing of illegal mines and is determined to work with them to help them convict anyone stealing from his people. And if Blake is found to be that man –"

Justin snorted. "That's rich coming from Akleelu. I – I mean, how could mines operate here without Akleelu? Just look at his new palace. Not hard to figure out who's involved and where all the money is going."

"True, true. But I wonder. Akleelu wouldn't dirty his hands with mining operations. No. He would ask a trusted man to handle the dirty work – for a cut, of course. And he will gladly throw his partner in crime under the bus. So, does Akleelu trust Blake?"

Logan noted a quick twitch before Justin looked away. "Akleelu may not want to get his hands dirty, but what makes you think that trusted man is Blake?"

"Fair question. Perhaps I've been away too long. Tell me. Who else does Akleelu trust?"

Justin's eyes widened. "Trust?"

"Yes. Who has his confidence? Who would he trust to get things done quietly. If not Blake, who?"

"Well, I guess there are a number of people." He glanced up at Logan as he downed the last of his drink. "Um. I think the generals would be in his inner circle."

"Like the generals who were shot?"

"Yeah. Well, not them. The other generals."

"I doubt he has much trust with anyone in his military. Isn't his political opponent a retired military man?"

Justin didn't answer.

"It seems to me Blake is the only man in his inner circle. And as such, he is a perfect scapegoat for Akleelu to hand over to the International Criminal Court." He threw a few bills on the table and stood up. He shook Justin's hand. "Thank you for the valuable information. I still want to talk with Blake, so if you hear anything or think of anything helpful, please let me know. I might be able to get him out of this big mess."

Justin followed him out of the Monk's Cellar where they parted ways. Justin glanced back a few times to check if Logan followed him, but saw nothing. With a bit of distance, he made a phone call. "Hey. I just had drinks with Logan. We've gotta talk. Okay, lunch tomorrow."

Logan lurked in the shadows listening to the call, and smiled in satisfaction.

On the way to his hotel Logan made a call. "Hello, could I speak with Jamie Moore?"

In the background he heard the elderly woman calling Jamie.

"Hello?"

"Jamie, Logan here."

"Logan. I didn't expect to hear from you."

"I know you're visiting your family in South Africa. I hate to disturb your vacation."

"No worries. What's up?"

"I'm in Zimbula and could use some back up. Would you be able to start in the next few days?"

"You want me with you in Zimbula? In Blake Talbot's territory?"

"Yes. He's missing. There's a few younger men here, but I could use a man with your skills."

"Of course. Let's see. It's Monday night. Would Friday be okay?"

"Good. Thank you for your flexibility, Jamie. I know you didn't plan to start with Ironwood for a couple of weeks."

"No problem. Honestly, ever since I heard Blake worked for

you, I've wanted to connect with him again."

"That's right. You two served together for a time."

"Yes – about six months and a couple of missions."

"I will see you Friday."

"Yes, sir."

Jamie hung up the phone and smiled.

His grandmother said, "Who was that, dear?"

"My new boss. I'm going to meet him in Zimbula on Friday."

His grandfather said, "Thought you weren't starting for a couple of weeks."

"Seems something came up." He smiled. "You know the movie The Talented Mr. Ripley? The one about the guy who kills this rich kid and takes his identity?"

"Is that the one with Matt Damon?"

Jamie nodded. "I'm about to meet Mr. Ripley for myself."

EPISODE FOUR – CLARITY

For psychopaths,

every human encounter is a contest of wills,

a feeding opportunity in which

one will dine and one will be the carcass.

They ruthlessly act without remorse.

Chapter 1 — Crossing the Legal Line

Tuesday, March 17

At the first sign of dawn, Dax quietly left the tent to use the bathroom facilities at the edge of the camp. Amedeo slept at the door on a lounger, guarding the tent.

She carefully stepped over his legs without waking him and weaved her way through staff tents. For sanitary reasons, there was a large expanse of ground between the camp and the bathrooms. The heavy morning fog shrouded the open area. Sounds of birds deadened in the thick air.

In the predawn darkness, she hesitated. Although everything looked normal, foreboding danced at the edges of her mind. She scanned the area again. Everything remained – undisturbed. Misty, but quiet.

What is bothering me about this? There's nothing here to worry about. Not even a mouse.

Then the thought struck.

This is the perfect place for some giant python to slither into the toilet and wait for a victim. After the whole drowning zebra story, a snakebite on my butt would place me firmly in the embarrassing encounters with wildlife category.

She shifted back and forth on her feet as she studied the ground for any sign of movement. *Okay, I have to really go. Everyone here uses these toilets without a snake latched on their butt. I'm sure it's safe.*

She carefully stepped her way past the wash station to the closest port-a-potty and entered. Peering in the dark hole, she banged on the walls watching for any sign of gliding scales. Seeing nothing, she quickly finished her business.

At the wash station Naga approached her. "I have prepared the mapsss you requesssted." He held several sheets of paper.

"I'm not interested. Thank you."

He pulled her arm, spinning her toward him. Slowly shifting his upper body back and forth he said, "No. You pay me." Several men encircled her.

From behind Naga and gang Amedeo said, "Boys. Something I can help you with?" He pressed through the wall of men and stood beside Dax.

"Doctor. Yesss." His hand darted out like an attacking snake. "You can pay me for these mapsss you requesssted."

"We declined your services. Not interested. Now move on."

Several men pulled out knives.

Dax moved in closer to Amedeo. He pointedly looked at the threatening men then at Naga. "One step closer and you'll regret it."

Dax felt his body tighten.

"Ssss. I regret nothing."

One man moved.

Dax felt Amedeo's reaction more than she actually saw anything. The aggressive man lay in a crumpled heap, moaning in pain. Amedeo, now behind Naga with the knife to the snake man's throat said, "Now do you agree, we will not be purchasing any maps?"

Naga struggled briefly, but stopped when the knife pressed deeper. "Yesss. I agree."

Amedeo removed the knife and pushed Naga into the watching

men. "Leave the camp and don't come back or you *will* regret that decision." He threw the knife at Naga's feet, burying the blade in the dirt. Resting a gentle hand on Dax's back, he led her away.

She glanced back several times, but Amedeo strode confidently back to his tent.

Naga touched the small thin line of blood on his neck then turned away.

"How did you know they wouldn't follow?"

"I have met many men like Naga and the boys. They are all hot wind – hmm – hot air, yes?"

She grinned. "Hot wind works."

Amedeo packed and when they settled in the Mercedes Benz SUV he said, "The border is 15 minutes from here. Remember, smile and don't get out of the car no matter what, even if they tell you to get out. We should be through in a few minutes."

"A few minutes? It took over half an hour to cross legitimately."

"This is Africa and Africa rarely makes sense. So, when we get there do not say anything. Leave it to me, yeah?"

She nodded.

He pulled out his camera instruction manual, written in Italian and ripped off the front and back page then tucked $20 American dollars inside, with an inch or so of the banknotes showing. He tucked that under his leg. Next he wrapped a plastic ring from a soda bottle cap in aluminum foil from a stick of gum and slipped it on his third finger. "This and twenty dollars will get us through in a few minutes."

Her eyebrows raised slightly. "So you are counting on corruption to get us in illegally?"

He got out his passport. "Oh dear Bella, I'm crossing legally. I am counting on *negotiation* to get you in illegally."

"That's what worries me."

He patted her hand. "I am having fun with you. Nothing bad will happen. We will smile at the guards. I will hand him some money and he will wave us through. Trust me. They want the money more than you want into the country."

At the border, they waited behind an aid truck loaded with rice and watched as the guards examined several heavy burlap bags.

Dax watched the inspection while her fingers drummed the side of her leg.

Amedeo noted her focus. "This is good for us. They won't be so inclined to give us a close look."

She drew in a deep breath. "That's good."

He winked at her. "It's going to be okay. I've done this many times and never landed myself in jail."

"You're not the one entering illegally."

"Not this time. But I have many times when I lived here."

They finally waved the truck through and Amedeo pulled up to the guard. He handed him his passport with his medical credentials on top. "Officer. I'm with Doctors For Africa and need a work visa."

The man looked at the credentials then at Amedeo and stamped his passport. "And the lady? She is a nurse?" He held out his hand for her passport.

Amedeo handed him the instruction manual with the money tucked inside. "Spending the day away from the wife. A little one-on-one with a pretty young thing." He clicked his mouth. "You know how it is."

The officer quickly slipped the money in his pocket. "Enjoy your visit."

Amedeo took the instruction manual back and smiled broadly. "I think I will." He waved and slowly pulled away.

She turned in her seat to face him. "Unbelievable."

He glanced in the rear view mirror. "Just takes a couple of minutes. You do not give them enough time to really think or assess the situation."

She nodded. "Man, you are good. This morning, the men with

machetes – now bribing a border guard. I've never seen anything so smooth. You talk of my kooky injury stories. I think you're packing some crazy stories in your background, Dr. Amedeo Ferrara. And not just amusing stories. No, I think you've danced over the legal line a few times."

He shrugged. "When in Africa, do as the Africans."

"So is bribe-your-way-across-the-border corruption rampant throughout Africa?"

"Oh Bella." He frowned at the distaste of her words. "This is not corruption. No, no, no. We are negotiating a *border crossing fee*."

"Oh, ri-i-ight."

"You see, these fees are a part of their income. When you see it as a negotiation then everyone is happy."

"I'm happy. Thank you."

They soon travelled into the hills heading northeast.

"Tell me about yourself, Amedeo."

"Ah, you want to know if you travel with a bad man."

"I know you are not a bad man. I'm curious about where you grew up. Do you have brothers and sisters? Why did you choose to become a doctor?"

"Ah, sí. My family is from the Naples area on the west coast. If you know Italy, we lived in Amalfi."

"I have not been to Italy, but I hear Amalfi is beautiful."

"It is very lovely. We lived well."

"What do your parents do for a living?"

He scratched his head. "I guess you could say Popà is retired. Mamma worked as a nurse."

"Ah, so that is how you became interested in medicine. What did your dad do before he retired?"

He shifted in his seat. "He was – how do you say – self employed."

She stared at him until he glanced at her. "What?"

"I'm a psychologist. I know hedging when I see it."

"What is this hedging?"

Her eyes spoke of her amusement. "You are avoiding my question. Now I am really curious. What did your father do for a living?"

"He was an engineer of sorts."

"Uh-huh. A self-employed engineer of sorts. That is crystal clear." Her eyes narrowed. "All this avoiding a straight answer – is your family part of the mafia?"

"No, no. Although I do know a number of guys in the mafia. But no, Popà was not a part of the mafia. He was a world-class –" He crossed himself. "Forgive me, Popà. He was a safe cracker."

"Oh wow. So what was it like growing up? Did you always know?"

"I think so. It was not a secret. I enjoyed my childhood. We visited many beautiful places in Europe and Asia."

"What did your mom think about it?"

"She did not like it – always worried something would go wrong. But she loved the man."

"She sounds like a good woman."

He nodded. "Made sure all of her children found legitimate work."

"Weren't you worried he would go to jail?"

"It never occurred to me until they caught him. He spent two years in prison. He was a proud man, but this devastated him. I remember visiting him once without Mamma and asked him how he was doing. He said, 'Son, do you know how to break a man? Make him see himself as the thing he abhors.' It broke Popà when they called him a crook. He was never the same after that."

"I'm sorry. What did he do when he got out of prison?"

"Nothing. He retired. Generally he sits in his chair for most of the day. He has little interest in life."

"Do you come from a big family?"

"I have six siblings. Niccolo and Allesandro are my two brothers. Nic is the oldest and a private investigator. Sandro is a photographer. And I have four sisters, Renata, Emma, Serapina and Angelica – Rennie is a nurse, Em owns a fine art store, Pina works as an accountant and Geli is a successful artist."

"Growing up with so many siblings must have been fun."

"I am the second youngest, so I am close with Geli, the youngest. And I earned money through my school years working for Nic."

"He's the investigator?"

"Sí."

"So you are a doctor who easily crosses borders without ID and a detective? I think we are getting to a very interesting part of your life. What is your best private eye story?"

"Let me think. Oh, I know one you will enjoy. The family of a wealthy Italian widow hired us. A man who claimed to be a cardiac surgeon courted her. He told her he needed investors for the development of a new bypass technology. The family wanted information on him before she lost millions. Turns out he ripped off other women, spent a bit of time in jail for fraud, and of course lied about his medical credentials and the invention.

"When confronted with this information, he told her we investigated the wrong man, not him. I showed her photo evidence. She filed for a protection order.

"With no chance of getting his hands on her money, he became vengeful. He posted compromising photos on the Internet, set her car on fire, destroyed her house, called all of her contacts and told them she hired a hit man, killed her dog and threatened to kidnap her grandchild."

"So the protection order didn't stop him. Did the police finally arrest him?"

"They would not accept our evidence."

"So what did you do?"

"Long ago this man worked as a janitor cleaning hospital operating rooms. He was familiar with hospitals and still had his old credentials. Several times when I followed him I watched him, dressed in scrubs, enter the local hospital and leave half an hour later. Afterward at his storage unit he removed a couple of cartons from his backpack."

The SUV bounced over a large pothole rock combination. That and a low section of the road flooded by a small river briefly slowed them down.

"What my father said stuck with me and I thought, how do I break this man?"

She said, "Make him see himself as the thing he despises."

"He was a janitor presenting himself as a heart doctor. The man desired respect and money. The family simply wanted to prevent him from getting the money. To break him I wanted to publicly expose him and make him an object of loathing."

As they crested a hill a panoramic view opened up. Her eyes danced across the vista. "Wow, that is a spectacular view. Zimbula is beautiful when not looking at the human mess." She turned back to Amedeo. "So you dragged his name through the mud?"

He let his eyes follow the rolling hills. "Sí. He had a secret. Those boxes from the hospital contained many vials of Rohypnol."

"Isn't that the date-rape drug?"

"Sí. Not to brag," his free hand waved," but I'm very good at picking locks – something Popà taught me as a young lad. I had no problem breaking into the locker to collect a few of the things he stored in there – drugs, syringes, zip ties and duct tape – all with his fingerprints. I found many disturbing things in there, like around 20 plastic bins labelled with names and dates, and each with a woman's set of clothes. Too many disturbing things."

Momentarily he lost himself in the memories. He drew in a breath. "So, I put my skills to work and made a duplicate key and labeled the ring with the address and locker number."

His eyes lit up. "And then the fun began. Geli struck up a conversation with this man at his favourite bar. I stayed nearby in case she needed help while Nic stashed all the drugs and paraphernalia in the guy's car including the duplicate key in his glove box. When Geli and the man left the bar together, I called the police and reported I witnessed this man snatch a woman off the street at gunpoint. I said she looked terrified and screamed for help.

"Within minutes, the police surrounded his car. Geli jumped out crying. The police searched his vehicle and found the drugs he stole from the hospital – and the key." He leaned forward. "The next morning the story in the newspaper depicted him as a serial rapist with storage unit full of evidence."

He put his hand on his chest. "The family was pleased with the outcome. The woman herself testified against the man. No longer living the high life of a respected cardiologist, he is now doing 20 years in jail. The world calls him a low-life scum. Even the prisoners despise him."

Dax studied Amedeo. "What do you like more? That you helped an innocent woman? Ensured a rapist is in prison? Or the thrill of the sting?"

He grinned. "You want to know if I am driven by compassion, or justice, or I am just a thrill-seeking rogue?"

"I'm curious about the unusual mix of a humanitarian doctor working in Africa, and the seemingly opposite investigator – like Robin Hood. It's a very interesting mix. You become quite animated when you tell this story. I find that quite telling. The psychologist in me is intrigued by this tucked away passion."

He thought for a moment. "I like the idea of Robin Hood – a hero outwitting evil in a very exciting and dashing manner. I think it's a little of all three – compassion for the underdog, justice and the excitement. "

"I see. So, why did you quit? You obviously loved the work."

"Ah, amore. I met a woman. She did not appreciate the value of that type of work. So I became a doctor."

"And did you marry your love?"

"No. It all fell apart. She moved on to a big politician."

"I'm sorry."

"Probably for the best."

They drove through a valley with thick high grass narrowing the road. Up ahead they saw bits of car scattered along the road. As they approached Amedeo slowed down to look. A dark car sprawled sideways across the road. A couple of suitcases lay open with clothes scattered everywhere. Two bodies lay face down in the road, a man and a woman.

He stopped a few hundred feet away. The hair on the back of his neck stood up. Being on edge, he pulled out a 9mm pistol and chambered a round.

Dax looked at the gun then Amedeo. "You are full of surprises."

"Something's wrong with this." He gestured at the road ahead. *An ambush? Am I being paranoid? No, something is very wrong.* "It looks staged."

Dax leaned forward in her seat, straining to see. "You think? It looks like a bad accident. Looks like those two people are hurt. We should check them."

"Have you ever seen what happens in a horror movie? No, we will not be getting out of the car."

Chapter 2 — Excursion to Pandora

He plotted a path through the wreckage – *pass the two people on the left, swing behind the car and we will be on our way.*

He tucked the gun under his leg. "Hang on." He approached the people slowly then punched it past the back of the car. A few hundred feet down the road he slowed.

Dax spun around in her seat to look out the rear window. As Amedeo glanced in the mirror they saw the two bodies rise up to their knees and stare at them. A group of people emerged from the tall grass.

"Look at all those people! We wouldn't have stood a chance. How did you know?" She turned back in her seat.

"The car looked undamaged, yet the contents and passengers were scattered on the road. All those car parts, they did not come from that car. Both bumpers were attached, so the one on the road was extra."

She looked at him for a long moment. "I didn't notice that."

"I see things not in agreement, things –" He waved his hand while searching for the word. "What is the English for incongruenze?"

"Incongruities."

"Sí."

She glanced back then settled into her seat. "So, do you still live on the Amalfi coast?"

"Many in my family do. I bought a wonderful cliff-side villa in Calabria – the toe of Italy. George Oppenheimer, a diamond dealer and nephew to Sir Ernest Oppenheimer, the man who controlled De Beers, the diamond company, built it in the 1920s.

"There is a story about young George, the villa and a famous missing Florentine diamond you might enjoy."

"Is it more interesting than my getting kicked by a drowning zebra story?"

He chuckled, his dimples on full display. "Perhaps. There is a very old 137-carat diamond called the Florentine Diamond. It has an unclear history going back many centuries. What is known is that it became a part of the Medici treasures of Florence. It passed by marriage to the Habsburgs in Austria. During World War I, the Florentine diamond ended up in Switzerland where it was stolen and transported to South America with some other crown jewels. Most historians believed it was brought to America and recut in the 1920s.

"Now, George Oppenheimer went to Cambridge College in the early 1920s where he became involved with the Cambridge Apostles. There, he met Charles Rothschild and became engaged to his sister, Elizabeth.

"George built a villa into a coastal cliff near San Nicola Arcella as a vacation place. Unfortunately, Elizabeth died of pneumonia shortly after they married. George lost interest in the villa, letting it fall into disrepair and eventually he sold it. It changed hands several times before I bought it five years ago.

"In the master bedroom I discovered a hidden compartment. Inside was the Florentine diamond along with several other diamonds. It seems George Oppenheimer frequently visited the States for business and came upon the Florentine diamond.

It is pure speculation, but perhaps he gave them to Elizabeth. Then she found the compartment and hid them for safekeeping and he never found them."

"So you found a world treasure? Was it yours to keep?"

"The last legitimate owner was the Archduke of Austria. Therefore, the man who currently holds that title, Karl von Habsburg, is the lawful owner. The other diamonds could not be identified as stolen goods and became mine because I purchased the house and all it's contents.

"I contacted Karl regarding the Florentine and he purchased the Florentine."

"Did you search the rest of the house for hidden treasure?"

He laughed. "I did stumble upon a hidden elevator and escape tunnel offering an exit out to the ocean, but no, it never occurred to me to search for more jewels."

"Interesting villa. Sounds perfect for a private investigator." She watched the passing landscape. "I can't imagine a 137-carat diamond. How big is it?"

"Like a very big strawberry."

"You're right. That is a good story. I think you have far better stories than me."

They talked of their childhoods, favourite songs, and spaghetti westerns until they neared the rendezvous point. As they rounded a bend they saw Logan's vehicle pulled off the road. They followed Logan to a small clearing in the jungle 200 feet from the mine. Logan noted that Amedeo parked the SUV with its nose pointed away from the mine.

Dax hopped out and hugged Logan. He held her close and rocked gently. "I'm very glad to see you. Any problems at the border?"

"No. We were through in a couple of minutes."

"You'll have to teach me that trick sometime." He pointed at her stitches and bruised leg. "What happened?"

"Bit of a tangle with a drowning zebra."

Amedeo circled the car, tucking his handgun in his waistband. "At least that is the explanation Dax gave me at the clinic."

Logan offered his hand to him. "Thank you for taking care of Daxie. A doctor you say?"

"Among other things."

"Indeed." *Carrying a gun in Africa is not that unusual, but no doctor I'm familiar with would know to park for a quick exit and how to successfully cross a border illegally.* "How about we take a look at this Pandora mine."

They trekked through thick jungle to an open pit with dirt piled up everywhere. Young men with machetes circled the edge of the pit. Kids, both boys and girls as young as five years old moved in and out of deep holes with adult men sifting through the excavated dirt. Lines of pregnant teenage girls traversed the dirt mounds carrying 30 lb. bags of minerals to the weigh station.

Logan said, "I see about 15 men overseeing the work."

Amedeo said, "No guns. I suspect the men at the weigh station are heavily armed."

Logan studied the weigh station. "You intrigue me, Amedeo. Do you have a military background?"

"No, private investigation."

"Ah. Very good." Looking at Dax he said, "Amedeo and I can go talk to the head guys. You wait here." His glance at Amedeo asked for and received his agreement. "We'll soon find out if Blake's been around."

Dax shook her head. "I'm going with you." With a determined look, she repeated herself.

"Daxie, people get killed here just for looking the wrong way. And we need someone to stay behind and call for help if we get into trouble."

"I'm going."

Logan and Dax locked eyes. He said, "Fine. Amedeo, could I ask that you stay back. Get help if things go wrong. Here." He shared contact information for Justin. "He works for me. On second thought, I'm going to give you another name. Jamie's not in country right now, but might be more reliable."

Dax noted the comment about Justin and added it to the pile of evidence weighing against him.

Amedeo recorded the information. "No problem."

Logan clapped Amedeo's shoulder. "Good man. Now Dax, stay close to me and don't look anyone in the eye. We will come in from behind and get a look inside the two buildings first. Follow my lead. If we're caught and someone asks questions, don't volunteer information. Ready? Let's go."

They circled through the brush to get close to the weigh station and the two buildings. Logan carefully moved to the back of the larger shack with Dax a few feet behind.

Amedeo repositioned himself to keep them in sight.

Logan looked in a window and saw three men playing cards. He gestured toward several barrels where they ducked before they made their way behind a nearby vehicle. They finally zigzagged their way behind the smaller building near the mine pit.

A large flatbed truck rumbled into camp, stopping in front of the weigh station. Two men from the small building greeted them. The driver pointed back to the road, describing the two vehicles he saw parked. The men listened for a moment then one shouted at the young men overseeing the pit.

The shouting brought three men out of the larger building toward the pit, trapping Logan and Dax. Within seconds they would be spotted. They tucked in beside a rusty steel drum along the side of the shack.

Amedeo muttered," There's nowhere to hide."

One man came around the building and immediately fired several shots in the air.

Chapter 3 — Drifting

Logan and Dax stood up with arms raised.

The gunman waved them toward the man in charge.

Logan tried to shield Dax from the gunman as they walked toward the boss.

The boss pulled a pistol and clicked off the safety. "Who are you?"

Logan said, "I have business with Blake Talbot. He told me to meet him here."

"There's no Blake Talbot here. How did you hear of this place?"

"Like I said, Blake told me to meet him here."

"*Like I said*, there's no one here with that name."

Dax pulled out the photo of Blake. "This is the man we are meeting."

The man looked at the photo. "Who did you say you are meeting?"

Logan said, "Blake Talbot." Thinking quickly he added," But you may know him under a different name."

"And who are you?"

"Logan Keyes, a business associate."

The man looked at Dax. "And you?"

Say nothing. She glanced at Logan, but remained silent.

"Right. I'm done playing games." He nodded at three hulking men with automatic weapons.

Dax said, "Wait. I'm this man's wife. This is his business associate. See? Here's a photo of the two of us together."

The man looked at the image. "You are not this man's wife. I have met Jack's wife and she's not you. Not even close."

The other men chuckled.

He nodded again. "Drop them in the new hole and one of you guard the opening until we get instructions."

A couple of armed men herded them on well-worn trails through mountains of excavated earth to a fresh hole. They called a young boy out and sent Dax and Logan down the rickety ladder.

Dax broke out in a sweat climbing down the narrow shaft. It ended in a vault barely big enough for two adults. She and Logan circled, trying to find breathing room for Dax. The ladder disappeared up the opening.

They sat hip to hip in the dirt. With her head back and eyes closed, Dax focused on her breathing for a few minutes until the panic subsided.

A dim light filtered down the shaft from 15 ft. above. Clods of loose dirt sprinkled down, threatening to turn the vault into a tomb and reignite her claustrophobia. Dax brushed a clump off her thigh near the curved arc of stitches. "I can try climbing out."

"No. Life is not valued here. They'd shoot you the second you emerged. We will have to wait until Amedeo gets help." *And hopefully it's before they bury us alive.*

After a long time Logan said, "They know Blake."

"And they think some other woman is his wife."

"Daxie, I haven't talked much about what I think might be going on here with Blake."

She pulled her knees up. "We have time now."

"Several people told you that Blake himself is hiring men to work these mines. I know you believe that Blake is not involved but is gathering evidence. Tell me more what you think."

"I think Justin has gone rogue and is in partnership with the president. And Blake is gathering evidence."

"I see. There are four major issues with that theory.

"One. Why would someone investigating and gathering evidence repeatedly visit the refugee camp to hire men for the mines?"

At the time, I thought maybe Black Rat wasn't actually talking about Blake, but told me that to get money. Now, I don't know.

"Two. While you were in Tanzania, I met with President Akleelu – at his new mansion. There's so much gold in there it's hard to imagine there's any left in the ground. The cost of his palace is astronomical. I'm telling you this because he told me Blake helped him gain that wealth in ten short years. The kind of wealth that comes from the low cost of child miners and the fabulous profit of selling copper, cobalt and diamonds.

But this isn't the Blake that I know.

"Three. These men running this mine know Blake, but under a different name. Presumably he has done this so if things go south, his name is not attached to anything illegal or immoral.

Screw Occam's Razor. There must be an explanation other than the obvious one.

"And four. I know Blake is alive, based on a couple of conversations I had with Justin and Akleelu. We've been here several days and he has not shown up. Now I know you think he could be sick or injured somewhere, but I think he's in hiding. I think things are getting too unstable with the election coming and the killing of the generals. So he's decided to grab his money and go. I think that is why he left the States so abruptly – right after the executions. That hit the news the morning he left.

"In fact, I think the reason he blamed you and told you your marriage is over was because he needed to bug out quickly and couldn't have you in the way."

Dax silently considered his points. She thought about the mountain of money in unnumbered bank accounts, the geological surveys, the detailed accounting information on seven different mining operations, and all the people who saw his photo then refused to talk. She weighed it all against the man she knew, the man who planned on starting a family, the man she respected, loved and lived with for ten years.

"I just can't believe Blake is a criminal running several child labour mines. You've known him for a long time. Do you really think he's capable of all of this?"

"It's the only way to explain everything."

"What about Justin? It could be that he's the one running the mines and Blake is trying to shut it down."

"I know Justin. He's just not this smart or gutsy. And he doesn't have the relationship with Akleelu. These mines only operate because they are in partnership with the president. That simply isn't Justin. Akleelu named Blake. And it wasn't Justin recruiting at the refugee camp."

"Okay, maybe not Justin. But it could be someone else, someone smart. Maybe even someone not with Ironwood."

He put his arm around her shoulders and pulled her close. "These are hard facts to come to grips with."

"That's just it. What are the facts? Yes, someone regularly hired men from the refugee camp. Yes, Blake was identified as visiting the camp. And one criminal looking for cash said that the recruiter was Blake. How much can we trust a criminal to tell the truth?

"Yes. These men here identified Blake as Jack. You say it's because he wants to keep his identity hidden for alibi purposes. But you don't know that. Maybe he decided to go undercover and didn't want Justin or whoever to find out who he really is."

Logan lifted his arm off her shoulders. "Jack, the recruiter was the name they called him at the refugee camp and it's what they call him here. And they even know his wife, who happens to not be you. These were photo identifications. Blake is Jack. Akleelu said Blake helped him become stupid wealthy. And as to his being undercover, how long has he been recruiting? Because if it's more than once or twice then he's working for the mine, not against it."

She shrugged. "Awhile. They said his manager does this work now."

Logan stared at her with expectation.

"What? If you want to deal in facts, we don't know that anything the Black Rat told me is true."

"No. But a couple of men in Zimbula told you they have seen Blake at the camp multiple times. His frequent visits to the camp is a fact. And the miners know him well enough here that they have met *his wife.* That implies many more than one investigative visit."

"Think what you want. I know Blake. I've been married to him for 10 years. He's worked for you for as many years. Do you really believe he is capable of what you are suggesting? You really think he's operating these illegal and immoral mines, making oceans of money on children's backs?"

He rested his head back on the dirt wall. "Africa is a tough place. No one escapes her malice."

Amedeo looked at his watch. *It'll be days before help gets here.* He glanced across the mine, his eyes landing on an automatic weapon. *I don't think Logan and Dax have that kind of time. So it's up to me.*

He watched the workings of the mine for a couple of hours then leaned against a tree to wait for sunset. *There are at least five armed men, three with automatic weapons. So I will need the cover of darkness. The mine will not be busy. Then I only need to quietly take out the one guard.*

The man in charge of Pandora considered his options – *kill the two outright. Jack always said to kill any intruders. But they claim to be related to Jack. I could tell them to come back when Jack is here.*

I've got a man who claims to be a business associate and a woman who claims to be Jack's wife. If either claim is true and I kill them, my life won't be worth spit.

He left a message and waited several hours for a call back with instructions.

Half an hour after sunset, under the cover of darkness Amedeo slipped into the mine camp. He crept behind banks of dirt and inched over mounds. It took over an hour to cover most of the distance to the guard. The door of the shack suddenly opened, blasting light across the pit. One of the men started toward the guard with a flashlight, calling to him.

Amedeo slinked into the shadows. The man passed a few feet from him and took over guard duty. Amedeo waited for the retiring guard to return to the shack.

In the darkness of the moonless night, the new guard lit up a cigarette. He leaned back to blow a well-practiced smoke ring.

Amedeo quietly eased behind the man, without a sound placed his gun to the man's temple and cocked the weapon. The man froze mid exhale.

"Not a sound or your brains will paint the ground."

The man dropped his weapon and raised his hands.

Amedeo moved his gun to the man's back and pushed him toward the mineshaft. "Get them out."

The guard nodded. The ladder dropped down the hole. Logan came up first, saw the guard under Amedeo's control and called Dax up.

The phone in the shack rang. "Yes ma'am. Yes, she said she is Jack's wife. Calls him Blake something."

The woman on the other said, "They are liars. Kill them."

"I really need to talk with Jack."

She let loose with raging invectives.

On her first breath he said, "As you say. Yes ma'am. I understand." He immediately left the shack with a couple of men. "Grab a couple of shovels. We'll bury them alive."

Amedeo saw the shack door open and three men head their way. He whispered into the guard's ear. "Remember, not a sound." He ordered him to climb down the ladder.

Three bobbing flashlights approached.

Logan jostled the ladder. "Hurry up."

The approaching men's voices carried over the open pit. Their light would soon reach them.

He and Logan violently shook the ladder, dislodging the man. They heard a thump and groan. Amedeo immediately removed the ladder and tossed it aside.

A matter of seconds separated them from the beams of the powerful lights.

They scrambled over a tall rubble pile.

One of the men told a joke. The other laughed.

Running along behind a wall of earth, they put some distance between them and the men. Logan took the lead. He took a sharp turn up the side of the pit and into the jungle. Halfway up Dax slipped. Amedeo grabbed her hand and pulled to the cover of the bush.

The men discovered the guard in the mine. One shot rang out.

Logan said, "One dead guard. C'mon. Get moving. They'll be on our vehicles fast." They ran while the mine sprang to life. When close to the vehicles, Logan turned and pushed Amedeo and Dax ahead. He waited until they both got in Amedeo's SUV then got in his.

Amedeo peeled out with no lights. He raced along the winding track. Branches snapped in their wake. Dax secured her seat belt. They skidded left. Rounded another bend. Slid right. Amedeo hammered on the accelerator. Took the turns at impressive speed. Logan fell behind. Behind Logan they saw the lights of trucks flashing through the jungle in pursuit.

At the main road, Amedeo waited for Logan then turned right to head north and further into the hills. He punched the gas pedal hard with Logan close on his tail.

By the time the pursuit vehicles got to the main road, Logan and Amedeo were out of sight. The mining men looked both ways, but saw nothing. The boss pointed left. "Catch them before they get back to the city."

After several minutes with no sign of any one following, Amedeo pulled over. Logan pulled up beside him and rolled his passenger window down. "I've not seen driving like that off track. Very nice. And good call in coming this direction. I think they assumed we went toward Mabezi."

"Prego." Amedeo nodded to the road ahead. "It'll take an extra three hours, but we can get to Mabezi this way."

"Lead on."

They turned on their headlights and continued at a more reasonable speed.

Amedeo glanced at Dax. "You okay?"

"That was some driving. I'm pretty sure a rally driver couldn't have done better. I love the way you threw the car into a slide and navigated around the tight curves. Amazing."

His dimples deepened. "Must be all the illegal street racing on the winding roads of Italy. That slipping bit is called drifting. When I was young I wanted to be a drifting racer."

"Car racing and private eye. You are quite the surprising doctor. Thank you for rescuing us."

"Prego. Did you get the information you were seeking?"

"Sort of. They know Blake – but they know him as Jack." She added nothing further.

Amedeo left her to her thoughts. *Jack? Didn't Greg mention*

Jack? Yes. He's Akleelu's partner in banking their ill-gained wealth. So, Blake is that man.

He glanced at Dax. *Blake must be incredibly good at hiding his true nature. Gutsy to marry a psychologist. That level of deception is impressive.*

After many miles ticked by she said, "Logan thinks Blake is involved with the president of Zimbula to become rich on the backs of children. He believes they operate these hidden mines. But the criminal and immoral person who would do such a thing is not remotely like the man I married and lived with for ten years.

Her fingers randomly tapped her leg. "I know there's some studies that suggest there is a benign version of psychopathy they call fearless dominance. These people don't know fear, are supremely self-confident, have good social skills, and are extremely resistant to stress, and with good education can rise to the top of business. From what I've read, they don't suffer from the antisocial behaviour associated with the negative form of psychopathy.

"I could see Blake as a fearless dominant. But the person who operates a bunch of illegal mines with child labour under a fake name, hires ruthless people, and fosters a violent environment where they shoot each other for a mistake – no one would accomplish all that without a number of antisocial characteristics.

"That then leads to the question of how well can a true psychopath hide their negative side? Do you think it's possible that a psychopath could pull off a happy marriage for ten years?"

"I don't know. I didn't do any specialized training in psychiatric disorders."

"You know people, Amedeo. You read people very well. Have you ever encountered someone who can pull off that kind of deception? To totally hide a core nature of truly antisocial qualities and live as a normal married man for ten years? Is this even possible?"

"I understand he worked here in Africa all of your married life, yeah?"

"Yes."

"How much time did he spend at home?"

She considered the implications of her answer. "Maybe a quarter of his time was at home. The rest of the time he was here. Yes, that is a good point."

Absently she ran her fingers over the rhythmic bumps of stitches on her leg. "If this is true and he's a world-class psychopath, I'm not much of a psychologist. I lived with him the equivalent of more than two years and never spotted any psychopathic behaviour. He had no problems with relationships. I didn't find him deceitful." She remembered remarking on how he found it easy to live a lie with her. "Well, not deceptive across the board. He was never cruel, violent, aggressive or manipulative. He was responsible, not impulsive."

He thought, *You don't see it coming, but truth is about to hit you hard.*

She shook her head. "I just can't wrap my mind around the possibility of such depth of deception. I get that psychopaths are super charming and tell you exactly what you want to hear. But they have no conscience and lack empathy. I didn't really see any lack of morality or an extreme level of narcissism. And inevitably a psychopath will hurt you in such a way as you don't see it coming."

Oh I can see the hurt coming.

"Again, that has not been my experience with Blake. Surely, something of their true nature would slip through the cloak of guile. Wouldn't some of his manipulative nature show over that length of time?"

Amedeo rubbed his face. *She is wrapping up his behaviour in respectable terms like Pop*à *did.* "The mind has an amazing capacity to frame behaviour in acceptable terms, and then happily live out of that lie. Most of my popà's life he never saw himself as a criminal. He refused to consider the truth and completely lived in deception."

"Blake is the son of two meth addicts who spent much of their short lives in jail. His aunt and uncle raised him. He never talked much about his childhood. I suspect he experienced some physical abuse. From the few stories he shared, they treated him like a third class citizen telling him his genetic heritage would determine his destiny. He lived like a pauper in tattered clothes while their own children lived a comfortable middle class life. There's probably plenty of reason for his mind to conjure up a more palatable version of life. Perhaps he's not a psychopath at all, but just a very damaged man struggling to prove himself worthy."

She missed the suggestion that she too is living in deception. "That's a rough start to life for anyone. All the people that work for your uncle come from the military?"

"Yes. Blake was a part of a special operations team before he came to Ironwood."

"So he rose through the ranks and proved his talent and worth to work in an elite unit?"

"Yeah. I get your point. The military is a pretty healthy dose of reality and he proved he was not destined to follow in his parents' footprints. So maybe he's not a deluded man trying to prove himself worthy." She let out a long slow breath. "I know what Uncle Logan thinks, but I'm not ready to go there. But I don't want to deceive myself either and perhaps that's what I'm doing.

"Alright. If I consider only the cold, hard facts, right now we have a few facts and a lot of assumptions. I need to find the truth wherever that takes me."

The three arrived at Blake's house in the early hours of the morning. Dax opened the fridge looking for something to eat and pulled out a bunch of food. After a light meal, they relaxed with a drink.

Getting sleepy, Dax left for bed. "Amedeo, please stay overnight. There are a couple of spare rooms. Make yourself comfortable. I'm tired so I'll see you both in the morning."

The men continued deep in conversation about the state of Africa. They discovered they knew a lot of people in common. An hour later they took their glasses to the kitchen.

Logan offered his hand. "Thank you for coming to our rescue today. I suspect you have plenty of experience in getting out of tough situations with the investigative work you've done."

"A fair bit. You're welcome."

Amedeo headed for the door when Logan stopped him. "I don't know your plans, but I'm wondering if I can impose on you for a few more days."

"No firm plans. I was going to check in on one of our doctors working here in Zimbula, maybe go out with a few friends, but that can wait. What did you have in mind?"

"It's now Wednesday morning. I have one of my men coming in from South Africa Friday. In the meantime there are a few people I'd like to see, but these are not the kind of places I can take Dax. I won't worry about her if you're here."

"Sure. I'll get a hotel room and come back in the morning." He looked at his watch. "Late morning."

"Stay here. The dark side of Zimbula is getting a little too close to Dax for my comfort. I would feel better about you staying here. And that gives me the freedom I need."

Amedeo thought of the crocodile tooth killer. "Certainly."

Chapter 4 — Stoking the Crazy Fire

Wednesday, March 18

At the sprawling waterside mansion in Malawandi, Blake downed his coffee. "I'm meeting someone here in a few minutes. I need complete privacy." He waited for a response. "Did you hear me?"

Salama set the magazine down. "I'm not deaf. You want to meet some creepy military guy and you don't want him to see me."

He kissed her cheek. "That's right. I don't want my creepy military friends to behold your beauty. Speaking of creepy military men, Justin is coming for lunch."

She brightened. "Justin? I will have the cook prepare his favourite meal."

He left to speak to the butler about directing his visitor.

Salama will not be happy when she discovers I'm leaving without her. Maybe I need to push her onto Justin. Give her something new to think about and not become a problem for me.

A few minutes later a knock at the library door announced the visitor.

"Good to meet you, Xander."

"Jack."

They sat opposite each other at the expansive desk. Xander opened his briefcase and pulled out a jeweller's loupe, a thermal diamond tester and a gadget labelled D-Screen. He put on cotton gloves. "I'll see the stone in question now."

Blake retrieved the diamond from the drawer.

Xander examined the raw shape of the stone from various angles. Satisfied, he confirmed the stone was a diamond with a thermal test. He moved out of the direct light coming from the window and examined the stone with the loupe and penlight. He returned to the desk and put the stone inside the D-Screen. In a few seconds the indicator flashed green.

He handed the stone back to Blake. Without saying a word, he carefully put his equipment away.

Blake said, "Interested?"

Xander folded his hands on the desk. "Perhaps. It could be a synthetic diamond. Worth about a quarter of the value of a natural diamond."

Blake smiled. "The green indicator says otherwise."

"Indeed." He thought for a moment. "We are talking black market trade. I can offer you $10 million."

"I know this stone, legally traded, would be worth a hundred and twenty million." He leaned back in the office chair. "Eighty million."

Xander chuckled. "Forty-five million."

"Seventy."

"I can see you are a determined man. Sixty million. That is my final offer."

Blake held out his hand. "You have yourself an Impossible Blue diamond."

"I will be back Saturday to pick up the stone. I only deal in unnumbered Swiss bank accounts."

"That is not a problem."

Xander stood up with his brief case in hand. "I will see you here Saturday afternoon."

During lunch Blake and Justin talked about mundane details of Ironwood work with the Zimbula military. When the meal was done Salama excused herself. She rested a light hand on Justin's shoulder. "It's good to see you."

Justin's eyes popped wide and watched Blake carefully for a reaction.

As many confident men do, Blake sat watching with his hand resting thoughtfully on his face. A slight smile softened his eyes.

Sensing that Blake was comfortable with the exchange Justin said, "Yes. Good to see you too, Salama."

Blake watched her leave. "She likes you."

"She loves you."

"Perhaps."

Justin said, "I had drinks with Logan."

"And what did the old dog have to say?"

"He's looking for you. The International Criminal Court investigators contacted him for information about you. They are looking into your involvement in crimes against humanity here – like five mines using child labour and the acceptance of intrinsic rape."

Blake shrugged. "Those toothless old women have been sniffing around for three years. They couldn't follow a trail even if it was marked with signs. Nothing to worry about."

"Logan spoke with Akleelu. Apparently Akleelu is cooperating with the investigators to find and convict the man running the illegal mines. Sounds like he's throwing you under the bus."

"So says Logan. It means nothing."

"You know they don't convict political parties, only people. And you are an easy bone with meat on it for Akleelu to throw to the dogs."

Blake considered Justin's point. "He can try. I've created enough evidence to bury him and clear my name." His hand absently tapped the arm of the chair. "A piece of advice. Anticipate betrayal. Always ensure you have more dirt on them than they have on you.

"I plan on leaving Africa on Saturday. You will never see or hear from me again."

"I understand."

"It's been a pleasure working with you, Justin. You're quite capable of taking over the relationship with Akleelu and the mines. Build in some protection should Akleelu go off the deep end. You'll be fine."

Justin weighed the threat of investigation against the irresistible attraction of unbelievable wealth. "I've learned a lot from you. Thank you."

"Remember, Akleelu is not a smart man, just a powerful one. He's a checkers player. You need to think like a chess player. As to the mines, the trucks will do a collection on Friday. Everything becomes yours as of Saturday. I have informed the men that you are taking over. You will want to visit each one immediately to assert your authority. Move men into key positions who you know will be loyal. Some of my guys could take this opportunity to grab the mines for themselves."

"Yes. I have several men in mind to move into position. If I'm as smart as you, in ten years, I too will be leaving Africa wealthy."

He contained an amused grin. *And once you are operating the mines, I have evidence to bury you in accountability. They will throw your ass in jail. Not mine.* "Two more things." He handed an envelope to Justin. "I have signed my house over to you."

Justin accepted the envelope.

"This last item is between you and me. I am not taking anyone with me when I leave." He gave Justin a meaningful look.

Justin looked surprised, his eyes briefly glancing at the door where Salama left.

"Yes. You understand." He looked out the window. "She has been an effective asset. I have used her to open doors that wouldn't have opened otherwise.

"It doesn't take much to keep her happy. I think she would make an equally effective asset at your disposal as well."

Justin focused his eyes on his hands while considering the implications of Blake's advice.

Blake started for the door. "It's clear she's attracted to you. Use everything and everyone to your benefit. Leave nothing on the table."

Blake offered his hand. "If all goes to plan, I won't see you again. Goodbye and good luck."

"Goodbye, Jack."

Blake smiled.

Sitting in his palace office, Akleelu pondered the meaning of Phil's visit. *First Logan. Now the crazy man.*

Phil followed the escort through the gold gilded halls. His tongue flicked with his anticipation of the opportunity. *Speaking truth to power. Speaking truth and grabbing some power for myself. Phil Kubwa. Everyone will know how important I am. One of the great thinkers of my time.*

The guard knocked on Akleelu's office door and announced Phil.

Akleelu continued working. With his head still bent he said, "Sit. Please make yourself comfortable."

Phil sat in one of the two chairs across from the desk. The sunlight streaming through the window impaired his vision. He shifted in the chair, but still couldn't see. He half stood, lifted the chair and shuffled, landing back in the chair with a thud.

I am the big dog. Meaner than a junkyard dog. Five breaths puffed out in rapid succession. His fingers twitched, the tremor quickly spreading up his arms. His whisper faded. "No mesmo now. No mesmo. No mesmo."

Something jangled in his pocket. "Forty nine. Forty-nine done.

Fifteen more."

He switched to the other chair.

Akleelu finally looked up. "Comfortable?"

"No. These chairs are not comfortable."

"Why did you wish to see me?"

"I have information – no, I have intelligence that the Americans are arranging a coup d'etat. They want to bring you down." A single tongue flick followed.

Akleelu rocked back in his chair. "And what evidence do you have for this claim?"

"Do you know Dakota Keyes?"

"No."

"She is a CIA operative, sent by the U.S. government. Wait. I have photos." He showed images of Dax meeting with the man from the embassy. "They arrived Saturday and the next day she had a secret meeting with this man." He pointed to David Perry from the Zimbula embassy.

"You said 'they'?"

"This man." He showed another photo of Dax and Logan. "He is their top agent. The agents call her *The Kingmaker*."

Akleelu looked at Logan in the image. "This is ridiculous." *This man is a fool. Logan is not with the CIA.* "You say this man is with the CIA?"

"Both of them are CIA. She's his niece and married to Blake Talbot." Phil got up to lean over the desk. "Look. Here they all are together. This man," pointing to David," is the grand spymaster. This was the first day these two came to Zimbula." He showed him photos from the refugee camp. "The very next day, under instructions from the spymaster, she travelled to Munyegera refugee camp in Tanzania. Here she met with a known Italian intelligence agent."

More pictures poured out on the desk. "And together they met with this man known as Black Rat, an arms dealer. They made arrangements for both mercenaries and arms to come into Zimbula."

Could this idiot have stumbled on to something?

"Next, they met with a map maker. Here. See. Here they are plotting rendezvous points on the Italian's map." Akleelu shuffled through the images.

Phil's tongue flicked several times. "You know they are funding this with money from mines in the remote hills?"

Akleelu's eyes narrowed. "Mines?"

"They are skimming money from five mines here in Zimbula, and a couple more in Tanzania. Millions. Millions for weapons and men."

Skimming? From my *mines? How dare these rats try to play me for a fool.*

"You know about the false documents the Italians sent to the U.S. to justify the invasion of Iraq? Here the Italians are again, contributing a false narrative. This stinks of an international dark operation, an armed insurrection in Zimbula.

Phil sat down. "They are coming for you."

Akleelu stood up. "Get out!" He yelled at the guard. "Get this idiot out of my palace." It took three men to subdue Phil and drag him out.

Akleelu paced the empty room. He boomed at his assistant. "Get me Blake Talbot."

The assistant left an urgent message for Blake.

In a few minutes Blake called the president on his private line.

Spitting, Akleelu said, "You're stealing from me? You worm. I will crush you."

"Hang on. What are you on about?"

"One of your men was just here. He told me of the coup you and your wife and Logan are planning."

"Who told you such nonsense?"

"Phil. He has photos of all their meetings."

"Meetings with who?"

"Arms dealers, Italian intelligence. I know your wife is The Kingmaker. Well, she won't be making any new kings here. I will squash all of you like a bug."

"Hold on. You believed Phil? You know he should be in an asylum. You can't believe anything that nutcase says. He believes there is a portal at the South Pole that transports people to a base on Mars. And he thinks half the world population isn't human but reptilian beings dressed as people. He has more screws loose than tight."

Akleelu laughed. "He really thinks half the people are reptiles?"

Blake smiled. "Yes. Ask him about it next time you see him. He's got about an hour's worth of evidence for that conspiracy theory."

"The idiot should be locked away."

"On the most part, his crazy ideas just swirl in his head and don't come out. I will talk to him about getting it under control. We okay?"

"Of course. I didn't really believe his mad ravings."

"Good. The elections are a few weeks away. Things look really good for you. There will be no problem with you winning by a landslide. But Etienne, you need to look legitimate. This is important. You have to stop killing your military men. Stop talking about a coup. I have my ear to the ground. There is no one talking about a coup but you and Phil, the idiot. And stop threatening to dispose of your opposition. You will easily win this election if you can contain yourself."

Akleelu's brows knit together. "You have heard nothing about a coup? Nothing from the military? You have ears in the opposition?"

"Nothing. So it would not be good for *you* to start rumours about a coup."

"No. No. I would not say anything. I am not a fool."

"Of course you aren't."

"Tell me, Blake. What are you doing with your share of the

money from the mines?"

"I plan on investing in a reindeer farm in Iceland."

Akleelu laughed. "You are one crazy bastard."

Afterward Blake called Phil and arranged to meet at a pub in Malawandi.

Phil swaggered down the street like a man of importance. A few steps from the pub door Blake hauled him into an alley. With a firm grip on Phil's shirt, Blake shoved him against the side of the building. He pressed into Phil's personal space, knowing it would torment him.

Very quietly Blake said, "Do you have a death wish?"

Phil vigorously shook his head. Beads of sweat dotted his forehead.

"Do you realize what you've done? The entire reptilian army has an order to kill you on sight."

Phil paled. "Wha – they're after me? What am I going to do?" His eyes darted to the street.

Blake released him. "One of them saw you talk to Akleelu."

Phil shoved his hand in his pocket to fondle the remaining crocodile teeth. "Fifteen left and the reptiles are coming for me, for their teeth." His tongue flicked over dry lips. "Blake, you have to hide me."

Blake stepped back and scratched his head. "I don't know, Phil. You really pissed them off."

"You can't let them kill me."

Blake shook his head then looked out to the street.

"Please, Blake. I'll do anything you say. Just don't let the reptiles kill me."

"Maybe."

"Anything, Blake. You've gotta help me. They will eat me."

"Eat your heart while it's still beating."

Phil's knees gave out.

"Alright. I will get the kill order stopped, but you have to stay out of sight."

"Yes, out of sight. Invisible."

"You cannot talk to Akleelu again. Ever. Do you hear me? They will be waiting for you, if you do."

"No. I won't talk to him again."

"You want my protection?"

Phil nodded.

"I don't want to hear another word about this CIA crap. I will kill you myself if any more of your whacked out paranoia comes out of your mouth." He glared at Phil. "Do you believe I work for the CIA."

"No."

"Then shut the fuck up."

Phil grimaced. "I will shut the fuck up."

"There is only one thing I want you to do right now."

"Shut the fuck up?"

"Besides that. I want you to do the job I'm paying you for – scare Dax."

"Okay. I will shut the fuck up and scare Dax. You can count on me, boss."

"Do this well and I have another job for you, one that you will enjoy."

Phil grimaced. "A job I will enjoy." His tongue flicked. "A crocodile tooth job for Phil."

"Alright. Go do what I'm paying you for and I will call you soon about the crocodile tooth job."

He watched Phil stumble out of the alley. *When that nutcase deals with Dax, I'll eliminate him. No loose ends.*

Chapter 5 — Rendezvous

Wednesday March 18

After their late escape from the Pandora mine, Dax slept in. A heavy rain pelting the window roused her. She listened to the blustery wind for a few minutes. As she sat on the edge of the bed letting her body wake up, her eyes landed on the night table. She scanned the table again for her missing watch. She ran her hand between the bed rail and the mattress, lifted the pillows and pulled back the sheets, but found nothing. After making the bed she headed for the bathroom.

When she returned she immediately noticed her watch carefully positioned on top of the pillow. Riveted, she scanned the room. *Nothing else has moved. Now I'm being paranoid. Probably Nakato found it and left it where I'd see it.*

She heard voices in the kitchen and listened at the door – a melodic African and a deep Italian voice. She strapped the watch on and went to the kitchen.

"Good morning, Amedeo. You decided to stay."

"Sí. Logan has some things he wants to follow up on and asked if I could spend another few days here."

"Well, you are certainly welcome to stay as long as you like. Good morning Nakato."

"Good morning, Mrs. Dax."

"I see you've met our house guest?"

"Doctor Amedeo, yes. Where did you find him? He's a handsome one."

Amedeo said, "Bellissimo. Talk like that can get you into trouble."

With a hand on her hip she eyed him up and down. "Your kind of trouble I can handle."

He grinned. "I'm sure you can."

With a fresh cup of coffee in hand, Dax said, "Nakato, thank you for finding my watch."

She turned from cutting a mango and wiped her hands. "I am glad you have your watch, but I didn't find it."

Then how did it suddenly appear on the bed?

Nakato handed her a bowl. "I thought you would enjoy some fresh fruit I bought this morning."

"Thanks, looks great."

Over breakfast Dax said, "I'd like to hire you, Amedeo. I could use some expert investigative help. You know Zimbula and you have contacts here. So what would you charge for this work?"

"For you, nothing."

"No, I'm serious. I want to hire you."

"Then I will help you in exchange for room and board."

"I'd like to pay you."

"I will help you and if we find Blake then we can talk about what my help is worth."

"It's a deal. So, where do we start?"

"There are two categories of missing people. Those that aren't in hiding. You simply have lost contact. And they are easier to find. And then there are those who are intentionally hiding. What have you done so far to get in touch? You have tried calling him?"

"Yes. I've left a number of messages asking him to call me."

"And you've not heard from him?"

"No."

"This is his house, but obviously he's not staying here."

"Right."

"And no one you know here has seen him."

"Correct."

"And we know that in some fashion he's involved in high-stakes criminal activity. These are the facts, yes? I think it is safe to assume that he doesn't wish to be found. That makes it a bit more difficult to locate him. And this is Africa, not Europe or America where people leave a huge digital footprint. So it's not assured that we will find him.

"Since the known associates are unable to help, I think we need more information about other people he mingles with here. He's staying somewhere. We need to figure out who he's with. Have you done an online search of his name?"

She shook her head.

The wind kicked up, blasting the heavy rain on the windows. "Because it's a monsoon out there today, let's start on the Internet."

They spent much of the day searching the Internet for information on Blake Talbot. There were a number of people with that name – a couple of engineers, a digital marketing specialist, a salesman, and a few project managers.

Dax spotted a photo of another man with the same military rank in the Special Forces. "I didn't expect it was such a common name. Imagine having two Blake Talbots in the Special Forces?" She read a bit more. "He's about the same age as my Blake. Oh, he died about 11 years ago."

They found a couple of stories on the AfricaNews site that included Blake. One article covered the first ball at Akleelu's new palace, which included several photos of Salama Mugisha, a famous supermodel. Blake was identified as her escort for the evening.

Another story detailed Akleelu's meeting with the leadership of the East African Community. Photos included Blake at the president's side.

A third story found on the Independent News site in the United Kingdom covered the International Criminal Court investigation into crimes against humanity in Zimbula. Several of the over 20 photos showed Blake and Akleelu together.

Amedeo said, "It is interesting that he is often seen with Akleelu."

"I know the Ironwood contract is with the president to train the military. I guess that's why Blake's with him."

"That would explain why Blake would appear with the military. If I hire a governess to train my children, it should raise suspicion if she always appears at my side."

"And not with the kids. I see your point. So, what are you thinking this means?"

He typed Awamaki Kubwa in the search engine.

She pointed to the screen. "Yes! The dead man we found at the refugee camp? He said this exact thing to me about Blake. What does it mean?"

He sat back from the computer. "Someone told you Blake is Awamaki Kubwa?"

She nodded.

"Awamaki means the god's dog. It is a name used 15, maybe 20 years ago or so, for a very secretive man that advised Akleelu. It was early in Akleelu's presidency and this man brought stability and sanity to the chaotic and often despotic behaviour. There were still problems, but for the first time under self-rule, there was a sense of future for the country. People had hope.

"In the last decade, the man people talk about is Awamaki Kubwa – the god's bigger dog. This new man is not a stabilizing factor, but violence and ethnic hatred has escalated with his presence. Coincidentally the International Criminal Court launched its investigation a few years after this Kubwa came on the scene."

She said, "And the Miami man called Blake Awamaki Kubwa. And he's now murdered." She swallowed hard.

He hit search and several results came up. Most posts mentioned the Kubwa in passing. Only one contained any information on who this man was, and most of that was conjecture, but nothing that confirmed or denied that Blake was the god's bigger dog.

It was late afternoon when Dax heard the radio in the kitchen. "I think I need a drink. Can I get you anything?"

He closed the computer and followed her. "Whatever you're having is fine."

Once in the kitchen he said, "Nakato. What are you making?" He lifted a pot lid. "It smells fantastic."

She beamed. "It is my mother's recipe."

"It's been a long time since I enjoyed a good African home cooked meal."

Dax handed a glass of wine to Amedeo. "Nakato is an amazing cook. Her meals taste even better than they smell."

She bowed. "Thank you, Mrs. Dax."

They took their drinks to the front room. Dax took a long sip of the smooth South African white. "Blake has a safe in his office. When we first arrived here, I thought there might be some helpful information in there, so I figured out the password and looked through the papers."

"And did you find any clues as to where to find him?"

"Not really. There are a couple of keys, one to a safety box in Switzerland and statements from three separate Swiss bank accounts, two of which are numbered accounts and between the two, there is over a hundred million dollars."

Amedeo's face momentarily flashed surprise.

"I thought maybe it's not his money, but he was collecting incriminating evidence. Maybe they were someone else's bank accounts. Then there are these recordings of Akleelu asking Blake to secretly run mines and selling the goods for both their gain."

"So if Akleelu tries to claim he's not involved in the mining, Blake can prove otherwise." He rubbed his temple with his hand resting on his face.

"Also, there are accounting books for the Zimbuli and Tanzanian mines. It shows all the transactions, all the minerals or gemstones sold."

"Because you thought he was gathering evidence, you thought he might be hiding in the refugee camp?"

"Or injured. I knew he'd been there before."

"Does anyone else know about what is in that safe?"

"Only you and I know about the banking statements and the mine transactions. But there's one other thing in the safe that Uncle Logan knows about. Photos of Akleelu murdering those three generals. Uncle Logan calls them a nuclear bomb."

Amedeo sat back shocked. *Blake might be the Kubwa, the one responsible for escalating this type of violence. And Dax holds the evidence of Akleelu's involvement? Just knowing about these photos puts her in peril.* "He's right. That is nuclear and you don't want it going off in your hands."

"The first crocodile tooth dead man that I told you about? The guy who was murdered out there at the gates? He dropped those photos off for Blake one evening. Then I found him dead the next morning – with a diamond in his pocket."

He rubbed his eyes, thinking about the implications of the contents of the safe. "Do not say one more word to anyone about a safe or what is in it. Your life will be in jeopardy if anyone finds out." He remembered something Greg had mentioned about the disappearance of the Director of Natural Resources in suspicious circumstances followed by no legitimate mining contracts. *Akleelu dismissed the man, and Blake probably eliminated him, then together they started the mines in secret and kept the proceeds for themselves.*

He looked at Dax. *Hard to get your mind around your husband, the treacherous criminal.* "What do you think about things now?"

She gazed out the window for a long time. "I don't know what to think anymore. I came here to prove Blake is alive and save my marriage. I don't have hard proof that he's alive, and who knows about my marriage. But there are a number of things that conflict with the man I thought he was.

She studied the rivers of rain streaming down the window, each losing speed until it incorporated another drop to gain momentum toward its inevitable destination. *Like me. I absorb this information and it propels me to an inevitable conclusion.* "Like maybe he's this Awamaki Kubwa who is being investigated for crimes against humanity."

The battle between her heart and the ugly facts created deep furrows across her brow. "Many have identified him as Jack, the man running several secret mines. That means those are probably his Swiss bank accounts. So if all that is true then he's not a good man investigating a criminal. He *is* the morally bankrupt criminal.

Unconsciously she fingered Blake's wedding ring hanging from her neck. "I keep thinking, this is not the man I married and have known for 10 years. So is this some kind of crazy frame up? Or is he a psychopath? In ten years, wouldn't a psychologist detect at least some antisocial behaviour? Maybe this is some kind of drug-related delusion.

She let his ring fall back to her chest. "I don't honestly know what to think."

After dinner Nakato cleaned up and took the garbage out. She returned frantic and yelling for Amedeo. Near tears she pointed next door. "The child. He is not breathing." She pulled Amedeo toward the door. "Please. Hurry."

In the heavy rain he made his way into the yard. The boy lay unconscious in the mud. Even in the dark, he could see the lad's lips were turning blue. He checked for breathing and a pulse then tried to give him a breath of air. He quickly performed the Heimlich manoeuvre and cleared an obstruction. The child coughed as he regained consciousness. Amedeo carried him inside and checked that he would be okay. The frantic mother thanked him through her tears.

Nakato and Amedeo returned to the house. She said, "Thank you, Dr. Amedeo," and pinched his cheek. "You are a keeper. I don't see a wedding ring. I'm going to find you a good woman. A man like you shouldn't be without a good woman."

He grinned. "You're not available, are you?"

She giggled. "Oh go on. You rascal."

Covered in mud, he tried wiping the water dripping from his hair, instead smeared his face in red mud. "Excuse me. I think I need a shower."

She said, "I'm on my way home now, but if you leave those clothes out, I'll wash them for you tomorrow."

Dax locked up after Nakato left then went to the kitchen to pour herself a glass of wine. In the front room she picked up the *Bourne Identity* to read the writing in the front again. "Salama. I thought so. Same name as the woman Blake took to the palace ball." She read some of the lines again. "Eternal lovers, like the sun and moon." She set the book down.

Who are you?

Feeling unsettled, her leg bounced a restless rhythm. She twirled her wedding ring.

I remember the dark, rainy night we met. And the Thai island where we shared our hearts and dreams over Sam Song. And the crazy night riding out a tropical storm on a sailboat without a captain. And the time you dove off the Florida Keys tour boat and lost your bathing suit. Or the night we hiked through the Andes – the stars were insane. We have laughed and we have loved. What happened to that man?

Her restless legs urged her to pace.

If this is a delusion, is there a possibility you can come to your senses and leave this sick life behind? Would a big scare bring you to your senses?

She shook out her hands.

Movement on the street caught her attention. For a moment her heart accelerated with a shot of fear. *Window pervert.* A stocky man stood still – just out of the reach of the light – staring. She stared back. *There's that feeling again – like a gazelle being sized up by a lion.*

"Screw you, buddy." Her hands clenched into tight fists. "This gazelle is going to fight." She strode to the front door. Slamming it open ready to challenge him, she found the street empty.

Salama found Blake reading in bed. She put a shot of Jack Daniels on his nightstand.

"Thanks, babe." He continued reading.

Her foot hit something heavy and hard in Blake's pants. She picked them off the floor to search the pocket. "What's this?" she said with what sounded like reverence.

Blake's head whirled around. *The Impossible Blue.* "It's nothing. Just a worthless piece of quartz."

"It's a beautiful blue. Diamonds come in blue." Her bright eyes locked with his. "This is a diamond."

"I deal in diamonds, honey. I know a diamond from junk."

She continued to examine it.

He patted the bed beside him. "Come here. I'll show you how you can tell it's not a diamond."

She sat beside him and handed him the weighty gem.

"See its overall box shape? Raw diamonds have six sides, not four. This has four sides, so it is a quartz – a pretty one, but worthless."

"I thought it was the opposite. Six sided ones are quartz."

"Who is the diamond expert here? You? Or me. Four sided is

quartz. Also, look at the clarity. There are very few flaws. Raw diamonds have way more flaws that they remove with cutting."

She watched as he tucked it in the night table drawer. "If it's worthless, why are you keeping it?"

"I thought I'd have it cut like a diamond. Maybe sell a bunch of the offcuts to people who don't know any better. I could make some money out of it."

In the middle of the night a noise woke Blake up. He saw Salama in the bathroom with the Impossible Blue, turning it in the light.

She didn't hear him get up. He startled her when he said, "I can ask the cutter to make you a quartz ring, if you love it that much." He took the stone back.

"I don't want any cheap thing that you might give your white wife. You can give her rubbish and tell her it's a diamond. She deserves that. I want a big blue diamond ring."

"Anything to keep my beauty happy."

He pretended to return the stone to the drawer, but instead he slipped it under the mattress and got back in bed.

Just a couple more days and I'm out of here. And best I slip away without the blood of the well-known Salama on my hands – or a beautiful American woman.

Tomorrow I will drive to Mabezi and lock this thing in my safe, out of the reach of Salama's greedy hands.

Now, how to deal with Dax? I need a way to get the stone into the safe without that one knowing.

A thought struck him and a grin tugged at his mouth.

EPISODE FIVE – DEEPLY FLAWED

If you seek truth, you may find comfort in the end.

If you seek comfort, you will not find either comfort or truth.

Seeking comfort begins with wishful thinking and ends in despair.

Chapter 1 — Finding The Kubwa

Thursday, March 19

Logan met his friend Colonel Jumai, the man in charge of the country's security, at the Ironwood warehouse.

"Thank you, Jumai. I appreciate your help."

"I owe you my life many times over. And I don't like what has become of our country under the Kubwa's influence."

Logan armed himself. "Where are we meeting?"

"At a historical site in the bush. Most people don't know it's there. It's become the unofficial headquarters for the opposition party."

"Good."

Climbing five stone steps they entered a 1500 yr. old palace through a crumbling archway. Several men stood. "Awamaki."

Logan shook each man's hand and stopped to briefly chat with the few men he knew. They sat on cut stones. Jumai said, "For the younger men, this is Awamaki. He is a loyal friend of Zimbula. Some of you will remember the stability and progress he brought to our country. And now he is looking for information on the Awamaki Kubwa." He finished with the traditional greeting between brothers. "Please open your hands to him."

Logan said, "Thank you, Jumai. I open my hands to you brave

men. I appreciate you coming to meet with me today. I'm so sorry to see what has become of Zimbula."

Many muttered their agreement.

Logan nodded to acknowledge their engagement. "Do you mind telling me what you know of the Kubwa?"

The men glanced around at each other. Several looked down at their feet. One young man said, "I know you only because some of these other men talk. It's been years since you've been in Zimbula. What do you think you're going to change by speaking to us?"

"You're right. It's been ten years. But I know the potential of the people and the natural wealth in the ground. There's –"

The young man stood up. "Yeah. Lots of money coming out of the ground, but it only goes to two people." The men grumbled in agreement.

Logan said, "And who are those two men?"

"Everyone here knows who they are. You know who they are. Why ask?"

Jumai stepped in. "You are a hothead, Mohombi. Respect your elders."

Logan said, "It's okay. Mohombi, you've seen your country fall into violence and wonder why your elders didn't do anything. And you don't know me, and for all you know, I'm another old man full of hot air.

"I worked with Akleelu for many years and saw much change for the good. But this cannot be said of the last decade. Akleelu started out with his eyes set on the welfare of the country. Power and money has corrupted him and it may be time for a change in leadership."

Mohombi said, "You think we will have an honest election?"

"No, not with things as they are now. The election, violence, change – all these things are currently in the grip of one man. The Kubwa. Remove him and all that you desire for your country and your people becomes a possibility. Leave him in place and none of it is possible.

"I am here to get the information required to bring this mongrel dog down. This is your opportunity to make a heroic change in your country's destiny – your destiny."

Mohombi stood inches in front of Logan and stared. Finally he said, "What do you need?"

Logan said, "I need to know who the Kubwa is and what is his weak spot, his underbelly."

Another man said, "He's a ghost. No one knows who he is."

Logan waited, giving the men time to ponder.

Another said, "It's a closely guarded secret. Akleelu doesn't want anyone knowing who his advisor is."

One man who sat back from the others said, "More importantly, Akleelu doesn't want to get his hands dirty."

Mohombi said, "So?"

The man stepped forward. "That is information that will lead to the identity of Kubwa."

Mohombi snorted. "That's stupid. How will that lead to the Kubwa?"

The man shrugged and sat back down.

Logan considered the man's thought. "Tell me about the dirty work."

An older man said, "The hatred between Abeesa and Jika burns like an inferno. And Akleelu's shadow forces pour fuel on the flames."

Logan said, "What specifically do they do?"

"They slaughter Abeesa like vermin. They publish editorials full of lies about the Abeesa to enflame the Jika. They advertise their atrocities to terrorize the Abeesa and make it acceptable behaviour to persecute. And they torture anyone who dares speak against Akleelu or the Kubwa."

The quiet man said, "The Kubwa's not afraid of dirt. He knows how to motivate and manipulate. He is skilled in handling presidents, the media, the military, the shadow forces – all to serve his purposes. He is a master chess player while everyone else plays tiddlywinks."

Mohombi said, "Yeah, yeah. That's right."

Logan said, "Tell me about the shadow forces. Who are they?"

Mohombi said, "They are not military. I can tell you that."

A more senior man said, "They are men that actually love getting dirty." He glanced at the quiet man. "My next door neighbour, for example. He lives alone. Often out all night. He's crazy as an outhouse rat. He's always going on about reptile people ruling the world.

"A couple of months ago Phil the lunatic told me about working for an important man. When I asked him what he did, because I couldn't imagine him holding down a job, he said 'Dark Services.'"

Blake hired a man named Phil to provide dark services. One tick closer to confirming Blake is the Kubwa.

"Just talking about these things got him excited. He started twitching in his fingers. It spread up his arms. It took over his whole body. His eyelids fluttered. His tongue flicked like a lizard. He groaned. It lifted a minute later and he continued to tell me about his secret garden in the jungle where he buries the bodies of all the people that he's been ordered to kill.

And the dead man in front of the house – he wrote Kubwa's dog Phil in the dirt. Strong circumstantial evidence.

"Since then I've seen him come home with bloodied clothes. I know this is Zimbula and we are mired in violence, but I couldn't believe some of the horrors he described. So I asked a friend in the police, and he said they know about Phil, but he's untouchable. He's protected by someone important.

Working for Blake and protected by Akleelu.

"That is who the shadow forces are. People who belong in a

maximum security prison along with the Kubwa. He that beats the drum for the madman to dance is no better than the madman himself."

Logan said, "So the Kubwa is not afraid of getting dirty. He's gathered a bunch of crazy sociopaths who will happily murder and maim. He knows how to motivate and manipulate. And he must be close to Akleelu for his protection. So who is close to Akleelu?"

The older man said, "The Kubwa sits between Akleelu and the military. No one in uniform has access to the president. We cannot answer that question."

Mohombi said, "Just sit outside his golden cage and watch who comes and goes."

Jumai said, "One of my sons works in the palace guard. We can ask him."

Logan said, "Thank you. That would be helpful. Listen. I want to thank you men for your willingness to speak with me, and your openness in telling me what you know. What you have done today will not be in vain."

As Jumai and Logan walked to their vehicle, the quiet man approached. "Awamaki, could I have a couple of minutes of your time?"

"Sure."

He gestured toward the road. "Alone?"

Logan rested his hand on the man's shoulder and they walked some distance down the road.

Jumai lit up a cigarette as he watched them. They stopped and faced each other. Logan listened intently for several minutes. The quiet man held up a hand a little over six feet from the ground. Logan nodded. He asked something and nodded again at the answer. The quiet man talked another minute. They shook hands and returned to the parked cars.

"Thank you, Gedeon." The quiet man nodded and continued to his vehicle.

Logan climbed in the vehicle. Jumai called his son and made arrangements for the three of them to meet in Malawandi.

With breakfast finished, Dax and Amedeo took a second cup of coffee to the living room. "I spent some time thinking about Blake and what I'm doing here. I know I came to prove Blake still lived and work out our marriage problems. But things have shifted. I think it now boils down to one thing. The answer to that will determine whether I need the answers to whether he's alive and whether we can make a go of our marriage.

"So, I want to focus the investigation on answering who Blake is. It's possible that he is a depraved outlaw. It's also possible he's the victim of a frame up. Or is suffering from delusional disorder – a psychosis. Is it feasible to get concrete evidence to confirm the truth, clear answers based on fact, not innuendo or circumstances?"

"Let me ask you, what evidence would you need to make a diagnosis of psychosis?"

"First, I would need to hear what he's thinking. Then if there's an indication of delusions I would use both interview and assessment tools to make the diagnosis."

"So gathering that evidence is dependent on a face to face interview."

"Yes."

"That may be difficult with him in hiding. We need to find him and he needs to cooperate to confirm or eliminate this one. Now, how would we prove a frame up? I would need Blake to lay out all the evidence and work with us to prove his innocence. It is possible that if he is being set up, he is trying to figure it out for himself.

"That would be a very desperate situation to be in. If he felt he was being framed I think he would reach out to Logan for help. Since our visit to Pandora, I am confident he knows you and Logan are here."

She tapped the side of her mug. "And he has not contacted Logan or me."

"As to the third possibility, is he a criminal? We have some circumstantial evidence, but you want something concrete. What does that look like for you?"

"I guess I was thinking if we eliminated the other two options then – I don't know, maybe I could find a way to wrap my head around the dissonance of the normal man I married and this horrific criminal."

"To prove a frame up or a psychosis we must locate Blake. If either of these is true, the truth lies with him. So, that leaves us with proving or disproving criminal actions. I think we should continue the search for him. In the process of finding him, we may uncover evidence that shows who he is. And Bella, in all likelihood we will uncover evidence that will be difficult to accept. Are you willing to continue?"

"You're right. I'm having a hard time accepting the evidence, but I came to find the truth. It just isn't what I expected or want to hear." She pressed her shoulders back. "I heard somewhere that the truth will set you free. I want my life built on a foundation of truth, not a story that makes me feel happy for a time."

She lifted her head. "We press ahead in our search. What should we do today?"

"You have visited a number of NGOs?"

"Yes. On the most part, people don't want to talk."

"That is not unusual for Zimbula. I'm going to call my friend Greg. He is the head physician here with our organization and has worked in the country for five years. I know he will talk to us."

Amedeo and Dax headed downtown to meet Greg at the Blue Rhino for lunch. The teeming rain turned the city watery grey. The wipers fell into a rhythm of brief visibility before the windshield flooded. Pelting rain ricocheting off the wet stone streets and the rising steam obscured the surrounding buildings.

After navigating a turn along the waterfront Amedeo said, "I have missed this smell – fog, rain, stone and mud – so Africa."

He parked in front of a long stone building painted blue. They dashed through a yellow door. Inside the Blue Rhino, they shook off some of the rain. Dax fingercombed her wet hair. "It never rains like this in Washington."

"Nor in Italy." He scanned the patrons. "There is Greg." He directed her toward a buff man with long wavy blond hair tied in a ponytail. "Dakota, this is Greg, a –"

"Careful what you say. I know most of your secrets." Greg stood and shook her hand. "I'm the lifelong friend that bails him out of his inevitable messes. Nice to meet you, Dakota."

She laughed. "Nice to meet you as well. You sound American." *That explains Amedeo's great command of English.* "How did you two meet?"

"We were next door neighbours growing up. My parents owned and operated a vacation villa."

Amedeo said, "Any story Greg tells you where he is the hero you can safely assume he got himself into trouble and I was the one who saved his sorry ass." The two men hugged.

Greg said, "Good to see you, Deyo."

"You too."

Drinks arrived as they sat down. "I took the liberty to order the house specialty."

Amedeo smiled. "Ah, the blue rhino. Careful Dax, it packs a rhino-sized punch."

Greg held up his glass. "To lifelong friends, old and new."

They clinked and Dax took a sip. "Ooh, that's good."

Greg laughed," Dax, you're a keeper."

After ordering their meals Greg said, "So you are looking for information?"

Amedeo said, "Can you tell us what you know about Jack, the

illegal miner?"

"The only mines in Zimbula are illegal and are operated by Jack, a man in partnership with President Akleelu. I say illegal in the sense that they do not pay for the land or mining rights. What those poor people are digging out with their hands belongs, at least in part, to the country and it is being stolen. And only two people benefit from the enormous wealth coming out of the earth – Jack and Akleelu. I understand you have been to one?"

Dax nodded. "Pandora. The treatment of people is hard to see. They send children down the narrow shafts to hand dig the minerals. A lot of young girls. I don't think I saw one of age that wasn't pregnant, raped I assume. And they were hauling the ore to the weigh station."

Greg said, "Life is not valued. Human labourers are an endless resource. So they are treated as disposable. And yes, the girls are brought in to keep the men happy."

Amedeo said, "How many mines? And where do they refine the copper and cobalt?"

"Don't know how many or where they are exactly, other than up in the remote hills along the Tanzanian border. I have seen heavily armed men guarding trucks passing through villages. The locals tell me they are transporting copper and cobalt across the border to refineries and merchants in Rwanda. It gets mixed in with legit copper and cobalt and becomes untraceable."

The arrival of their meals interrupted their conversation. Greg took a bite of his burger. "I hear you're looking for your missing husband."

"Yes, here's his photo. I'm wondering if you've met him, maybe know something about him."

He hesitated as she'd seen others do before.

"Greg, please tell me what you know. I want to know the truth."

"Yes I've met him once, at our clinic in the north east." He shot a look at Amedeo. "He visited with another guy in tow. They wanted to search the clinic for a man. The guy with him made the nurses very uncomfortable, so much that they got me out of an exam room to deal with the two men.

"I found them carrying multiple weapons and wandering about in the ward. I informed them no guns were allowed in the clinic. Your husband said, 'We won't be long. We're looking for a man.'"

"I said, 'And that takes two of you armed to the teeth?'

"Your husband looked at me for several seconds with the frostiest stare I've ever received. He then smiled and nodded toward his companion. 'It's his best mate.'

"I insisted they leave their weapons outside. Your husband smirked. Ignoring my request he said, 'Is this all of the patients?'"

"I said 'People with guns attract more people with guns and these sick people don't need to be caught in a firefight.' To my surprise he handed his gun to the creepy second man and sent him out. He then looked behind curtains and lifted sheets to look at each patient. 'Anyone with a gunshot injury?'

"I told him no, and insisted he leave. Only when he was satisfied I told the truth he said, 'If a man with a gunshot wound shows up you call me.' He wrote a number on one of the charts. I asked him who he was. He grinned. 'Jack Daniels.' Then he turned and left."

Dax thought, *Jack Daniels, his favourite drink. That's why he goes by Jack.*

Amedeo said, "We are looking for people that Blake associates with. What can you tell us about the man that came with him."

"Like I said, he creeped out the nurses and I consider them fearless. His piercing blue eyes were arresting. He has a scar down the middle of his face, and he has the habit of flicking his tongue out, like a snake tasting the air. From the things he said, he was quite delusional. I couldn't tell if it was drug-based or medical-based, but if I had to guess I would say he is suffering from a severe psychological illness. As they say in the Old Bailey, his madness was spectacularly on view." He added," They seemed an odd pair – the cool and collected leader and the sinister sidekick with uncontrollable impulses."

Sounds like Dumbo, the creep in the grocery store.

Amedeo said, "And that's the only time you've seen Blake?"

"Yes." He rubbed his face, letting his hand rest over his mouth. He studied Dax.

Amedeo said, "There is something else?"

"This is just my opinion, but my sense of Jack, or Blake I guess, was that he was equally as evil as his friend – in a cold, ruthless, Hannibal Lector sort of way. The only difference between the two was the bizarre anti-social behaviour of the other man."

Dax didn't react. She stared at her plate of partially eaten food.

"I'm sorry. I can't imagine how difficult it is to cope with searching for a missing spouse, let alone hearing some jungle doctor's opinion."

Dax held his wrist. "It's okay. I really do want to learn the truth, as dark and incomprehensible as it may be. Thank you, Greg. I do value your opinion."

"Anything else I can help with?"

Amedeo shook his head.

Dax lifted her eyes and smiled. "Yes, as a matter of fact there is." She looked at Amedeo. "Tell me about some of your adventures. I suspect he has a very interesting past."

Greg shuffled his chair closer to her. "Ah you want to hear about Deyo's past and all the trouble he got us into."

An hour later Greg excused himself, needing to get back for a meeting. "Listen, most of the staff are hanging out at the bar tonight. Why don't you both come along?"

[illegible]

Chapter 2 — Your Psychopath is Showing

Thursday, March 19

In the late afternoon, Logan and Jumai met his son Kofi on the shore of Lake Tanganyika. Kofi smiled when he saw Logan. "Mjomba Logan, it is very good to see you."

"Look at you, Kofi. I see you've got a few inches on your dad."

Kofi wrapped his arm around Jumai and knuckled his head. "Yeah, he's gotta look up to me now. Right, Baba?"

"Careful, my son. I can still take you down a notch or two."

Kofi clapped his hands, laughing. "I love getting a rise out of you."

Jumai looked at Logan. "I wonder why I had children."

Logan said, "You are a blessed man. I see a lot of you in him."

They loaded the fishing gear and case of Heineken into a battered aluminum boat and navigated into the middle of the lake. Rocking in the gentle waves, the three men cracked open a bottle each.

Kofi said, "Baba said you wanted to talk to me about who comes and goes from the palace?"

Logan said, "I'm looking for the identity of the Kubwa."

Kofi's face flashed with surprise. "And you think I might

know?"

"Perhaps. He would be a frequent visitor, and one who commands preferential treatment, like not having to submit to the usual checks, or not requiring guard escorts."

Kofi took a long swig.

Leaning his arms on his legs, Logan studied Kofi. "If you don't want to say anything, I understand. I'm asking for information that could get people killed."

Kofi shook his head. "No, I will help. Are you going to take him on alone?"

"Other than information, I don't want you or your dad involved."

Kofi looked at his dad then Logan. "It is my country. If you are going to take down the Kubwa, I want in."

Logan leaned back and patted Jumai on the shoulder. "You raised a brave and patriotic man."

He and Jumai clinked their bottles. He turned his focus to the young man. "Thank you, Kofi. Let's start with names of who might be the Kubwa."

"A number of top governmental officials often visit."

"I understand from one of my contacts that I'm looking for either an American or European man."

"Well, that eliminates most people. I can think of two or three that frequently visit and bypass security. Two are Ironwood men – Blake and Justin. And another guy. I think he works for one of the aid organizations. His name is Francoise, or something like that. There have been a number of white men that visit occasionally, but these three are regulars."

"Tell me more about Francoise."

"I don't know exactly which organization he is with – something about social justice I think."

Jumai said, "Is he about 45 yrs. old, short blondish hair?"

He thought for a moment. "Yeah. Bald up front."

Jumai said, "I know him. His entry forms say he's with a world economic development organization called African Trust. Nice enough man, but strikes me as a bit – um – not simple, but –"

Logan said, "Gullible?"

"Yes, gullible. Believes anything you tell him. Apparently he really enjoys fishing." He started laughing. "One of the young guards told him the best eating fish in Zimbula is the furry trout. Francoise became quite excited and asked about where to find them, what lures to use and how to clean the fur off the fish. Every time he comes through the border he tells us that he has not caught one, but he keeps trying."

"So either he's too naive to be the Kubwa or he's exceptionally brilliant at his cover." He mulled over the likelihood Francoise the furry trout fisherman is the perpetrator of the near collapse of a society. *Not likely.*

Logan pressed on with the other options. "I know both Blake and Justin, but Kofi, I'd like your impression of them."

"They both work for your company, don't they?"

"Yes."

"And you think one of them could be the Kubwa?"

"I'm not so foolish as to not consider all possibilities."

"Okay. Well Justin comes maybe once sometimes twice a month. He seems like the cub and Blake the lion. Blake is definitely in charge. And he's at the palace quite a bit. Sometimes two or three times a week. He and Akleelu can spend several hours together. I've seen him giving orders to the military generals."

He leaned forward. "There's quiet talk of a dark Special Forces unit. And Blake commands their missions – not missions like the American navy seals. More like the hit squad of the mafia, only worse. But that is all rumour. I cannot say whether any of that is true."

Jumai said, "I know Akleelu never attends political or diplomatic summits without Blake."

Logan said, "I may be a bit biased when it comes to Blake. Jumai, you're a good judge of character and you've seen him in action here. What is your assessment?"

He thought for a long moment. "What services does Ironwood provide to Zimbula these days?"

"Same contract as always. Train the recruits. Work with military leaders on strategy."

"Like Kofi, I have no evidence of any offence, but his frequent and long visits with Akleelu and his attendance at international meetings with Akleelu does seem odd. I'm sorry, my friend."

"Indeed – that is action beyond the scope of the contract. It is I who should apologize to both of you. I hoped you would tell me of someone else who was close to Akleelu. But more and more things suggest the Kubwa can only be Blake. I still need something concrete though, something that clearly proves he is the Kubwa."

They sat quietly rocking in the boat, each draining their bottle.

Kofi said, "Speak to Rosa Romano. I know of your past with her. But I think if anyone has the information you seek, it would be her. She works with Akleelu's political opposition. For some time now she's built a large underground movement. We meet in small secret groups, and the numbers of people are growing fast. I can take you to talk to her if you want. I'm sure with her connections she will have a better idea who the Kubwa is."

"Interesting. As you know, Jumai, I came to Zimbula with my niece to find Blake. He'd gone missing. The Tanzanians suspected he was killed in a helicopter crash. I wasn't with my niece at the time, but she talked to Rosa the first day we were here. She wanted information on Blake, but Rosa refused to tell her anything. Maybe she didn't want to say anything because Blake is the Kubwa. I'll have a quiet word with her."

Kofi looked at his dad. "Baba, did you tell Mjomba Logan about what happened to your career?"

Logan's eyes narrowed.

Jumai glared at his son.

Kofi said, "He won't tell you, but I will. Dad was moving up the ranks quickly. Everyone said he would be the top general one day. Then about nine years ago, he was sidelined – sent to oversee border guards. Why? No reason."

Jumai said, "Let it go, Kofi. It's okay."

"It's not okay. I think Akleelu somehow found out that Dad viewed him as the cause of what was becoming a brutal regime."

Jumai said, "I thought that many times, but I never said anything."

Logan gathered everyone's empty bottles. "I'm sure you didn't."

Kofi said, "And yet he was sidelined. Why? Holding an opposing opinion is the only explanation."

Logan handed out a second round of Heineken. "Indeed, it sounds like someone wanted you out of the way, my friend. I doubt your career path has anything to do with what you think or believe. I suspect the real reason is because you are a friend of Awamaki, and the new dog wanted to ensure people loyal to him held the power positions."

Kofi said, "Yes! I think that is right. Wait until the election and all of the garbage is swept away. I'm sure you will move into a position worthy of you, Baba."

"If I am needed, I will be happy to serve. But this is no longer important. It is all water that has flowed out to the sea – long gone and forgotten."

With Nakato off for the day, Amedeo made chicken cacciatore for dinner.

As Dax finished the last mouthful she closed her eyes. "That was fantastic. You could have been a chef."

He laughed. "No. Chicken cacciatore is the only proper meal

I know how to make. Momma always said we boys should know at least one good recipe to impress the women."

"I'm impressed. Thank you." She sat back to let the meal settle. "So you and Greg grew up together, and both became doctors. Was it a rivalry between you two?"

"He spent so much time with my family we all treated him like one of us." He looked off lost in thought. A smile broke across his face. She saw the mischievous boy for a brief moment. "We had a good childhood." He sat back and stretched out his legs. "This morning you asked that we find out who Blake is. What do you think about the information from Greg?"

She bit her lower lip. Watery eyes looked away. "I came to find the truth. I thought the big question was whether he was dead or alive. It turns out the big question comes down to is he a bastard or a psychopath." She took a sip of wine to give her eyes a moment to clear.

"The story about Blake and some freak at the hospital searching for a man with a gunshot wound – and I think I've met that freak, by the way. Why would he need guns if he's looking for a friend? And what is he doing looking for a man who's been shot?" She set her wineglass down. "And why is he hanging out with a psychopathic freak? Goodness knows, there seems to be a lot of them here.

"Then there's the whole Jack Daniels thing. It's his favourite drink. I guess that explains why he'd use the name to conceal his identity. So that is another weight on the scales tilting the evidence away from a frame up."

Confusion washed over her face. "I just don't get it." She looked at Amedeo. "You know those movies where the person they know suddenly and dramatically changes then it turns out to be an evil twin? The difference between Blake in America and Blake here is nearly impossible to reconcile as the same person. I could more believe in an evil twin than one person being so polar opposite.

"We are – I am moving toward embracing the evidence, but it's still quite a stretch for me. I know it might be impossible, but I'd really like irrefutable proof. It's hard to accept a truth of this magnitude on circumstantial evidence."

She stood up from the table and stacked the dishes then leaned down. Resting a hand on his shoulder she kissed his cheek. "Thank you, Amedeo. I really appreciate your help."

He held her hand for a moment. "You are welcome, mia Bella."

They took their dishes to the kitchen. He checked the time. "Are you sure you want to stay home? They are a good bunch of people."

"No, thank you. Perhaps another time. I'm a little tired." All she learned about Blake made her think about the things she found on his computer and the paperwork in the safe. She planned on sending digital copies of everything to her email.

"We will probably be out very late – middle of the night late."

"Here's the gate key and house key."

He tried one more time. "Are you sure you'll be okay here alone? You are more than welcome to come out with us."

"Thank you, no. I think I'll get an early night tonight. I'm tired. I promise I will keep the doors locked."

"Okay. You are sure you will be okay? I can cancel and see them another time."

"Go see your friends. I will be fine."

Shortly after Amedeo left, she walked by the front window and saw a man standing in the middle of the driveway.

Her breath caught in her throat. *The creeper is back.*

She moved toward the door then hesitated. *There's something –*

The man approached. She backed away from the window.

He finally stood in the light.

Her hands flew to her mouth. Tears welled.

It's Blake! He's here.

She ran to the front door to meet him. "Blake! It's you."

"Dax."

"Where have you been? We've looked for you everywhere. They think you're dead. Why didn't you call? Did you get my messages?"

He didn't answer any of her questions, but silenced her with a demanding kiss.

She melted.

He picked her up and carried her to the bedroom.

She could hardly believe he was home. She kept touching his face and kissing him. They made love, as passionately as she could ever remember. She fell asleep with the scent of his cologne and the sweet taste of his mouth still lingering.

As soon as her breathing became steady he got up, pulled on his pants and padded to the safe in the office. A few minutes later he returned and sat on the bed to put on his shoes.

She woke up. "What are you doing, honey?"

He pulled on his second shoe. "Get out of Africa. Forget about me. Use the death certificate to collect on the insurance."

"What are you talking about?"

"Logan is not who you think he is. Ironwood is a military services group, not financial. When he worked here, he was known as Awamaki, which means god's dog. He and the President are very close. He does his dirty work."

Awamaki maybe. Not Awamaki Kubwa. Not the bigger dog. "What are you talking about? Logan isn't dirty."

She rolled out to sit beside him. "Whatever. That doesn't matter. Blake, I'm so glad to have you back. And tonight, well it was amazing. The world feels right again. And who knows, maybe we started our family tonight." She laid her head on his shoulder.

He shrugged her off. "I had a vasectomy before we were married. I never wanted kids."

The statement hit her with physical force. "What? A vasectomy? Why did you let me think we could have kids?"

"That was your dream. Not mine." He pulled on his T-shirt.

"Okay. Well. Forget about all this. Come home with me. We can make a life together, without kids."

"Make a life with you? In middle-class suburbia? Are you out of your mind? Go home, Dax. I already told you. It's over." He stood up.

She stood in front of him, resting her hands on his chest. "It doesn't have to be over. We still love each other."

"Dax, it is *over.* In fact, *it* never was. I never loved you." He held her wrists tight enough to bruise. "I used you to get close to Logan to bypass his usual background checks. And I used Logan to get close to Akleelu and set up the mining operations. I've got my money and now I'm through with you."

His eyes narrowed. "You happily let me use you because you liked the idea of a husband and companion in life. Honey, it was all an illusion. Blake is dead. Take the insurance money and find yourself another man. Shouldn't be hard with your good looks and a bit of money. And you're entertaining enough in the bedroom."

She pulled free of his grip.

He laughed.

She stepped in close, her face inches from his. "I get that you are trying to push me away. And you know exactly what to say to hurt me. But it's not too late. I still love you."

He pocketed a few items from his dresser. "You want something to love? Get a puppy. Find yourself another man. I don't care. I've done ten hard years. I'm not interested in a life sentence. Never was."

Tucking in his shirt he said, "And you can tell Logan to stay out of my way or he will regret it."

"You're not acting yourself. Is there something wrong? Something we can deal with together?"

He clamped his one hand on her throat, pushed her back and held up a finger to signal she remain quiet. "I don't need your psychobabble." He glared at her.

He squeezed a little tighter. "Now, I have a few things to deal with. I'll be back here, in *my* house, in two days. Be gone by then. Do any different and you won't live to see the weekend." She stumbled as he pushed past her.

For several minutes she stood alone.

Chapter 3 — Uninvited Monster

Friday, March 20

Walking out of the house he smirked. "I've done my time." He drew in a deep breath of the damp air. Like a boa constrictor easing out of its old skin, his muscles contracted. His shoulders pressed back in seeming rebellion, mentally slipping out of social constraints. "Unstoppable. Untouchable. Unrivalled. The byzantine man."

Even the house felt like a penitentiary and he the prisoner who begrudgingly gained a release from a long sentence. Relief shuttered down his back. *I'm done living like a suburban saint. It's time to walk the ledge, to shed the chains of conformity, and inject some fire into this dull grey life.*

He made a call. "Phil? She's ripe. Scare her back to America tonight."

Dax poured a second glass of wine and sat curled up in the third bedroom. *What the hell just happened?* She swallowed hard with the memory of his vice grip on her throat. The lamp filled the room with cold light.

Confused thoughts windmilled without grinding the events into base truths. *Why would he tell me to go home? Be gone in two days or I won't be alive to see the weekend? How could my husband make passionate love then turn around and threaten me?*

Half a glass of wine later, her heart entered the conversation. Like a metronome, a tick of charitable thoughts and a tock of confused ruminations clicked back and forth.

Tick. *Maybe he knows of some danger and wants me out of the way.*

Tock. *But a loving husband doesn't leave in the middle of the night. Then there's the choking threat seemed to naturally erupt. Now that leans toward psychopathic behaviour.*

Tick. *But none of this ugly behaviour is Blake. He's not cruel and heartless. No. This has to be him trying to keep me safe.*

Oh I don't know what to think.

She poured herself another glass of wine and the clicking back and forth continued.

Tock. *And he's had a vasectomy? Can that be true? Why would he talk of starting a family for the past year if he's been shooting blanks for the past decade?*

Tick. *This doesn't make sense. The man that I woke up to is not the man I've known for ten years. He's always been loving, attentive, sweet – maybe a bit of a workaholic, but not psychopathic. Not mean or ruthless.*

Tock. *But then it's like a switch flipped and he suddenly became the opposite.*

Absently she rubbed her thumb along the texture of the covers.

Maybe he has a brain tumour? That can dramatically change a personality.

But then why would he be normal earlier then suddenly act like a jerk? No, I don't think cancer explains it.

Is he on drugs? Like LSD or coke? And he's deluded and acting out of that delusion? Maybe grabbing my throat stems from coming down off a high – like a meth psychosis after several days without sleep.

Or maybe he really is a world-class psychopath who complete-

ly suppressed his nature, character and personality for ten years without slipping once.

Tick tock. Tick Tock. Her mind circled until she fell into a fitful sleep. In her grogginess she heard a noise. Thinking it might be Blake coming back she pulled herself awake and looked at the alarm clock. 2:02. The bed creaked as someone sat down. She rolled over. "Blake, you're back."

She froze.

Her heart hammered in her chest.

A man sat on the end of the bed with a knife in his hand.

Her mouth opened, but no sound came out. She couldn't move. Suddenly she felt starved of oxygen.

He mumbled something then without warning, sprang across the bed. Straddling her, his scarred face hovered inches from hers.

She fell back. *The lunatic from the grocery store!*

High on his knees he hoisted the knife above his head then plunged with full force into the pillow, inches from her head. His tongue flicked over an evil grin. He moved in close, his breath hot against her face. The stench of 80-proof alcohol filled her nostrils.

"I am the wind bringing destruction."

She struggled to free her arms. He pressed his legs tighter, pinning her down.

"I am the moonless night bringing death.

"I am the terror in the shadows."

Blood throbbed through her neck.

He leaned in close to her ear. "I am the echo whispering, whispering, fiendish whispering." His tongue briefly darted in her ear.

She groaned in revulsion.

"I am the heartbeat pounding a message of dread."

She turned away. Seizing a handful of hair, he pulled her to face him.

"I am the silence shrieking in your mind.

"Listen to the moaning drifting through your thoughts like a cold curling smoke, pushing you into lunacy.

"I am the uninvited monster in your wee hours.

"I am the keen blade, eager to taste your blood."

A vehicle pulled through the gates into the driveway. The beam of light swung past the window.

Amedeo.

Phil pulled his knife out of the pillow, pushed off the bed and casually walked out. The rarely used iron gate on the back door groaned open in protest. A few seconds later his cast shadow drifted across the bedroom curtains.

She held her breath and strained to listen. The front door opened and locked. Steps approached down the hall.

She tried calling out, but no noise came out. She tried again. "Amedeo?" squeaked out.

The steps stopped.

"Amedeo?" This time with some volume.

"Yes, Bella?"

"Thank God."

Confused he stood at the spare room door. "Are you okay?"

"There was a man. With a knife."

He pressed the door open and flipped the light on. With his gun drawn, he entered the room.

"He left out the back when you pulled in the driveway."

Amedeo locked the back door and returned, tucking his gun away. "Did he hurt you?"

"No. He stabbed the pillow."

"I think he wanted to scare you."

"He did a good job of it. I know him. He's the crazy man I met in the grocery store." She tried swallowing. "My mouth is dry."

"Do you want a drink of water?"

She nodded. As he turned to leave she said, "Wait. I'm coming with you."

On the way down the hall he said, "How did he get in? You left the door locked, yeah?"

She groaned. "I don't know."

He stopped with a puzzled look.

She leaned against the wall for support. "Blake was here earlier."

He steadied her arm. "So he's alive and come out of hiding."

"Yes, but he left." She sniffed and looked away. "Anyway, I didn't check the doors after he left. Maybe he didn't lock up."

"Did he leave through the back door?"

"No. The front."

And the front was locked, but the back was not? "This has not been a good night."

In the kitchen she turned on the stove light and saw a note on the counter. Something fell out when she picked up the paper.

Amedeo picked it up. "The crocodile tooth killer."

Under the light they read," Leave Zimbula. Next time my knife will cut out your heart."

"Oh Bella." He leaned on the counter, his brows gathered together as though the gravity of potential cost weighed heavy. "I'm sorry I went out this evening. I should not have left you alone."

Their eyes met and held for a moment. He broke away. "I will not give this maniac another chance." He got the chilled water out of the fridge and poured a glass.

She drank a few sips of the water. "Blake snapped. He's not the man I know. I can't imagine what would have happened if he found you here." She set the glass down and hugged herself. "He came in all kisses and sweetness. We made love then he turned into a bastard. He said he never wanted kids – apparently had a vasectomy before we married. And said he used me and Uncle Logan to get close to Akleelu. Said the whole marriage was an illusion. Told me to go home – in two days or I won't live to see the weekend. Grabbed me by the throat."

"What? He tried to choke you?" He turned on more lights. He

could see the forming bruises. "Do you have a sore throat inside? Does it hurt to swallow?"

"No, I'm okay."

He checked the whites of her eyes. "Let me see your tongue."

He carefully examined her neck for swelling. Satisfied there was no serious damage he said, "This is strangulation. It is abuse."

"Yeah, I guess."

He ran his fingers through his hair. "This is crazy. He is crazy. Crazy surrounds him. You have to leave."

"No, not yet. He's involved in this mining thing. I get that it's not good. But I just can't believe that he's *really* a bad man. I think if I found a way to stop him, maybe bring him to his senses then maybe he'd come home."

"Bella, your loyalty is beautiful. But you know he's not going to stop doing the things that bring him millions of dollars just because you want it. He's been mining and collecting money for years. Now he's tying up loose ends, and you, my dear, are a big loose end. With all your poking around, you know too much. He choked you. He threatened to kill you. Do you think it was a coincidence that he just happened to leave the back door unlocked and shortly afterward his lunatic compatriot comes and threatens you? He's the psychotic Greg ran into."

"He matches Greg's description."

"So the crocodile killer is Blake's best buddy. And they were both here tonight. Sounds like he's wanting to eliminate you."

"If he wanted me dead, I'd be dead by now. No, I think deep down he still cares. He's trying to get me out of the way. Maybe something bad is about to go down and he's trying to protect me. Or maybe this is all a bad delusion in his head. I just want to rattle him. I want to do something that makes him rethink the direction he's taking."

"Take off those love-tainted sunglasses. I think he spoke more honestly tonight than he ever has. You heard truth for the first time. He stated it in clear terms. He used you. Period. And he used Logan. His goal was to become wealthy, in the easiest way he could find. He doesn't care about you. I doubt he ever did. I am sure there's a reason he has not killed you yet, but I promise you it is not love. The psychopath is finally showing his true nature. Time to go home. It is over."

"I've got to believe he's harboured some feelings for me. It's been ten years. That's a long time to pretend to love." She rested her hand on his arm. "I've got to try, for the sake of our marriage."

"What ending to this story can you live with? Logan killing Blake? Blake killing Logan? Blake killing you?"

"There's been far too much killing already. No, I don't want Blake dead. Or Logan. Or me."

She rubbed her temples. "I guess if I'm really honest, I feel partly responsible for this mess. He used me for ten years to scam all this money and hurt hundreds of innocent people. Because I never identified his antisocial character, I enabled him. So here's the cold truth, with no sugar coating. I want to stop him – permanently.

"I've thought a lot about why one would break a man. That seems extreme. I want to stop all his illegal activities, stop using child labour, stop looting Zimbula. But I don't know if I have the heart to *break* him. I've dedicated my life to healing people, not breaking them."

"And what of your marriage? Are you hoping he will come back?"

She stood firm for a long moment then her shoulders slumped as truth won the mental battle. "No. The marriage is over. And maybe it was all an illusion, a front. Maybe the romance and passion were his means to an end."

"You told me you came to prove he's alive and determine if your marriage can be saved. You now know the answers to those questions."

She fell against the counter and lifted her face to the ceiling. Her eyes pressed closed. "That's true."

"Then go home. What he does with his life is his own business."

"I can't stop thinking of those young children, all the pregnant girls –" Her hands unconsciously went to her throat. "– all the violence."

"Brutality is rampant in Zimbula. I agree, it's horrible. But neither you nor I can change that."

"What if there was a way to stop those seven mines tomorrow? We don't need to save all of Zimbula, but what if we can make a difference for a few hundred people?"

She could hear the scratch of his day's growth as he rubbed his face. "What do you have in mind?"

"I'm going to throw a monkey wrench in the works."

Chapter 4 — Monkey Wrench

Friday, March 20

The grey dawn held little promise of sunshine. Logan picked up Jamie Moore at the border mid morning.

Over the bumpy drive to Mabezi the two men carried the conversation of new boss and employee getting to know each other. Jamie talked about his time with the navy seals. "I joined the unit a little over 11 years ago. Seven years later I was one of the instructors. As technology progresses, so do combat tactics. There are some base things that never change, but with the flow of technology, ground tactics have shifted dramatically from when I started. As the tactical officer, I proved effective at using technology in new ways to disorient and overwhelm.

"Between missions I taught combat and personal defence to civilians back home. I really enjoyed working with the teenage boys, many of whom went on to join the forces.

"I'm pretty pumped about the opportunities to train the recruits here and get back into training tactics."

Logan said, "I'm glad to have you onboard. Guys like you, fresh from the military, bring the latest knowledge and skill. I've had a long relationship with President Akleelu, working with the military here. And there's plenty of opportunity for both tactical and recruit training."

At the edge of Mabezi, Logan drove past a row of shacks washed out by a massive landslide. People scoured the debris field down by the river despite the ongoing threat of more slides. Further into town, the assembled bits of tarp, salvaged boards, tree trunks and corrugated steel called shacks crowded the road.

A wooden ditch lined one side of the dirt road – a noble attempt to divert the heavy rains from flooding the ramshackle homes. In front of each door a rickety collection of boards acted as a bridge over the trench. Piles of garbage and unused building materials lay scattered about. Shack after shack, desperately thin people sat on the ground in front.

Logan finally stopped in front of one with nothing that distinguished it from the dozens before. "Leave all weapons in the lockbox in the back seat. Take nothing in with you."

Jamie glanced up and down the street before removing his holster, gun and hidden knife on his leg. They both jumped the 4 ft. moat rather than trust the homemade bridge.

Standing in front of the ill-fitting wooden door, Logan scanned the area then knocked. While waiting, he looked back at the Tahoe, the only vehicle in sight.

A young man answered and invited them in. Logan ducked under the short doorway to enter the dark room.

It took a few seconds for their eyes to adjust to the dim lighting. A female voice said, "Logan."

He turned in her direction. "Rosa?" He noticed the woman in the darkest corner.

"It is. This is my assistant, Pierre."

He patted them both down, checking for weapons.

"And this is Jamie Moore. He just started with Ironwood."

Pierre said, "All clear."

"Sit. Please make yourself comfortable." She directed them to a couple of homemade chairs that looked more flimsy than the bridges outside. "What can we do for you?"

The two men sat down, gingerly testing the weight-bearing capacity. "I'm hoping you can provide some hard-to-come-by information."

She steepled her fingers. "Ah. Information you cannot get anyone else to share."

"Perhaps. I think it more likely that it is information that only you might know."

"I see. And what are you offering in exchange?"

"What would you like? What is your price?"

"Ask me your question then I will name my price."

He laughed. "You were always a tough nut, Rosa. I couldn't even buy you a drink without negotiating on your terms."

"You mean you could only get me in your bed on *my* terms."

"The first time, perhaps."

They looked at each other an uncomfortably long time, each one with a slight smile. Pierre stared at the far wall. Jamie studied his fingernails.

She brushed her hair back. "I have missed you, Logan."

"We're not too old."

She smiled. "Ask your question, you old hound dog."

"Alright. I'm sure you are aware that Blake Talbot heads the Ironwood operations here in Central Africa. A couple of weeks ago, he was thought to be aboard a helicopter that crashed in western Tanzania. No one survived the accident. There is some evidence that he is still alive."

She shifted in her chair, showing no reaction.

"Since coming here to look for him, I have heard about Awamaki Kubwa. Reliable sources tell me he manipulates Akleelu to the severe detriment of the people. There is also some circumstantial evidence that this Kubwa is Blake.

"I understand you are building a grassroots movement against

Akleelu. I know you are a formidable adversary. You will have extensive intelligence on Akleelu, probably enough to throw him in jail for ten lifetimes." He leaned forward. "And I know you have equally good intelligence on the Kubwa.

"Like you, I am devastated at what has become of this country – the out-of-control violence and hatred boiling over. As Awamaki, I feel an obligation to end the Kubwa's reign. If it's Blake, I have an additional axe to grind with him.

"So, my question is this – who is the Kubwa? And I will need concrete proof."

She waved at Pierre. "Get the Kubwa file please." Pierre placed several folders on the table in front of her. She rested her hands on the pile. "We must address the price – business before pleasure, as they say in America."

"Business before pleasure." He looked directly into her eyes. "Reminds me of that long hot summer."

She flushed. "Mangoes and marshmallows."

He reached across the table and held her hand. "Passerotto."

She rubbed his fingers with her thumb. "That was a long time ago." She pulled her hand away.

"I was a fool to let you go."

"Two fools collided." She sighed. "Indeed that was long ago, and we are here today to negotiate a deal."

"So we are. Name your price."

"There are two things I want. But first, what are your plans once you know who the Kubwa is?"

He hesitated, glancing at Pierre.

"I don't need to know the details. I want to be assured that whatever it is you do, the Kubwa will be permanently removed."

"Of that I can assure you."

"Never to wield influence of any kind in Zimbula again?"

"Agreed."

"And this will be done before the election?"

"Yes."

"Then we have a deal. The Kubwa is –"

"Wait. You said two parts to the deal. One is dealing with the Kubwa. What is the second thing?"

"It is of a more personal nature. We can talk about it when the first part is paid in full."

His old eyes wrinkled at the corners. "As you wish, Passerotto."

She looked at him for a brief moment with the soft eyes of promise. Then she returned to business. "Blake is the Kubwa. We have many witnesses and, as you can see, a lot of documentation. We know he ordered a lot of people killed, but he is careful to appear squeaky clean. He built a dark forces unit and filled it with mentally unstable men and ruthless killers to do the bulk of his dirty work."

"Dark Services. Yes, I've heard a bit about that."

"But he has plenty of blood on own his hands. For example, a number of people in power positions disappeared within a couple of years of his arrival here, many were last seen with him. Anyone who publicly spoke ill of the Kubwa lives only a few days before they are found with their throat slashed. Doesn't matter who they were. Journalists. Business men. Top ranking military. Forward thinking government heads. Murdered. A man who worked closely with Blake witnessed this. We have the details of his testimony. He is in hiding out of the country.

"If you are looking for proof that he has killed, here's a series of photos taken from a video. You can see him executing a young woman – a relief worker at the Munyegera refugee camp. She told her friends that he was going to marry her."

Logan flicked through the images. "That is the camp he frequently visited to recruit men to work the mines."

"She was often bruised after he visited. I understand he killed her because she became a liability. He couldn't afford Salama finding out about another woman."

Logan examined the images more closely before passing them to Jamie. They clearly showed the woman begging and Blake pulling the trigger.

Logan said, "Thank you. That is all I need."

Jamie handed the images back to Rosa.

She tucked the photos back in the folder. "There's one more thing you should know. One of our supporters was a photographer and graphic designer. He worked in a downtown office during the day. But he has a sideline of producing hard-to-acquire documents. You know what I mean?"

"Fake identification, passports, visas."

"Yes. A few months ago, Blake came in and ordered all the documentation associated with a new ID. My friend said it would take about three weeks to get the appropriate blanks and complete the work. The day Blake was scheduled to pick up his documentation the man disappeared. No one has seen him since."

"Blake is preparing to run."

"We believe so. But Zimbula cannot afford for us to be wrong. The Kubwa's reign must end."

"I agree. Do you know the new name on the identification papers?"

"James Winslow." Her gray eyes studied Logan. "Are you travelling with your niece? And is she married to Blake?"

"Yes. Dakota and Blake have been married for ten years. She wanted to come here to find Blake."

"I met her. She came to the warehouse looking for information."

"And you called her a pretty chicken."

She smiled. "I did. Tried scaring her back home before she got herself into trouble. Seems she's a lot like you – doesn't scare easily."

"She's a strong and determined woman."

"I didn't know she's your niece, so told her nothing. When I saw her leaving with you I realized her connection. I sent one of my men to promise her information on Blake if she would go to Tanzania. I wanted her safely out of the country before giving her any information. Unfortunately, Blake's sidekick killed my guy before he could tell her anything. Please let her know I'm not really a crusty old bird."

He smiled. "Crusty is not a word I'd use for you. I will let her know."

"She is back in Zimbula?"

"Yes."

"You need to get her out. Blake will not tolerate her poking into his business. Many have been killed for less. The only reason she's not dead yet is her murder would attract too much attention."

"Easier said than done. One more question. Do you know where Blake is hiding? Anyone who he associates with?"

"He normally spends most of his nights with Salama Mugisha. They have been an item for a number of years. She is a supermodel and has a large estate in Malawandi. I would think you can find him there."

"Thank you." He held Rosa's hand. "It was good to see you again."

She squeezed back. "You too, my old friend."

Driving back to Logan's hotel he noted Jamie deep in thought," You're quiet."

Jamie watched the passing scenery. "I'm trying to figure out what kind of man you are."

"And what do you think?"

"Your answer to one question will clarify things."

"My day is full of negotiators. Okay, ask away."

"Were you playing Rosa to lighten the deal, or do you really have feelings for her?"

"Ah. Am I a prick or a straight shooter?" He glanced at Jamie. "A good thing to know about your new boss, I imagine. Will my answer make a difference to you staying with Ironwood?"

"Perhaps."

Careful and ethical. I knew he was a good hire.

"Fifteen years ago when I worked here full time, Rosa and I lived together. Best year of my life. Then her ex showed up. He wanted them to give their relationship another go. She was torn, but finally agreed. I put up a good fight and almost convinced her to stay with me. But she went back to Italy with him. It lasted six months. She came back to Zimbula alone.

"It took a long time before I wanted to see her again. Eventually we got on good footing, but she said it was too late for anything more than friendship."

"Seems open to something now."

"Then I will be a very lucky man."

At the hotel Jamie unloaded his gear. "Can we grab a beer? There's something you should know."

When the waitress dropped off their drinks Jamie said, "I'd like to tell you something from when Blake and I were in Special Ops together. Before I do, would you happen to have a good photo of Blake? The ones Rosa has are not real clear."

Logan showed him one from his phone.

"Yes. I thought so. Here's a photo of the Special Ops team when I first joined the unit." He handed his phone to Logan.

"Yes. There's you." He zoomed in. "And Blake."

He gave the phone back to Jamie who pushed the phone back. "Take a look at this guy here – third one from the left."

"Uh-huh."

Jamie took his phone and navigated to a website. "Here's his graduation photo in the local newspaper."

Logan looked. "Yes. Younger, but the same man."

Jamie pointed to the caption under the image.

Logan read," Blake Talbot, valedictorian." His brows knit together. "I don't understand."

Jamie pointed to the newspaper photo. "He is the real Blake Talbot. The guy who you think is Blake is Geoffrey Barber." He showed him a high school yearbook archive with Blake's photo and the name Geoffrey Barber underneath.

Logan studied the photo for a moment then turned away. Jamie watched as Logan processed the information.

Logan's finger tapped the side of his glass. "Geoffrey Barber."

"Yes. He targeted the new recruits, trying to build his personal empire. He tried to engage with me but I wasn't interested.

"I watched him catch another new guy in his web. He whispered comments questioning the captain's orders, said the captain had complained about the new guy, undermining the guy's confidence. Once he had the new guy unsure and nervous Geoffrey promised to look out for him, be his protection. He convinced him to break some rules and the guy was busted out of the unit."

"For what purpose?"

"He wanted the captain to look unable to effectively command and incompetent at choosing new recruits.

"He used a young female lieutenant to meet the captain's wife then threw the young woman over. He started a relationship with the captain's wife, and got her talking about issues in their marriage. He used that information to expose the captain and had him removed from the team. As a result, the navy looked within the unit to promote to team lead.

"The real Blake Talbot was a good soldier and well-liked by the men. He brought cohesion in direct opposition to all of Geoff's efforts to undermine and divide. Both Geoff and the real Blake were in line to lead the unit.

"As we geared up for what would be our final mission together, a shouting match broke out between Geoff and the real Blake. I don't know what it was about, but Geoff began taunting Blake and pushing him. Blake deflected Geoff's efforts and told him to stand down. Both stood in each other's face. Blake, too smart to become ensnared in Geoff's plots finally said, 'Don't threaten me, little man,' and walked away. After a few steps he spun back and said, 'Your days are numbered.' That threat pushed Geoff's buttons. Things escalated and a couple of us stepped in to bring the temperature down.

"In a few hours we were on the ground – invading a compound to acquire a high value target. While clearing a large warehouse, Geoff followed the real Blake into a side room and immediately fired several shots. When the dust settled, Blake and our target were both dead. I saw Geoff plant a gun on the target. So, a couple of us retrieved the weapon.

"Once back on base, I met with the colonel. After explaining what I suspected, I showed him the footage from my head camera, which included the plant and the collection of the gun. I also gave him the gun. But Geoff is slippery as an eel. Nothing sticks. The results of the investigation were inconclusive. I personally think with the forensics on the bullet and gun they had him dead to rights, but I suspect he had something on the commanding officer. Regardless, they dismissed him for a lesser infraction.

Logan said, "So Geoff then stole his victim's identity and transformed from Geoff, the unit's snake to Blake, the all-American hero." *And it explains why Blake didn't want Jamie on his team. I wonder if my suggestion was the trigger for all of this – the dumping of his marriage, disappearing, planning to run.*

"Yes. You can imagine my surprise when you told me I would be working with Blake Talbot."

"About as great as my surprise that the man I know is not Blake Talbot. Thank you for telling me. It explains a lot. Like how Blake, I mean Geoff, could be the Kubwa."

Both Amedeo and Dax got a late start to the day. It was the first day in several without teeming rain. Nakato opened the windows to air out the house. With coffee in hand, Dax peered out the window to listen to the hoo-hoo-hoop of a bird calling its mate.

Amedeo joined her in the living room. "So, what is this monkey wrench you wish to throw into the works?"

"I've thought about engaging the International Criminal Court investigators and give them some evidence." She turned around. "But that would lead to Blake in jail."

"I would not bother. An investigation means nothing because Zimbula is not a member country. So the court holds no authority. They investigate. They lay charges. But it goes no further than that."

"Alright then my plan is to talk to Akleelu. Do you know anyone who can get me in to see him?"

"Akleelu? He is a homicidal maniac. One tiny push in the wrong direction and he will go off like Krakatoa. When the ash settles there will be nothing left but a big crater where Zimbula once was."

"And one tiny push in the right direction and he shuts Blake down."

"You do not want him going off on a killing spree."

"You know how I had to trust you to get me across the border? You need to trust my psychological training to manage the president and achieve my ends."

"Dakota Keyes. You are fearless."

Let's hope it doesn't get me or anyone else into too much trouble. "The question is how to get an audience with the president."

He rubbed his brow. "I hope I do not regret this. I know someone who can get us in to see him. One of the women in the group last night, Claire, manages to squeeze money out of him regularly for medical supplies."

After speaking with Amedeo, Claire called the president and arranged for a meeting mid afternoon at his palace in Malawandi. Amedeo and Dax met her in front of her organization's office.

Once Claire settled in the back seat Dax thanked her for her help.

Claire took one look at Dax and said, "You will have no problem with Akleelu. A beautiful woman and Akleelu trips over his tongue."

Akleelu greeted Claire with his standard manhandling hug and kissed both cheeks. He rested his hands on Dax's shoulders. "And you must be Claire's twin sister."

Dax held out her hand. "I'm Dakota Keyes, the wi–"

Akleelu pulled her into a bear hug and kissed her left cheek then her right. He went for a third cheek kiss. Unfortunately, Dax thought he was done and turned to face him. His third kiss landed on her mouth.

He took full advantage. When he saw her reaction he threw his head back in a deep laugh. "Come, the lovely Miss Dakota. Join me for afternoon tea."

He chatted with Amedeo and Claire over the finger sandwiches and scones. Two scones later he stood up and offered his hand to Dax. "I will show you my gardens." He looked at Claire. "Please entertain Amedeo."

Claire glanced at Dax. Amedeo stood up and started to protest. Dax accepted the president's hand. "I will be fine. I'm sure President Akleelu will ensure no harm comes to me."

"Of course. My guards protect against evil entering my home. And I personally guarantee your safety." He led Dax off the marbled terrace. "You say you are not related to Claire."

"We do look a lot alike, but no, we are not related."

"Remarkable. You look like twins. What is it that you want to speak with me about?"

"I believe you know my husband, Blake Talbot?"

"Yes, the Ironwood man." He looked her up and down. "And he left you in America? I don't understand American men at all."

"We are so honoured to have the opportunity to work with you.

I respect all the good that you have done for the country. You are an outstanding leader and, I must say, now that I've met you, you are an impressive man."

"An impressive man. That is good. Does Blake call me an outstanding leader?"

"Like many men, Blake doesn't talk about his work. But I have studied you. You bring the steady hand of a good father to a desperate people. They really should crown you king."

He nodded thoughtfully.

"I want to thank you again for taking the time out of your very busy schedule to see me."

He took her hand. "An emperor rarely hears acknowledgment of the good he does. You have brought joy to my soul."

"I am a great admirer of your leadership. You are strong, yet fair. You bring the wisdom of Solomon to your people. They are blessed indeed."

He bent to pick a flower and gave it to her. "Blake is a blessed man to have a woman such as yourself as his wife."

"Thank you, your highness."

He linked her arm in his. "Please, call me Etienne."

She bowed her head. "You do me too great an honour."

He turned her to face him and took her face in his hand. She glanced up at him then cast her eyes down.

"We are good friends, yes?"

She nodded, her face still in his hand.

He returned to strolling, patting her arm in his. "Then Etienne it is."

"Thank you, Etienne. You are a very generous man. That is partly why I came to talk to you."

"Yes, I am known around the world for my generosity."

"And that's what concerns me. The most important thing to me is to honour and respect you. I want to be sure Blake's business dealings with you are fair and above board – that your generosity is respected."

"You have a concern?"

"I came across a paper and I can't find Blake to ask him about what the numbers mean. I certainly don't understand this business. It may be all right. I just don't know. But my concern is that you, the revered leader, receive all that is rightfully yours."

She pulled a paper out of her purse. "Maybe you can look this over. I hope you can relieve my heart that all is as it should be."

"My dear, we can't have you worried. You have too pretty a face and too good a heart to worry." He scanned the paper then turned it over. "Was this the only paper?"

"Yes, it was the only one. I presume there are others because there's a number at the bottom indicating it is the 14th page. I found it on the floor. I assume Blake has the rest. Please tell me, is this right?"

He did some calculations in his head.

"If anything is amiss, I want to ensure it is corrected immediately."

He muttered several numbers and did more calculations. When he looked at Dax, a couple of tears rolled down her cheek. He rubbed them away with his thumb. "Sweet lady. You do not need to worry. I will straighten things out with Blake."

She drew in a deep breath and let it out. "Oh thank you. That is such a relief. I feel so privileged to know you and to play a small part of making a difference in your country."

"Blake doesn't deserve you."

"Thank you. You will work it out with Blake? You are such a gentle man. I appreciate your time. It has been such a thrill to talk with you." She held her hands to her heart. "I can hardly believe that I've met you. And I will tell everyone what an extraordinary leader you are. I'm so excited. You know, I have a friend that's a journalist. I'm going to ask her to write a story about your great leadership and your gracious and fair treatment of Blake and me. She writes for the Washington Post."

He looked at her a long moment. "Indeed. The Washington Post." He held up the paper. "May I keep this?"

"Oh, of course. And if there's anything I can do, you only have to ask. It would be a great honour to serve you."

They returned to the terrace. Amedeo and Claire stood up. Dax gave them a quick smile.

Akleelu said, "Well now, I have other things I must attend to. Amedeo, good to see you again. I am glad for what you and your staff do for my people. Claire, it was lovely to see you as always. You and Amedeo should get together. He's a good man, you know. And a doctor. Women love the doctors."

Claire said, "Are you trying to set me up, President Akleelu?"

"Just pointing out the opportunity before you."

He turned to Dax and held her hands in his. "And Dakota, thank you for coming to me with your concerns. I can assure you that I will straighten things out with Blake. You do not need to worry. And be sure to tell your journalist friend what I am doing for you."

"Thank you, Etienne. I will for sure. I can send you a copy of the article when she writes it, but it may take a month to get it published."

"A month?" He pondered the implications of waiting a month before dealing with Blake. "I look forward to reading it."

Guards escorted them to their car. Once out of the palace grounds Amedeo said, "So? What happened?"

Dax smiled. "He was all you said he would be, Claire. Thank you." She sat back in her seat. "It was perfect. I told him how great I think he is, and when fully buttered, I told him I wanted to make sure everything is above board between Blake and him. So, I gave him a copy of one page from the red accounting journal – I suspected it details the massive skimming above the agreed to rates. Generally that's the reason for two journals – one legit and one with the incriminating details. Funny, he didn't like the numbers."

Amedeo said, "You did what?"

"Now before you panic, I asked him if the numbers were right. I shed a couple of tears. He said he would straighten it out with Blake."

Amedeo said, "I think you have just written Blake's death warrant."

"Except I said I was so impressed with his Solomon-like wisdom that I was going to get my Washington Post journalist friend to write a glowing article about him."

Amedeo laughed. "And it will not be published for another month. Akleelu cannot kill Blake or it will hit the papers right before the election and he will lose everything. In the meantime, he will stop Blake, but you tied his hands. He cannot kill him if he wants to win the election. A well executed monkey wrench."

I hope so.

Chapter 5 — Finality

They got back to Mabezi in time for dinner and the three decided to celebrate at a lakeside bar and grill. While they lingered over drinks, Dax got a call from Logan.

"Hi Daxie. Gotta make this quick. A couple of things. First, Jamie came in this morning, but we have a few more things I need to do. There's a couple of bits of information I've uncovered. I have proof that Blake is the Kubwa."

"You're sure?"

"Yes. I am. I've seen photo evidence. And the other piece of info is that Blake Talbot is not his real name. Geoffrey Barber is his actual name. Jamie was in Blake's, or rather, Geoff's Special Ops unit a few months before Geoff left. There is eye witness evidence that Geoff killed the real Blake Talbot then assumed his identity and record."

He waited, but the long silence concerned him. "I'm sorry to not tell you in person. Time is tight. I have strong evidence that he's acquired a new identity – James Winslow. That means he's going to disappear – soon."

"So – then what does this mean? I'm married to a dead man I never met? I'm not actually married?"

"I don't know exactly but I checked. You can get the marriage annulled on the grounds of fraud."

"So, I guess I am married to – what's his name?"

"Geoffrey Barber."

"Right. Wow. That's a lot to take in."

"I'm sorry Daxie. I really am. But I thought you should know."

"Thanks."

"You stay safe. I'll be in touch tomorrow some time. This will all be over shortly. Could I speak to Amedeo?"

She passed the phone.

"Amedeo, thanks for watching over Dax. Jamie is here now, but we have a few things to wrap up. Can you stay with Dax a little longer?"

"Certainly."

"I'm sure you heard a bit of my conversation with Dax. Blake's real name is Geoffrey Barber. I think Dax may struggle with all the implications of that."

She is already dealing with a lot of garbage around a failing marriage. "Sí."

"I plan on dealing with Geoffrey Barber once and for all. He has hurt Dax, me, Ironwood and countless people in Zimbula. His vortex of opportunistic manipulation and pain will end. I need to know as the dust settles, you'll make sure Dax is okay."

"You have my word on it."

"Thank you, Amedeo."

"Prego. Caio."

"Caio."

Akleelu paced his office. "He has been skimming? From me? He will pay. I will personally blow his brains out." He yelled out the window," You are a dead man, Blake Talbot. Dead!"

He threw a small glass figure he picked off his desk. It shattered on impact. "But I cannot kill you right before the election. No. That would be bad press. I cannot afford that." A wake of vultures circled over a distant field. "You're days are numbered, you worthless snake. My vultures will soon be circling over your carcass. And I'm going to watch them pick your bones clean."

After raging for several hours, Akleelu called Blake.

"Hey, Jackhole."

"Etienne? What's wrong?"

"Your wife tells me you've been stealing from *my* mines."

"Who? Salama?"

"No, you idiot. Your wife. You know, the beautiful and sweet Dakota Keyes. I notice she didn't love you enough to take your last name. More proud of her own name than yours?"

"I have no idea what you're on about."

"She apparently found a paper on the floor. I guess it fell out of your journal of mining transactions. It is very clear that the mine is producing far more than you said. You owe me a lot of money and I'm going to make sure you pay every penny."

"I can show you the books again. I am not stealing from you."

The veins in Akleelu's neck bulged. "I've seen a page from the real books, you snake. They are *my* mines. *My* cobalt. *My* diamonds. *My* money. You will pay 50% interest on everything you have stolen. You are done."

"I don't know what document Dax forged. Doesn't matter. It's garbage. I have been abundantly honest with you. I'll bring all the books over right now and we can go through them."

With spit flying out of his mouth Akleelu said, "You will never set foot in my home again. I've ordered the guards to shoot to kill the moment they see you coming. And all the dispensing with problem people? All your murders? The three generals? The National Resources Director? The journalist? All of them. It is on you. It's all you. You think you are the Supreme's bigger dog? The Kubwa? You are nothing. You are –"

"I will call you tomorrow and we can sort out this confusion when you are more calm."

"There is no confusion! There will be no sorting out anything! You are a dead man, Blake! A dead man." He threw the phone against the wall then crushed it with his foot.

Geoff raked his fingers through his hair. "What has Dax done? I gave her the opportunity to leave. Instead she's talking to Akleelu? About some forged piece of paper?

"I needed one more day without complication. One day. Then I will leave all this behind. Dax has become a serious liability. An irritating loose end.

He strapped on his leg holster. "And tonight is the night of dealing with loose ends, starting with you, Dax."

Rage shortened the drive to Mabezi, yet enough time to brew his rage, concentrating and focusing it. He already planned on Phil eliminating Logan. *He's been a thorn in my side since I started with Ironwood. Yes, eliminating Logan and his little investigation before he uncovers and exposes too much is critical to keeping my new identity hidden.*

But Dax? How dare that little mouse interfere? Her meddling ends tonight. Done and done.

Over the years, Geoff exploited his relationship with Akleelu to ensure the president no longer trusted Logan, but it never occurred to him to harden him against Dax. And getting bested by Dax fuelled his hatred.

I wanted to get out clean. No more murders. No fresh blood on my hands. But oh it will feel so good to choke the life out of her.

She is probably with Logan. They probably conspired together to turn Akleelu against me. And if they are together, that simplifies my evening.

As the sun set over Mabezi, he stopped at his house. He didn't expect to find either Dax or Logan there, but it was the easiest to check. No lights. He walked through the house. No one home.

Next stop, the hotel. Logan's truck was not in the parking lot, but he knocked on the door anyway. No answer.

They must be out for dinner somewhere. He scoured the city, slowly coasting by the better restaurants and pubs looking for them or the Ironwood truck.

I'll find them and wait for the moment when they are separated. Then grab Dax as a hostage and force Logan into the trunk. Take them both out to Phil and let him have a bit of fun.

He called Phil to stand by at their favourite secluded location, promising him a night of revenge on the reptile people.

Finally he spotted Dax at an outdoor restaurant. *What is she doing dining with a stranger? Not with Logan.* He tapped the steering wheel. *One bullet and I can move on to other loose ends. Not quite as satisfying as slowly squeezing her throat until the life leaves her eyes, but I've got a few things to wrap up tonight.*

He parked his vehicle across the street and lined up the shot. *Always thought I'd make a good sniper. A quick shot and her death will be attributed to some random drive by shooting. Pre-election violence. Nothing to see here folks.*

Patiently, he waited for a clear shot. Almost had it when the waiter walked by. Then a patron. A woman sat down with them. Finally a clear view of Dax. He squeezed the trigger slowly, just as Dax leaned forward. The bullet buried into the cement wall.

Amedeo yelled. "Get down."

People scattered. Amedeo knew within seconds the people would clear. They would be exposed targets. "We must get out of here now."

They ducked behind a car, moving with the scattering crowd. He steered Dax and Claire close to the buildings, keeping other people between them and the street.

They rounded a corner into an alley. "Hurry."

At the end of the alleyway, Amedeo peered around the corner. "The street is quiet. Get in the truck quickly and stay low in the seats."

Within seconds Amedeo took off. He made a couple of quick turns. Glancing in the rearview mirror he said, "I think we have a tail."

Dax spun around. "Looks like an Ironwood truck."

"You think it's Logan?" He eased up on the gas.

She shook her head. "No, I don't think –" The truck rammed them. "Get us out of here."

Amedeo pressed the pedal to the floor. With deft handling, he expertly slid the truck around corners and bends, putting a bit of distance between them with every turn.

The rear window shattered. "Get down. He's shooting."

Amedeo took an impossible corner, sliding sideways and missing the building by inches. The vehicle behind chickened out.

Amedeo made several turns hoping they would not be found, but the tail raced out of a side street and fell in behind again. More shots.

"He's not giving up."

Dax peeked over the seat. Light flashed from a nearby building revealing the driver. "Oh crap. It's Blake. I mean Geoff."

"I imagine he heard from Akleelu."

More shots.

Geoff tried to ram their vehicle off the road. But it proved difficult to keep up. The lead driver exhibited great skill at speed and controlled slides. *Who is he? Drives like a pro.*

Early in the chase, Geoff stayed hot on the guy's tail. But the driver turned at the last second. He cranked the wheel. Momentum rocketed him toward the buildings. He hit the brakes hard. Tires locked. Violently he spun the wheel. Narrowly missing the building he careened across the road. More violent wheel spinning. He finally regained control of the vehicle.

He hit the gas and gambled on what direction they went. Making a couple of turns, he spotted them on a parallel street and soon caught up. Hoping to kill the driver, he fired several shots into the vehicle. They raced, pedal to the metal.

Several corners Geoff approached too quickly for his skill level. Hitting the brakes hard reduced his speed enough to navigate a few, but he fell behind. Attempting a couple of the turns proved too difficult.

The lead car lost him again on another turn he couldn't manage at speed. He gambled again, but this time they were nowhere in sight. He continued scanning the quiet evening streets. Little traffic simplified his search.

Street after street, he searched.

After 10 minutes he rounded a heavily wooded curve. Ahead, flames rose 20 feet into the air from Dax's vehicle. He stopped in the middle of the road.

They wrapped their vehicle around a tree. Haahaa. Not as good a driver as you thought.

The passenger door was slightly ajar.

With a fresh clip of bullets in his gun, he carefully approached the burning car. An exploding tire pushed him back a few feet. He moved in closer to look inside.

Flames engulfed a single body. Immediately, he scanned the area. Satisfied he was alone, he moved in closer. It was a woman.

But who?

Despite the heat of the flames he kicked the door open. The body fell across the seat, her left hand hung out the door. He stared at the ring on the third finger.

It's Dax.

EPISODE SIX – BRILLIANT CUT

Three things cannot be long hidden – the sun, the moon, and the truth.

Buddha

Chapter 1 — Loose Ends

Friday, March 20 (continued)

While concentrating on keeping distance between themselves and Geoff, Amedeo considered their options. *He is relentless and wants Dax dead. And we can't keep running. Think.*

Nearly missing a sharp turn shifted his focus back to the road for a moment. *We could head for the hills, but isolation is risky. We need to do something that causes him to give up the chase. And only one thing will stop him.*

He thought for a moment. "I have a radical idea."

"Anything."

He pulled another hair-raising turn, inches from a stone wall. He navigated back the way they came. "I'm going to need about three feet of rope or something to use like rope."

She checked the glove compartment, the pocket in the door and under her seat. She turned to check with Claire. "Any luck?" She leaned over the seat. "Claire? You okay?"

Claire lay unconscious on the floor of the back seat. Dax shook her then felt something warm. "Oh God. Amedeo. She's bleeding bad."

He glanced over the seat. "Check for a pulse."

She checked on her neck. "No. Nothing. She's dead. One of the bullets got her."

"I am sorry to ask, but crawl back there and see if you can find anything we can use."

She rummaged behind the passenger seat. "How about jumper cables?"

"No. I have a better idea. Here. Help me off with my shirt. I need you to rip it into strips. Tie them into a rope. When everything is ready we will have to be quick. There's a gas can in the back. We will need it. Do you have any matches or a lighter?"

"No." She grabbed Claire's purse. "Claire was a smoker. Yup. Matches. Got it."

"The only other thing we need is a very large stone. Let me know if you see one on the side of the road."

"There. That pile there. Will one of those do?"

He stopped and threw in the largest one he could find. They took off again. "Now, I need to find the right spot." He glanced at Dax. "Geoff isn't going to stop until you're dead. So we need to make you appear dead. And Claire is going to help us with the illusion. Dax, Claire is dead. And we are going to stage a crash and make it look like you, okay?"

"Yes, it's okay, but one look at Claire and he will know it's not me."

"Not if she's engulfed in flames."

She spun her wedding ring on her finger. *Geoff has gone too far. Killing Claire. Trying to murder me? Well, now I'm furious.* She pulled her ring off. "We do what we need to." Carefully she pushed it onto Claire's finger. "That should help with the illusion."

"Brilliant."

He found a perfect spot and backed up into position. They quickly worked together to position Claire in the front passenger seat where Dax had been. Amedeo left the door slightly ajar. He sprinkled a bit of gas on the shirt-rope then tied it around the steering wheel to secure it from turning.

They doused the interior with gasoline. Dax stood on the passenger side ready to toss in the lit book of matches. Amedeo worked from the driver's side. He pressed down the brake while positioning the stone on the gas pedal.

With the engine revving he shouted," Ready?"

She lit the matchbook. "Ready!"

He slid out of the vehicle and stepped off the brake. She threw in the flaming matches. The vehicle took off in a straight line for the trees. The flames from the cab soon swallowed the vehicle.

It crashed into a tree at a good clip, rupturing the rad. Stream screamed out of the engine.

"Come on. We cannot stand here." They climbed down a slight embankment and hid in the heavy bushes.

Soon Geoff rounded the corner. They watched as he kicked the door open. The incinerated body of Claire fell over. Geoff moved in close. It took a moment, but he stepped back with a smile.

"Good riddance. The world will not suffer from your death, you useless piece of skin. I told you to leave Africa. But you always think you know better. You deserve this hell for all the hell I put up with for 10 years." He watched the flames for a minute. "One loose end dealt with. Onto the others."

He got into his vehicle and drove off.

Amedeo helped her up the embankment and onto the road. She watched his taillights disappear.

"You okay?"

"I'm great. No. I am enraged. Beyond enraged."

"We need to get out of Zimbula before he discovers you're not dead."

"This was no delusion or drug addiction or crap childhood. He is a full-on, world-class psychopath. So screw the marriage. Screw Blake – Geoff – whatever his name is. I will break him." She ripped the necklace with his wedding ring off her neck. "If breaking you is my protection, so be it."

She paced back and forth. Stopping in front of Amedeo, she pointed where Geoff left. "I will break that man. Break him financially. Break him for any future opportunities. Break him of his freedom to perpetrate a marriage fraud on anyone else again. There will be nothing left when I'm done. It'll be the sweetest, most satisfying moment of my life."

"I'm in favour of breaking the bastard, but we best not hang around here. I will see if Greg can pick us up."

When Greg arrived, she stared at the burning vehicle for a moment. *My marriage – up in flames. Actually, no. I never had a marriage. It was all an illusion. Rest in peace, real Blake Talbot. You will be cleared of all the horror perpetrated in your name. I promise you the honour you deserve.* She thanked Claire for helping in her escape.

In the front seat, Amedeo and Greg discussed the details of the chase. Turning around, Dax watched the flames fade into the distance. By the time they arrived at Greg's she knew how she would break Geoff.

While pulling on one of Greg's shirts, Amedeo suggested she call Logan. "I am concerned he is one of the remaining loose ends."

She tried, but got no answer.

Greg said he would be travelling back to Italy in a few days, but offered them a couple of rooms for as long as needed. Amedeo agreed that it would be best to not go back to Geoff's house.

Dax thanked Greg, but declined his offer. "I have a plan to break Geoff, and there are things I must do immediately. I know it's asking a lot, but could I borrow a vehicle?"

Amedeo said, "Where are you going?"

"Back to the house."

He shook his head. "If you run into Geoff, he will kill you."

"That's why I must go now, while he's out dealing with his loose ends."

"I still think it is too dangerous. What is so important that you would risk your life?"

"I must get the safe contents." Looking directly into his eyes. "I want to break him – really break him."

He slowly understood. He shifted as the full implication hit him. "To Zurich?"

She nodded.

His dimples popped.

Greg moaned. "Oh man. I know that look."

Still eye-to-eye with Dax, Amedeo said, "I've got a backpack at the house. Greg, we are going to need one more. And your motorcycle. We may need to go where trucks cannot. And we will need a flight out of the Democratic Republic of Congo." He turned to Greg. "Do you have any contacts in the DRC?"

"I assume you are talking about not quite legal entry and exit?"

"We will have our passports, but I do not want anything traceable leaving Zimbula or even the Congo."

"Then I think Voodoo is your man."

Dax said, "Uncle Logan talked with a man by that name in the Congo before we came to Africa."

Greg said, "Probably the same man. You can trust him."

Amedeo said, "Where is he located?"

"In the Congo, up near Uganda."

"Right. We can be to Butembo in 10 hours. I will call you for a specific location to meet once we are clear of the border."

They arrived to a dark house around midnight. With no vehicle in the driveway, they quietly entered the place Dax had called home while in Zimbula. Creeping down the hall, they listened for any sound that would indicate the presence of another person. The house remained quiet and still.

She grabbed her identification, wallet, important papers and a few clothes and filled Amedeo's bag. Her hand hesitated over the cute little black dress. Back in Washington, she hoped to find Blake and celebrate a renewed marriage. Instead she found Geoff and a fraudulent marriage. She ignored the dress momentarily then threw it in the pack at the last minute. *No sense in leaving a perfectly stunning dress behind.*

In the office she fumbled the code on her first attempt to open the safe. She blew out the tension and tried again. It popped open.

Amedeo held the second backpack as she filled it with the photos of Akleelu killing the generals, the two journals, and bank statements. Amedeo put the diamond from Jimmy James and the safety deposit keys in a side pocket. At the back of the safe she found a cloth bag that had not been there before.

Inside she found a blue crystal stone the size of a plum. "Now what is this?" She handed it to Amedeo.

He turned it over. "This looks like a diamond to me."

"Not a surprise I guess. Geoff operates a couple of diamond mines. It's kind of large, even for an uncut diamond, isn't it?"

He laughed. "Monstrously large and impossibly blue." He handed it back to her. "Do you know what this kind of stone is worth?"

She shrugged. "I guess a lot – being a diamond."

"A huge, beautifully clear, vividly blue diamond?" He turned it over several times. "Impossible Blue. Well past $50 million. Maybe even more than $100 million."

"Cut and polished, you mean?"

"No. Just like this. When I found those diamonds at the villa, the jeweller who appraised them taught me quite a bit about diamonds and how to recognize quality. This beauty will set the diamond trade on fire."

"Then it comes with us." She stuffed it in the backpack pocket.

He watched her, pondering the implications of carrying around the Impossible Blue. "Sometimes life gives you things that radically change your life forever, and not always in a good way. This is a dangerous stone. You take it, it may bring you nothing but pain."

"I plan on leaving him nothing. He gets nothing to start over with."

"Alright. Let's get out of here. Is there anything else we need to grab before we go?"

She smiled. "One more thing I need to do." She left a note in the empty safe then locked it up.

Saturday, March 21 (the small hours of the morning)

As they neared the border to the Democratic Republic of Congo Amedeo took the Impossible Blue out of the backpack and hid it on the motorcycle. "Remember, stay cool. Leave the talking to me. Do not get off the bike. No matter what, remember, this is all about negotiating the entrance fees. Nothing more."

She nodded.

At the border, the guard ordered them off the motorcycle. Amedeo shrugged. "I do not understand." He handed the guard a few scraps of paper with $30 American dollars.

The other guard reached up the tailpipe and pulled out a small bag of white powder. He waved it around, yelling.

The main guard pointed at the bag and yelled.

Dax broke out in sweat.

Amedeo laughed. "Ah, so you found my stash. Just something to keep the lady sweet. You know what I mean?"

The guards both laughed.

Amedeo added another ten dollars to the pot.

The first guard flagged his arms about, yelling at Amedeo. Two more guards came out of the hut with automatic weapons.

Dax unconsciously tightened her grip on Amedeo. She choked out, "Oh no."

He squeezed her hand then reached into his wallet and pulled out an ID card. "I am with the press. I am really glad to meet both of you. I am writing a story on police corruption for the papers in Europe and America. Would you be willing to go on record? Give me a quote or two for the piece?" He leaned over to read the name on the man's badge. "Maybe a photo of you, Samuel Kasongo?" He handed the press card and the money to the guard.

The man took the cash. He politely declined the photo and interview, pushing the ID card back. "Welcome to the Democratic Republic of the Congo," and waved them through.

Amedeo smiled broadly, and slowly drove past the raised gate. Shortly after two in the morning, they safely entered into the Congo with no trail for Akleelu, the police, the military or Geoff to follow. Without a trail, no one would suspect they exited through the Congo.

Geoff called Logan. "I think it's time we talked."

Logan said, "A place of my choosing."

Geoff silently considered his options. "Fine. Where?"

"The abandoned air field. At the base of the control tower. Half an hour. And come alone."

"Only if you do. I will see you there."

Geoff called Phil and Justin. "There is little cover. I will keep Logan facing south. When you are within shooting range, call my phone. And Phil, when I scratch my ear, kill Logan."

Phil's tongue flicked in excitement. *The big dog is mine. Number 49. I will pick the biggest tooth for you.*

Geoff pocketed his phone. As he drove to the airfield he thought, *it would only take one shot from Phil to eliminate Logan.* Geoff counted on Logan arranging backup. *Once Phil kills Logan, the backup will eliminate Phil. Then Justin will eliminate the backup. And while all that goes on, I will slip away unnoticed. Nice and neat. And Justin will be left holding the bag. Voila, no loose ends.*

Logan waited in his truck. He was at the control tower shortly after speaking with Geoff. Jamie positioned himself at the top of the tower with a good view of all movement on the ground.

A vehicle entered through the gates. Logan stepped outside of his truck to wait.

Geoff parked a few car lengths away and approached Logan in the glare of his headlights.

"Geoffrey Barber."

"So you know who I am. You were easy to fool, old man – as easy as Dax."

Jamie watched two men creep through the darkness to positions near the talking men.

Logan stood steady. "You can't get away with all the criminal garbage."

"I have achieved all I have set out to do because, unlike you, I do not have a conscience to hold me back. And most people happily swallow shit if it's wrapped up pretty. I learned that in the back seat of a Chevy at 14 years old." His phone buzzed.

"You degenerate bastard."

"Everyone has their dopamine button – the promise of anticipated reward. Push that button every so often and people will give you whatever you want. I told Akleelu he could have a golden palace and he danced like a puppet. Never checked the amount coming out of the mines. He was blinded by his desire.

"Dax's dopamine was a happy marriage. Come home for a few days a month. Say a few I-love-yous and she was very compliant. Never bothered to inquire about my life here. The illusion of family kept her happy. And I needed her to keep you off my back.

"You have the easiest button. Keep your niece happy and you would have turned over your company to me, but that's chump change, you old has-been. I wanted Africa and Akleelu. And you gave me both without question. Yes, you made all this possible."

Logan refused to take the bait. "You will not walk out of here tonight."

Geoff laughed. "You are predictable. Predictable. Soft. Blind. You've lost your sharp edge, if you ever had one." He caught a faint glint from the top of the tower. *And there's the backup.* His eyes squinted as he thoughtfully considered Logan. "You are the old dog. And the new dog kicked your ass. And now, a final blow." He scratched his ear.

Three seconds of automatic fire and Logan was down. The tactical vest protected his chest, but he took a couple of rounds to the legs.

Jamie swung his gun to the source of gunfire and let loose, killing the shooter.

Justin spotted Jamie and the two engaged in a prolonged exchange of gunfire.

While they kept each other occupied, Geoff turned his attention to his old boss.

Logan reached for his holster.

Geoff approached with his gun pointed at Logan's head. "Do it, old man."

Logan relaxed.

Geoff squatted beside him. "Good riddance, old fool."

Logan made a desperate move for his gun. Geoff knocked it out of his hand. He held his pistol to Logan's head. "You are not the first member of the Keyes family that I will kill tonight." He pulled the trigger.

Geoff peeled out, leaving Jamie and Justin in a fire fight.

Desperate to get to Logan's side, Jamie ignored the spray of bullets. He took careful aim. His shot connected, embedding in Justin's shoulder. The split second it took Justin to recover, Jamie took the lethal shot.

He hurried down the outer staircase and across the tarmac to

Logan, but he was gone.

Chapter 2 — Breaking the Man

Dax tapped Amedeo on the shoulder and yelled into his ear. "Was that your stash of drugs? Or Greg's?"

His dimples deepened. "Neither." He pulled over to the side of the road. "Border guards plant something incriminating when they want to up the fees. I'm willing to pay a bit more, but not much more. So, I called their bluff. No police officer in his right mind wants his photo plastered across international newspapers depicted as a corrupt official, even if he is. Exposure of a drug frame up is not going to be well received by his superiors."

She shook her head. "I was in a sweat."

He patted her leg. "It's all part of negotiating the entrance fees."

"And you just happened to have a press card?"

"You never know when one of those will come in handy."

"So, how do we get to Zurich fast?"

"Before Geoff, you mean?"

She nodded.

"We should have several hours lead on him. Maybe up to a day. However long it takes for him to discover the empty safe. I will call Greg and find out what arrangements he has made."

When Voodoo heard it was Logan's niece looking for help, he arranged their entire trip to Switzerland, not just a flight out of the DRC. Voodoo planned to meet them in Butembo. A small aircraft would fly them into South Sudan. From there he booked them on a flight to Cairo then on to Zurich with a stop at Athens.

Dax took the opportunity to call Logan again.

Geoff answered. "Hello?"

"Geoff." *What is he doing with Uncle Logan's phone?* With a sinking feeling she realized there was only one way he would answer Logan's phone. "You bastard."

"Dax. So that wasn't you in the car. Shame. I didn't think you capable of that kind of deception."

"You will pay for what you've done, for killing Uncle Logan."

He laughed. "You? You think you are going to make me pay? Honey, living with you, I've already paid and then some."

She ended the call.

Grateful the rain held off, they continued the long drive to Butembo.

Geoff arrived home and checked the clock. *Two thirty a.m. Twelve hours and I unload the Impossible Blue, collect my money, and five minutes later I'm outta here – to life on easy street. A new identity and it won't matter what that little life-sucking worm thinks she's going to do to bring me down. Blake is dead. And soon Geoff will be dead forever. Just 12 more hours.*

He went to bed satisfied.

The next morning dawned grey, the clouds heavy with rain. Shortly after 9 a.m. Amedeo and Dax arrived at the meet up location in Butembo. Dax slowly climbed off the bike, stiff from hours of hanging on over rough roads. She peeled off the backpack as she watched Amedeo stretch out his wrists.

He dropped his backpack and rolled his shoulders. "We are going to Zurich to clean out his bank accounts, yes?"

"Yes. I want to leave him with nothing."

"And what about all the evidence we have." He tapped the backpack.

"I haven't spent much time thinking about it." A broad smile brightened her face. "That will be the icing and cherry. I only thought about cleaning him out, but I have enough evidence to put him away for decades. Truly and thoroughly broken."

"Icing and cherry?"

"The best parts of a cake and the finishing touch on a sundae. Knowing he's in jail is the sweetest thing we can do with this stuff," she said tapping the backpack with her foot.

"He won't be put away for decades if Akleelu is protecting him."

"Why would he? Geoff has been stealing millions from him."

"Ah, but if Geoff is exposed, he will bring Akleelu down with him."

"Hmm. That's true. But if I release evidence against both of them, Akleelu will do his best to throw Geoff under the bus to save his own hide. And – I've got my investigative reporter friend. The Washington Post has international exposure. The story will be picked up by every big news agency and that will bring public opinion to bear. That will bury him for a lifetime."

She dug out her phone and dialled her friend. After relieving Libby's concern for her health and welfare, they chatted briefly about the story.

"It's a story that every journalist dreams of writing, the kind that earns a Pulitzer prize. You're in Africa?"

"We are heading to Switzerland now. We should be there Sunday night."

"We? You and Logan?"

"No. Not Uncle Logan. Amedeo and I. I'll explain later."

"I look forward to hearing that explanation." She scanned her calendar. "Best I can do is Thursday. I'm at London right now, but I will be in Rome on Wednesday. Where would you like to meet?"

Amedeo said, "Tell her to meet you at my villa. Invite her to stay for the weekend. We can send the address once we are in Europe."

"Okay. Amedeo says we can meet at his villa. It's in southern Italy on the coast. You're invited to stay for the weekend."

"A villa – on the coast of southern Italy. You're joking. You meet the most interesting people in Africa."

"You have no idea."

"Can't wait to hear everything. I will be there on Wednesday evening."

Voodoo arrived minutes before the Lear jet. He apologized that he couldn't send them through to Cairo on his private plane. He outlined their travel itinerary and arranged for his contact in Sudan to meet them and ensure everything goes smoothly.

They both slept for the majority of the three-hour trip to South Sudan, arriving at the airport in Juba late Saturday afternoon. The officials asked few questions. Perhaps it was because they came in on Voodoo's jet, or it was policy to not question people escaping a troubled nation. Either way, with their passports stamped, their contact took them to a hotel for the night.

They invited the man to join them for dinner, but he chose to dine alone at a table nearby, keeping a close eye on his charges.

"I've been wondering what I'm going to do with all that money. It's dirty."

"There are a number of good charities."

"Yeah, I've thought about that. It's *a lot of money.* The money alone is more than a hundred million. And then there's that huge blue diamond."

"You have the transaction journals, so you know how much came from the Tanzanian diamond mines and from the Zimbuli cobalt mines. You could return the money to each of the governments, but that means giving it to Akleelu."

"I don't want it in the hands of anyone that will continue the atrocities on the people. It really belongs to the citizens."

"So what breaks your heart the most? What would you change if you could?"

"I think changing the lives of the suffering girls and women. Empower them to earn a living and not fall victim to the violence."

"So start your own charity that does just that."

"I don't know anything about running a charity."

"You're smart. I'm confident you can figure it out."

"And I can always call you up for advice."

He clinked his glass to hers. "To the latest NGO in Zimbula."

"Thanks. What do you think about asking Nakato to help?"

"I think you could not find anyone better. She is connected with the people and great role model. She is someone the younger women will look up to."

"So, now the big question. How do I convert the diamond to cash? They track where the diamonds come from to ensure people don't purchase blood diamonds."

"Blood diamonds are sold and the money is used to fund wars. You are not using this money in any negative way. What if you found it while wandering about the jungle? You would have the right to sell it for whatever you can get for it."

"I guess."

"I can introduce you to the man who worked with me in dealing with the bunch of diamonds I found in the villa, if you like."

"Thank you. That would relieve my mind."

Three hours before his Saturday afternoon appointment with Xander in Malawandi to sell the Impossible Blue, Geoff opened his safe.

Everything was gone. He stood aghast.

Everything but one single sheet of paper. He unfolded it and read,

Geoff

You choked me. You threatened to kill me. You tried to assassinate me.

You are right about one thing. It's over.

I will break you.

D

The note fell from his hand as he stared at the empty box.

That worm has the Impossible Blue.

He looked away but the bare vault gripped his attention. As the realization of the truth settled in, a rage fuelled by entitlement exploded. The empty safe dealt a crushing blow to his perception that he held unshakable control over others.

"I will break you." He snorted. "You're a mouse. You cannot touch me. I will squash you, you piece of snail slime. You will pay with your life for crossing me." He ripped the reindeer painting from the wall and smashed it on the desk, scattering desk items across the room. Several blows left the canvas torn and the frame in pieces. It failed to quell his fury. A wood chair fell victim before he stormed out of the office.

He paced the hall. "I've got to get control." He returned to the office to determine all the missing items – *the Impossible Blue* – He shook his head. *Okay, I've got to focus. What else does she have?* He paled. *The transaction journals.* A record of all the diamonds, cobalt and copper – and who paid for it. His mind flooded with the realization that if she leaked that she had this information, it could get him killed by any number of men. He kicked the wall leaving a hole.

"Okay. Calm. Think"

His eyes rolled. "Banking statements with account numbers. And the safety deposit key. Holy crap. The money. And that key will unlock the names of everyone." He fell to the desk chair. "Now what will the little mouse do with that information?"

He let out a deep breath, feeling relief. *She can't access any of the accounts or the safety deposit box, as I am the only account holder.*

He looked out the window pondering why Dax would take the banking statements. Then the unthinkable possibility dawned on him.

Everything is in Blake's name. And she's got a death certificate from Tanzania. She just has to stroll in there with that document – and Blake's will, which leaves everything to her. Shit.

Would her ethics allow her to steal everything? He shook his head. *She put her ring on a dead woman and let her go up in flames. A cold move. Yes, perhaps she has the guts.*

His eyes landed on the note. *What did she say? "I'm going to break you."* His jaw clenched. *She's headed to Zurich, that bitch.*

"I will crush her. Force her to give me the journals and the diamond. Move my money into James Winslow's account. Then I will take great pleasure in choking the life out of her." Unconsciously, his hand tightened, leaving fingernail prints on his palm.

He checked his watch. *At best she has a 12-hour lead on me.* A quick estimate indicated she could be in Zurich sometime on Sunday. *I need to get to the bank first thing Monday morning to intercept her. Move the money first then deal with her.* He grabbed his passport and drove like a madman to Kigoma.

At the airport he discovered he missed the last flight of the day. The next flight out to a hub was early Sunday morning. It would put him in Nairobi by two in the afternoon. *Maybe another 15 hours to Zurich. If the flights line up, it is possible to get there before the banks open.*

"Any flights available from Nairobi that will get me to Zurich before 8 a.m. Monday?"

The agent clicked through several screens on her computer. "Yes. There's one that leaves Nairobi at 6:00 Sunday evening. There's a layover in Rome. You would land in Zurich at 7:30 Monday morning."

"Nothing from Rome that would get me there sooner?"

"No, that is the earliest."

"Book it. When does the flight leave here?"

"It leaves at 6:30 tomorrow morning and lands in Nairobi at 1:30 tomorrow afternoon."

"And I catch the next flight at 6? Okay. That works."

Chapter 3 — Out of Africa

Sunday, March 22

By six a.m. Sunday morning Geoff was on a flight to Dar-es-Salaam. He looked at his watch. "Everything is going to plan. Nairobi by two. Zurich Monday morning."

Despite the cloud cover, Sunday morning in South Sudan started hot with the temperatures quickly rising to sweltering. At eight a.m. Dax and Amedeo boarded a small commuter prop plane for Cairo. They expected to land just after noon and catch a 3:30 flight to Athens and on to Zurich by midnight Sunday night.

They felt the luggage doors bang closed beneath them.

Amedeo said, "How are you feeling this morning about breaking Geoff?"

"Are you asking if I still have the heart to take everything from him?" She pursed her mouth and nodded. "Yup. Everything I can lay my hands on."

"I was thinking that he is probably on his way to Zurich by now."

The luggage doors banged again.

"You think he's figured out that I'm headed there?"

He shifted to move closer. Speaking quietly in her ear he said,

"I think in the clear light of day he will check the safe and discover it empty, except for a note in which you promise to break him. You took his diamond worth tens of millions of dollars. That alone would put him on your tail. And you took evidence of his criminal activity. For that, he will again try to kill you. But you have all his banking information and the key to his safety deposit box. And that is what will bring him in a hurry to Zurich. He needs to open new accounts so he will be on his way to get to the cash before you."

The doors banged a couple more times.

She looked out the cloudy, scratched window across the tarmac to the hazy scrub beyond. "Funny. A week ago I would never have considered breaking anyone. Just the other day I told you I'm a healer, not a breaker." She turned to look him directly in the eye. "I am not that woman anymore. My indignation and anger squashed any feeling I had for that fraudulent man. Everything he did in the marriage – all hollow, all done to keep me quiet while he used me as a means to a criminal end. My need for justice overwhelms any need to heal the man. I will break him financially and do all I can to ensure he spends many years in jail."

He smiled. "Just checking."

Over the public address system the pilot announced," There will be a slight delay on our flight today. The luggage compartment is not locking shut. A mechanic is effecting a repair now. It will be about a half hour delay. Thank you for your patience."

Her hand tapped on the armrest between them. "How much does a delay impact us? Can we still catch the flight to Zurich?" She forced out a breath. "Now that we suspect Geoff is on his way there, I'm concerned."

"If this is only a half hour delay, we should still have more than two and a half hours layover."

Geoff's flight landed in Dar-es-Salaam on schedule just after nine in the morning. He had a few hours before his noon flight to Nairobi.

Dax said, "Let's hope this mechanic guy gets the problem fixed."

Amedeo craned his neck to look out the window. "They've got enough men working on it," and sat back in his seat.

"I really liked the idea of leaving the note in the safe at the time. He left a note for me ending the marriage. I left a note for him ending his life as he knows it. It felt really good – like I gained some control. I'm regretting it now. It made it clear who took all his stuff. This wouldn't be so nerve-wracking if I didn't think we were in a winner-takes-all race."

"He's a bright boy. Even without the note, I think he would figure out it was you and that you would be running for Zurich."

The doors banged again. She half stood up and peered down the side of the plane, but only saw a couple of men with orange safety vests. Another bang. "I guess they don't have it fixed yet."

A big burly man got into a golf cart and took off for the hangar. Another talked into a walkie-talkie. Shortly the pilot informed the passengers that there would be a further delay.

The hot African sun of Sudan soon overheated the interior. A flight attendant served cold drinks.

Amedeo wiped the sweat from his face. In checking their tickets he realized they fly into Terminal 1 at Cairo, but their flight to Athens and on to Zurich leaves from Terminal 2. Online he found that it is a 10-minute shuttle from one terminal to the other. "We need to get to Cairo by 2:30 to make the connecting flight. We need to leave here by 10:30 if we are going to make it."

She looked at her watch. 9:40. "If we are a few minutes late, will they hold the plane for us?"

He shrugged. "Sometimes they do, but we cannot count on it."

She nodded. Her hand tapping continued.

The burly man returned. The plane rocked as he worked.

Finally the pilot said, “I have good news and bad news. The mechanic can force the doors locked. This will allow us to fly to Cairo. Unfortunately, it will delay the unloading of luggage at the other end by at least an hour. If anyone wishes to not take this flight and deplane, please speak to the flight attendants. They will have your luggage removed before the repair is completed. For those of you staying onboard, it will take 30 to 60 minutes to remove luggage. Once that is done, the mechanic will quickly get us on our way. Again, thank you for your patience.”

She glanced around the plane. “Let’s hope not too many deplane.”

“Doesn’t much matter. Even one and they will have to pull the luggage out. If their luggage is on the first cart in, they will end up pulling out all the luggage.”

A family of four, a young man and a businesswoman all deplaned. It took an hour to remove the luggage from the cargo hold, search for the correct bags, and reload. It was close to 11:00. They waited for the mechanic to complete the repair. Thirty minutes later, the doors banged closed. The plane rocked as they checked the repair.

Finally at 11:30 the pilot said, “We are cleared to take off. We should land in Cairo by 3:30. If we have fair winds, I will try to get us in a little sooner. Thank you for your patience.”

She looked at Amedeo.

“We land when the Athens flight is scheduled to leave and we will be in the wrong terminal. I’ll talk to the flight attendant and see what they can do.”

As soon as the seatbelt lights went off, he discussed their situation with the lead attendant.

An hour later she brought the details of a solution. “We will arrive too late for you to catch your flight. They have moved you to a flight leaving two hours later. You are going on to Zurich?”

They nodded.

"Yes. You will still have a layover in Athens, and will land in Zurich a little after two in the morning."

Dax said, "Thank you."

"Here is the flight information for you. If you will wait and deplane last, I will take you to an agent to issue new boarding passes."

Amedeo said, "Thank you."

He patted Dax's hand. "It's going to be okay. We will have several hours in Zurich before the banks open."

As they approached the Cairo airport Amedeo pointed out the Great Pyramids. Their shadowed faces stood in stark contrast to the tawny, sun-baked desert stretching out past the horizon.

Dax said, "That's the first of the seven wonders of the ancient world I've seen. Too bad we don't have time to stop and look."

"It's a three-hour flight from here to Rome. You can come back."

They landed in Cairo a little before four in the afternoon.

At 6:00 Sunday night Geoff's flight left for Amsterdam. He was on schedule to land in Zurich by 7:15 Monday morning. *Enough time to get to the bank and lie in wait for the mouse to show up.*

While Geoff boarded his flight from Nairobi, Dax and Amedeo boarded their flight to Athens. An hour into the flight, a flight attendant leaned in close and asked if Amedeo was a medical doctor. She indicated one of the passengers needed medical attention.

Amedeo followed her to the area in front of the first row. Dax moved to the aisle seat to watch. Amedeo took a minute to assess an older man lying on the floor. He pulled the airline's stethoscope from his ears and spoke with the flight attendant. She nodded and disappeared while he propped the man up to ease his breathing. She returned with a medical kit. He selected a couple of different pill packets, which he gave the man.

Amedeo spent the remainder of the flight monitoring the man.

When they landed, the ambulance crew boarded the plane and spoke with Amedeo before transporting the man to the hospital. The pilot chatted with Amedeo for a moment and shook his hand, thanking him for his help before Amedeo returned to his seat for the flight to Zurich.

"Do you think he will be okay?"

"I suspect so. A little nitroglycerine relieved the pain in a few minutes."

"That's good. Listen, I've been thinking about what I need to do at the bank tomorrow. I think we should be at the door as soon as it opens. Get in. Get the money moved to new accounts. Then clean out whatever is in the safety deposit box. And do it all as quickly as possible."

"I assume you are not an account holder."

"No, but I have his will and death certificate."

"In Blake's name."

"Yes. I guess if the accounts are not in his name I'm out of luck."

He nodded. "Assuming they are in his name, I have two pieces of advice for you. One, be confident. Give them no reason to hesitate with your request. And two, stay alert. It is very likely that Geoff will be there. I think we should get to the bank before it opens and keep an eye out. When you go in, I will stay outside and keep watch. If I see him, I can text you."

"Okay. Any more advice? You've pulled at least one successful sting. I value your thoughts."

A pondering finger rested over his mouth. He turned with a slight smile. "I think I am a bad influence on you, Dakota Keyes."

Her eyes sparked. "Perhaps. But I'm not putting up any resistance."

"No, you are not. I think under that healer lies the heart of an adventurer."

"Just like you."

"Like attracts like. So, you are looking for advice. Let me think. The bankers are used to dealing with the demanding wealthy. So act like the woman from *The Devil Wears Prada*. You know that movie?"

"Yes."

"And dress like her, if you can."

"The only thing I've got is that little black dress."

"Good. Push the banker to speed up the process. Say you have a flight you have to catch. And don't forget to check your phone. It is the only way I can communicate with you. And one last thing. You don't know what will be in the deposit box. You should take one of the backpacks."

"Oh, right. I hadn't thought about that." She considered the implications of using the backpack. *Do I want to take all the evidence into the bank? Not really. Better to be unencumbered.* "Can we fit everything into one pack? I only want to take an empty pack in with me."

"I think so."

As they approached Zurich the pilot announced a warning light indicated a landing gear malfunction. "Sit back and relax, we should have this resolved shortly."

"I'm thinking I shouldn't be flying today. Everything that can go wrong is. Perhaps next time for your own safety, you should take a different flight."

"Think of it as a grand part of the adventure." His eyes danced with delight. "It is these things that make for a great story."

"True. If we're alive to tell it."

"Commercial planes are built with backup systems. Right now they are trying to deploy the landing gear a few more times. If that doesn't work, they can manually crank them down into place. And if none of that works, they can belly land the plane. It trashes the plane, but we will get down safe and sound."

"Then my escape from Africa is a great story that no one will believe."

He looked puzzled.

"How many people can claim they've been on a plane with a sketchy, improvised repair, followed by a heart attack, then landing gear that doesn't deploy. Very few people have had all that happen in a lifetime of flying, let alone all in one trip."

"Like how many people sport a scar from a drowning zebra?"

She laughed. "Only me."

The pilot aborted the landing and circled. After half an hour of burning fuel, the flight attendant moved people from the front of the plane to the back to keep the weight off the nose.

Dax watched the people as they made their way to the back of the plane. Most wore their fear on their face.

At 4 am the pilot announced they were going in for a landing.

The woman across the aisle hyperventilated. A teenager behind them quietly wept. A man several rows ahead kept saying," Jesus, save our souls."

The plane slowly glided in. The pilot brought it down to gently kiss the tarmac and discovered the landing gear fully deployed. It was a fault in the indicator.

They landed flawlessly. Outside, all the emergency crews lined the runway – a line up of fire trucks and ambulances and piles of security officers. The plane taxied to the terminal without further incident.

People gratefully shook the pilot's hand as they stumbled off the plane.

Chapter 4 — Moments Apart

Monday, March 23

Dax and Amedeo stepped off the jetway into the massive glass and metal terminal at Zurich. The architecture of enormous sweeping curved lines spoke of the power of Zurich and of its hustle and pace. On the way to customs, they walked past floor to ceiling windows, the black of night slowly yielding to the light of dawn.

As the first arrival, the waiting customs agents efficiently cleared the passengers.

Dax felt the tension increase as time ticked relentlessly toward the critical hour at the bank. She secretly pondered how she would handle running into Geoff. *What would he do? What could he do in a public setting? Like Amedeo said, he's on my tail to get the diamond and the evidence of transaction journals from me at all costs. That's enough reason for a psychopath to kill. He's already tried once. If he catches me at his bank cleaning out his accounts, that will push him over the edge of rationality.*

He finds me here, he will kill me.

She blew out a long breath. *This is no time to get nervous. I must be cool and collected if I'm going to convince the bank to release the funds.*

In the bathroom, she splashed water on her face, combed her

hair back into a bun. She slipped into her little black dress, put on fresh lipstick and examined the effect in the mirror.

Nailed it.

Alright. Time to break the man – for Uncle Logan and the real Blake Talbot, I make this promise. Geoff, you will not win.

When she stepped out of the bathroom Amedeo stood up. He eyed her up and down and smiled. "Perfect."

"Not too much?"

"You clean up alright. Try to get a male banker. One look at you and he will be falling over himself to do whatever you want." He led her to a ticket agent. "I think we should get our tickets now for Naples. As soon as you are done at the bank, we will get out of Zurich as quickly as possible."

They decided on a flight leaving at 12:30 in the afternoon. They would have three hours at the bank, if needed. "We will need to leave for the airport by 11:30 at the very latest."

She nodded.

As they headed for the taxi stand, he wrapped his arm around her shoulders. "Are you okay? Nothing requires you to go through with this."

"You don't know me too well. Once I decide to do something, I'm determined to follow through. No, I have no doubts about breaking Geoff."

"But something is bothering you."

Sheepishly she grinned. "I guess you read me better than I realize. Yes. I've been thinking about Geoff's reaction if he sees me." She leaned in close. "I know he wants to kill me. And with his Special Operations training, he could accomplish that goal quite easily. I don't stand a chance against that skillset."

"He cannot afford to kill you immediately because he wants to collect the diamond and the accounting books. And they will be with me. But he could try to strong arm you out of the bank into a secluded place."

He steered Dax to a quiet area to avoid the increase in people traffic. "There are two things we will do to prevent that from happening. One. I'll be watching from the outside. If I see him, I will discreetly follow him in and keep you posted on his movements. With this information you can avoid him. And two. If this fails, any trouble at all, and I will be moments away."

"Okay. Thank you, Amedeo. Thank you for everything."

They negotiated with a taxi driver, booking him for the entire morning.

Dax drew in a deep breath. The Zurich spring morning offered cool fresh air after the oppressive heat on the tarmac of South Sudan. In the distance, the white-capped Alps stood on a bed of cool colour – nature's majestic version of pyramids.

The drive into the banking district took them through the northern part of the city. The streets bustled with activity. Frequent buses, trains, and trams hustled around both old and ultramodern districts.

Dax felt the culture shock of moving from dirt roads with shacks to the luxurious lifestyle of Zurich. *I'm not in Oz anymore. No negotiating border fees here.*

The cabbie took them to an early morning diner for breakfast. Power men and women in expensive business suits drank coffee while reading the newspaper. The industrious waitress brought their food in minutes, moving diners through with speed and efficiency. At this time of the morning everyone moved briskly – quick orders, fast service, speed reading – all to ensure an early start to the business day. Even the flags energetically snapped in the breeze.

The cabbie drove them past the bank for Amedeo to scout out a good spot to wait. They watched as bankers flocked to their offices with the first rays of the sun.

Geoff's flight landed at 7:30. He checked his watch. *Get through customs and a 15 minute drive. Get to the bank by 8:30? It's tight, but possible to get there before it opens.* A flood of travellers clogged customs. He leaned out to determine the length of the line. Then checked the time. Frustration threatened to erupt. He willed himself to calm down. *No time to appear anxious and draw undue attention.* Rage bubbled and brewed inside. The culmination of his ten-year plan lay in jeopardy. And every minute spent in a customs line put him further from his goal.

Every few minutes he checked his watch. He engaged the elderly couple ahead of him in conversation letting it slip that he had an important meeting at a bank. They encouraged him to go ahead. He continued working his way up the long line.

At exactly 8:30 the bank opened. Amedeo escorted Dax to the entrance, scanning the area for danger. "No sign of Geoff. Maybe something happened to him. You got your phone?"

"Yes. How do I look?"

"Gorgeous. I'd give you whatever you asked for."

"Let's hope I get an equally impressed banker."

She expected marble floors and walls, high arched ceilings, dark carved mahogany, and huge crystal chandeliers. She found the opposite. Spacious and bright replaced dark and heavy. With a glance she took in the shades of light grey, bright pot lights in the walls and 20-ft. ceiling, glass elevator with wrap around curved staircase.

The woman at the information kiosk contacted one of the financial advisors. "Nolan Francks will be with you in a moment. Please have a seat. May I get you a coffee or tea?"

Keep with the impression I am in a hurry. "No, thank you."

Within a couple of minutes Nolan came down the staircase and introduced himself. He pushed the elevator button and asked if this was her first visit to Zurich.

"Yes." *Keep my answers short. Keep up the pressure. No chat-*

ting. No time.

He nodded and asked no further questions. His second floor office was the third in a long line. He offered her a seat as he rolled the frosted glass door closed.

Good. If Geoff comes by, he can't see me.

He carefully sat down and slowly rolled his chair forward. Several askew pens required straightening. He brushed off invisible dust then rested his interlaced hands on the desk. "Now, how may I help you?"

Great. I get the one slow poke in all of Zurich. He moves at the speed of a snail.

She made it obvious that she checked the time. *No messages from Amedeo. At least that's good.* She produced the death certificate. "My husband died in Tanzania over a week ago. I wish to move all the money from his three accounts into a new account and I wish to empty the safety deposit box into one of my own."

"My condolences."

"Thank you."

"Let's take a look at what you have there – a death certificate, is it?"

She pointed out the pertinent information on the document.

He read the entire document. "Tanzania. Interesting. This is the first time I've seen a death certificate from Tanzania."

Who cares? I am not interested in chitchat. Let's just get this done. "He worked in Africa."

"I see. Blake Talbot." He mumbled a couple of things. "Died of burns. My, my, my. That is terrible. The coroner –" He tried a couple of times to pronounce the name. Finally he set the paper down on his desk and adjusted it to sit straight. He removed his glasses. "Yes. This will need to be verified, of course. And you are the executor of the will?"

"Yes." She handed him the will, indicating the section that named her as the executrix and sole beneficiary.

He put his glasses back on. "I see. Yes. The date. Uh huh." He mumbled through the first couple of paragraphs. The glasses came off. "Well now, what happens in these circumstances is we will need to verify these documents."

I know I'm going to regret asking this. "What is involved in the verification?"

"Oh. Certainly I am glad to explain our procedures. For the death certificate, I will have my assistant call the Tanzanian authorities to confirm all the details. And then I will have our lawyers examine the will and confirm the accounts you wish to close as belonging to Blake Talbot. I will need photo identification that shows you are –" He picked up the will and read. "Dakota Keyes. You have a passport with you?"

"Yes."

"And what do you do for a living?"

"I'm a psychologist. I run a clinic in Washington, D.C."

He nodded, made some notes then called his assistant on the phone.

"Could you have the lawyers look over the will *while* your assistant confirms with Tanzania? I have a flight I need to catch and am pressed for time."

"Certainly. Yes. Of course. Let me see now. I think I will send along the numbers of the accounts you wish to close. Get a final approval on everything." He looked up at her over the rim of his glasses. "Seeing as you are in a hurry."

"Thank you." She handed him statements from each of the accounts. He carefully copied the numbers, reading each number aloud before writing it down. Then double checked each one and handed her back the papers.

You deal in numbers all day long. Is this the fastest you can work? She almost offered to read the numbers to him.

A young woman entered the office. Nolan gave her instructions, the paperwork and asked to prioritize the verification.

He turned his attention back to Dax. "Now. While the documents are being dealt with, let's talk about what you want done. Your husband had three accounts. You don't need to open a new account. We can simply –"

"No. I want everything moved into a new account." She waved her hand then clutched her chest. "It's too emotional. My therapist says I must let go and move on." *Oh crap. That sounded stupid coming from a psychologist.*

He looked at her for a moment. "Yes, I understand. Certainly losing your husband is a great loss. A new account then." His phone buzzed. "Nolan Francks." He pulled his glasses off and leaned back in his chair. "Yes. That's right. Oh. I see. Yes indeed. That is a problem. Fine. Yes. I will inform her. Yes."

Her heart sank.

"Please excuse that call. My wife. Now –" His phone buzzed again. "Nolan Francks. Yes?" He put on his glasses and made a couple of notes. "Yes. She's set up in the system? Thank you."

He tapped through several screens. "Ah, yes. Here you are. Excellent. Well, seems things are moving along."

She checked her phone. 8:50. *Not fast enough for me.*

Once through customs, Geoff bolted to the line of taxis. He told the cabbie the name of the bank and promised an extra $100 if they got there in ten minutes.

At 9:00 a text message came in. She glanced at the notification. "No sign of Geoff. Hope things are going well."

She responded. "Good. Okay here, but slow process. Awaiting review of documents and approvals."

Nolan's phone buzzed. "Nolan Francks. Yes? Good. Yes. Okay, thank you." He checked the information on the computer. "Yes. Here it is. The death certificate is confirmed."

Excellent. One down. One to go.

Minutes into Geoff's ride into town, the cabbie slammed on his brakes. He barely avoided a collision with a sudden pile up in front. The truck behind, unable to stop in time, rear-ended them. Geoff screamed at the driver to drive past and get him to the bank. The cabbie explained the legal requirements to remain at the scene and asked dispatch for a pickup.

Unwilling to wait, Geoff got out of the cab. The truck completely blocked all through traffic. *Unbelievable.* He tried flagging down a cab on the other side of the highway. Several drove by with passengers. Finally an empty one stopped. He checked the time. He might arrive at the bank before 9:30. He pressed the cabbie to hurry. "There's $200 if you make it quick." *I've got to get there before I lose everything.*

Nolan said, "Oh look. The lawyers have had a look see. Seems everything is in order, Mrs. Talbot – er – Ms. Keyes. My apologies. Let me just check one more thing. Yes. A signature approval. That is critical. Sometimes they forget to include a signature. We can't go ahead without the signature. But here it is. So, everything is in order."

You are going to drive me crazy. Stop blathering and just get on with the job. She glanced at the time. 9:12. She caught her leg dancing out her anxiety and quietened it down.

Nolan opened a filing cabinet and pulled out a brochure. "Now, we have various types of bank accounts available." He opened the brochure and turned it so she could read. "As you know, we have named and numbered accounts. The difference between –"

"A numbered account."

He picked up a pen and moved his notepad into position. "A numbered account. With the numbered accounts, we will need an initial deposit of $100,000."

She smiled. "No problem."

"Good. A numbered account it is. We will issue you a debit card to access the account. If you are in Switzerland, you can walk into any of our branches and withdraw cash with no record of the transaction. If privacy is important to you, you may choose to use travellers' cheques. There is a small fee for going this route. I presume you will not be requiring regular cheques as they defeat the purpose of a numbered account."

She nodded. "That's fine. I will need twenty thousand U.S. in travellers checks."

"Certainly." He repeated her request as he wrote it on his notepad. "Now the last thing to think about is what currency do you want the account in? If Swiss francs, there is a small amount of interest earned, but there is also a withholding tax. Most foreign account holders choose –"

"American, please."

"A numbered account in U.S. dollars. Excellent. Now you said you are a doctor?"

"I'm a psychologist and I own a clinic in Washington D.C."

"Yes." He made a note. "A psychologist and clinic owner. Fine." He looked over his notes. "Yes, I believe that is all the information I need to open your account."

Thank heavens. She checked the time. 9:15.

After a couple of minutes of tapping through several screens he said, "Good. That looks like everything is filled in. Now, we send this for approval."

She almost rolled her eyes. *Oh c'mon. Another approval?*

His phone buzzed at 9:21 with a question.

Hurry up. I don't have time for this.

A few minutes later Nolan said, "Oh here it is. Congratulations. You have an account."

She checked the time. 9:24. *Finally. I'm close. Just got to empty the accounts now.*

"Let's see now. I guess I will need the three account numbers again."

She handed him statements from the three accounts. Her fingers tapped the week-old and suddenly itchy stitches on her thigh as she waited. Her phone pinged with a text message.

"Geoff is here. Following him into the bank."

Her heart doubled its already rapid rhythm. *Get a move on, man. Let's go.*

A minute later Nolan said, "There we go. The first account is cleared and closed. That would be the named account."

Chop. Chop.

He picked up the phone and buzzed his assistant. "Yes. There is money in Ms. Keyes' account. Please draw up–" He checked his notepad. "– twenty thousand in travellers' cheques, please. Yes. As quickly as possible." He peered at her over his glasses. "Seeing as you are in a hurry."

"Thank you." Another text came in. "Following Geoff upstairs. Where are you?"

"Third office, second floor."

"He's going past you now."

She glanced behind her to see a couple of dark shadows pass the frosted glass windows. A shutter rolled down her back. *We have maybe a minute before he accesses his accounts.*

"Looks like the second one is cleared and oh – hold on. Let me see now – yes, it is closed."

Down to the wire. Two down. One to go.

Another minute passed. She strained her ears, waiting for the explosion when Geoff discovered two empty accounts.

Nolan said, "And there we have it. The third account is closed. All the funds are in your new account." He handed her a balance statement. "I presume you will find everything correct?"

One hundred and eleven million dollars. I can't believe it. I've actually done it.

She folded the statement and put it in her purse. "Yes. That is correct. Now, I'd like to deal with the safety deposit box."

"Of course. Let me give you all the paperwork on your new account. Here is a temporary card to access your account. A credit card will be mailed to your address in Washington."

The assistant interrupted to hand Dax an envelope. "Your travellers' cheques, ma'am."

"Thank you." She tucked them into her purse.

Nolan handed her some papers. "And here is some information on the type of account you have chosen. Oh and here is a list of our branch locations. And of course, my business card. Please feel free to contact me should you need anything."

She stood up to encourage him to get moving.

"I really must deal with the contents of a safety deposit box."

"Certainly. Follow me."

As they exited the office, she peered out the door and scanned the hall. *All clear. Let's get going*. As Nolan rolled his door close she heard Geoff yelling several offices down. Nolan ushered her quickly to the elevators. "Please excuse the disruption."

"No problem."

They waited at the elevators. She glanced down the hall then up at the floor indicators. One at the tenth floor and one at the ground floor. Down the hall, Geoff raged then became quiet.

C'mon. Let's go. She whirled around at the sound of one of the office doors rolling open. Another advisor and client hurried toward the elevator.

Finally it arrived. They rode it to the basement. The safety deposit advisor was busy with a phone call.

Nolan offered his hand. "I will leave you in Elena's competent hands. Thank you for your continued business."

As she waited she kept an eye on the stairs, elevator and her phone. *Please. Please.* She quietly said, "Is there someone else that I can speak to?"

The woman finished her call. "I am sorry for the delay. How may I help you?"

"I would like to clean out my deceased husband's deposit box and open my own please. All the approvals are in the system. If you could please hurry. I have a flight I absolutely cannot miss."

"Of course. The woman asked for her name. "Yes, I see legal has approved. You have the key for your husband's box?"

"Yes."

Dax sat down while the woman prepared the paperwork to set Dax up with a new box.

Five offices from Nolan, Leon tried to calm down the maniac in his office. "Please sir. If you do not calm down I will call security."

Geoff growled," I am calm. Check your damn computer again. These are my accounts. There should be over a hundred million dollars in there."

Leon searched again. "These accounts do not exist."

"That is impossible. Here are copies of the bank statements."

Leon looked over the pages. "Nonetheless, these accounts do not exist."

"How is that possible?"

"Perhaps a second account holder closed the accounts? Closed accounts are completely removed from our system."

"There was no other account holder." *Dax.* "You have made a big mistake and your bank will pay dearly. I want to check on my safety deposit box then I wish to speak with a manager."

"Certainly." Leon gladly escorted Geoff to the basement.

Amedeo sent another message. "Geoff on the move. Getting on elevator. Watch out."

Elena said, "Here's your new key."

Dax glanced at the elevator. The number indicated the second floor. It flicked to the first floor. *He's on his way here.*

Elena said, "Please follow me to the vaults." They turned left down a long hall lined with massive safe doors as the elevator dinged and the doors opened.

They stopped at vault D and collected Geoff's box then continued to G to open her new one. Around the corner at the front desk, she could hear Geoff arguing with someone. Elena showed her to a small office on the opposite side of the hall. "When you are ready you can return your box and use your key to lock the deposit door. Leave the other box on the desk." She closed the door as she left.

Dax checked the time. 9:40. She texted Amedeo. "In a private room opening the deposit box now."

"Geoff is somewhere in the basement. Be careful."

"Yes. I hear him down the hall yelling at one of the bankers."

"Do not take any chances."

"I'll be careful."

She opened Geoff's box to find a title deed to a huge estate property on a private island off Belize in the name of James Winslow. There was a list of three-digit numbers with names and notes beside each one. And a pistol.

A fresh round of yelling started. She cracked the door open to listen.

"I have a safety deposit box here."

"I have no record of it. Do you remember the number?"

"No. I don't remember the number. Do you know the serial number of your phone?"

"I am only trying to help you, sir."

"I know. I am sorry. Please look again. Blake Talbot."

Dax moved the gun to her box, using her dress to avoid her fingerprints – *probably has Akleelu's prints on it.* She threw the remaining paperwork into the backpack. Ready, she stood at the door listening. All was quiet. She peeked out the door. *No one in the hall.* She dashed across the hall to G and slipped her box in the compartment and locked it.

At the vault door she heard Elena's and Geoff's voices approaching. Louder and louder. Then they turned into one of the rooms. She glanced out. The hall was clear.

She crept toward the voices, stopping at the entry to D.

"It was in this area here."

Dax stole a quick look in. *They are both facing the other way. It's now or never. I've got to get out of here.*

She clutched the backpack and quietly crossed the door. Once past, she hurried to the stairs, taking them two at a time. As she neared the top, Amedeo stood up and set aside a newspaper. He took her elbow and they quickly left the bank.

"Let's get out of here. Geoff is moments behind me. And he's pissed."

They hurried to the waiting cab.

"You okay? Get everything taken care of?"

She nodded. "Let me catch my breath."

To the driver Amedeo said, "Take us back to the airport."

The cabbie signalled and waited for traffic to clear from a red light

Her face flushed with excitement and the thrill of success. "It was so close. He was right there. Just feet away."

Before they could pull into traffic, Geoff stepped out of the bank and scanned the area for Dakota. *She's here somewhere. The bank has only been open for 75 minutes. So I've just missed her. With the accounts drained, where would she go? That mouse will run back home.* He looked for a cab.

Amedeo spotted Geoff and knocked Dax's purse on the floor of the cab. As she leaned over to collect the scattered contents, he hustled the cabbie. "Let's get going. We can't miss our flight."

The driver nodded. "As soon as the light changes."

Geoff approached their cab.

Amedeo rested a hand on her back. "Stay down. He's right outside the door."

Geoff ducked to look in their cab, saw a male passenger and moved on to other cabs.

They pulled out into traffic. Amedeo glanced behind them. Unable to find an available cab, Geoff ran down the street in hopes of finding one on the cross street.

She sat up, pulled her hair out of the bun and watched him out the back window. "I see why you like this work. It's intoxicating." She turned in her seat." He was just a few offices away. Then down in the vault, I crept past while he argued with the advisor. If he'd turned, he'd have caught me. I felt my thumping heart in my neck. It almost got the better of me. I wanted to yell all the way up the stairs. Oh my goodness. It's like an addiction. So exciting."

Five minutes later Geoff hailed a cab, and offered $500 to get him to the airport quickly.

Amedeo checked the time as they hopped out at the airport. "It's ten o'clock now. Let's get through security in case Geoff shows up."

At mid morning, the line up to go through security extended several switchback lengths of queue.

At the departures level, Geoff threw money into the front seat of the cab and noted the time. *Five after ten. She can't be far ahead of me.* He entered the airport at one end and worked his way to the other end searching for long sandy blond hair.

Several dozen people filled in the line behind them. Dax stood with her back to the main terminal. Amedeo faced her to watch over her shoulder. He plopped his ball cap on her head. "Tuck your hair in. You'll be harder to find. He will be looking for your long hair." He reached around behind her and tucked in a bunch of strays.

"Yeah, no one will notice a woman in a little black dress and baseball cap."

"Several rows of people block the spectacular view of this dress.

Most will only see the cap."

With only a couple more lengths of line before they went through security, he scanned the moving traffic coming from the main area. They shuffled a few feet ahead. He dropped his backpack between his feet. "Getting hungry? Want to get something to eat?"

"A little. I guess it will be getting on in the afternoon before we get out of the airport in Naples."

"We should be on our way to the villa by two or two-thirty." His eyes skimmed the crowd over her shoulder.

"Yeah. Maybe we should –"

In a heartbeat, she found herself in his arms. His mouth touched her lips gently, like a delicate butterfly. Startled, she inhaled the scent of his cologne. His rough unshaved face rasped against her skin. She melted into his tight embrace.

He paused briefly, his lips still joined to hers. They passed breath between them. His grip tightened, pulling her head toward him. He pressed his mouth to hers with intensity.

Her heart fluttered. She felt her blood pounding in beat with his. For a moment, the world fell away and she floated in a universe of comforting heat.

Her welcoming lips ignited a fire in his belly. A lifetime passed between them in that moment. He pulled back. "Bella." His lips brushed hers as he spoke.

He glanced over her shoulder then gazed into her eyes. "I saw Geoff checking out people in the line."

She swallowed. With the barest of whispers she said, "Is he gone?"

"Sí."

A young boy behind them said, "Mommy, look. He's stealing her bubble gum!"

Several people in the line chuckled.

The moment ended. The reality of the airport, the press of people watching, and the moving line pulled them apart. They caught up with the people ahead. He turned to the onlookers. "Just married."

The lad's mother grinned. "Congratulations."

He bent down to the boy. "Her bubble gum is the best I've ever had."

He giggled and hid behind his mom.

Best bubble gum I've ever had too. Even my toes felt that one. She studied his ruggedly handsome face. *Is life compensating me for the ten years stolen? Karma tossing me an apology? "Here. Life's given you quite a blow. How about a handsome, Italian doctor who blows your socks off. A little bit of adventure and we'll call it even."*

A few minutes later, they cleared security.

While they waited for the boarding call, Dax phoned the Washington lawyer that wrote up their wills. She briefed him on all that transpired, that Geoff Barber assumed the identity of Blake Talbot, and that according to Tanzanian authorities, Blake is dead and they issued a death certificate.

"My question is this. Is the marriage over because I have a death certificate, even though the actual man is not dead? Or is the marriage automatically invalid because I did not actually marry Blake Talbot? Or is it valid, so the marriage must be annulled? I want to protect my assets."

"Death certificate in the name of a man that doesn't exist. And the man's real name is Geoff Barber. He is still alive?"

"Yes."

"Do you have any children?"

"No."

"How long have you been married?"

"Ten years."

"Well, first thing. Yes, you are married. You can go the route of annulment. He entered the marriage based upon a fraudulent act or representation. On this basis, you can receive an annulment via court decree."

"And how long will that take?"

"A couple of weeks to gather the evidence and appear before the court. Because there is ten years worth of joint assets, a divorce should be considered. The complication is that it will take longer, and will involve mediation to divide the assets equitably."

"No. He tried to kill me. I want out of this as quickly as possible. And I do not want to meet him or discuss anything with him. In fact, a story of his criminal activities will hit the newspapers and he will be hard to find."

"I see. In that case, I think we can expedite an annulment. It would help to have evidence and witness testimony regarding the attempted murder.

"In the meantime, I recommend you immediately revoke your current will which names Blake Talbot as beneficiary by replacing it with a new one. And as to protecting your assets, not that Geoff Barber is *legally* allowed to access your bank accounts in your and Blake's name, he still retains identification as Blake, therefore has access to your property. Can you drop by the office in the next day or so?"

"No. I am in Europe right now."

"I'm going to put you on with my paralegal. She can gather the information required for a new will. Once we have it done, we can send you a digital copy. You can have your signature witnessed there. That will revoke your current will. I strongly suggest you move your share of the assets to non-joint accounts."

"Thank you."

He transferred her to the assistant.

Amedeo bought a couple of burgers, fries and drinks. They chatted about Italy when her phone rang.

Caller ID read Blake.

Amedeo held her hand. "Let it go to voicemail. You do not need to speak to him and in his frustration and anger, he may leave an incriminating message."

She nodded and waited for the phone to indicate a new message. She picked it up as soon as it showed. Leaning close so Amedeo could hear, they listened.

"I will find you. I will hunt you down and slowly kill you. You will soon regret crossing me. I know who took you to meet Akleelu. And I know where he lives. My friend Phil terrified you in the middle of the night. That will look like child's play compared to the night you woke up to me. Tell Amedeo I know where he lives." He hung up.

Amedeo scanned everyone in their vicinity and all the traffic passing by.

"He knows about you?" She rolled her eyes. "Our visit to Akleelu. Oh I am so sorry, Amedeo. I've involved you in something you don't deserve."

"It could be Akleelu said something. More likely it was one of the palace guards. Some guy in his pocket, keeping him informed of all palace visitors. He is bluffing about knowing where I live, other than Italy." He checked the departures board. "Two flights to Italy – ours and one to Rome. That will not be of any help." He checked his watch. "We should board in a few minutes. So if he buys a ticket and searches for you at the various gates, we will be out of sight shortly."

"Unless he buys a ticket for Naples." She scanned the crowds. She gasped and grabbed his arm. "He'll have looked you up by now and know what you look like. And that means he probably remembers you from the cab. And that means he knows for sure we are together. I thought the worst was over."

They heard a commotion at the security screening. Several guards ran past the gate toward the disturbance.

She said, "What do you think?"

"It is worth a look."

She packed their food and they walked toward the noise.

Guards scrambled to subdue a man. One guard tased the man. He still fought hard, pounding on the guard. When they got a clear look she said, "Geoff always was tough as nails."

An announcement called for their flight to board.

As they turned, Geoff caught sight of them. "This isn't over. You are dead." He struggled to get out of the hands of security. One of the young guards clocked him in the jaw, dropping him to his knees.

Amedeo took her elbow and led her away.

Seated onboard for their final flight to Italy, Dax let her head fall back on the seat.

Amedeo said, "You are safe now."

Tears flowed. "No, I'm not. And neither are you, or anyone in your family. He will use any means to get to me. And that includes threatening your family."

"It will be a mute threat if he believes I do not know where you are." One dimple creased.

"You have a plan."

"I do."

"I didn't realize the extent of the fear inside – of him, of even seeing him. The thrill of the caper held it down. Excitement trumped the fear, but it still lurked there." She rolled her head to look at him. "Going in the bank, getting the money moved right under his nose – I thought that would be the hard part of breaking Geoff. The rest would be easy."

"This is nothing. It is a simple thing to deal with. Trust me."

She searched his eyes for any indication of anything less than confident. A slow smile threatened. "Okay."

"We have one bit of serious business between us that must be dealt with."

"Oh? What's that?"

His finger tapped his mouth. "I recall a discussion where we established terms of a deal." He looked at her with fun dancing in his eyes. “I said I would help you and if we found Geoff then we would talk about what my help is worth.”

She laughed. “I see how it is. Hitting up the vulnerable, wealthy woman for money. There’s a word for people like you.”

He rubbed the three days growth on his face. “Oh Bella, I do not want your money.”

Chapter 5 — Exposé

The flight attendant closed and locked the door. Underneath, the baggage handlers slammed close the luggage doors. Dax drew a breath and looked at Amedeo.

"So – you don't want money in exchange for your assistance? I don't know if I dare ask what you've decided your help is worth."

He leaned over, his shoulder touching hers. "If you are afraid, we don't need to talk about it now." His entire face displayed his delight. "Just wanted you to know there is an outstanding debt."

"Right." She delicately scratched her stitches. "Before we talk about my debt I want you to know that from my perspective I can never repay you for all you have done. I was lucky enough to have you looking out for me. And you haven't stopped. Uncle Logan wasn't so lucky." Her lower lip quivered.

"Bella." He held her hand in her lap, fingers intertwined.

She looked out the window lost in her thoughts. "I don't even know where he is. Maybe I will never find him, like so many others in Zimbula." She wiped her cheeks with her free hand.

They remained holding hands, each lost in their own thoughts.

Once through Naples customs, they exited the secured area into the main terminal. A middle-aged man approached them grinning. He and Amedeo hugged each other warmly.

Amedeo said, "Nic. Thanks for coming."

"This is a favour I enjoyed. And you must be Dakota Keyes." He held out his hand. “Deyo told us a bit about you. He failed to mention how beautiful you are. I’m this guy’s big brother Niccolo. And this is my girlfriend Maria.”

“Thank you. I’ve heard a bit about you too. Nice to meet you both.”

Nic tossed Amedeo a set of keys. “It’s parked in the third row, about halfway down. How long are you back? Maybe we could go out for dinner? I’d like Dakota to hear the true version of your stories.”

“I tell it like it is. Sorry if that makes you look bad, big brother.”

Nic wrapped his arm around Dax. “Maybe we should leave him at home, yes?”

She laughed. “I can see the similarities between you two. You’re both charmers.”

Amedeo glanced at Dax. “How about Friday night?”

“My friend Libby will be here.”

Nic said, “Bring her along.”

“Okay. Sounds like a very interesting evening. I look forward to it.”

The brothers fist bumped and Nic waved goodbye.

“You look a lot like your brother.”

“Yes, people say we have the *Ferrara* look. I have a surprise for you. I asked Nic to drop off my car. I thought you would enjoy a ride in a fine machine as a change from a rickety old African truck or a cab with no shocks.”

Her right eyebrow lifted. “I am intrigued. What kind of fine machine are we talking about?”

He just smiled and led her to the parking lot. They made their way down aisle three. “Ah, there she is.” He nodded toward a metallic blue 812 GTS Ferrari.

Her eyes popped. “Are you kidding? It’s beautiful.”

“And drifts like butter.”

"You know how to sweep a girl off her feet."

He put the backpacks in the trunk then held the door for her. She slid into soft leather. As he put on his sunglasses she said, "When did you arrange all this?"

"When you were in the bank. Ready for the sweetest sound in the world?" He started the engine. The entire cabin rumbled with pure promise. A ferocious creature roared with every rev of the engine. "Nothing sounds quite like a Ferrari."

With the top down, they rolled out of the airport for a spectacular run on the highway, south to his villa on the northern coast of the tip.

The engine grumbled in protest when he geared down and took a detour on a quiet road. After turning the corner, he stopped in the middle of the road. "Let's see what this baby can do." He hit the gas. The acceleration plastered her to the seat. It passed 60 mph in three seconds.

She watched the needle cross two hundred before he rapidly geared down.

Her eyes danced with the thrill of speed. "I need to get me one of these."

He laughed. "They are addictive." He turned down a long winding road, hitting the curves at speed, executing the perfect drift every time. When he geared down for a stop sign she said. "So good for the soul. The ride of lifetime. I actually forgot about Geoff for awhile."

He revved the engine a couple of times just to listen to the beautifully tuned engine sound then pulled into traffic.

They turned into his driveway around six in the evening. The entry post indicated the name – Villa del Mare Sereno. Beyond the house, the stunning blue of the ocean washed into sky. The house perched atop a small cliff with an expansive view of the bay.

Running along the side of the villa a road cut through the cliff giving vehicle access to the waterfront. He parked in the garage located on the side of the villa.

Inside, the architect built every room with an expansive feel. The interior designer capitalized on the spacious high angled ceilings with cream coloured slatted wood and beam. The walls, furniture and flooring matched in hues of light sand. Floor to ceiling banks of windows gave a spectacular view of the infinity pool and the ocean beyond.

She dropped her bag and stared out the window. “What an amazing place. If I owned this, I might never leave.”

He stood beside her, pointing out various points of interest – the marina far down the west side of the bay, a historical church on a peninsula of land to the right, a small island bird sanctuary.

“Do you use the pool much?”

“Every morning when I’m here.”

She looked up at the darkening sky and spotted the first star. “Looking up at the stars while floating sounds like heaven. Villa del Mare Sereno, indeed.”

“Want to go for a swim?”

“I don’t have a bathing –”

A bright female voice said, “I would love to go for a swim.”

Amedeo said, “Geli. How did you know we’d be here?”

“I had lunch with Nic and Maria.” A shorter, beautiful version of Amedeo introduced herself to Dax. “I am Deyo’s baby sister Angelica. Everyone calls me Geli.”

“Nice to meet you, Geli. I’m Dakota Keyes and everyone calls me Dax.”

“I brought dinner. I didn’t think Deyo would have much to eat in the house. Hope you like pasta.”

Amedeo hugged her, kissing the top of her head.

After a laughter-filled meal Geli said, “I heard you talking about the pool. It is spectacular at night. Want to come for a swim?”

“I would love to, but I don’t have a bathing suit.”

Geli looked over Dax. "I'm sure Deyo has something that will fit."

She cocked her head. "Um, Amedeo has women's bathing suits?"

He laughed. "With six sisters and sisters-in-law who always pop in unprepared, I have an assortment of bathing suits. You're welcome to help yourself."

Geli said, "Come on. I'll show you the collection."

Picking through the options Dax said, "Amedeo is quite the shopper. These are all high-end."

Geli laughed. "I got his credit card and did the shopping for him."

Dax chose a flattering bikini in shades of blue and green. When the two ladies got out to the pool, Amedeo was already in. As Dax stepped into the shallow end, Geli stood behind and held two thumbs up to Amedeo. Dax dove in and swam underwater to the far end. Geli moved beside her brother. "She's gorgeous – and sweet. This one's a keeper. Don't screw it up."

He looked at her pointedly. "Keep your pretty little nose out of my business."

She laughed. "Not likely."

He picked her up and tossed her into the deep end.

Tuesday March 24

Over coffee the next morning Amedeo said, "I called Lorenzo Russo, the diamond expert I told you about. He can see us today if you like."

"Okay. Where is he? Naples? I'd like to shop for some clothes."

"Rome. It's an hour flight from the local airport. I presumed you would want to go shopping. My buddy Pietro the pilot, offered to bring his wife along. Martina knows the shops."

"Oh, that sounds fantastic – clothes shopping in Rome with someone in the know. When do we leave?"

He laughed. "I'll let him know. I expect he will want to leave in half an hour."

Once they landed in Rome, Amedeo and Dax left Pietro and Martina to deal with some personal business while they went to the jewellery store. They planned on meeting up for lunch.

Lorenzo, aware of the potential value of the impossible blue, brought them into a private room to examine the gem.

When finished, he handed them back the stone. "This is a find of a life time." He looked at the stone again. "Actually it is the find of all time. It is rare to find a white diamond of this size. A vivid blue this size is unheard of. And the clarity is breathtaking. Thank you for the opportunity to actually handle this treasure. How did it come into your possession?"

Dax said, "It came from an artisanal mine in Tanzania."

He nodded. "And you are bringing it to me rather than the mine's diamond dealers."

She glanced at Amedeo. "Yes."

"Do you possess it legally?"

Amedeo said, "Her husband ran several mines. This stone, we call the Impossible Blue, was his, but Blake is dead. Dakota is now disposing of his estate. Since she doesn't know or trust the dealers in Africa to give her a fair appraisal, I recommended you."

Not one word of a lie. Well done, Deyo.

"My condolences. Given a legitimate providence, this could easily fetch you $100 million. It could go as high as $120 million because of its rarity and uniqueness."

Dax stared at the man.

He laughed. "Yes. It is worth far more per ounce than gold. You are a very wealthy woman."

She sat forward in her seat. "So, how do I go about selling it?"

"Some people sell raw diamonds online, but for one of this size and quality I would strongly recommend you put it up for auction at Christies."

"Okay. I don't know anything about diamonds or auctions. Is this something you can help with?"

"Certainly. If you wish to learn, I can shepherd you through the process, or I can handle things for you."

"I would like to be involved."

"Excellent. In the meantime, I recommend you insure it. I can give you an appraisal certificate today and give you the names of a couple of insurance companies that cover this kind of thing. One is just down the street."

"Thank you for your help, Lorenzo. I much appreciate it."

By the time they met Pietro and Martina, the Impossible Blue was insured and on the cusp of its world debut.

After lunch Dax and Martina visited a number of stores from elegant dresses and Italian leather bags to casual shirts and shorts, and a variety of things in between.

That evening Amedeo got a call from Greg at his home up the coast in Paola. Amedeo invited him to del Mare Sereno to spend the next couple days.

Wednesday March 25

Wednesday dawned an exceptionally warm sunny day. The sky and sea an endless expanse of azure with the occasional puff cloud dotting the horizon. Mid morning a voice announced, "Single male. Driving a black Lamborghini. Front drive."

Amedeo picked up the small walkie-talkie. "Thank you. He is expected and will be staying a few days."

"Roger that."

Greg came through the front door. "Hey, Deyo."

"Hey, buddy. Did you see anyone out front?"

He glanced back. "No. What's up?"

"Come on in. I will tell you and Dax."

They took their coffees out to sit on the terrace. Amedeo slowly scanned the property.

Greg said, "What gives?"

Amedeo said, "Geoff called Dax at the Zurich airport. Said he knows she's with me. He's threatening to hunt her down."

Dax said, "But you have a plan, right?"

"I do and it involves both of you." He laid out his plan and their part.

Dax grinned. "That is perfect. But I would like to include Libby with me. Geoff knows she's my best friend and a perfect target to force me to do whatever he wants."

"And Libby too."

Greg said, "So now we wait until you get word Geoff is released by Zurich police and one of your guys radios that Geoff is here."

While Amedeo took a phone call, Greg handed Dax a piece of paper. "This is the contact information for Jamie Moore. He brought a man to the clinic very early Saturday morning. Unfortunately, he was dead. The man's name was Logan Keyes. I immediately remembered you mentioning your Uncle Logan."

Tears welled up in her eyes.

He leaned forward, elbows on his knees. "I spoke with Jamie and confirmed that Logan is your uncle. Jamie said he just started working for Ironwood and your uncle specifically asked him to come to Zimbula to help him with the situation there.

"Dax, I am so sorry."

"Thank you, Greg. I – we knew Uncle Logan was dead. I thought we would never find out exactly what happened or where he ended up."

"Jamie asked if I would pass along his contact information. He would like to speak with you. Said you can call any time. Sounded like he urgently wants to talk. He also gave me all of Logan's personal effects to give to you. They are all here in this box."

She wandered out to the far side of the pool and called Jamie immediately.

"I'm glad to hear from you. I am so sorry about your uncle. I didn't know him well, but he struck me as an honourable man."

Dax asked what happened and Jamie gave her an overview of his time in Zimbula, up to the moment when Logan was killed. "Logan met Geoff at an abandoned airport. I witnessed him kill Logan. If you wish to pursue this, I want to testify."

"Thank you, Jamie. I plan to expose Geoff and ensure he spends decades in jail. Your testimony will make a huge difference, I'm sure."

"I would like to arrange for Logan's body to be shipped back to the States. Is there a funeral home that you would prefer?"

She gave him the pertinent information.

Before signing off Jamie said, "One more thing. Could you tell me who inherits Ironwood?"

"Me, I guess. I'm his only relative and the full beneficiary of his will."

"I don't know your plans for the business, but I'd like to talk with you about buying it. He was a highly respected man and built a phenomenal business. I'd like the opportunity to carry on with the business."

"Oh. I had not thought about what to do with Ironwood."

"I'm sorry. Perhaps this is not the right time. My apologies if I have offended you."

A little smile tugged at the corner of her mouth. "No need to apologize. Uncle Logan put his heart and soul into Ironwood. I'd like to hear what you are thinking. And Jamie? Thank you for being there for Uncle Logan. It means the world to me that he didn't die alone. He must have trusted you tremendously to ask you to come to Zimbula. That says a lot about who he believed you to be."

"You're welcome. Logan impressed me as well. May I call you in a few weeks when I've put together a proposal?"

"Yes. I look forward to it."

She joined the men talking. Amedeo gave Greg a blow-by-blow description of their escape from Africa. He got to the bank part and invited Dax to tell him about how close Geoff came to discovering her at the bank.

Greg shook his head. "You're both nuts. And you both seem to think of this as harmless fun. You do realize this could have turned out very badly. And he's not done yet."

Her eyes twinkled. "A wise man once told me it's all a grand part of the adventure."

Amedeo said, "Speaking of your grand adventure, how about I remove those drowning zebra stitches? Let me look. Yes, that has healed nicely."

When he finished, she examined her leg. "There's barely a mark. Nice work Dr. Ferrara."

Libby arrived Wednesday evening. After briefing her on their plan to deal with Geoff, the evening conversation flowed as many do, wandering and meandering through many topics. At midnight, Dax excused herself and went to bed. Amedeo left a few minutes later leaving Libby and Greg talking for several more hours, barely aware the others left.

Thursday March 26

Libby and Dax got an early start the next morning. Over coffees on the terrace, she laid out everything as Libby took copious notes. Greg and Amedeo hung out by the pool. Greg seemed unusually attentive to the ladies' coffee and snack needs, much to the amusement of Dax.

During lunch Libby peppered both Greg and Amedeo with questions, extracting all the information she could on the country and Akleelu.

"Thank you everyone. I will need to do a pile of research and talk to a number of people, but this is a fantastic story. I think when I've gathered all the facts it will require several articles. I will make sure Geoff is toast when I'm done with him."

They spent the afternoon on jet skis on a perfect blue ocean. That evening the four celebrated the success in Zurich, the upcoming sale of the Impossible Blue, and the future success of Libby's articles.

Friday March 27

Dinner at a restaurant on Friday evening included most of Amedeo's siblings and spouses along with Libby and Greg. They were a boisterous group, full of laughter and teasing. Dax and Amedeo regaled everyone with their adventures – Dax of fleeing the scene of a bombing on her first day, Amedeo of his rescue of Logan and Dax from the mining pit.

Emma said, "I knew it was not a stable country, but I had no idea of the violence."

"And lots of mentally ill people who get no help." She told of her encounters with Phil the crocodile tooth serial killer in the grocery store, then in her bedroom.

Amedeo said, "Phil was the worst, but there was also snake man Naga. The African map maker who thinks he is half white cobra."

Emma asked about where and how the two of them crossed paths.

Amedeo said, "I found Dax wandering lost in the jungle with a gash in her leg from a drowning zebra."

Everyone leaned in for an explanation, curious to hear about her tangle with a zebra. Dax described her first illegal border crossing, the homemade vine bridge, the desperate zebra, the killing of her driver, Terrance, and climbing out of the pit to escape the human traffickers.

Serapina, her hand resting on her mouth, stared at Dax in utter shock. "How in the world did you carry on? I would have left for home after the bombing on the first day."

She shrugged. "I don't know. I never thought about it I guess. I had a purpose for being there. I wanted to find my husband."

"And did you?"

"Yes. Well, sort of."

Allesandro said, "Now that sounds like an interesting story."

"I thought I married a man named Blake Talbot. It turns out Blake Talbot was not his name, but the name of a man he served with in the navy seals. The man I married, Geoff, killed Blake then assumed his stellar identity to get a job with my uncle. He married me to get that job without my uncle looking into him too closely. All that so he could become insanely wealthy operating illegal mines in Africa under the cover of a security company."

Around the table people reacted with shock.

Geli said, "So according to the marriage license you were married to someone who doesn't exist? Does that mean you were never married? And did you find the bastard?"

"I'm not sure how the law sees the marriage. My lawyer is getting it annulled. And yes, we did find him – or rather, he found us. He choked me. He tried shooting me, but Amedeo cleverly saved me."

Nic looked at Amedeo. "Did you kill the bastard?"

Dax said, "We went back to Geoff's house, grabbed a pile of evidence out of his safe and escaped the country in the middle of the night. And now Libby is going to write a series of articles that exposes all the atrocities and brings all that evidence to light."

A glance between Greg, Amedeo, Libby and Dax silently confirmed the rest of the story is not yet written and best they share nothing about Geoff's threat to find and kill Dax.

Serapina shook her head. “I can’t believe how brave you are. I would have been a puddle of tears.”

Geli said, “I think Deyo has met his soul mate.”

Amedeo gave her a warning look.

She looked at him “What? Tell me I’m wrong.” She looked at him expectantly. “No? Then I’m right and you know it.” She poked him in the chest.

Emma said, “Geli. You’re impossible.”

“What? I’m just saying what *every one of you* is thinking.”

Dax glanced at Amedeo for his reaction.

He said, “I’m sorry. You can’t choose family.”

She said, “As you say, it was a grand adventure, and I’m glad much of the story includes you.”

As the party broke up, Geli pulled Dax aside. “I’m sorry if I embarrassed you. Sometimes my mouth spills out whatever I’m thinking.”

“It’s alright. Really. I can see you deeply love your brother. You are so blessed with a wonderful family. You are all quite lovely people. Don’t change on my account.”

“Thank you for understanding. I really do hope things work out for you and Deyo. He really deserves a great woman like you.”

Dax laughed at the woman’s frankness. “Thank you for your generous compliment. He’s quite a man and anyone would be lucky to be with him.”

“See? I knew you were sweet.”

Amedeo joined them. “Dax, I came to rescue you. Geli, what are you up to now?

She rolled her eyes. “I’m apologizing. You’re as suspicious as a cow at the slaughterhouse.”

“Yes. Cows at the slaughterhouse have good reason to be suspicious, as do I.”

“Humph.” She walked off.

“Geli is really a wonderful woman, but she does speak her

mind."

"Honestly, it's okay. She's not wrong. I think we are made of the same stuff."

On the way home, Amedeo got a text message. After reading it he said, "Geoff is released from police custody. I think we can safely assume he will arrive tomorrow."

At the villa, Dax said her goodnights then wandered down to the dock. While closing up Amedeo noticed her. Concerned that either Geli's antics had bothered her or something of their plan bothered her, he went down to the waterfront. "Mind some company?"

She turned around. "No, of course not. The stars are spectacular tonight."

He helped her into the boat and they sat on the deck seats, rocking in the gentle waves.

She said, "It has been quite a grand adventure. I must admit there's a big part of me that really enjoyed myself. It's crazy. We could have been killed a number of ways by a number of people, or thrown in jail for illegal entry into a number of countries. We encountered a number of crazy people and unbelievable situations. And I don't think I would change anything."

"Even though the man you married turned out to be a fraud and criminal?"

"He is what he is. The marriage was a fraud. It wasn't real. And I don't want to live a lie. The whole –" She counted on her fingers. "Unbelievable. It was only seven or eight days in Africa. Those eight days needed to happen. The thing is that without the constant craziness to distract I would have been overwhelmed by the ugly truth. The adventure kept me from sinking in too deep.

"Instead, I kept all of me intact until the breadth and depth of revealed truth ensured anger not feelings of loss and pain. I survived. I will live and love again. All the danger and constant jeopardy was my mental protection. After talking about it tonight with everyone, I realize the adventure and excitement was actually more than protection. It's the heart that beats inside me."

They watched a lone boat passing through the bay.

"At home, Libby and I climb rock faces, some quite terrifying when I can talk her into it. I treasure those moments, hanging from an impossible overhang or roof." She shook her head. "Moments of pure joy. I now think excitement is something I need, like food and air. I find life in adrenalin-pumping adventure. And I wouldn't trade all that happened in Africa for anything because not only did I find the truth about Geoff, but also I found a truth about myself. And that is priceless." She looked at Amedeo. "I led a predominantly boring life in Washington, D.C. interspersed with occasional moments of something that makes my soul sing."

"So what will you do with this truth?"

She dipped her hand into the water, splashing it. The droplets caught the light of the moon and for a brief moment looked like fireflies. "I don't know. I suspended my practice to go to Africa. There's nothing requiring me to get back to it immediately so I have time to think about what I want to do.

"You know how when a person loses their spouse, it changes them and inevitably their lives forever. Things that once seemed so important suddenly look pale and feel pointless. I feel the same about my life. I don't know the path ahead yet, but I don't think I want to or even can go back to the life I led three weeks ago."

"Then stay here. Take all the time you need to sort it out. Even when we're done throwing Geoff off the scent, he could continue to hunt you down, particularly when Libby's articles are released."

She stared up at the stars. "True. He's probably raging angry now and when the articles come out, he will be a ferocious vindictive animal. I can't go back to Washington for now, at least until he's in jail for a long, long time. It just occurred to me, once the Impossible Blue sells, I have no requirement to earn a living. Wow. It hardly seems real.

She sat up, drying her hand on her shorts. "You know, it's funny. Libby and I were rock climbing shortly before all this started and I told her I felt my life was on the cusp of something significant. What an understatement."

She turned to look at Amedeo. "Thank you. I accept your offer. I'll stay, at least until I sort out where I want to live."

"Bella, I want you to stay until Geoff is in prison. There is the chance that he could track you down if you rent a place in your name. He knows you have plenty of money. So aside from your home in the States, he will be checking every recently rented expensive European place, and expand his search from there. It's too risky to go out on your own."

Their eyes locked. In a low voice she said, "There is a danger in me staying here too."

"Is that a risk too great?"

"Is it for you?"

"I'm not coming out of a fraudulent marriage."

She broke the increasingly intense eye-to-eye connection and walked to the far end of the boat. After a moment she turned, her arms wrapped around herself. "It's hard to explain, but it feels like I was never married. It wasn't real, and in my heart I don't feel anything. Not loss. Not nostalgia. And really, not even anger now that I know the articles are going to expose him."

She leaned back and looked at the stars. "It feels like the real me has been lost in a fog for a decade. The day is now dawning clear and bright, and I'm ready to embrace whatever life offers."

Amedeo drew a breath to speak.

"Hold on. There's one more very important thing you need to know. In the midst of a crazy adventure I landed into your life. You dropped everything to help me, to keep me safe – and maybe you did so mostly because Uncle Logan asked you. And I thank you big time for that. I wouldn't have survived without you. I know we need to deal with Geoff one more time, but I do not wish to continue to be an obligation. I don't need another relationship built on something other than love and passion."

"I didn't stay with you for Logan's sake, or even for the thrills." He stood in front of her, taking her hands in his. "Bella."

She tipped her head back to look into his liquid eyes. For a moment their hearts whispered their secrets. She stood on her toes and kissed him.

The next morning, the walkie-talkie squawked the warning code.

Amedeo said, "This is it. He's here."

Dax grabbed Libby and disappeared upstairs.

Greg and Amedeo refilled their mugs and sat out on the terrace to wait for Geoff.

Cautiously observing the villa from the line of bushes, Geoff spotted the two men casually chatting and watched for a number of minutes expecting Dax to appear. She didn't. He crept onto the terrace and in behind Amedeo. Silently he held the gun to Amedeo's head. "Get Dax."

Amedeo turned to look at Geoff. "Oh, it's you. I thought I was done with the pair of you."

"I know she's here with you. Call her out."

"She's not here. After all the help I gave her, she left me feeling like a jackass in the middle of the street in Rome. I offered to carry her bag and all hell broke loose. She ranted about men. Totally lost it. Called all men bastards. I didn't catch most of what she screamed. I was trying to calm her down because a crowd was gathering. Then she howled about how some aunt and uncle had you pegged from the beginning. Buddy, she's some kind of angry that you fooled her for ten years. Repeated many times that men are slime. Said if I ever contacted her again, she would blow my jewels off and feed them to the rats. She's gone off the deep end and I want nothing to do with either of you."

"I don't believe you."

"Grab a beer in the fridge and have a look around if you want. She is not here."

Geoff backed away and looked about the great room behind them. He wandered a short distance to think and then circled back and stared at the two men relaxing.

"Seriously. Help yourself to a beer. Have a good and thorough look around. She's not here. Never was and never will be. I plan to keep the family jewels intact."

"Don't move. You move from here and I will shoot you."

"Whatever." He and Greg carried on with a conversation about the non-profit organization. They heard Geoff searching the house, floor by floor.

When done, Geoff stood looking at the two men relaxing on the terrace.

Amedeo said, "Told ya."

"Did she say where she was going?"

He shrugged. "Don't know. Don't care."

He pointed the gun at Amedeo. "Where did she go?"

"Man, some chick threatens to blow off your balls, you don't hang around and ask her forwarding address."

Geoff turned away to gather his thoughts.

Amedeo watched him struggling. "For the sake of the brotherhood of men I will tell you this. I overheard Dax on a call to a friend, Lindsay or Lindy?"

"Libby."

"Okay, Libby. They made arrangements to meet in California. Said something about going to Joshua Park, I think."

"Joshua Tree National Park."

"Yeah, that sounds about right. Planned on renting a place and spending a month there."

He studied Amedeo's eyes then muttered," They've talked about going there for years."

Finally dropping the gun to his side, he paced, as if thinking it through. "It figures she would run to Libby." He stopped, looking out to the horizon. His jaw clenched as he growled," So she thinks she has outsmarted me? Stupid mouse."

Amedeo scratched his ear. "Is this Libby some type of journalist?"

"Yeah."

"Yeah well, she talked to Libby about writing an article on what is going on in Zimbula and your involvement. I heard her say she had enough evidence to bury you. Mio amico, she is incazzato –" He looked at Greg for help with a translation.

Greg said, "Pissed off."

"Sí, she is pissed off. What is it they say? Hell has no fury like a woman scorned."

Geoff cursed under his breath. "That's what she meant by break me." He stalked to the door. "I will break her, make her pay. Ten years of her crap. Now she threatens me with a newspaper article?" The front door slammed behind him.

Amedeo and Greg waited for the all-clear signal from the men outside then went up to the attic.

Throughout the house they saw evidence of Geoff's search. Furniture was moved, doors left open, in the attic boxes were shifted, and a couple of chests were left open. Amedeo went to the far corner and pressed a hidden lever. A panel swung open. He called down a long shaft," He's gone."

A small elevator started up from an old escape tunnel that ran along beside the basement and went out to a cleverly hidden opening at the base of the cliff. Dax and Libby stepped out of the small cage with their luggage.

Dax gulped a couple of breaths after the dark confinement of the very small elevator. Between breaths she said, "How did it go?"

Amedeo said, "You okay?"

"Yup. Just need a bit of air."

Greg laughed. "You should have seen his face. He totally bought the California thing."

Libby said, "While in the tunnel I heard back from the Senior Editor of the Washington Post. He wants the first article in the next couple of weeks."

Greg said, "Oh, that's great news, Libby."

Amedeo said, "How far is the Joshua Park from Los Angeles?"

Dax shrugged. "An hour or two, depending on where in L.A. you are going."

Amedeo said, "Good. It will easily take several weeks for Geoff to search the area for you two."

Dax said, "Nicely done, Amedeo. Thank you, again."

Libby said, "Yes, thank you both. I will make sure the first article has Geoff running for his life. He will have no time to think about you, Dax."

Greg said, "And once the evidence is public, there's no point in tracking you down."

Amedeo said, "Except revenge." He held Dax's hands. "Stay. At least until he is in jail."

The following afternoon Amedeo's phone rang. "Sí. Solo un momento." He handed the phone to Dax.

"Hello?"

"Is this Dakota Keyes? The woman who found her missing husband in Africa?"

"Well, yes I guess. I was in Africa looking for my missing husband."

"You're the one! I heard from a friend of a friend of Emma Ferrara Cataneo about what happened and how you found him."

"Oh, yes." *Man, news travels fast here.*

"I'm Maria and I'm hoping you can help me. My husband is

missing and I'd like to hire you to find him."

"Oh, I'm not a private investigator."

"I know. But you sound perfect." After a long pause she said, "Please just think about it." She gave Dax her contact information.

"Okay, well I –"

"I think he might be in trouble."

Dax closed her eyes, remembering when she thought Blake might be in trouble. *I would have done anything to find him.* "I understand. Really I do. It's just that I'm a psychologist, not an investigator. I was determined to find him, but I didn't know how. You should speak with Amedeo. He has a background in this kind of work and helped me enormously."

"But you pursued without wavering, without giving up. I really need someone who will work that hard for me. I'm desperate. Please."

As Dax thought about what to say, the woman said, "Have you read about the art theft in Florence?"

"No. I haven't followed the news for a few weeks."

"I'm worried that my Massimo is involved. He's an art curator who was wrongfully dismissed. Since then he's struggled to earn a living because no one will hire him. But over the last year, big money deposits have gone into our bank account with no explanation from Massimo. I mean really huge amounts of money. And now, he's gone missing.

"You can understand why I cannot go to the police.

"Let me think about it. Can I call you back tomorrow?"

When she hung up she passed the phone back to Amedeo. His raised eyebrows questioned her.

"Seems your sisters have been talking. Our story is travelling faster than a cat on fire. This woman wants me to find her missing husband. She thinks he may be involved in some art theft."

He grinned. "Interesting."

"Yeah, I know. It does sound intriguing, doesn't it. But I'm no investigator. I don't know how to find missing people. My heart goes out to her. She sounds like me when Blake went missing. I know exactly how she feels. I want to help her, but I have no clue how to find a missing person. I told her I'd give her an answer by tomorrow."

"Think about our conversation on the boat – the new day dawning, ready to embrace whatever life has to offer, how adventure is your very heartbeat." He leaned forward, resting his elbows on his knees. "Now, what will you do?"

She copied him. "I think it's time we talk about what I already owe you and your fees going forward. If I agree to this, I will need your help. So what do I owe you so far?"

His dimples deepened. "What I want I cannot be bought or sold, yet to me it is beyond the measure of money, beyond the value of the Impossible Blue. And the fees for my help with this woman? Same as last time. Let's find her husband first then decide what my help is worth."

"I already owe you my life. Anything else is a bargain."

Epilog

Two weeks later the first of five articles detailing the atrocities in Zimbula, with a particular emphasis on Geoff Barber's role, was published and picked up by newspapers around the world.

As a result, Geoff went on the run and Akleelu lost the election. The new president and government charged and convicted Akleelu.

Several months later, Geoff was found in Prague and extradited to Zimbula to be convicted for a number of crimes, including fraud, theft, conspiracy, hate crimes, and multiple murders.

Both Geoff and Akleelu sit locked up in a dingy Zimbuli prison, the warden a man who lost his family to the country's violence.

After the Zimbuli election, Dax used some of the money from Geoff's bank accounts to fund Logan Keyes Mining, a legitimate operation of the mines in Zimbula, and retained a small interest in two new legitimate Tanzanian diamond mines.

Working with Nakato, Dax started Impossible Blues, a non-profit organization offering microfinancing and entrepreneurial support to women in Zimbula.

Jamie Moore offered Dax a deal to purchase Ironwood over time. In the meantime, she is a silent partner.

Ironically, the Impossible Blue sold on April 25 for an unprecedented $105 million, the same day the court approved her annulment.

It is in the compelling zest of high adventure and of victory,

and in creative action,

that man finds his supreme joys.

Antoine de Saint-Exupery, author of *The Little Prince*

Thank You

If you've enjoyed *Blue Thief* won't you please take a moment to leave me a review at your favourite retailer? I am so appreciative of you sharing your thoughts.

Your review does two valuable things. One, your review will help other readers decide on this book. And two, I love to hear what you liked about the story. Your thoughts encourage me to write more of what you love.

Yes, *your* review is priceless to me.

Thanks so much!

If you have never posted a review on Amazon, it's easy. Here are some instructions.

Log in to your Amazon account.

Go to the *Blue Thief* product page and select the book format you purchased.

Scroll down to the Customer Reviews section and click on the "Write a Customer Review" button.

Next to the title of the book, you will see five light grey stars. Counting from the left, click on the appropriate number of stars you wish to give. The selected stars will turn blue.

Under the stars is a text box where you can write or paste in your review. You may also add a headline for your review. When done, click the "Submit" button.

Amazon will thank you and indicate they are processing their review then send a congratulation email when it is posted.

Cheers!

Join Dax for another exciting adventure in *The Azurite Project,* the next book in this series.

About the Author

I've raced in a corvette with the needle buried. Not a pilot, but flown a piper aircraft. Been attacked by machete welding natives hunting for heads. Swam with an alligator. Hightailed it in a sailboat racing a monster storm threatening to capsize. And found myself face to face with a growling lynx.

Love living the adventure.

Serenity McLean, Adventurer and Author

Connect with Serenity:

Pinterest: https://www.pinterest.com/mclean3963/
Facebook: www.facebook.com/Serenityauthor
YouTube: https://www.youtube.com/channel/UCt82lzlc7NDixFAH-fuFZXfg

Other Books

Final Moments Series

- Rainswept
- Veiled Agenda
- Certain Thunder (to be released in 2021)

Heartwarming and Inspiring Collection

- The Flawless Life, Finalist of the Word Award 2016
- Weeping Dune
- Leaving Lost
- White Sands Black Heart

Dakota Keyes Series

Under the author name S.E. McLean

- Blue Thief
- The Azurite Project (to be released in 2021)

Non-Fiction

- Honest Grief
- Supporting Honest Grief

www.ingramcontent.com/pod-product-compliance
Lightning Source LLC
Chambersburg PA
CBHW050733230626
47052CB00002BA/4
* 9 7 8 1 9 8 9 4 4 7 0 3 1 *